Praise for

THE
SISTERHOOD

'A gut-wrenching, heart-breaking journey through
the looking glass of *1984*. Compulsively written,
Julia's is a story begging to be told'
Freya Berry, author of *The Dictator's Wife*

'A shockingly relevant take on a classic'
Claire McGowan, author of *This Could Be Us*

'Much love simmers beneath the surface of
Katherine Bradley's fast-paced and suspenseful work.
The Sisterhood's greatest gift, however, may be in its message
of hope, capable of surmounting even the most formidable
of odds and the most uncertain of futures'
Katherine J. Chen, author of *Joan*

'Nothing short of a triumph'
Mara Timon, author of *City of Spies*

'A heart-pounding look into a secondary character's legacy'
Grazia

'Sinister, chilling and heart-breaking, it's a worthy
successor to Orwell's dystopian classic, allowing readers
to explore a new version of Julia's story'
Culturefly

'As a massive fan of *The Handmaid's Tale* and *1984*,
I had high hopes when reading this book and I am pleased
to confirm that I was not disappointed in any way'

'Bradley skilfully writes of Julia's heart-wrenching
story as she fights against the oppressive regime, forcing us
to consider what it really means to be brave, selfless and loyal.
By introducing these more positive values and characters,
Bradley ensures that *The Sisterhood* stands apart from its
dystopian counterparts, giving readers an inspiring and
ultimately satisfying tale'

'I never knew that I needed a retelling of *1984*, or indeed,
a feminist retelling of *1984*, until I read this book and now
I know I absolutely did need those things. I love that we get
Julia's perspective in this book as I was always fascinated
by her in the original. A really good read'

'I honestly don't remember the details of George Orwell's
1984 so I approached this as a dystopian stand-alone novel,
not a retelling. It was everything you expect from the genre,
oppressive, tense and disturbing. Recommended!'

'This is the book I have been waiting
for and it is so satisfying done'

'Absolutely loved this book, was gripped from the start'

'A brilliant retelling of a classic'

'Beautifully written ... A must read'

Katherine Bradley enjoyed a twenty-year career managing services for homeless people in Brighton, before retraining as a teacher. She now teaches English in a secondary school academy, finding time to also teach creative writing to adults. She holds a first-class degree in English Literature, in addition to qualifications in teaching, creative writing and coaching. She has published two suspense thrillers under the name Kate Bradley, and her work has been described as 'addictive, original and brilliantly twisty' by T. M. Logan and 'heart-stopping' by David Nicholls. Katherine lives near Brighton with her family.

Follow her on Twitter 🐦 @kate_bradley

Writing as Kate Bradley

To Keep You Safe
What I Did

THE SISTER HOOD

KATHERINE BRADLEY

**SIMON &
SCHUSTER**

London · New York · Sydney · Toronto · New Delhi

First published in Great Britain by Simon & Schuster UK Ltd, 2023
This paperback edition first published 2024

Copyright © Katherine Bradley, 2023

The right of Katherine Bradley to be identified as author
of this work has been asserted in accordance with
the Copyright, Designs and Patents Act, 1988.

1 3 5 7 9 10 8 6 4 2

Simon & Schuster UK Ltd
1st Floor
222 Gray's Inn Road
London WC1X 8HB

Simon & Schuster: Celebrating 100 Years of Publishing in 2024

Simon & Schuster Australia, Sydney
Simon & Schuster India, New Delhi

www.simonandschuster.co.uk
www.simonandschuster.com.au
www.simonandschuster.co.in

The author and publishers have made all reasonable efforts
to contact copyright-holders for permission, and apologize
for any omissions or errors in the form of credits given.
Corrections may be made to future printings.

A CIP catalogue record for this book
is available from the British Library

Paperback ISBN: 978-1-3985-1428-7
eBook ISBN: 978-1-3985-1429-4
Audio ISBN: 978-1-3985-2263-3

This book is a work of fiction. Names, characters, places and incidents are either
a product of the author's imagination or are used fictitiously. Any resemblance to
actual people living or dead, events or locales is entirely coincidental.

Typeset in the UK by M Rules
Printed and Bound in the UK using 100% Renewable Electricity
at CPI Group (UK) Ltd

MIX
Paper | Supporting
responsible forestry
FSC® C171272

For Juliet and Dorrie.

Here's to sisterhood.

'Women are powerful and dangerous'

AUDRE LORDE

PROLOGUE

Rebirth. Is this what this moment offers me?

It occurs to me, that in this too-hot bedroom of my father's, this feather-filled pillow I hold, could be how I wrest my life from a place of pain and powerlessness to something ... *else*. Something better. A new start.

Eyes shut, he lies prone, a sick, ageing man on his bed. My grip tightens against the softness; I am actually considering this. I see it in my mind's eye – placing it across his face. Holding it down as he struggles. I imagine different versions: where he goes gently; where he fights and wins; where someone (Mother?) walks in and finds me engaged in an undisputable sin.

A log in the hearth pops like a child's cork gun and I'm startled from my reverie.

In this damask-draped room, apart from the gap in the curtains, the fire is the only light. Now sound is smothered: quiet only broken by the sounds of his breathing, my heartbeat, the faint tick of his mantel clock, the sounds of licking flames on logs – but together the room hushes, waiting to see what I will do. I'm waiting to see what I'll do.

1

I feel dangerous.

Even in the gloom, his bedroom is familiar to me – too familiar my mother would say if she knew. But she doesn't know. Just as it used to be, it's now just me and him. I am not just here now – this room, his suite, is a palimpsest of memories, each laid over each other, different images, different emotions, different times. They are all within me.

The clock ticks on.

I have not got long – they are coming. I did not come here to do this, I feel like telling him, but despite my pro-testations, I have not put down the pillow.

In the gloom I study my father's face; jowls hang, his charcoal and ash-coloured hair swept back from his forehead, smoothed out of place perhaps, by my mother's anxious hand. She could come back – or the men – and find me here. I need to decide now, while I still have time. Is my rage enough?

Ceaseless, cold and candid – my rage *is* enough. I move the pillow closer to his face. Part of me watches with horror, challenging me: you won't really do this, will you? Yes, I tell myself. I will. Because I want the chance to start again, to become someone else. I want rebirth.

I will become Julia.

PART ONE

*'Any woman who chooses to behave like a full
human being should be warned that the armies
of the status quo will treat her as something of a
dirty joke . . . She will need sisterhood.'*
Gloria Steinem

Chapter 1

'Julia,' Cecily murmurs, her voice light, her touch on my arm lighter. Even in this thick, jostling, stinking crowd, she is grace personified. Her wavy, blonde hair is caught under a strip of blue material she's reused from our uniform of blue overalls. With her hair pulled back, it is easier to appreciate her square, smooth face. Although I always feel calmer for Cecily's presence (is it the carefully modulated cadence of her voice? Her reluctance to rush anything?), I don't acknowledge my friend – not here where Big Brother watches us. Too much togetherness could look suspiciously like friendship. In Oceania, our relationships can only be like the uniform we wear: plain, basic and functional. Friendship is dangerous – why would we deflect any love owed to Big Brother into each other? It would be theft – and theft from Big Brother is punishable by death.

Instead, we part as we wait in the crowds for the others to arrive.

It's not the law for proles to attend the weekly public screenings of the lottery – because there are no laws in Oceania – but every eighth day on each Fraterday, the effect is the same because it feels like every prole in London packs into every square, waiting for the numbers to be drawn.

Around us is the press of unwashed bodies in the unexpected first spring heat of late March sunshine; their sour smell is pungent as they push and shove against me. 'Why are you even here?' snarls a dead-skinned woman.

She can say that to me because as a prole she's free to come into the squares, but as an Outer Party member, if I were to be caught in the prole parts of town, the patrols might take me in for questioning. She growls and shuffles as she readjusts her focus back to the stage. Just as well – she won't get an answer to her question. The truth is, I've come to meet my Sisterhood. And today's Sisterhood meeting promises to be special: Ruby has news for us.

Every face is tipped up towards the mammoth screen that sits on top of a stage. It's showing clips of brass bands, intercut with interviews of proles who've allegedly won the lottery. Now it's mid-interview of a prole who claims he's worked out the perfect system for forecasting the winning numbers. He admits he hasn't won the big cash prize. What he doesn't know, unlike party members, is that the big wins are a propaganda lie. Actors celebrate fake wins.

I pretend to be interested in the interview – maskface – but I'm looking for the others. I spot Prisha in the crowd; she's rowing with a man younger than her thirty-odd years. Jaw set, brown eyes burning with disdain, it looks brutal, but I know she's just looking to blend in; blending in isn't skulking in the shadows, it's doing the same as others. She's spitting swear words at him whilst pushing against his chest; she's feisty – tenacious. He doesn't stand a chance. He's a prole in ordinary clothes and because she's wearing the Outer Party uniform of blue overalls, he soon backs down. Just as well for him – she's got a right hook on her that would make any prole slum-fighter proud.

I spot a couple of other tussles in the crowds – Hate is encouraged and expected in Oceania – but no others involve members of the Sisterhood. Mostly it's a party mood; for the proles it's a welcome fanfare, a weekly anomaly amongst the grey dirge of reality. Around me, the often too-thin faces are transformed with inner-lit lanterns of hope, their excitement palpable. It's the twenty-minute countdown before the major lottery winner is announced and for every prole it feels like – for them – the monotony and poverty of their lives is about to change.

Meeting amongst proles is one way we make contact with each other. We've got a practised plethora in our arsenal; three years of life in the Sisterhood dodging detection has made us experts. Although surveillance cameras spy from high stands, pointing directly down into the crowds, we also know that Big Brother is less interested in watching proles.

Society is divided into three tiers: at the top, the Inner Party; the middle is the Outer Party and at the supposed bottom are the proles.

Proles: the majority; the mass underclass; the poorer; the less educated, the decategorized at birth. Unlike the Inner Party, who form the Ingsoc government (Big Brother), and my strata, the Outer Party, who are little more than skivvies to the Inner Party and serve it by forming the huge bureaucratic machinery that enacts Inner Party orders, both are united in their dislike of proles. Proles are considered unfortunates by the Inner Party and Outer Party. The Sisterhood are seemingly alone in their secret envy of the underclass for the lesser restrictions on their daily lives they experience. It seems we alone can see what is real: proles are no different to any one of us. Any idea of difference is a myth sold to those who wish to believe they are somehow better than their equals.

I look through the thick crowds and can see Leona now. I know that Leona adores her older sister, Ruby, but because she is Black and Ruby is white, I know the disparity in their treatment has left an indelible mark on Leona. Today, she wears her hair in a neat tight bun; it fits her well – dressed in Outer Party overalls, she is neat and tight in the way she carries herself, except when she is especially animated, when she gestures with her hands with the lightness of a puppeteer. To me, I see beyond the beauty of her bright eyes and skin and see Leona for her serious, quiet determination. Her resilience. Her self-control. She is a true soldier of the Sisterhood.

She stands near me, ready to draw tighter when needed. But where are the others?

With Leona, Cecily, Prisha and me here, there are only two to go before we are all assembled to hear Ruby's news. We are waiting for Ruby herself and for our leader, Eleanor.

Ruby announced two days ago at our weekly meeting: 'I have something to tell you. Comrades, on Fraterday I'm going to observe the lottery in Endurance Square. I've realized I have not been attentive enough to how proles gain strength in Oceania – it's big news because there's simply so many of them. You should all attend so we can plan our next move on how we can educate the troop about Oceania's greatness.'

This is doublethink – proles have no strength. But we understand this nonsense is to obfuscate Big Brother who is always listening.

We, the Sisterhood, have heard the real meaning: *I have something to tell you. It's big news. You should all attend, so we can plan our next move.*

The troop are the girls we look after, under the guise of our public persona as the leaders of the Anti-Sex League Steering Group. The ASL is a façade. Publicly, we are concerned only with the leadership of the forty-strong troop of girls, aged ten to eighteen, guiding them in the world of Anti-Sex, of chastity, of loathing for the old way of baby-making.

Ingsoc values us because science is working hard to eradicate the need for the womb. Officially, it's because infertility levels are rising. Unofficially, pregnancy is too nurturing, and like sex, creates the bonds they wish to break.

I've seen the propaganda films Big Brother shows at the cinema which champion the progress of the lifelabs. Row upon row of artificial uteruses constructed out of opaque fleshmesh, each growing a clone. At the moment, the utebubbles can't yet support a foetus beyond two months. But that's not the lifelabs' only aim – their ambitions are greater. The films tell us that the Ingsoc scientists have been inspired by the Komodo dragon and its ability to impregnate itself. They are trying to rear a new generation where, like the dragon, they can asexually reproduce.

I look at the faces of our young girls and fear for their future. Will females even be wanted in this unknown world? Although I sometimes loathe the spiteful girls in our troop, we fight for them. We fight for us. We are the Sisterhood.

As good troop leaders, Eleanor nodded sagely and told Ruby that the proles were, indeed, interesting. We agreed, yes, we should observe them and feed back our ideas to the girls. 'Perhaps,' Leona said, 'we could initiate a Prole Observation Badge.' Everyone agreed it was genius – the children of our troop love to earn badges and sew them on their red sashes.

Although Ruby summoned us through oblique language, we do not need permission to be here. As Outer Party, we're allowed to come along to gawk; the squares are shared ground and we can be here as long as we look like we don't want to win. There's more than a smattering of Outer Party blue overalls here – they come for the noise, the snobbery and amusement of seeing how the proles conduct themselves.

I remember once that a someone from the Outer Party *did* win a small prize – a man who worked in the Ministry of Plenty. His face flashed up on the screen with his name and he stuttered, pink with panic, sweating and straining in his Outer Party uniform of blue overalls. I wanted him to say: *Sorry but we are poorer than the Proles! We are more unhappy than them! It's the Outer Party that truly suffer and want to change their lives!*

But, of course, he didn't. Instead, he cried, 'I don't want the money – give it to the Party! I didn't buy the ticket – I love Ingsoc! I love Big Brother!' and everyone cheered. The usual chanting started: 'B! B! B! B!' and the camera shut off.

I never saw him at work again.

Poor man – I believed him. I think he was set up. Sometimes, people are for no discernible reason. After all, why would he buy a ticket to something he knew wasn't real?

I see Ruby first. I don't signal I see her – it's not safe – but she weaves through the crowds and then she's beside me. Like me, she's wearing an overcoat because it's permitted and helps hide our blue overalls to the more cursory glance. A knot of blue in a sea of prole mixed clothing would not be unusual, but we want to save it for when we are ready to communicate. The early spring sun has heated her face and the sweat has gathered along her strawberry-blonde hairline. The warmth has brought her cheeks to a pink shine. She has a gap in her front teeth she hates: I think it's beautiful. She is a mass of beauty, freckles and energy. Being with her is sunshine; she is my most favourite friend. Although I keep my secrets from her, she is still the person who knows me best. Around us, the thick crowds buzz with excitement; their voices are the duvet of noise we will hide under.

'E here yet?'

I say nothing – which means no. There's no need to waste words. We have to assume there are spies everywhere – physical spies, dro-cams, the dreaded Thought Police. Even now, a black Thinkpol helicopter buzzes in the distance, a wasp around rotting meat, its interrogation of the several blocks of flats that line the skyline reminding us we are never safe.

'You have news?' I ask. There's something about the way her face shines with joy that means I can't wait for Eleanor.

'Julia, I have had a *result*.' She says nothing else and even though I hate myself for it, I risk another glance at her. To the casual observer, she wouldn't look out of the ordinary, but I know her well enough to know that she is incredibly happy. Joyous, even. Perhaps she can get away with it here – there's only a few minutes now until the numbers are drawn and around us, every prole already considers themselves a winner.

'I met a man who is in the Brotherhood.'

I can't speak. This is what we've been waiting for, for three long, long years. Can this be true? Have we finally, finally done it? The Brotherhood is the secret underground organization that works to bring down the Ingsoc government. Emmanuel Goldstein is their leader and is the main enemy of the state. But the enemy of the state is our heart's desire. Men hold all the power – I'm unusual to even have the responsibility of running a Ministry team – most women, even Outer Party women, are no better than proles in the work market. The limits of money held by us is capped; we can't apply for senior job roles. Our wombs are being replaced; there's rumours of depleting girls being born. Certainly, in crowds, at work – everywhere but the food markets – there seems to be fewer and fewer women about.

But we are here. We can offer our help to the

Brotherhood. We are willing. The six of us (Eleanor, me, Ruby, her sister Leona, Prisha and Cecily) are strong. There will be a role for us. Eleanor has always been tireless in telling us feel that. I look for her, instinctively wanting her to hear the news. The *Brotherhood*! Finally! After all this time of seeking them out, Ruby has done it!

As I look for Eleanor, I ask Ruby, 'How?'

'Can't explain now, but the short version is I heard my new contact talking to his colleague. I made my approach.'

'Do they want to meet us?' I bite my real questions down: *Will they even want us? Will they accept the Sisterhood as collaborators?* My biggest fear – even bigger than of Big Brother – is that like the rest of society, they, too, will be dismissive of us; they, too, will tell us women don't count.

'I haven't told him about the Sisterhood. Want to wait for E's approval. Just said I was a Goldstein fan.'

To even admit she's an admirer of Goldstein is enough to guarantee her execution if she were caught. Goldstein – if he really exists – wants to end Ingsoc's rule over the country, over the whole of Oceania, even. To follow him is to be a rebel and traitor of the state.

Perhaps she sees the sudden doubt on my face because she squeezes my hand briefly. 'Jules, you know me better than most – this life is agony to me. I can't bear it. And I don't want to wait any longer for change. I heard him and just reacted – didn't think. He was so clear though and I just thought, *this is my chance*. I took it. You would've done the same.'

This is true. Ruby and I are both impatient and we suffer because of it. During one of our recent walks, we both confessed that when we joined the Sisterhood, we imagined something would happen almost instantly. But three years later, the waiting for something to happen has become painful. The Sisterhood hasn't yet achieved anything – but maybe that's now changed. 'So, what happens now?'

Ruby pauses as there's a stage announcement about the lottery. 'He says he will get in touch with me. He's promised me I will know when the Brotherhood is upon me.'

We both fall silent as the crowd boils around us. The excitement for the numbers being called – now only minutes away – is feverish.

Against their clamour is my internal thunder: our world is going to change now. We have sat on our secret for so long – looking, hoping, being ready for . . . what?

We've never been quite sure for what. A hope. A chance. Something bigger than us.

There is no one in this crowd who wouldn't have heard the rumour of the Brotherhood. Their leader, Goldstein, is a national figure of Hate. All of Hate Week in late summer, the daily Two Minute Hate and every other Hate activity, is directed at him. I've seen grown adults faint at the whipped up, state-organized Hate-worship of Goldstein. Big Brother tells us there is no one more dangerous to our society systems.

But what if you want to break our society systems?

This is why we seek Goldstein and his Brotherhood.

Shortly after Eleanor brought our little group together, naming it in homage to our heroes, I remember Ruby telling me why she was joining. 'They hung my mother in the town square. They came and took her

14

in the night – just burst into our flat – all these men in black boiler suits. I remember looking at Leona as she just screamed and screamed and screamed. Can you believe one of those fuckers came in and struck her with an electrobaton?'

I shook my head, but of course I believed it. We all have our own stories of Big Brother cruelty.

Leona had said, 'I didn't know about the electrobaton.'

'You were only five, hon,' Ruby told her. 'Sorry – me and my big mouth.'

Leona looked dreamy. 'No, I want to know, I want to remember. I can't even remember much about Mum. I just wish we knew why they took her.'

'I wish we did, too, but we will never know. At the time, we just had to move on and survive. To not get arrested ourselves. And for that, we had to pretend nothing had happened.'

Leona's still remembering: 'When I was eleven, Dad found me rubbing bleach on my arms. Fortunately, he got it off before it did too much damage. I thought they took Mum because me and Dad are Black, and you and Mum are white.' She looked down at her hands for a long time. 'Ruby, you've been through so much – your first dad dying when you were young, then Mum's killing, but you've never moaned, never complained – you've just looked after me. You're amazing.'

Ruby rested a hand on her arm. 'You're the best, most beautiful sister I could hope for.'

'I don't remember the electrobaton. I should, but I don't,' she said slowly. 'But what I do remember is that you stood in front of me. When the Thought Police broke into our bedroom and ordered us to get out of bed and stand up. I do remember the noise: Mum screaming in the corridor and Dad shouting, the booming commands of the Thinkpol and their dogs barking – but through it all, you stood in front of me.'

'It's what Mum would have done herself – if she could.'

I listened to this with horror. Now, as I briefly glance at her profile, I realize that Ruby is the bravest of us all. We've vowed to find the Brotherhood, to petition them to let us help in any way we can and now she might have done it. She has taken the first step and declared herself to someone outside the Sisterhood as a rebel – a dissident. She has done it regardless of the consequences.

And now this is it – the moment of change is upon us.

The crowd starts yelling and screaming in abandonment as the lottery man from the Ministry of Plenty appears on screen. Like Pavlov's dogs, they know the winning numbers are now moments from selection.

Their uproar hits me in the sternum, a true power blow and with it, something about the intensity of the noise shifts inside me – makes me feel vulnerable. Yes, everything has changed, but how I feel about it now tilts again: surprise, relief, optimism now feels ... *frightening*. The reality of Ruby's statement floods cold through my belly and I squeeze against the sudden urge to pee. The initial elation is now lost under a tidal wave of fear. Tension clamps pain into my shoulders.

I am afraid for Ruby, for my sisters.

As if sensing my fears, she reaches and rescues my hand

and holds it briefly in her own. 'Always forward, Julia,' she tells me, reminding me of the Sisterhood's slogan. *Always forward*. But it has never felt more uncertain – forwards into what?

'Comrades!' trills the lottery rep, an eager young man with the oily combed parting. 'Attention! Attention! We have stupendous, glorious news for one of you – someone is about to become the big winner! But fear not, comrades! When one of us is a winner – we all become winners! With Big Brother watching over us, our happy life is constantly improving, constantly developing with greater strength and greater glory!' I've seen this man before – his voice is piercing and he skips from side to side when excited, repeating his mantra about 'our happy life'. He repeats endless phrases I've heard before: 'Big Brother gives us so much!' 'Oceania has never been more plentiful!' 'Ingsoc is the party of plenty!'

Hungry people, people dressed in rags and who live in cold homes, will clap and cheer these statements without irony.

To blend in, I'm forced to listen to his speech with a rapturous look – to show irritation or boredom could mark me out. There's something about his smooth, shiny face, his confident maxims, that make me feel weakened. *We can't beat them!* I think with a maddening voice. I feel a deep sense of panic that Ruby is wrong, that Ruby has made a terrible mistake.

As greasy-parting finishes his speech, everyone surges forward. This is the point the numbers are called each week and their focused mania is overpowering. I'm desperate to get out of the press now and perhaps Ruby feels the same because she's moved to the periphery of the crowd. I can see that Prisha and Cecily and Leona are moving nearer, coming to join us and I wonder if they have already heard Ruby's news. But where is Eleanor? I badly want to see her now because I know her wisdom and guidance will give me confidence. I want to hear that she is pleased with Ruby, that Ruby has done the right thing. When she says it, I'll feel it.

I break out of the main crowd and buy time by stopping to tie a shoelace. Cecily joins me – I know her large feet anywhere. Prisha joins us and they talk – some nonsense about the glory of Oceania that's designed to be heard. *But where is E?* I think again. Eleanor's late and she's never late: she is the queen of routine. That in itself is making me anxious, and coupled with the incessant circling of the Thought Police helicopter – which is so loud and so close it looks like it's going to land, in the square or in the scrubland just on the other side of the road – I'm unsure what to do. It all feels wrong. I want to leave. Cecily, Prisha and Leona are just killing time waiting for Eleanor – has Ruby already told them her news?

I decide to call Ruby over.

The helicopter does land but on a low, flat-roofed building on the far side of the crowd. The huge blades are loud, but the noise and music being pumped from the speakers is even louder. Is it intentional to cover the noise of the helicopter? The crowd are expecting the winning numbers, but there's another filler interview. It feels too late to leave now; it could look suspicious. Who would stay all this time only to leave just as the numbers were called? Cecily has finally stopped talking about the glories of Oceania and I can tell she's uncertain, too. Prisha is looking at the helicopter but Leona is at least doing the right thing and is cheering loudly.

Ruby has moved quite far from us now – far from the crowd, almost across the square. Her back is to me. I wish I could see her face. Why has she pulled away from us? Why is she not coming together as planned?

Then: joy! Eleanor is finally here! She's coming through from the nearby street, dead ahead at thirteen o'clock. She's walking at speed, pulling her shopping trolley behind her. She's moving with an arrow-like purpose towards us.

'Comrades! Sorry for the delay. First number coming now …!' Coloured balls (a promise in prole-grey lives) are turning in a clear drum. Every prole clutches their tickets with such concentration a bomb could land and they wouldn't notice.

Leona is clapping and cheering, and I pretend to do the same, but really risk a glance at Eleanor. She's closer now, moving so fast I can already see the grim determination hewn into her face. She's now pushing her shopping bag trolley ahead of her, pushing it like it's a lawn mower cutting a path through the crowds, but looking to my right. It feels like time has slowed down as I turn to my three o'clock, to see what she's looking at to make her look like that.

From the landed helicopter, six – no, seven – black-suited bodies of the Thought Police emerge. They are bent low, to evade the slowing blades. Now they are running towards the square. Are they coming for us? This is wrong ... this is wrong.

I notice so much, it's as if time has been stretched. Leona has stopped cheering – perhaps like me, she can see their expressions are flint axes. I see the numbers being called and then flashing onto the screen; I see the crowds staring at their tickets, not seeing – even as the black boiler-suited police scythe through the crowd. I see Prisha tug on Cecily's sleeve in a gesture that reminds me of a small, uncertain child. People in the crowd who see them coming back away, faces falling instantly from lottery excitement to Thinkpol fear. Those who don't see them are hit with jointed electrobatons and fall flopping to the floor, popping and fizzing from a dose of electricity. But they are lost under the press of the crowd, who even stand on the fallen as they close up the path created by the running police.

We can't help it – we shouldn't, but we press closer together. Our knot isn't complete though, because Leona has moved closer to the stage and Ruby is in the other direction, and Eleanor is still too far away.

Before I can move, the Thinkpol rush at us. It seems to be me they are staring at. Fear means my next thought isn't fully formed, but is something pathetically, shamefully self-ish like: *me, me, it's me*. But then they run past us. I turn to see Ruby who is now over fifty metres from me; she's backing up and she can see it's her. Now all I can think now is: *her, her, it's her*.

Over the oppressive noise of the brass band music and the cheering crowd, I can still hear Leona's gasp of horror. She's already started to sprint towards her sister and the men in black uniforms. I see how this will end for her. She will try to save her sister from the armed Thought Police and will fail. She, too, will be arrested. I know Ruby's thoughts will be of Leona's safety.

You stood in front of me to save me from the Thought Police.

I will do what Ruby did for her. I move suddenly, cutting in front of Leona's path. She's quick and strong and her momentum is already great, so when we collide, the impact knocks the air from her – I hear her expulsion of shock and grief (so sorry, Leona, so sorry). I put my arm around her and use the force of the collision to pivot her around into Cecily and Prisha. They collect her from me almost as if it was a practised, elegant dance. They press against her, holding her, saving her.

I turn back to the arrest. The Thinkpol are on her now. She is in the centre of a scrum – she stands no chance. I can't see her face, but through the gaps in their black shod legs, I see her blue trousers. They buckle and with that comes the irrational idea: it must be me who saves Ruby.

It's not a real thought – save her with what? – but the feeling is a powerful emotion. I can no more save her than Leona can, but instinct propels me to turn towards her, and I start to move. But in the seconds of that movement, I feel a sharp shove and then pain in my legs, and I'm pushed to the ground. My head hits the pavement and for a few blissful seconds I don't think about anything other than the white pain in my head and the nothingness that brings.

I breathe through the grey. For a moment, there is only peace.

Then it's Eleanor standing above me and she's apologizing formally, her hand extended to help me up and she says something stupid, something I don't understand until later, something like, 'Oh, silly me, this silly wheeled thing! So sorry, I didn't see you there.'

I was played at my own game.

Cecily reaches down, too, even though she has one arm around Leona, and she and Eleanor both help me to stand. Leona's eyes are shut and her body is limp like someone cut a circuit.

The final number is called and the noise of explosions is loud. Around the square, there are devices filled with glitter that pump into the air. I watch the gold and silver pieces fire into the sky. The pieces turn, catching the sunlight; a moment of glitz against the grey. Music plays. Everyone is cheering.

Eleanor is half holding, half restraining Leona. But the fight has gone out of her as it has for me because now there is only the helicopter and its door sliding shut. The blades are speeding up, and the noise of the engine has started again. Someone is screaming and for a moment I think it is me. Prisha appears in the crowd, her face slack with processing emotion, but it's not her screaming. Then I realize it's someone in the crowd and he's pushed to the stage. He takes a microphone and announces: 'I've won!'

We've lost.

The absurdity of the timing – him winning just as Ruby is taken – is an insult. It's a fix. The chances of the winner being in this very crowd – is it just a stunt to distract the crowd? Do they know about us? Or has Ruby been betrayed by her new contact? Or is it none of these things?

As the helicopter takes off, I want to run to it and beat the doors and warn Ruby what she already knows – that they are taking her to her death. Dear Ruby, sweet, steadfast, try-hard Ruby is gone and all Eleanor, Prisha, Cecily and Leona have is a crowd of cheering people too blind to see the reality of their world.

Chapter 2

Gone is the brief, hot sun of the day of Ruby's arrest, five days ago. Now, standing in the bleak, mizzly rain, the bruised clouds and drab sky is the perfect pathetic fallacy to this sad mission today.

I'm at the address that Eleanor gave me. I look at the three-storey, brick-built ugly box of a building. The grey walls are pockmarked by bomb debris, like many others in London. I know this country used to be called Great Britain, but now it's only known as Airstrip One. As an airstrip to the rest of Oceania, it remains a main target to our enemies.

We are war-bombed and our economy bleeds to produce weapons to retaliate. Hate has a high cost. There is no money for anything else — least of all for housing the masses. Little is built and nothing is maintained. This unloved building's guttering is choked with weeds and the window frames are blistered and rotten; part of the roof is patched, like many, with corrugated iron. There is a sign above the door:

Chastity House: An honourable home for single women.

There are grim homes like this all over London; most singles under thirty live in hostels. If anyone asks, I tell them I live in a hostel, too. Better that than the truth. And better than the clusters of shacks with open sewers and no power or running water, that occupy the many bomb sites all over London.

This is where Ruby lived and where Leona still does. No one has seen Leona since Ruby's arrest. We all want to help – we all know we can't dissolve her grief. But there is something else I might be able to do and I'm here to find out.

There's a door buzzer and I press it a few times before I realize that it's broken; I test the metal push handle and it opens. Inside, the air is stale with the smell of fried liver. Behind the counter sits a middle-aged woman in the blue overalls of the Outer Party. Her dead, steel-coloured eyes are transfixed on a telescreen fitted on the far wall, and even when I approach the desk, she doesn't shift her gaze from it.

The telescreen listens more than it talks – and it never shuts up. Although it's a propaganda tool, spouting endless diatribe from the Party of Ingsoc, its real purpose is that it downloads our every conversation. Monitoring, scrutinizing, analysing our every utterance. It cannot be muted. It cannot be turned off. To cover the microphone would result in instant arrest. Big Brother is watching and listening.

Always.

But obedience is not enough. Subservience is not enough. Fear is not enough. Big Brother demands love – constantly.

And not just love – it's greedy and selfish enough to demand all love is directed towards it. The only thing I am allowed to love has been Big Brother. The face of the Party, the face of Ingsoc, demands our lust, worship, adoration. Our mania. Our eros. Our agape. Love is dead – unless it is for Big Brother.

I don't look at it.

My mother told me when they replaced the televisions for telescreens, everyone wanted one. People already had listening devices in their homes, silently uploading their conversations, their arguments, their silences. To switch to being watched was less of a leap, more the natural small step for society. What they lost in privacy, they gained in connectivity, features and the latest must-have pride. Two decades later, those features were erased, but the twenty-five hour, eight days a week observation remained. But my mother and I – despite our differences (*you're such a cold fish, Juliet!*) remain united across the years of our deep and centred loathing for being watched.

'You new?' she asks, scratching her face, eyes still transfixed on the screen.

'No, I'm here to see Leona Rayer.' I see lots of hand-written signs stuck around the reception. 'Curfew is at 11.00pm – NO excuses.' 'No smoking ANYWHERE.' 'Rent MUST be paid one week in advance.' 'NO men.' And in pride of place, the huge poster of Big Brother in his white military uniform. His stern, handsome, moustachioed face looking at us with eyes that follow. Underneath is printed: BIG BROTHER IS WATCHING YOU.

As if we could forget – how I wish I could. This image

is posted all over London – even stuck on the outside of houses, street corners and prole shop windows.

'No visitors,' she says in a granular voice.

I'd got this address from Eleanor. To get it from her, I'd had to hang around the market, waiting for her. Eleanor does her shopping every morning at the same time, and I'd made my murmured approach at the veg stall. I knew I'd leave with broccoli – for the last two weeks it's been the only veg available. It makes a foul soup, but I cannot eat any more of it baked or boiled. As I paid for it, I told Eleanor what Ruby told me about her alleged Brotherhood contact. She shut her eyes against it, but told me she was glad she knew that. She said it was settling and I realized she'd been living with the fear that it would be us next.

Eleanor had warned me that the woman's hostel didn't allow visitors, so I am prepared. 'I don't want to see comrade Mayers particularly,' I say to the side of the woman's face. I notice she has a large scar by her temple. I've seen scars like that before. The thought of how she might have got it, mixed with the overpowering smell of liver, is starting to make me feel a little sick. 'What I want is for her to get back to work. She's needed on her preparations for Hate Week.'

'Someone told me Mayers is sick.'

Sick. She's not sick – she's grieving. But of course, no one can admit that. To admit that would be to admit that her sister has gone, and gone would be to admit that she was once here. But she's been vaporized: she's never officially existed. Every record, every image of her has been expunged. To even utter her name and be heard could result in arrest. Normally, arrests happen at night. Normally, it's just as they came for Ruby's and Leona's mother: dead of the night, arrest by torchlight. But Ruby's happened in public. One day, we will spend time considering this, but at this moment Leona is our priority.

That, and trying not to fall apart ourselves.

But I don't think about that now. It is instinct to second-guess that everything said or done is being uploaded, recorded and analysed. With this in mind, I reset my jaw to appear annoyed. 'Well, *when* is she going to be better? I need her to stop lounging in bed and get back to doing what she's supposed to.' My lack of compassion is pitched at the same level that most people have for their comrades. 'There are flags and banners to be made and she's not making them.'

The woman sighs. She waves her hand behind her, indicating the rows of post pigeonholes. There are about thirty of them. 'You can leave her a message.' Each pigeonhole has a name underneath – no gaps. I scan the alphabetical names on each one – since Ruby and Leona have the same surname, last week I know I could have seen Ruby's name next to Leona's, but it isn't there now. Ruby's name, like its owner, is gone. But as much as it makes me want to have some reaction, I know the telescreen behind me, whilst it is pumping out its pulp about the width and breadth of this season's harvest yields, is also fulfilling its real purpose: watching, filming, listening to everything said or done.

'Can't you go and tip her out of bed or something?' I persist. 'Don't you run this place? Isn't that sort of your job to make sure everyone does their bit for Big Brother?'

'I don't like your tone.' Her eyes stay on the telescreen, but I detect an edge in her voice.

I give a clear sigh. 'Look, sorry, comrade, I'm just really fed up. I'll get stuck with her work on top of my own, you know? I just don't want to do my day job, and then do my work for Hate Week and then start hers, too. You know that feeling?'

Her silence makes me push that final bit. 'I just don't want to be down on what we've told the ministry we are going to provide for Hate Week. They might ask us to write a report as to why we've under-delivered. I'd hate to identify the barriers.'

The woman didn't move for a moment, but then she finally gives a little nod. 'You can go up. Third floor, room twenty-three. You've got fifteen minutes. But tell her, the other women have been moaning that she didn't clean the kitchen when she was rota'd to do so. Tell her, if it happens again, she's out.'

At the sound of a buzzer, I am admitted into the hall. Inside, it is even more dismal. The lino flooring is old and cracked; the tang of liver metallic and livid. At the end, I can see the door open to what is a large kitchen – the source of the smell. Opposite the stairwell, is another BIG BROTHER IS WATCHING YOU poster above another telescreen, and in case anyone was in any doubt, as I trudge up the stairs, there are more posters and telescreens. On the third floor, a little way down the dingy corridor, I find Leona's room. I noticed every door I passed was shut, no one gathered in the corridors. I wouldn't expect to see anything different – friendship can be dangerous.

Since I moved to London, I've known that intimacy and affection is not permitted – not even between children and their parents (although there are no laws, there is still undefined crime that might result in death or detention in a forced-labour camp). A girl in our Anti-Sex League group, Chantelle, ratted her own mother out for thoughtcrime to a patrol – said she thought her mother was thinking about the wrong things (knowing Chantelle that meant just not thinking about Chantelle every waking moment). The thrill of power I saw light Chantelle's eyes, the sneer twisting her mouth as she told us that she'd got her mother arrested, sickened me more than most things in this sick world.

I knock the door gently. Then I notice a sign to the right of the door: 'Strictly NO visits to bedrooms.'

It's like I can hear the roaring of the lottery crowds again – am I losing my nerve? The Sisterhood have systems in place to help us move conversations forward – they are tried, tested. They don't involve obvious crime. This does. At the end of the corridor I can see a window. I can't help it – even though I'm being watched by the telescreen, I check the sky, almost expecting to see the approach of a helicopter. There isn't. I remind myself that I have no choice: Ruby was my best friend. She would want me to get Leona up and to help her stay off the radar.

There isn't a lock because privacy is also undervalued. Separating people is a way of fragmenting society, to maintain control. Deciding to assume I have permission to do otherwise, I knock again, a little louder.

A head pops out from a neighbouring room. 'She's in,' a young woman tells me.

'Thanks, comrade.'

'Tell her she's down to clean the kitchen tomorrow. Tell her if she doesn't do it this time, we'll grass her to Holmes.'

I wonder if it's Holmes with the scar and the love of telescreen downstairs.

Trying the handle, keen to get away from the woman who is now watching me, I step inside. The room is in darkness. I allow the light around the thin curtains to let me adjust to the gloom. It's quiet, and although I can sense that Leona is in here, I can't see her. It's clear there's no telescreen in here – telescreens are not fitted in bedrooms as they are always watching, can never be turned off, never be muted. For two people to meet in here is dangerous. I could be arrested just because Holmes or Leona's neighbour alerts the authorities. Desperation is hazardous.

As I consider Holmes might be calling this in even at this moment and I might've been set up, my eyes adjust to the gloom. There's a single bed under the window. I can make out a shape under the covers: Leona. I think of when I was at the scalpel blade of grief, and I feel tears well.

I take a moment before I sit on Leona's bed. I reach out in the gloom and gently touch what I think might be her shoulder. 'Leona?' I pause, and then just as I try again, I hear a whisper.

'I can't,' is all that she says.

I think about this and believe it. I wish I could accept it, but for her sake, I can't. Her grief is thoughtcrime. Punishment could be death. How can I allow her to do what is right – and mourn her loss – if it leads to her arrest, too?

'Leona, I ... am so, so sorry.' My voice is a whisper – there might be no telescreen, but there could be microphones. For a long, long moment, I just sit and let the weight of my hand rest against her. I wish I could do something tangible – cook for her; take her to my home and look after her over the next few months; simply rescue her and take her somewhere brand new, somewhere she can forget – just as my brother did for me.

'Is there anything I can do? I know that sounds ... trite, but ...' I pause, hating my choice of vocabulary, remembering what it gives away about me. I must be careful: my distress for Leona has made me careless. 'I would do anything to change what's happened.'

I think of Ruby bristling with life. We are all different in the Sisterhood and to some extent, play different roles. If Ruby had a role, it was (*was*! How I hate the past tense!) that she was our zest. Our energy. Her vitality, melded with Eleanor's wisdom, and Prisha's fire, gave us hope that change was possible. They were our triumvirate and under them, Cecily, Leona and I are their (or were? Without Ruby, is our hope now past tense, too?) willing foot soldiers. Can we still plunge on without Ruby's enthusiasm?

I'm left with these thoughts in the dark of Leona's room. The clock is ticking and I don't want to enrage Holmes. 'Leona, let me help you. I daren't do your cleaning for you in case it makes others suspicious, but can I get you some tea? Have you eaten today?' I glance around the room; even in the gloom, it doesn't take long to see there's not even a kettle in here. There's a lonely chair in one corner; there's an open set of shelves and I can see Leona's regulation Outer Party uniform of three blue boiler suits folded up. Hanging from a hook is the red sash we wear to show we are part of the Anti-Sex League – to symbolize our allegedly chosen but ridiculous façade of chastity. Like all of us, she has scarce belongings; Outer Party life means enforced frugality as we endure the boundless realities of a country stripped to its bones by never-ending ravenous wars.

I decide I'll have to risk irritating Holmes, otherwise my visit will be purposeless. 'I'm going to get you something to eat,' I say vaguely and pat her hand, like she's a delicate great-aunt.

Back in the corridor, I'm returned to the observation of the telescreen. There's a programme running on wheat production, huge red combine harvesters crossing great, golden fields, showing the might of Big Brother, the great wealth he provides us. How do people swallow this crap? It's not even crop harvest time. There's been no bread in the market for nearly three weeks. People collapse hollow-cheeked with distended stomachs, at the roadsides.

I look up and down the corridor – there's a woman wearing a towel coming out of what I assume to be the communal bathrooms. I walk in the opposite direction.

At the other end of the corridor is a small kitchen. Balanced on top of the fridge is a small telescreen; the continuing programme still talks of abundant food and smiling families eat chunks of break covered in lavish, melting butter. This room tells a different story: the countertop is burnt and broken and the cabinets either miss handles or bear other damage. One with a missing door reveals shelves are labelled with names; I open and shut doors until I find Leona's shelf. There's a tin of soup, two wrinkled beetroots and an exhausted carrot. I root around tacky drawers until I find a tin opener; I'm glad the cooker uses gas because for the last few weeks, there's been no electricity during the day. Electricity is reduced as part of the economy drive in preparation for Hate Week. The flame is small though, limited for the same reason, and I have plenty of time to fish a cup from the scummy water-filled sink and carefully clean it before the soup is even lukewarm.

As I pour it into the cup, I think of all those I have known who have been vaporized. Vanished. Unpersoned. Disappeared. It all means the same. A woman went missing from my building in August because a child spy from the same building said that she heard the woman singing in the lift and reported her for thoughtcrime. Thought Police removed her the next day. Brianna in my department at work developed an eye infection; the woman who serves us our vegetables in the canteen then reported her for 'looking at her funny'. I miss Brianna; she was generous with her stationery allowance. I even saw a man called Peter at work stand up and announce to the room that he could no longer Crimestop about his wife; his voice was reedy but insistent as he called for 'someone to please do something as I can't do it myself anymore'. Crimestop is a catch-all term to describe bad thoughts. For example, the ability to stop oneself thinking about anything anti-party or perhaps failing to understand the illogical diktats laid on us by Ingsoc – here he was applying it to his wife. His self-disgust was evident. He started shaking, his whole body almost convulsing, and another man quietly got up and led him out of the office.

We never saw him again.

We will never see Ruby again.

I carefully carry it back and a girl with tight curls and patched overalls follows me out from the dining room next to the kitchen. 'Hey, no eating in the rooms.'

I can't be caught being kind – that would be worse than two people discovered away from a telescreen. 'She's sick.'

'Do you mean Leona?'

I carry on walking.

'She's got to clean up! Tell her she's on the rota!'

Hearing this for the third time, I feel like hurling the soup at this girl. Instead, taking the opportunity for the telescreen, I shout back: 'I know, you prick, I'm here to get the lazy cow out of bed!' I glare at her. 'If you'd done it like a good comrade, you'd have saved my evening.'

Glad to see the girl take a step back, I feel an unusual press of gratitude for my brother, Ephrem. Our relationship is complicated, difficult, but I cannot deny the kindness he has shown by securing me a decent flat. To live amongst childish crones like this would've stripped me of the will to live. I make a mental note to try to reframe what I perceive as loneliness and instead recognize the benefit of solitude.

I slip back into the dark of Leona's room. I help her sit up. She has a single, thin pillow, so I fold one of her overalls to bolster her into recumbency. She takes a single sip and pulls a face; it said vegetable soup on the tin, but no vegetable is grey.

We battle politely for a few moments as she tries to put the soup down and I try to make her drink it. She wins. I can't force-feed her, particularly as she's started crying. She doesn't say anything for several minutes, and then as I'm struggling with what to do for the best, she finally speaks: 'I'm sorry you are stuck with me instead of Ruby. She was the better of us both, always was.'

I remind her to whisper and then add in my own: 'That's not true. We adore you, for you.'

Leona shook her head. 'Ruby was always brave, kind, clever – even when she was a little kid. I have never been like her.'

My voice drops so low, I can barely hear it. I want to reassure her, but I also want to live. My mouth is next to her ear. 'Can we be heard?'

She shakes her head. 'I check for mics all the time,' she whispers back.

I touch her cheek. 'Lee, you are brave, kind and clever. You are a brilliant tactician. Think of all the things you've done. It was your idea to apply for the old church hall for the group. It was also your idea to raise the group's age to eighteen, in case we identify anyone else for the Sisterhood. And it was you who—'

'Do you know at school the teachers said – because I'm Black and Ruby was white – do you know they told us we weren't even sisters? Well, we bloody *were* and now she's gone, I am nothing without her. I can't bear to be alive without her. I wish I was dead.'

'No!' I give her a little shake – perhaps too rough. 'Please don't say that! Listen to me! Think of Ruby, think of what she would want for you.' I take a deep breath, understanding the importance of my words that perhaps can now be measured in a life not taken. Suicide – a marker of society if there ever was one – is rife. 'Ruby would want *you* to stay *alive*. Say you know that's true.'

She doesn't answer. I smooth her forehead, as if I can stroke away the grief. 'Please, Lee, I know the pain is so, so bad now, but you will find a space in which you can live with it – just as Ruby would want you to.'

For a moment, I even consider the unthinkable and nearly offer the pretence that Ruby could still be released and return home. But even if we did see Ruby again, it would be better we didn't. Sometimes death is not the worst outcome.

I don't want to think of Ruby in the Ministry of Love. Also known as Miniluv, it's a huge frightening building even from the outside – like the other ministries, it's a vast pyramid. Unlike the others, it's windowless, and impossible to enter unless on official business. I have never met anyone who works there – my assumption is that it is staffed only by Inner Party and the Thought Police. Around it, there is a hulking perimeter fence, topped with curled barbed wire and machine gun nests scrutinize from each corner. Maddened dogs salivate on chains at numerous checkpoints. There are whispers that inside, personalized torture and electrocution await the prisoners, who are chained for years in their own filth. The thought of my darling Ruby in there is sickening.

I also hate to think that the sand is running down on us, because if she's there, she may not have any choice but to give us up. And if that happens, it won't be long until they come for us in the night with flailed electricity cables and cattle prods and long-nosed tweezers.

A sour taste like curdled milk coats my tongue.

I try to reassure Leona: 'Don't give up – you are not alone. We will help you with whatever you need.'

'Do you promise?' she asks me through her tears.

'Of course, I promise.'

For some reason, my words only make her cry harder. She waits to speak so her voice remains soft. 'Do you know what Ruby did to help me when I was little? After our mother was taken, I had panic attacks at bedtime. My dad was freaking out because I couldn't stop screaming at night. I was only five when my mother was arrested, and because it happened when I was asleep, all I could think of was that when I slept, either my dad or Ruby would be gone in the morning. Nothing could reassure me. After a few nights of this, my dad even threatened me, said that Big Brother would hear me through the telescreen or the neighbours would tell and would send the Thought Police after me. Ruby was distraught and threw her dinner at him. Now, I realize, he was just desperate, trying to make me stop before that exact same thing happened to me.'

She keeps her mouth next to my ear. 'You know what changed it? What probably saved us from arrest? Ruby offered to stay with me in my bed. She slept in my single bed with me, for years. But that doesn't sound exceptional, does it? Not even when I say I'd wake kicking and screaming every night from terrible dreams. That's still not exceptional, is it? A lot of sisters would do that, wouldn't they?'

She doesn't wait for me to respond before she adds, 'But it *was* exceptional, because right up until I was a teenager, I wet the bed, *every* night. *Every* night she slept in my urine. Never complained. Never left me. Didn't even stop when they turned off the bath and showers because of the water shortages. Like they do with the electricity now. Remember that?'

I'm too ashamed to admit that I don't.

'No showers went on for years and Ruby just put up with it. She had to go to school and suffer being mocked and bullied for stinking of wee. My wee. But she never left me on my own again. *Never.* She was prepared to sleep in *my cold piss* if it meant I felt safe! Never mentioned it, not even after we'd grown up!'

I hate to interrupt her, but since Ruby's arrest, I'm struggling to get a hold of my nerves. 'Let me check the door,' I tell her. There's no shadow under it, but to be sure, I crack it open to check the corridor is empty.

Leona then continues her whisper: 'But now she is gone – and do you know what I lie here and think of, Julia? That I've done nothing to help her. *Nothing.* She might be alive, in the depths of the Ministry of Love being tortured, or she might be dead. But I'm tucked up safe in my dry bed and all I can think is that I've done nothing to help her. And I never did.' She shudders, and when she speaks again, I can hear the anguish despite the quietness of her voice. 'I can't think of a single time when I gave her something she needed, or when I sacrificed anything for her, or did something that improved her life. I hate that – *hate it.* I wish I had – I wish that so badly. I hope you don't know what it feels like to let someone down.'

She's crying silently, her body shaking a little and it's so dark, I can only be glad that she doesn't know that I'm crying, too. I've lost so much, and I never told any of the Sisterhood. I think of those who are gone, how I let them down. I can't bear it.

After a minute, I have a hold of myself – I need to. I can't risk discovery. 'Lee, I've got to get going soon.' I can't help it – I have an unshakable feeling that we'll hear a helicopter again or the door will be kicked down with Holmes standing cross-armed in front of a squad of Thinkpol.

'I'll only be a minute. Don't worry about Holmes – she spent a year in Miniluv. I'm trying to ask you something – trying to explain. I would be dead, Julia, if I hadn't thought of something I could do. I decided to take a jump off a tall building at one of the Hate Week prep marches. Do you remember that woman you knew who did that? Jumped off and died in front of everyone – you said she did it so we knew it was her choice that she died, that she didn't just become one of the disappeared. Well, I was going to do the same at the next one. No – please don't interrupt, I want to ask you something and it's difficult. I've been lying in bed and all I can think of is this plan. But I need your help. Will you help me, Julia?'

'Of course.' I pat around the duvet a little and our hands meet, and I grip hers between mine. I'm desperate now – desperate to make the best impact I can, as quick as I can. 'Anything, Leona.'

'Even if you think me terrible and manipulative?'

'Lee, I just want you to not give up. To stay alive. If I can help with that, I will.'

'The man who tricked her ... I want you to find him. And tell me who he is so I can kill him.'

For a second I think: this is it. This is what I came for. I feel I knew it somehow – that I wasn't here to make soup. Instead this is the start of the journey to how I die.

In our silence, I can clearly hear the sound of the corridor telescreens leak into this room. It's an orator I recognize screaming his hate and preaching war: ' ...disgusting Eurasian soldiers ... vile torturers ... molesters of children ... rapists of mothers ...' Although I listen to this all the time wherever I am, there's something about the detached voicelessness, like a threatening stranger whispering threats just out of sight, that feels worse.

I dry swallow, audibly. I move my mouth even closer, so my lips graze the skin of her ear. 'Are you sure there are no mics in here?'

'I wipe the walls with vinegar most days to check.'

'Ruby told me she'd made a Brotherhood contact – or she thought she had.'

'Yes, but I don't think he was in the Brotherhood, do you?'

'Difficult to know.' The truth is, we don't know anything about the organization, other than what we learn from whispered gossip. The reality of the Brotherhood might be nothing more than a tale told to help the Thought Police track dissidents. Yet it might be a huge organization populated by half of Oceania, poised to take control of at least London. Or they may have been crushed decades ago and only the rumour remains. It is hard to find something when you don't know what it is you seek.

'No, we can't know, but, Julia, I want you to find out. I want you to see if he is in the Brotherhood and if he is, great, we could join them. But if he isn't, then I want you to find him and tell me who he is so I can kill him. For Ruby. So I know I did something for her, in the end.'

'Leona, Eleanor will never—'

'*No.* You mustn't tell her – or the rest of the Sisterhood. They'll never allow it because it is too dangerous. But please, I can't find him without you because I don't have security clearance to the Ministry of Truth where Ruby told me he works. Only you do. That's why it has to be you. You and he are both there together. I wish that I didn't have to ask you to get involved, but without you, I wouldn't know how else to find him.'

I think she's finished and I start to sit up, but her hand placed gently against the side of my head implores me, and I bend again to hear her whisper: 'Besides, you're good at getting information off men. You are clever and beautiful, no one can resist you – you could draw him close, lure him in. It's what you do already for us, isn't it? Does that help you forgive me asking you this, because you already sugar trap for us? And this is a proper lead, don't you see? Ruby always said you were the bravest – if anyone was going to save us, she said it would be you and I know—' She's whispering so fast, it's hard to interject.

'Leona, I—'

'Isn't this what we wanted? A possible lead? Julia, I know I am asking so, *so* incredibly much of you. I realize the risk. But what if he is the way for us to link with them? And if he isn't, you'll be better prepared than Ruby was because you know what happened to her. You can be careful – more careful than her – to not give anything away until you're completely, *completely* sure.'

In her silence, I can hear her breath in gulping pants as if she's been running. Fleeing. I know that feeling – that need to be away from oneself, that the grief is so overwhelming, it can't be borne.

I go to the door and check again. 'Two minutes, Lee – then I need to go.'

Mouth back to ear. 'If you do this for me, it'll give me something to look forward to. I know it sounds like blackmail, and Julia, I don't want you to feel that, but if I can't be honest with you, then who can I be?'

'I . . . just don't know what to say. I would want to act with the Sisterhood's agreement as we always—'

'No! They'll stop you. Too dangerous. Just promise you'll think about it. If you consider it, I promise – *promise* – I won't do anything rash even if you say no, you don't want to do it. I'll respect you've thought about it and discounted it and swear I'll play fair. I'll get out of bed, and I'll turn up to Hate Week without jumping off any building.'

I want Eleanor. The thought is as basic as a heartbeat. Whilst my mother is still alive, it's Eleanor I want to see. Because that is what Eleanor's become to us all.

'I'm not promising anything, but tell me what you know about this man.'

'She said he works on the same floor as you in Minitrue.'

'What's his name?'

'Not sure – but his first initial is S and his last is W. I'm sure that's what she said.'

'What does he look like?'

Her face turns downwards. 'I'm sorry, she didn't say much other than he looked pathetic, weak and a bit broken. They were her exact words – she thought that was a true sign he was Brotherhood, before she even heard him discussing it. Didn't we always say that is what they would look like? Didn't we say that's how they'd hide from Big Brother, by seeming like they were nothing? But couldn't that also be the double bluff? That he's a powerful Thinkpol agent, but hides it by appearing weak?'

I feel breathless with fear. There is danger everywhere – even in the darkness of this single room.

She continues: 'She also said he knows a hatchet-faced man with glasses – she definitely said that.'

'How old is this SW?'

'I got the impression he was older than her – but most people in the ministry are, aren't they? I do know he's white.'

It feels like precious little to go on.

She finally sits up, her eyes grey in the dim light. 'That's it.' She grips my hands. 'Know this, Julia, as soon as I can do something brave for the Sisterhood, I will do it and I will not hesitate. Know I will do it for you. Because you came to see me, because you have not walked out on me when I've just asked something terrible of you.'

My words trail away. The truth is, we do rely on each other to be brave. And Leona has not asked anything from me that I wouldn't ask from the other members of the Sisterhood. We swore we would lay our lives down in the fight against Ingsoc. Their strike against Ruby is not just a strike against Ruby and Leona, but against each and every one of us in our Sisterhood.

I promise nothing except I'll think about it, and she tells me she'll get up and dress.

On the way downstairs, I hide my fear from the telescreens, which have now switched to playing brass band music, which is so jolly and reminiscent of the music at the lottery that it's jarring and sickening and bounces bold notes on my nerves. What's clear to me is that the Sisterhood's usual method of coded conversations in plain sight is much less stressful than breaking the rules. Whispering behind closed, forbidden doors would draw trouble quicker than our legitimized activities of the ASL.

By the time I reach reception, the visions of the Thought Police waiting for me are electrically alive. My excuses for my delay are so well rehearsed they crowd my mouth, but as soon as I see Holmes, they die. Holmes' face is still propped in her hands, but there's a leaden, corpse-like stillness about her. She stares dead-eyed, but from this angle, I can see it's not the telescreen she looks at all, but at some point above and to the right of the screen. I thought she'd been watching it, but perhaps she never had.

I remember Leona's words: *Don't worry about Holmes – she spent a year in Miniluv.* And afresh I see: Holmes has the slackness of flesh as if someone with a neat scalpel had cut some crucial wiring in the soft folds of her brain.

Perhaps psychosurgery is the treatment in the Ministry of Love that we fear the most.

Unsure, I almost pause, but a fly lands on her cheek. Pity turns to revulsion as the bluebottle crawls unchecked across her face. As it reaches her eye, the image is so disturbing I want her to flick it away. But instead she just stares on and on, so I turn away, not wanting to see the inevitable.

Chapter 3

I meet Eleanor back in the market the next day. Today is the first day of April and with it, winter temperatures have returned. The northerly wind bites my nose and I pull up my scarf around my face. It's a joy really that we can cover our mouths with scarfs so cameras can't lipread: survival is reductive.

Around me, the same miserable clutch of stalls huddle in the square. The daily markets are frequent throughout London, but there's no variance – one is the same as the other. The stalls are metal frames and thick wood boards; there's no pretence of anything other than basic need, and what they sell reflects the same. Proles still have shops in their quarter – often small dark affairs, which dodged the bombs and the bulldozers. But Outer Party people understand organically that it is prohibited to visit prole areas. People do – there are things they sell in their shops that we can't get, but if the patrols catch you, you might not go home again. With severe rations in place, shopping for food is a daily chore – it's a time-filling exercise and just another way the Inner Party keeps the Outer Party and proles busy.

If you're always battling to feed yourself, then you're less able to raise a rebellion.

But we've made it work for us. Eleanor and I visit the same market each day and, whilst a whole week could go past between us when we don't need to speak at the markets (because we also have our Anti-Sex League weekly meetings with our troop at the church hall, *and* the ASL steering group meetings at Prisha's for planning and prep), we know we can talk here if we need to.

The stallholders all have the same weathered walnut-shell skin and hard-calloused hands. The man on this stall is boldly shouting out his deals as if the prices are any different to the others. The prices are going up and the portion sizes go down. If others notice, they don't say. But today, there is a welcome change: the broccoli has gone from the veg stalls and now there are *both* new potatoes and cabbage. It feels like the promise of something – spring perhaps, at least, but whatever is changing, it is badly needed. But it doesn't pierce my fug of gloom and despair; I dreamed of the arrest again last night, but this time, Ruby was screaming at me: 'You left me behind! You left me behind!' I woke with a headache that felt like a screwdriver gouging into my brain, and the bright, cold sky harsh in my eyes. The significance of Ruby's words were not lost on me. My worst – very much worst – errors of my life have been leaving people behind.

Very softly, Arthur closes the door behind him. I can hear the latch clicking into place like yesterday and he is gone.

There is more than one way to leave someone behind.

My breath has gone from me, my lungs places of emptiness. I can't breathe as I think it again: *there is more than one way to leave people behind.*

I *need* to see Eleanor; as much as I love the others, she is my centre point. My fulcrum. I need to see her, reconnect. My dream – and now memories of Arthur – has left me so anxious, I need her to ground me. Only she can help me.

Then I see her coming towards me, towing her shopping trolley. Eleanor is tall, majestic even, and moves with the air of one who was once a practised dancer. I don't know if she ever danced in her youth before the dancing stopped forever – I often mean to ask her and always forget – but she has an elegance that defies even in her Outer Party boiler suit and Anti-Sex League knotted red waist sash. In her late sixties, her blue eyes are steady, direct, unquestioning but with no harshness – just quiet compassion. There's clear intelligence in her face, but I've seen her switch it off to a blank nothingness when the situation has called for it. Her height and her intelligence give her gravitas, but her leadership is more than that. She has Cecily's ability to be calm, but it is not Cecily's easy, relaxed stillness she possesses; instead, Eleanor's comes from a place of certainty, of resilience and of wisdom. She has lived; she has seen – she *understands*.

It was Eleanor who established the importance of routines as the bedrock of our communication. She taught us we are strong if we communicate with each other – and that by breaking communication between people is one way the Inner Party controls us. Therefore, we all hold our routines so that if we need to get word to each other, we can do.

She raises her hand to attract the stallholder's attention. 'Half kilo of potatoes!' As he serves her, we indulge in a glance – it's heavy with woe. Her normally clear eyes are cloudy with our shared pain over Ruby. Reddened and puffy, they tell of the story we can't tell each other: endless private grief. She returns to the stallholder and waves a finger at him: 'No mouldy ones!' I notice her wrists are a little thinner, too, and suspect she's lost weight she didn't have to lose. She moves a little closer and speaks to me in a low voice from behind her scarf. 'I saw Leona this morning. She was up early and came to clean the old church hall. A transformation. Damaged – of course, so damaged – but alive. To think I was concerned that she mightn't pull through . . .'

To hear of Leona dragging herself out of bed to clean before work makes me both want to sing and to cry. This is the news I needed. She is heroic. I want to hold her close and tell her how proud Ruby would be. Even the implications for me – that she wants me to find the man who snared Ruby – can't dampen my relief for my friend.

The stallholder passes a brown paper bag of potatoes to Eleanor, and she pays. I wonder if Eleanor knows what Leona has asked of me – I know she didn't want me to tell Eleanor, but did she change her mind? We've sworn to share everything in our fight. 'Did L say why she got up.' My question is flat like a statement – it's better not to sound interested in anyone.

'Only that—' Eleanor pauses as the woman in front

momentarily moves, which means that Eleanor's mouth can be seen. She tilts her face down and looks at her potatoes as if checking them. 'That your visit had given her something to hope for.'

I can't speak and I can't look at Eleanor.

'She became evasive when I asked her,' she murmurs. 'Would you know what she's hoping for.'

My friend is shrewd. I want to confess all – even open my mouth to do so but shut it again.

I decide I will tell her – just not yet. I need to first honour the deal with Leona, especially now she has kept her side of the bargain; I will try to find out something about SW, but I'm unsure of the wisdom of anything more. I reason, if I don't find anything, I'll never have to trouble Eleanor with it. Besides, as I look around, I notice that the market is fairly quiet away from the immediacy of the stall – and we can't linger here much longer.

'Only that she hopes we will find the Brotherhood,' I equivocate. I call out to the stallholder my request for half a cabbage.

Eleanor doesn't say anything – we both know the lie when we hear it.

We both pause momentarily with the Ministry of Truth in our sightline. Like the other ministries, its white pinnacle can be seen from anywhere in London, towering above the decaying city; perhaps now we are both thinking of Ruby who also worked there. It's where I am headed now; it's time for my work shift.

Eleanor wraps her scarf around her and leaves, but I continue to just stand for a moment, the cold on my face.

The Ministry of Truth – Minitrue in Newspeak – is magnificent and terrifying. A huge pyramid constructed of concrete, its surface polished to a finish that nears wet bone. Terrace after terrace builds to a masterful three hundred metres, the tomb-like building's pinnacle pierces the sky. There are four such government ministries, and I can see the tops of them all now, because if anything was ever taller in the city, it has long since been bulldozed to rubble or bombed to dust in the old wars. All four white pyramids stand imperious over enslaved London, the design a reminder of Big Brother's eternal promise to lord over all.

Within Minitrue, today, I'll try to find a middle-aged man who works on my floor, average height, white, in possible ill health and whose initials are SW.

Eleanor has already crossed the road and is out of sight. I didn't say goodbye to her because we never do – but today it sits badly with me. I dislike that I can't get her opinion on how to find SW without rousing suspicion.

I think of Ruby saying to me 'always forward' just before her arrest, but reflect that she misquoted Eleanor's slogan. The Sisterhood's proper slogan is 'always forward *in safety*'. As I start the walk towards the Ministry of Truth, I wonder just how safe I can realistically keep myself looking for someone who might be in the Brotherhood but is more likely to be a spy for the Thought Police.

Chapter 4

I am jubilant. Yesterday, at work, an opportunity opened up for finding SW and it means today I know I will find him.

I keep excitement tight within me, locked down under maskface, but I do feel it. I already have a plan – and it is already in action. I am hours from securing my target, of finding who SW is. It's changed so quickly: just yesterday, seeing Eleanor in the market, I wondered if I could successfully find SW, but today doubt has gone because everything changed almost as soon as I got to work.

Almost immediately, the path of how I might succeed in finding SW laid out in front of me, so clearly, so honestly and with only marginal risk, it seemed like a gift that could not be returned. I was sitting opposite Dreadful Grahame who I have sat opposite for four grinding years, when the solution to finding SW opened up to me. Finally! The years of staring at Dreadful Grahame's disturbing face become worthwhile. Although he's so thin, his face flesh is too big and appears unsecured to his skull. Worse – he dribbles and mutters to himself when thinking. The combination is a disaster – the muttering causes me to look up from my work, to which I then have to see the dribbling, which not only lands on the chin, but also onto his shirt. But Dreadful Grahame has finally proven to be an asset – he presented the way to find out who SW really is.

Dreadful Grahame is always cold, so has numerous jumpers, cardigans and little rugs dotted about his desk and chair. Yesterday, as he got up from his chair and walked past me to the photocopier, a jumper he had draped across his shoulders fell to the floor right by my desk. It's not the first time – he drops woollens like Prisha drops expletives. Normally, I throw them onto his chair or if feeling irritated by the dribbling, leave them so he can trip on them on his return.

But yesterday, I saw the plan in an instant. It was easy to put into action: I got up to go to the watercooler and gave the dropped jumper a swift nudge with my foot, pushing it under my desk. After three hours, satisfied Grahame hadn't noticed (he sat down, rooted around for another one and replaced it apparently without noticing), I was able to drop it into my bag also under my desk. Grahame's blue, regulation issued Outer Party unwashed jumper had become mine. At home, I locked myself in my bathroom (no cameras) and with a pen, added the initials to the label.

Now, I have Grahame's modified jumper in my bag and therefore half of my plan is already completed. An hour early for my shift today, I also have time to find SW before I have to be at my desk.

As I approach the ministry, the harsh sunlight has thrown the huge pyramidal-shaped shadow out in front of it. The road to the Ministry of Truth is wide, straight and pedestrianized. The start of every shift sees a steady line of comrades filing silently, obediently, like worker ants into the ministry. We don't talk; we don't walk in pairs or groups; faces are grim and set. Small trees line the route, silent sentries no doubt loaded with cameras and mics; it certainly feels like they watch as I and the others approach. London is filled with homelessness and litter – it's not uncommon to see skeletal people starving by the roadsides – but this road is clean and clear of any possible offence. CCTV on tall poles and patrols sweep constantly; to be caught in any way disfiguring the area outside of a ministry would result in swift retribution.

As I step into the shadow, I look up and draw in my breath. The anger I feel over Ruby's death makes me feel like I could tear it down. *Perhaps*, I think, as I walk through the ministry's triple height double doors, *I will yet*.

I step into the vast-heighted hall, just like I have for the last eight years, when my brother had pulled strings to get me this job. Set against the opposing wall so that it's the first thing one sees on entry, is an enormous gilt-framed painting of Big Brother; he stares down on us, crown prince of an empire that allegedly covers a third of the entire globe. There is no need of the slogan here that he is watching us: we know. Underneath, instead, is a repetition of what is carved into the ministry's outside walls:

WAR IS PEACE

FREEDOM IS SLAVERY

IGNORANCE IS STRENGTH

And there's many to see it – the hall is a cacophony of noise, bustling with workers (watched from the periphery by armed guards), all heading off to their various rooms. Every worker's role is to ensure that the three slogans are digested by the masses in a number of forms. For example, in the fiction department, AI bots will write crappy penny dreadful books that didactically explore what happens when a character decides that war is *not* peace. Short answer: they die. I am probably the only person in this entire building of over five thousand staff who studied Shakespeare and Sophocles' *Oedipus the King* at school, and the alignment between the party's new books with the classic tragedies is not lost on me. I think of Oedipus and my own father and wonder if I, too, am fated to destroy everything, including myself.

Just like every morning before work, I have to be processed by security. I remove my coat and place it with my bag in the plastic tray on runners; today I have something that could provoke trouble in my bag. But, because it's only a jumper, I have a degree of confidence and try not to watch the man who stares at the screen to check I'm not carrying any bomb or weapon into the building. After it's through, I step through the scanner. Someone else checks my pass and I grab my bag – I'm cleared for work.

I take a lift (the electricity is never cut off in the ministries – nothing stops us from carrying out the duty of Ingsoc), but don't get out on my floor. I've arrived early for work so I can carry out my idea. The lift doors open onto a noticeably different environment to the lobby. Gone is the smooth, polished, impressive gloss of the exterior and entrance hall – although I don't doubt that it's continued in other parts of the building. But here, like my floor, the routine parts of administration of the ministries' work is sustained by greige, stained carpet tiles, tired furniture and a smell close to farts and boiled cabbage.

The sign announces HUMAN RESOURCES. There are ten men and women sitting behind desks and I approach the nearest one, holding the jumper.

A man looks up – on his desk is a metal sign: Jahin Sundar, section leader. 'You're not supposed to be here. Message the HR team if you have a human resources issue; standard response is seventy-five hours, unless it falls on a Fraterday and then it's one hundred hours.'

I ignore his welcome. 'Found this,' I say, holding the jumper out of his reach. 'It's got the initials SW written on the label.' I pull it out to show off my handiwork. 'I'm in early today to serve Big Brother, and want to help a cold comrade out. If you want, tell me what floor SW works on – I could drop it over to them.' I hold it from pincered fingers to show it's unpleasant. 'You'll not want it. Stinks.'

Jahin looks at the ragged jumper and sniffs. 'I've got better things to do than bother with this.'

'Comrade, surely if the owner of this jumper is well clothed, he will preserve his health and therefore will serve Big Brother better.' I raise a quizzical eyebrow. 'You wouldn't want to stand in the way of a comrade's service?'

Jahin pulls a face, but taps into his computer. 'I've got twenty-five people with the initials SW – no, twenty-four as one retired two months ago.'

Twenty-four! I hadn't imagined that many. 'Well, take out the Inner Party.'

Jahin narrows his eyes at me, 'Don't worry, I did not include them.'

Stupid of me – of course he didn't. 'Well, let's see if we can narrow it down. By the looks of this jumper, it's probably a man's.'

Jahin's voice is haughty. 'I don't know why you think that.'

And I can't tell you why, I feel like hissing at him. He's right, though – men and women wear the same clothes. But I need the point made. 'Trust me, comrade, the smell of it – no offence.'

Jahin's lips push to a line. 'None taken,' he says dryly.

'And I found it on my floor. So, you could narrow it down to just the men on the fifth floor?'

He taps on his computer and then leans back. 'Lucky you. That narrows it down to just two.' Now obliging because he's got rid of me, he writes down the names. 'I'll put down their departments, too.'

'Thank you, you are a true comrade.'

I look at the names – Simon Whitstable and Steven Winter. Time to go and find the man who might just be Ruby's traitor. I feel sick but also bubbling excitement – there's a chance (slim but possible) that Ruby had found the Brotherhood. This man could be the person we are looking for and not our enemy but our true comrade.

But probably not. He is probably exactly what Leona and I suspect: Thought Police. And he's used to hiding in plain sight. Perhaps this is the right thing to do after all, because as I get in the lift to my floor, I realize something: I could kill this man. I could kill the person responsible for

Ruby's death. And I think I want to. I try this thought on and decide it fits well.

I take the lift back to my floor to check these men out. I just have to remember to be very careful.

Chapter 5

I'm looking at Simon Whitstable sitting at his desk typing and I know it's not him. I don't even bother to make an approach. He's at least sixty, maybe seventy, and has a white milky eye. I've seen this guy around – his blind eye is so distinctive, Ruby would have mentioned it in her description. And the age is wrong, too – he's old enough for her to have been more definitive.

One left. Steven Winter. It has to be him. I tighten my jaw and remember to take a deep breath. I roll my shoulders a little – not enough to be detected by any of the numerous telescreens, but just enough to ease some of the tension. When I get tense, I always feel it in my shoulders.

Instead, I walk down the long corridor, clutching the jumper. For the telescreens which are hung at regular intervals, I check the jumper label again as if thinking it over. I walk past my area – the fiction department. I'm not due to start my shift yet, but I make sure I pick up pace and turn my face away so they don't see me. I don't want Grahame to see me carrying a jumper in case he's missed it. It could be awkward if he reclaimed it and then found the initials written into the label.

No one sees me and after a few minutes and a couple of turnings, I make it to the Official Documents department. I can't scout around so approach the first person on the desk. 'Is Steven Winter here?'

This woman doesn't even look up from her work but just thumbs over her shoulder at a young man of about seventeen, who is tapping away on his computer. He looks up at the sound of his name. I recognize him. I've noticed him before, because he's one of the few people who will hold the lift door if he sees someone coming. And I know it's not him.

'Can I help?' he asks.

But I feel crashing disappointment because the SW I'm looking for is white, and this young man is Black. 'Are you Steven Winter?'

'Yes,' he says, puzzled.

'Is this yours?' I say, holding up the jumper, forced to continue the charade.

The crushing disappointment I feel as I turn away at his 'no', is so, *so* much more than I expected. I didn't want this mission, but it's become – in my grief for Ruby – my focus. Somewhere between leaving Leona and now, I had come to feel that this was the answer. Finding SW would lead us to . . . the end? I keep my face passive but realize something significant: I never thought we would just get quietly old. I considered that we would be caught by a patrol or arrested by the Thought Police; I even thought we might find the Brotherhood and do something important. Yes, society says that women are worthless, but Eleanor has told us otherwise. I – rarity that I am – have seen enough of another world to know that anything is possible. Knowing that, how can one not strive for better?

I'm not done yet, I decide, heading back to my desk. This can't be it. I know there's someone significant on my floor and even if it doesn't feel it at the moment, I know I have enough information to find him. I just have to believe enough and try enough. My father, when I still called him Daddy, told me that when jumping my pony. 'Dig in,' he used to tell me, 'and you can do anything.'

I'm not sure he used to believe that of me, but now I have to.

Chapter 6

For nearly two hours I sit at my desk, and tap some keys, and ignore Dreadful Grahame and the others, and I can only think that I've blown it in some way. I'd hoped my plan would yield a result, but now it hasn't, I have to think of something else.

Frustrated at no ideas, in the end, I just can't stand sitting still. I wait until Grahame is elsewhere, then I let a couple of others know that I'm on a mission to find the owner of a missing jumper. 'I've got a cramp in my leg that won't shift, so I might as well combine the two.' If they look suspicious, I don't notice because I've already turned and gone.

I walk around knowing that I haven't got long before I'll be back at my desk. I clutch it, a little desperately, and walk the long corridor before I realize it's just a few minutes until eleven hundred – in my fever, I've forgotten the Two Minute Hate. The Records Department are dragging out chairs from their cubicles (so paranoid is the work of Records, they dare not even let each other see their work and huddle, crouched, behind their cubicle screens). They are lining the chairs up in the centre of the hall opposite the big telescreen. Everyone is obliged to Hate at the right time – and in the right way – so I'm here for the next few minutes. Good. It gives me a chance to look for the 'owner' of this jumper and work out if there's anyone here who fits the description.

And then I see him. He's taking his seat on the middle row of chairs and I know it's *him* before I even have a logical thought. First, a memory, an impulse of Ruby, hot-faced and laughing. *I have had a result!*

My first rational thought, therefore, is a reflex of her memory, how she made me feel and of the description she gave and then I feel a certainty, a deep, visceral knowing when I look at him. *So, it's you.*

You.

Chapter 7

Winston Smith.

I've seen him in the corridors and there's something about him that feels unpleasant – that feeling like biting on an apple and then seeing the wormhole or having to put on yesterday's underwear. I've never considered why he invokes such distaste – not least because I don't look at him long enough to know. In a show of being helpful, I help arrange the office chairs into neat rows in front of the big telescreen to get ready for the Two Minute Hate and it gives me ample opportunity to take quick glances at Smith. In his mid-forties, and shorter than the average man, like most of us, rations have kept him too thin, but there's also something frail about him – looking at him now, as he shuffles to make himself comfortable, he appears more than a little pathetic.

I sit down feeling a strange, overwhelming feeling of tumult. I let Grahame's now misused jumper sink to the floor – I'll leave it here and let someone else deal with it now, because I don't need it. I have found my mark.

'Older than Ruby': *check*.

'Works in Minitrue on my floor': *check*.

'White': *check*.

'Pathetic, weak and broken': *check*, *check*, *check*.

Even the initials are correct, albeit inverted. A very easy mistake for Leona to make, especially given her considerable grief.

It is him.

Around me, people fall silent – a member of the Inner Party has joined us. O'Brien. Dangerous. Dressed in black overalls – even if one didn't know him, his uniform marks him as Inner Party. I've seen him around many times before. He works on the upper floors and if he ever looks in my direction, I make sure I'm looking the other way. He checks his watch and makes a show that he might as well stop here for the Hate that's about to start. But I don't trust it: what if he's here for Smith? A tall, muscly man, with glasses, with sharp cheekbones and an air of cruelty, he could certainly be called 'hatchet-faced'. This seems even more likely when he sits down here, in the row in front of me, just one person, a small, blonde woman, between him and Smith. I squeeze crescent moons into my palms with both fear (he must be Thinkpol) and anger (I want to kill them both), but also excitement (it's as if Ruby is helping me).

The Hate is starting. A mandatory coming together, it is like an anti-worship that everyone must participate in. It starts with a grinding speech of Hate about Goldstein as his face flashes onto the screen. Goldstein – who the Sisterhood want to find. I risk a look at Winston – does he know him? Is he affiliated with him or is he sworn to destroy anyone associated with him? I wished I wasn't behind him so I could get a clearer sense of him.

Goldstein is speaking on the screen: his ideologies about freedom of thought; freedom of speech; freedom of the press – and a grinding unpleasant voiceover cleverly dismisses his arguments as Goldstein's soundbites are made. Goldstein himself looks like a kindly grandfather, with a lean face and gentle eyes. Allegedly he was once friends with Big Brother himself and helped shape the state – even now, on this clip of him, he complains about the rebellion being betrayed and thumps his fist to palm as he does so. Is this true? Was he ever affiliated with the government? Is Goldstein even real or a CGI creation to give the masses focus? I don't know.

The effect of watching Goldstein against the grinding, hideous voiceover and the whipped-up hate is having a palpable effect on everyone around me. We are trained to Hate – as we do this, children are doing the same thing in schools; babies cradled in nurseries witnessing the one who holds them scream their Hate. Here, adults have lost control; raise their own fists; shaking; sweating; chestbeating. The more one Hates, the better party person you are. Winston himself now shouts: 'Swine! Swine! Swine!'

I hate now. I hate *him*.

I hate him and like a scratch to an itch, I pick up a heavy Newspeak dictionary and fling it at the screen. Although I throw it at Goldstein, in my heart I am throwing it at Winston Smith who, very likely, trapped my friend.

Around me the Hate is reaching its zenith. The image of Goldstein has been modified to a sheep and his voice to a bleat. It's vile and childish and seems to create a deeper repugnance in those around me. I'm suddenly angry – so angry it's like the hugeness and brightness of the sun is in me, overwhelming me. My grief for Ruby; grief for Leona; my increased fear of arrest is just burnt up in the fire of this all-consuming anger.

I hate these people who have taken a good, kind, decent woman. So much punishment, so much death. I hate that everyone around me is so easily whipped up into such fervour about the wrong things. Goldstein, to my knowledge, has done nothing. Yet these men in the row in front of me have orchestrated the death of someone good. It's all wrong. People are stamping, kicking chairs, crying with anger. The worst part is I don't know how much they truly feel it. I think they do, that they are so easily pitched to a fever because our lives are so awful – grinding poverty and the never-ending fear of being caught or turned in for doing something against the Party.

Now, the crowds have started their monotonous chanting of B-B-B again (almost a hymn, a prayer, muttered zombie-like through half-closed eyes and swaying bodies). I see Smith exchange a look with O'Brien. He turns his face to him and O'Brien turns his to Smith's. It is such a strange look; if I was not sitting directly behind them, I wouldn't have seen it. But it was a shared look of contempt. Of wry amusement. They are mocking the people around them.

And it's significant because it's facecrime. To commit facecrime, to show anything other than zealous commitment to the party – against Goldstein and to those who participate in the Hate – is unthinkable. But they have shown they are united in their thinking.

The Hate over, I help them put away the chairs. I try to catch Smith's eye and think of Ruby telling me that she couldn't help it – that she was tired of waiting and when the opportunity presented itself, she had to act. I cannot act so impulsively and go back to my desk before I give myself away. I need to be careful and decide my next steps. Do I take it to the Sisterhood, even though their debate could halt me doing anything – leaving us still achieving nothing? Or do I act as Leona wants me to and attempt to flush him out on my own?

Chapter 8

I smooth the flag under my hands, scrutinizing my hand-work of small stitching, and take a moment to gather the courage to speak. I've spent every hour between the Two Minute Hate yesterday and now, trying to decide what to do.

It's clearly risky to pursue Smith – particularly as the reality is that he is probably Thought Police. I'm scared – looking for an owner of a jumper is one thing, but this would be something else entirely. Last night I heard the helicopter in my dreams and when I woke, had the compulsion to check the sky again.

To make big decisions whilst hurting so badly is impossible.

But as the morning dragged on, I wondered how I could do nothing. How could I pass Smith in the corridor and ever forgive myself for walking on by? Seeing his thoughtcrime with an Inner Party member; the fact O'Brien was even *there*; the way Smith felt empowered to commit thought-crime in front of anyone who happened to look; Ruby's sudden arrest so soon after contact with him; even his physicality: it all feels like the most certain one can be in

Oceania, where nothing is certain at all. Ruby was right – Smith is exactly the type of puritanical, shuffling bureaucrat who could be a Brotherhood comrade hiding in plain sight.

By the time I arrived at Prisha's for our meeting, I had made my decision. I had no choice. I would pursue Smith as I would any mark as part of my role in the Sisterhood – but I'll hold back the truth of Smith's connection to Ruby. I have to: Leona and I made a deal. And seeing her now, slumped on the dining chair, puffy-faced, shows she's keeping her side of it. Really, what choice do I have?

If I find out Smith had a role in Ruby's death, it'll be Leona who hears that first. If he's Brotherhood, I'll lift him up to my sistren. But I do need to tell them something – enough but not the full truth. I know Eleanor would never agree to it – she would say it's too dangerous. After all, it's the persecuted we seek – not the persecutors.

What's left of the Sisterhood is seated around the dining table in Prisha's front room. The room, currently set up as a sewing workshop, is small and crowded by the large table and chairs. It's changed around to suit whatever we need it to become at the time. Normally there are six chairs, but now Ruby has gone, Prisha has taken one away. But we are not alone: the mandatory telescreen hangs above the fireplace.

Inadvertently my gaze instead flicks to Cecily, and just glancing at her, pins in mouth, as she sews the word SEX in black velvet against cornflower blue linen, calms me. The look of concentration on her smooth, broad face, allows me to breathe. To settle. This is just another sewing meeting, I lie to myself.

I am ready to speak.

My charade starts: firstly, I intentionally focus on my flag. Then, leaning a little closer, my eyelids narrow – just enough – but not too much. I am hyper aware of being watched – if they took Ruby because of something connected to the Sisterhood, then they will be watching us now. But we also can't be paralysed by fear: we still have to move forwards because without moving forwards, nothing changes and that is simply a different type of death.

I lift the material to the lamp-shaded light and scrutinize it. My nail grates against the linen. I shake my head a little. Now I must speak: 'I have found a mark. A new one.' Despite my Sisters' understanding of the real meaning of the term *mark*, none of the women's faces lift away from their sewing. I wonder if Leona was waiting for this.

I add: 'Any thoughts?'

For the sake of Big Brother and the Sisterhood's public persona as the steering group of the Junior Anti-Sex League, they agreeably chat as they sew, sharing ideas on stain removal, continuing the pretence of my 'mark'. Tips are exchanged; the veneer maintained. Publicly, we are poised, perfect women, subservient and only concerned with petty, domestic matters. But my Sisters, they know what I'm suggesting – even if they don't know why.

Leona ties off her sewing with elegant fingers and bites the thread with small, neat teeth. She comments on Prisha's stain-removal technique. 'I want to say thank you, Julia.' She grabs my hand. 'For caring about . . . the details.'

I feel my throat thicken and work hard not to look at Eleanor. Don't guess, don't guess, don't guess, E.

Leona continues, mercifully covering up her real intention. 'Sorry, but nothing *really* removes tough stains. You must throw it away, start again. Your flag represents the ASL troop and our girls deserve immaculate representation – because they *are* immaculate. To have dirty flags will only encourage the dirty minds of the sexual deviants. To even see the mark could result in sexcrime.' Her voice, always a soft growl, which earnt her the nickname lion by her sister, now crumbles to a half cry and someone passes her a tissue.

My heart bruises for her. Despite her puffy face, she must have lost another three pounds since I saw her last week.

'Leona,' Eleanor says, 'we can't throw material away – the Ministry for Plenty can only be plentiful if we are observant. The corn starch or vinegar will work.'

Eleanor turns to me, words sodden with subtext: 'Julia, you must pursue the mark by agitating it. It is a good cause. You are right to be diligent. If it yields, your work will be rewarded. If it doesn't, you were still right to try.' And then unnecessarily for the Sisterhood, but for the all-observing telescreen, she adds without missing a beat, 'If only because it's such a lovely flag you are making. It will make a big impact at Hate Week.'

Prisha and Leona nod. Only one does not react at my news. Without pausing, Cecily continues to slowly take pins from her pursed mouth and pierces the material, weaving each silver shard through, marrying the velvet and linen. Her actions are careful, precise. I have never encountered such gentle deadliness. If she's unhappy, her voice is silent. Instead, she finishes her pinning and shakes out her new banner. The rippling sound unsettles me. If there isn't peace within the Sisterhood, we have nothing.

'That's a beautiful banner,' says Prisha. 'The blue and black are really powerful.'

Cecily smiles her thanks. Materials are hard to come by, but there's a lot of support for the Junior ASL, from both the Ministry of Truth, responsible for education and entertainment, and the Ministry of Love, responsible for law and order. They both find value in our work and regularly give us access to resources. It's not much to have a supply of otherwise scarce biscuits and sweets to entice the girls into membership, but the old church hall we were gifted (where we never dare talk about business as it's probably filled with mics) gives our group a weekly sense of place. We have purpose under the watchful eyes of government: all the time people are getting pregnant the old way, there is a demand for us to try and stop it. Family bonds are based on love – it is love that Ingsoc seeks to eradicate.

'I think you should forget it,' Cecily finally says in her slow, deep voice. 'You could end up damaging the material. Leave it, find—' Her voice catches. *Another way.* I know she wants to say this because she doesn't agree with looking for marks anymore. She and Prisha want more direct action. 'Find a *different* answer.' For context she adds smoothly, 'Or learn to live with the stain. With all the Hate Week celebrations, one little mark is likely to be incidental.'

Nobody says anything. Prisha gets up at one point to serve us more too-cool blackberry leaf tea from the pot.

The telescreen shifts to a programme on Eurasian's water shortages. We watch malnourished Eurasian children and their mothers cry at empty water tap stands, and we all praise Ingsoc that they deliver us a society where children don't have to die of thirst. Privately, we wonder how much of the propaganda we see is true. The programme switches to a huge water turbine and the juxtaposition from the thirsty to the crashing abundance of the river and the huge toiling water wheel, is obvious. There is an announcement, telling us that there is great news, that Oceania has converted another power station from water to oil. It makes no sense but as 'Oceania, 'tis for thee', is played, we all dutifully stand and sing.

Leona finishes another banner for the children to wave at Hate Week and we all congratulate her on it.

I keep sewing as if nothing's happened. Because slow equals survival, nothing but sewing happens for the next hour. Then finally, Eleanor says, 'Who has got the crimping scissors?'

Prisha's voice is light. 'They're in the usual cupboard. In the hall. Help yourself.' We always meet at Prisha's because she has a secret cellar. Her house was her parents' and she says her grandad dug it out when he saw the way the world was going. It seeps damp through the wood-banked walls and smells, but we hope and pray that it's as underground as it feels.

'Your big cupboard where you shove everything? I can never find anything in there. Julia, you know what's what – can you show me?'

Although the ASL steering group meeting is weekly, we

only have this conversation once a quarter. Last time, Ruby came with us.

So, with Ruby an unperson, it's now just me available for reconnaissance work. I say, 'If it means we can have better banners for the beloved Big Brother, I'm already up!'

Eleanor and I are still chuckling when we make it into Prisha's darkened hallway, but away from the telescreen, our smiles drop as if severed from a puppeteer's strings. We can still hear its monotone, but it's muted here. Just blind whispers in the shadows. It can't see us. Of course, we are meant to position ourselves in front of it all the time, but we risk small snatches of time each quarter.

It's musty here in the dark hall, like stale air and damp-stored linen. We open the cupboard door and pull the shelves out. The unit then partially lifts out. It conceals an opening.

If they found it, we would be put to death. No question.

We move quickly. I can't do this on my own and Eleanor is helping me. I hate that I am putting her in danger. I think she hates what she's going to do to me and why.

The *why* is the biggest heart scratch.

The opening gives way to steps that drop into the dark. A cool air uncoils from below and reaches for our faces. But we don't hesitate.

Eleanor and I move fast: we go down into the cellar.

Chapter 9

The cellar steps are lined with old yellow brick. There are other places around London where I still see these old bricks and every time, they bring me back to these steps. It's dark but we step quickly out of memory and the fear of being gone long enough for our absence to be detected.

The room at the bottom is open to the staircase. There is no cellar door. Arthur's father told me once that 'cellar door' was considered by some to be the most beautiful phrase in the English language. That couldn't be said now. Beauty and language must not be celebrated.

The cellar is small – the size of Prisha's kitchen. A bomb shelter. I love this man who had the foresight and sheer effort to dig this out when a sofa and a cold beer must've beckoned. Perhaps others laughed; perhaps he kept it secret. We owe him everything. Yes, there are fewer bombs now, but everything still to shelter from.

Eleanor reaches up to a shelf and takes down a biscuit tin. The air is lung-moist here, warm and humid. The tin is rusting – really, I'm surprised this has gone on long enough for the tin to decay. She opens it and takes out a vial and a syringe. She wipes it with alcohol. Eleanor's mother was a doctor, she once told me, perhaps to reassure me. I don't remember. Maybe that's not even true. I spend so much of my life dancing between the truth and a lie, I don't even keep track.

I've turned away from her and I'm pulling down my trousers. Then I pull the material of my pants up to expose my buttock.

Eleanor is swift. She's already drawn up the contraceptive. 'Upper outer quarter, miss the sciatic nerve,' she mutters to herself, just like she always does.

The pain is sharp but brief. I think of Cecily's needles darting like minnows, flashes of silver. Eleanor plunges the syringe's fluid further into my muscle; it's a cold flush and then it's heading for my bloodstream. We pause briefly and she looks at me closely. 'I *know*, Julia – about you. But I want you to tell me yourself. No time now – we'll arrange a crowd.'

My breath is held in my lungs, tight. She knows. Is this true? Has she found out my secrets? No. *Not* possible. How could she? She must mean about my engaging Ruby's contact.

But even the fact she's chosen to whisper in the cellar is alarming – normally we never speak as it's too dangerous to even pause and whisper. Then, it's lid back on tin, tin slid home and she's up the steps behind me and without speaking, we are back in the hall and replacing the wooden shelves.

We pause in the gloom of the hall and our gazes snag together – a frisson of understanding.

Then, after impossible seconds, I blink and smile. The movement feels stiff and false because inside I'm panicking. *Don't panic, Julia – she can't know.*

I want to forget this and enter the front room. 'Now you've got the crimping scissors, what are you going to use them for, Eleanor?' I hate the fact that my voice is overfilled, water-balloon tight.

I thought I might get something from Eleanor, some nuance or depth, but her voice is strong and clear, the moment gone: 'I want them to edge the FUCK for my flag – the crimping edge will make the word in my slogan stand out.'

'What's your slogan?' asks Prisha, looking at us across the table.

'Fuck Sex!' Eleanor laughs. Her laugh is surprisingly girlish, and I am always enchanted by it. I recall the clear-sighted look she gave me like she knows about me and think *I imagined it, I imagined it.* Just jumpy. Ruby's arrest has made me see worries where there are none.

Perhaps.

We carry on, sewing and chatting about finding the perfect maxim for the Anti-Sex League. We drink our substitute tea and continue the rest of our meeting talking about the things that the telescreen can download about us. Our conversation is inhaled in, pulled through the digital arteries, pumped towards the mega computer that is the brain of Big Brother. There are files on all of us since we were born – *before* we were born. Files on what our parents read, bought, watched, ate, shat and made them horny. We exist to Big Brother before we've even seen the sky. He predicts our tastes, our temperament and our abilities. We are earmarked for Party (only Outer Party, *never* Inner Party – no, that is *quite* a different thing), or prole before our mother even pushes us into the world.

But there are no files on the Sisterhood.

Perhaps.

Ruby.

When we say goodnight and step out into the early evening, Eleanor says to me casually on the doorstep: 'There's a saucepan sale at the Waverly Street market.' She speaks slowly, enunciating the date and time – she wants to be clear. Then adds, 'I hear they are good pans – I expect they will draw a crowd.'

My heart quickens but my face and voice do not betray me. 'Thank you. I need a new pan. The Party is the perfect provider.'

'Don't tell anyone, girls,' says Eleanor. 'The Party has placed new pans – in their wisdom – at the point of high demand. If we tell anyone, we might not get one.'

When I was a child, Cook used to say: tell someone something and they might tell one person; tell someone it's a secret and they will tell ten. We all know this is true. 'I won't tell anyone,' I murmur.

'Nor me,' says Prisha.

'Nor me,' promises Leona and Cecily, all understanding the lie. We will each repeat this line to every woman we will encounter between now and then. If enough people attend wanting pans, there will definitely be a crowd.

We silently spill into the street. For a moment we are a group, our scarlet sashes bound over our overalls and around our waists – signs of our chastity, our membership to the ASL – both unifying and homogenizing us.

But then we break apart. Leona leaves in one direction, Eleanor crosses the street and turns north, Prisha shuts her front door. None of us say goodbye. None of us can pretend to care about each other.

As I leave, Cecily says in a bright, clear voice, 'I'll walk with you, Julia, to the corner. I have an errand to run.'

I don't nod – it feels like trouble.

Chapter 10

It feels awkward to walk next to Cecily; my nerves make my body feel clunky, as if the muscles and joints have forgotten and are learning again how to interact. It's not just the surveillance, but I'm almost more bothered by the possibility that Eleanor could glance back and see our illicit (how does it feel so wrong when it isn't? *Is* it?) change in routine. Eleanor's approval is all I have. I can't bear that I might not even have it now.

I know, Julia.

Could she?

No. Impossible.

It takes concentration to relax. I listen to the sound of my thick soles hitting the pavement and it steadies me.

We walk along for a few minutes and make light conversation about the girls in our troop – who Chantelle hit most recently and why Gerta insists on stealing biscuits. The grey street is empty; the pavement dirty; the air muzzily grim, almost as though the April weather feels enough schadenfreude to dampen our clothes but can't summon the energy to pour properly. A helicopter buzzes in the far distance and I can't watch it lest they see my scrutiny, but it frays me; they still edge my dreams.

The wind complains through the gaps in the buildings. Beneath the wind and our footsteps, we whisper into our knitted scarves. 'Prisha and I want you to know that we want change.'

Relief: for a moment I thought this was connected to Eleanor's unnerving comment about me.

I know, Julia.

She continues, 'I went to see Leona after you saw her, and she told me a secret.'

Just the mentions of secrets makes me feel sick. Too many, there's too many.

She pauses and we turn down an even quieter street. She stops to tie a shoelace, so I know what she's about to say is important. I don't breathe so I can't miss her whisper: 'She told me about her real work in the Ministry of Peace. It's not what she told us.'

Now I'm intrigued. Leona is perhaps not just mobilizing me. She has always said she sits on a conveyor belt, attaching two bits of metal together. Sometimes, she tells us snippets about her life in Minipax. With its remit for war, law and order, it sounds a terrible place to work. She told me once that sometimes, on cold winter days when noise travels more easily through the aircon tubes, people eating their lunch in the ministry's canteen can hear the screams of the weapons tests from the vast laboratories below. She says if it's really bad, they turn up the telescreens and switch them to music – usually something with brass bands.

'The truth is, she helps assembles bombs.' She finishes her knot and then gets up and starts walking.

For a moment, I'm so stunned, I simply stand as she moves away. When I catch her up, she continues: 'She didn't want us to know because she didn't want us to judge her. She was ashamed that she makes things that kill people.'

I say nothing. Poor Leona. No one has a choice in what work they're assigned.

'But she says you're doing something for her – don't tell me, I can guess, but know this: Prisha and I don't want you to. But whatever you've agreed it's changed her – she says she owes you. She told me she is inspired by your bravery. Says it's lit a match in her and now she has a plan and wants to tell us. This led to me and Prisha talking, and well, we want change too. At our St Paul's meeting next week, we're going to push for a different direction for the group. We want to stop looking for *them* . . .'

No more searching for the Brotherhood? That is the point of our group. What if we are so close? What if our link is Smith? 'E won't like it,' I say unnecessarily. It's our purpose as the Sisterhood.

'We need to try something new. A proactive plan – one where we don't rely on men anymore. One that doesn't rely on rumours that might not even be real. It doesn't feel like there's a point to it.'

Three years ago, the Sisterhood's dreams felt possible. Now, with no gains and only the loss of Ruby – and with not even the slightest rumour of any kind of dissent against the Party found, let alone a murmur of the Brotherhood breathed to any one of us, I realize it's not just me who's worried we are truly alone.

The Party supposedly covers most of the world. We are told that there are three world governments, with Ingsoc controlling Oceania (the Americas, the Atlantic Islands, Australasia, and Brazzaville). If we can rebel against Ingsoc, there must be others in these countries who feel the same as us (how could there not be?), but I fear we are too small, too infrequent, too spread apart to ever connect. I fear we are only flotsam in a huge, silent sea; the space between us is just too huge, too immense, too empty to find others like us, and we're operating in a huge nothing.

'But if not this, then what instead?' I ask. Searching for the Brotherhood is the only plan we have. Joining small groups, becoming networked, gaining size and strength, felt like the way to grow. We don't look for other women – why would we when they have no money and no access to power?

Cecily doesn't answer my question. I know she worries about her input (her 'weight', she calls it) in the group – like Prisha, they both teach at a nearby secondary school. Usually, women are only allowed roles that are entry level or involve childcare. She doesn't talk about her job – I think it makes her sad. I think about what Arthur told me about his school and I can understand why. Obviously as teachers, although they are connected to the Ministry of Truth and still Outer Party, they are very far from any connection to power. Not that she or Prisha ever countenanced the idea of using sex for spying ('dangerous and unproven'); now she's in a relationship with Prisha, no one would agree to it either. But it's frustrating, I can see that. We want to do so much, but to get a foothold – until now – seems impossible. 'Think it over,' is all she says.

It makes me feel ashamed. I want to tell her the truth about why this mark could be different, could be worth the personal sacrifice, but I can't make the angles work. Nothing fits. To settle one of the Sisterhood means being disloyal to the other. The noise in my head is deafening – all I can hear is the indecision on how much of myself and my past I should turn in – and if Eleanor knows now, have I left it too late? But when I turn to my dearest friend to speak, Cecily has already peeled away unnoticed, and I am left alone.

Chapter 11

Eleanor's plan has worked better than expected: we must have all told a dozen who told a dozen who told a dozen and now this market square is packed with hundreds of women. Whenever there are huge crowds, the mood often sours. If there's not the possibility of winning the lottery, then crowds can be dangerous places. The crowds around us pulse like it's a single homogenous mass feeling the same emotion. It's anger, I know it's anger, but sometimes it feels like . . . hunger.

What are we hungry for?

It's not saucepans. We are here for pans, but we don't need them. This visceral emotion is something completely removed. Big Brother ignores occasional rioting to allow the anger to vent from its controlled populace. The Two Minute Hate is not enough to remove all the pus from the boil. If there weren't eruptions of emotion it would build, perhaps into something useful, something significant. It's normal for people to become angry over nothing – now it's pans. Next it will be shoes. The day after, the wrong colour bread.

People have kicked each other to death over knitting needles before.

There is a middle-aged woman next to me. Her mouth is open and screaming, strings of saliva like spun webs or wires between her teeth. The cords on her neck are standing out. She is shrieking to the point of loss of control.

Two women are having a punch-up over a pan that continues until the handle is wrenched from the pot.

Pans are passed over our heads, but they are passed back in an orderly manner. The pans are rejected. These people don't want to be soothed, they don't want to be mollified. They want to *feel*. Hate is all we are allowed to feel and to feel it – to feel anything – makes us feel alive. A pan passes close by but the woman beside me does not reach for it. Her irises are encircled with white and are focused on the vendor, I think at first, until the vendor runs away, cowed by the pressing crowd. She is actually staring at nothing. Her anger is for nothing. It is for everything. It is for our fear-sodden, cold, controlled lives.

I move away.

The crowd lows, cow-like, in unison. As one, it pulses, elbows me, deadens my toes and blows stale gin breath my way.

We are atavistic; we are primeval.

In this breathing animal of a crowd, birthing anger, I raise my fist and shout savagery. I'm good at it. I look like everyone else – I look like the perfect citizen of Airstrip One. Next to me now is an unusually short woman. Her clothes strain against her bust; I push against her and she falls against the next woman. I grab her shoe – it's laced but easy to pull off. It releases a quick pungent smell of sock and sweat.

Prisha then is in front of me and smiles. She holds her fist high. 'Fuck pan theft. Fuck all of you!'

To answer her – to make her laugh later – I then hurl the shoe across the crowd at the pan vendor. 'Fuck you! Oceania is the greatest!' We catch each other's eye again, amused – moments of friendship scaffold me long after the event.

The woman struggles to a stand and looks up at me. She is obviously bewildered – it's not every day that someone takes and weaponizes your shoe. To her credit she pulls off the other one and throws it in the same direction. 'I love Oceania!' she exclaims, pleased to love our nation state. Then bizarrely, the woman next to her pulls off her shoes and does the same.

Prisha laughs and then is gone. The shoeless woman reaches for the woman's feet next to her, and I'm finished. I'm not prepared to get caught in some strange shoe throwing fetish, even if I started it. Instead, I seek what I came for. Eleanor wanted a crowd and I fear I know what she wants to talk about that couldn't wait until our next St Paul's visit next week.

Now I see her. It takes only a few minutes before we are able to edge closer, two torn cloths seamed together.

'I know what you are doing,' says Eleanor. 'But I want you to tell me yourself. I need to hear it from you. What is your plan for the Sisterhood?'

I am not going to tell her the truth – I can't. I decided a long time ago that I'd keep my secrets and I will. Instead,

I choose to think she is asking me about Smith. Sorry, Leona – I'd rather renege on our deal than to reveal who I was before I became Julia.

So, I tell her the truth about Smith.

I'm expecting her to say: *No, not agreed. Don't kill him. It's too dangerous. Stay safe and keep away.* So when she says, 'Do it,' I realize I haven't understood her at all. Nobody is acting like they should anymore. Ruby making independent contact; Prisha and Cecily and now Eleanor. Do we even know who we are now?

But this is still what I want, and her word is enough. Eleanor and I let the crowds carry us away from each other. I think she has gone and think, *I have permission to hook my fish.* My mark is now my mission.

Winston Smith, watch out.

I am coming for you.

Just as I think this, Eleanor is back. She is behind me, tight against my shoulder. She is close to my ear and her voice a whisper, but her mouth is so close I can feel her breath on my cheek. 'I am trusting you with our lives.' She grips my elbow briefly. '*Trust*, Julia. Don't let me down.' Her grip is strong – any stronger and it'd hurt – and I am now afraid: she *does* know about me.

She does.

Chapter 12

The park gate is coming up on my right. Rattled by the change in Eleanor, I decide to take the shortcut home, and the green space might help me calm my mind. I need to settle my thoughts – *She knows, she knows, she knows* – before returning to the closer scrutiny of my flat.

I've turned into the park, and have already made a start across the grass, before I realize I have made a mistake. Today there was a hanging. Every month there's a well-publicized execution, and today there was a clutch of Eurasian prisoners. Everyone goes – is expected to, not just to increase the prisoners' ignominy but to keep us all in check.

Perhaps that's why there was such a large crowd just now – perhaps they came from the hanging and needed an outlet.

I usually go to show what a good citizen of Oceania I am, but since Ruby . . . I couldn't face going and risk seeing her there.

So I've stayed away from the park, but I've been so consumed by seeing a different side to Eleanor, my feet have found the children's play area: the home of the hangings.

No one questions that the public gallows are situated in the play area – Oceania is perfection. The gallows are set up in the middle, near the roundabout (a popular place to sit on, to watch) and the baby swings (the perfect way to distract fractious toddlers anxious for the fun to start). When there's no hangings, someone had the bright idea of replacing the rope with a springy rope thing. Kids hook their feet through a loop at the bottom and there's a short bar looped through at hand height, so the kids can use it as a suspended pogo stick. They bounce and swing and kick out against it, mashing their faces against the gallows pole. It's the most popular play facility in the park.

Today, though, there's just a straggle of kids gathered around the gallows post. It was once a telephone pole – the numbers are still visible in the wood. I can't resist but draw nearer; there's something about the combination of fascinated horror on their faces as they take turns to peer closely at something on the post, and the abandoned pogo string, that lures me. What's better than their favourite plaything?

Without wanting to, I open the gate and go into the children's area.

'What is it?' I ask, nearing the group. I hope it's a dragonfly or rude graffiti that's holding their interest.

But it isn't.

Chapter 13

Nailed onto the gallows post is a smorgasbord of human flesh laid out for our inspection. There is one eyeball and one ear and a tongue. The children – the youngest can only be six – move away, now watching me narrow-eyed, curious for my reaction.

The ear is like a pink shell, with glistening white gristle visible beneath the flesh. The edge is rough as if it's not been removed smoothly, but instead hacked off with more than one blow. The eyeball iris is flecked hazel and stares at me with a three-inch iron nail jutting rudely out from the middle.

There's something in my eye.

It's horrible. The optic nerve trails from behind it, an unwanted loose thread.

The tongue looks like a stabbed slug. No – worse – it looks like what it is: a human tongue that has been cut out and nailed to a post. My eyes drag upwards; above it is a poster with printed words saying: SEE, HEAR AND SPEAK NO EVIL AGAINST THE LOVE OF BIG BROTHER.

I look back at the eye – Ruby had hazel eyes. I can't help it and now look at the ear. I don't want to but how can I not check to see if this is her? *Is it?* I don't want to know–

–I do want to know. I want to know what happened to my friend. I want her alive–

–but I don't want her alive, held in the bowels of the Ministry of Love. If she is there, I wish the escape of death upon her–

–but I don't want her dead.

I look again at the eye. I've never met anyone so given to hiccups. She was adorable. I would've given anything to save her. There's a small freckle up in the fold of the ear. Did Ruby have a freckle there? The ear is pierced, and the size suggests it could be an adult female.

'What do you think, miss?' asks a boy narrowly. He's the oldest and looks like he'd nail my eye to a post, given half a chance. The second-biggest, a girl, and a boy younger than her, are dressed in the blue shorts, grey shirt and red neckerchief uniform of the Spies. All children are dangerous but the children who attend the Spies' clubs particularly so. Spies would turn their own parents in for thoughtcrime just for the glory.

'I *think*,' I say slowly, lifting my chin and pulling myself to full height as I meet each of their eyes, 'I think that I *don't* think. You shouldn't be thinking either. Thinking will get you in trouble – like this person. You remember that Big Brother does all your thinking for you and that's how it should be.' I narrow my eyes. 'Now get off home to bed before I call someone … I'm always looking for crimethink.'

Five and a half pairs of eyes are rounded at me, not moving.

I lean closer. 'She's only here because of me,' I say, hoping it's not true. I clap my hands suddenly in front of the boy's face and he turns and scrams, the others following afterwards. I need to get going and fast. I don't want them coming back for revenge.

With fast legs, I'm out of the children's area, out of the park and down the road, without looking back. I feel sick, the image of the nailed eye imprinted on my own. When I blink, I only see it more clearly. I dearly want to grip the nearest railings and throw up in the gutter, but to do so would be to reveal my feelings, and like everything else, that would be dangerous.

All I can do is get home, and hope that the child Spies aren't following behind me. Or Eleanor – but perhaps she already did and that's the secret she knows about me. Knows that I don't live in a hostel like I've claimed. Perhaps she knows where I really live.

Chapter 14

I keep walking home, trying not to see the nailed eye in my mind (I must not pass out; I must not pass out; I must not). My footsteps carry the mantra when I cannot.

The streets are empty, the biting wind savages my extremities; I wish I could go somewhere – anywhere – where I could cry, release the hysteria. I think of the two neat cuts to the tongue – this world is a cruel one. Was that Ruby? Was that how she died? The grey, cold sky gives me nothing when I have never needed the warmth of the sun more. My head is a muddle of shock, revulsion and fear.

But the worst emotion is paranoia.

I want to shake the feeling that the dead body parts *were* Ruby's – and laid out just for *me*. I often cut through the park, missing the pastoral views of home, country girl that I am. It would be easy to leave them there for me to see. Hazel eyes – commonplace, but the small beauty spot on the ear? I'm observant but can I trust my memory that Ruby had one? Really? If it was Ruby and it was for me, that would be a clear indication that I am walking dead.

—there's something in my eye—

It *is* a warning. I *know* it. It would explain why Ruby was arrested during the day, instead of the night. That carefully constructed public arrest in front of me, right under the prole noses, but when they were least aware of what was happening. Could they be linked? Sickeningly, I think so.

I take the crossroads and after checking over my shoulder – once, twice – I head for home, towards the smarter, more salubrious suburbs. Perhaps Eleanor followed me here. Perhaps that's the 'truth' about me that she knows. But I've always been so careful – I've always known that if the Sisterhood see where I live, they'll eject me from the group immediately. If not worse.

London has different areas – the slummy prole areas; the equally bomb-ravaged underinvested areas of the Outer Party that are supposed to be better, but in many cases, have areas of worse deprivation. The Inner Party live in luxury mansions, grouped together in gated communities. It is challenging running Oceania – they need every comfort, of course. While most of London live in often unheated – fit only for farm animals – accommodation, the Inner Party have the finest of everything.

But Manor Towers is an anomaly. Near the Inner Party area – but definitely not in it – it's next to the grey and rubbish-filled Thames. When I moved into the twelve-storey building, it was brand new, but eight years later, it still stands almost empty. I rarely see any other inhabitants. To my knowledge, in my time here, there have been one or two, but when I see someone I never see them a second time.

My eyes are scanned at the entrance to my building, and the door opens. The warmth should comfort me, but it doesn't. Like the black marble floors, the teak panelling is tasteful, and it always smells of lavender furniture polish (although I've never seen a cleaner). Reception is always empty; above the empty desk is the obligatory picture of Big Brother, but this is different to the others. First of all, it's an oil painting, an original, and it's the only one I've ever seen where he is wearing a dinner suit rather than a uniform. At the desk, I insert my finger into the machine that holds messages – the screen tells me there are none.

My footsteps echo across the floor. I don't like being here because in this construct of modernity and almost Inner Party luxury, I suspect there is more sophisticated observation than the old-fashioned residences such as Prisha's, where there is only the telescreen to deal with.

I take the noiseless lift up to my flat (there's no power supply issues here either), for once choosing to sit on the lift's velvet bench cushion. My legs feel so weak, I feel so sick, I'm worried I'll collapse. But I keep my maskface intact – tired, yes, I can admit to that, devastated, no. What's there to be devastated about? Despite the obvious reality of our world, we can only embrace that Oceania is perfect.

The lift door opens – I'm on my floor. Opposite the stairwell, there's another enormous, framed picture with Big Brother's face staring impassively back at me. His eyes watch me.

'Open,' I say to my door. My eyes and voice are scanned again and it opens, but there's no hiding – he watches me here, too. The eye of the super brain of Ingsoc, always watching.

Always.

The telescreen murmurs into life at my detected presence and its cameras and mics click into life. *Julia, welcome home*, intones Big Brother in its deep, smooth, too-familiar voice I hear every day. *Did you enjoy your ASL steering group meeting?*

'Yes, Big Brother. Thank you for asking.'

Did you enjoy your walk through the park?

I've been ready for this: the CCTV is extensive. 'I was pleased to see that enemies of the state aren't given a chance to prosper and harm citizens of Oceania.' My voice is even as I stow my shoes on the rack.

Big Brother loves you, Julia. I would never allow anyone to harm you.

'I know.' I shrug off my coat and hang it on the hook. Shut the fuck up.

It was good that you reminded the young people that there is no cause to think.

There must have been a close-up camera. *Of course* there was a camera. Does my face give me away now? Did it then? I think of the revulsion as I peered at the trailing optic nerve.

Do you require anything, Julia?

I don't even breathe out now we are back on normal territory. This is our usual conversation. I can order anything from Big Brother – food, clothes, gin – and have it delivered straight to my door. Except because of the war, there's so little available that there is nothing to order. If

I did, it would say: *Julia, your choice would diminish the war effort – do you wish to proceed?* I could say yes, but the next day, be arrested for thoughtcrime and taken to the Ministry of Love. How could anyone place their own selfish needs above Oceania's?

So, instead I say, 'No, Oceania is everything I need.' I look in my fridge. There is a camera in here, monitoring my food – but not just my food. Nothing to see here. My mind inches towards abuse about the surveillance, about the ear freckle – I picture Ruby tucking her strawberry blonde hair behind her ear; was it there? But I'm fast to get a grip on my thoughts: survival forces quick wits.

Your period will start tomorrow. You have forgotten to restock sanitary products, so I have ordered for you. They will arrive at 07.00 hours.

Because there is a camera inside my bathroom cabinet, I remember to go through the monthly charade of having a period, lest they guess at the contraceptive. Big Brother notices everything. 'You take such good care of me. Praise to the party.'

Praise to the party, Julia. Enjoy your meal. Don't forget you have a group spin session at 06.40 hours. You must look after your heart.

The irony of its statement just makes me hate it more. I keep my face relaxed as I prepare a mundane supper in my beautiful kitchen. The cabinets are American walnut and there would not be many Inner Party members who could beat me for gadgets – I have them all. The whole flat is polished chrome, underfloor heating, sunken jacuzzi bath. The huge windows even have privacy glass, meaning that although I daren't stand on the balcony in case I'm seen, I can gaze out across London. But here I am a prisoner – arguably less free than Leona in her hostel room. Because what I must do to live here rent-free costs me a price higher than I can bear to pay.

And yet choiceless, I do.

Day after day. Year after year.

PART TWO

'If women want rights more than they got, why don't they just take them, and not be talking about it.'
Sojourner Truth

Chapter 15

Prisha and Eleanor and I are all leaning over the balcony inside the Whispering Gallery at St Paul's. We look united – but I fear we are not.

This is the first time I have dreaded this meeting instead of looking forward to it. Normally, I love to see Eleanor, but now I just feel edgy. I swear I can still feel where she gripped my elbow. The St Paul's meets have always been our major meeting – up in the huge stone, lead-covered roof we are freer to speak than anywhere outdoors. No one comes up here and even better, we've never seen a mic up here – we think the dome's unusual acoustics or the thick construction might be why.

Today's meeting will – for the first time – bring trouble. So much seems to have changed since Ruby's arrest.

We are half watching the Junior Anti-Sex League as they run amok in the apse below. Half watching, because that's the required charade; we occasionally call out a sharp reprimand that echoes and multiplies into a thousand imperatives. Because we mostly leave them alone, the girls' screams and shouts are largely unchecked; they are free to run up and down the space, whooping and jumping from pew to pew. The dean and canons are all long gone, along with the nation's Sikhs, the Muslims and the Buddhists, banished by Big Brother (in increments – legislation against prayer, followed by membership, then identity, until people of all faiths disappeared). A few pews linger for the children to climb on, sad and abandoned by their congregation.

Gerta, a jug-eared twelve-year-old, has one booted foot on the seat of one, her other on the back support. Gerta laughs, the sound bouncing like a thrown ball against the walls. Her arms aeroplane and with a measured pump of her legs, she attempts to launch off the back of the pew. For a brief moment, she is magnificent – arms out straight, the pew balancing under her captaincy. But of course, it totters and falls. The back slams oak to stone, the crash ricochets and everyone turns to look. The noise is explosive; the echo slams on and on and on. The girl tumbles, but she doesn't crash – instead, she catches her step before squawking a victory.

Girls whoop and Gerta takes an answering bow.

Their indecorous behaviour is perfect. The less reverence shown, the better, because this is what is wanted. Faith in anything other than the Party has been scourged and scrubbed away. Big Brother has to be placed above all.

Most wouldn't even know this building had once been a church. Anything obviously old is simply described as being built during the Middle Ages – an indeterminate time. But Ingsoc is obsessed with erasing truth from history – streets; squares; parks; anything that might give an insight into the past has been methodically altered.

Now the idea that this was ever a place of sanctity is beyond lost; rather, it is a space to examine the past – the Ingsoc-approved past. Huge posters depict vivid, violent scenes, taken from each faith's history. It's the same propaganda used against the queer community – at the doctor's, hideous photos of a vicious flesh-eating disease are displayed, a so-called record of fact and the reason they give for zero homosexuality. It was done with 'love' – to save '*them*', of course. The answering bravery was magnificent – I've seen the photos of the time before – when crowds remind the world of '*us*'. Then the anti-homosexuality laws were abandoned along with all laws, but there was no victory. The revolution fizzled with no battle, with the apparent surrender by Ingsoc. There was an announcement that a civilized society required no laws.

But then the vocal dissenters disappeared. The clerics, the leaders of the gay and queer community, the journalists, the opposition leaders ... then the tech began to be unreliable until one day it simply never worked again.

Fear did the rest. I don't remember this. This happened before I was born. I would suspect that most people know none of this – how would they? But what we all know is this: if Prisha and Cecily were to walk down the street hand-in-hand, they would not be in their flats the following morning.

We've created a regular habit of bringing the Juniors here to this stone ghost of what was; a giant against its sister gravestones, markers of a time now long buried, cold and dead. We tell them we come here as a vital part of their educational programme. The whole thing is a ruse, of course. We say it's the critical examination of how the pre-Ingsoc society failed to limit promiscuity.

We bring them here a lot – we've made sure it's a favourite outing for the troop. The troop are all girls, some of them only eight, all the way up to eighteen. We save any sugar we get for biscuits and present them on this day. Anything special we get, chocolate, sweets, we keep back for this. Like Pavlov's dogs, we train them to salivate at the thought of the St Paul's trip. We want them hyped; we want them to drive the visits with pleading caught on microphones, so our submission appears organic.

We want them to beg to come and beg to stay.

When we pack for the trip, we mutter to ourselves in front of the telescreens about how dull the whole thing has become. We then remind each other that in doing so, we are being 'good women', sacrificing our time to help stamp out the 'scourge of sex'.

We do this because coming here is vital. This quarterly meeting at St Paul's has become the solid buttress of our group. Outside of snatched conversations hidden in crowds, here we dare to build the Sisterhood. We have the conversations we need. It defines us, structures us. We raise our ideas here, give them walls and cap them with possibility.

Then when we step away, we press our lips together, draw the scarves over our heads, and bend our heads down. There is nothing to see here. We are nothing. Only women. Only women doing our best to improve society. Trying to scrub out human attraction and family life. Despite its apparent infallibility, the rise of famfarms – taking babies from birth into large, purpose-built institutions – continues. Big Brother tells us family life is costly and time-consuming, parenting outdated and damaging to the child; it's clear that there's a movement towards relegating family life to the history rubbish heap.

Clever Eleanor used to be a scientist working in the lifelabs – it was her job to try to get the fertilized female gametes to stick inside the utebubbles. It was her experiences later visiting the famfarms that started her to turn from Ingsoc. Unlike the rest of the Sisterhood, Eleanor's rebellion comes from her ideological pursuit of right. She was the only child of older parents – one was an academic, the other a doctor. She says they poured all their ideas into her and it created a 'fertile thinking environment'. She winked when she said that, enjoying the pun. She told me her parents remembered the time before and passed on their memories to her. When she started, she was the only female scientist working in fertility. She said she was flattered which stoked her ambition. But that soon changed and her experiences – which she told me is a story for another time – started a fire in her.

Eleanor was the one to suggest our nothingness had weight. Rather than drift away, unseen, unfelt, into nothing, we could use it, by holding it tight, we could make it count. She told us: 'I'm an old woman – no one notices old women. We are the unimportant; the uninteresting; the unseen.' She told us we could weaponize female invisibility and make it our strength. We saw we could subvert our situation and add definition to the billowing emptiness of our lives.

She told us that here, long ago. Prisha, Ruby, Leona, Cecily and me followed her up here to the Whispering Gallery. She'd got us on the cleaning rota and pressed supplies into our palms. In hers, she carried a bucket of soap water. I watched her ahead of me on the stairs, carrying the heavy pail as if it was nothing. Her feet solidly met each riser as if it were a promise she'd vowed to keep. Rubber sole on ancient stone; *I will, I will, I will*.

She never spilt a drop.

I followed her up the steps, just as I followed her into the Sisterhood. I knew Eleanor before; we were both in a group called Women Against Freedom. Everyone in Oceania is a member of some group or other – it's not mandated but to not take part in something to promote the love of Big Brother would result in a visit from Thinkpol. Eleanor also brought Leona, who in turn brought her sister Ruby, then Ruby brought Prisha. Eleanor had selected us – we thought – to set up a new branch of the Anti-Sex League. Up the steps we went, curious as to why our new ASL steering group should be on St Paul's cleaning rota and why we were now heading for the hardest to reach Whispering Gallery.

At the top, she set her bucket down, lowering herself next to it. I remember that I thought: she is so strong. Eleanor is so strong!

On our knees she whispered her ideas to us. She told us she saw a sisterhood, a group that would try to find its way back to the old ways. She spoke of the fabled group led by the hated Goldstein. Could it be, she said, if Emmanuel

Goldstein is real, then so could his rumoured group of men, the Brotherhood, also be real? And if they are, could this group of men need us? Could we find them and offer our support to overthrow Ingsoc?

We scrubbed the stone with suds, bristles scourging old, ingrained dirt. We said little, but we cleaned hard and listened hard. We knew how brave she was to even voice her rebellion. It gave us hope.

'There might be a role for us. Women have worth. We are strong.'

She muttered these golden words into the bucket of greying water and they fell with the hope of coins into a wishing well.

That was just the start of us. Still we come. Sometimes we bring the girls up to the Whispering Gallery; they like to turn upwards to the dome so they can be heard.

We turn outwards, hoping not to be.

We pause for minutes sometimes, just so it doesn't appear that we are in conversation. Thumbnails dig at ghost food in gums so fingers obscure the mouth; hair curtains over tilted faces. Words hiss through already-parted and immobile lips, vowels so light they are more air than sound. Anything to ensure we can't be lipread. But mostly we are free to use as many words as we need. And by the look in Prisha's brown eyes, we are going to use them right now. But these words will not be welcome to Eleanor, so for the first time, I wish I wasn't here.

'Eleanor,' she says softly, 'we need to talk.'

I shut my eyes, coward that I am, and think: *oh no here it comes.*

Chapter 16

'I'm suggesting,' says Prisha, voice light, but knuckles paling as she grips the handrail, 'a change in direction for our group. I'm sorry, E, I know you set it up, but I, for one, no longer wish to be part of a group whose sole purpose is to pursue men.'

'Then how will we find the Brotherhood?' Eleanor murmurs.

The line between Prisha's eyebrows – her '*I want*' line, Cecily calls it – deepens. 'I'm not convinced they're there to find. They're just a rumour that we don't know is true. And if they are true, what have they ever achieved? Really? A few ineffectual attacks perhaps, probably staged by Big Brother to keep the group alive in people's minds. I fear they're just part of the Hate construct – something to unite people. Something to draw out anyone against Ingsoc.'

Eleanor's face remains passive.

I'm terrified; I just want to please her and have her promise she knows nothing about my secrets.

Prisha – always clear and determined – tucks her dark

hair behind her ears. 'And now Ruby has gone, how can we justify more loss in the same direction?'

Leona makes a small noise and bows her head.

'Our society's construct is that men have the power. To destroy it, we're going to have to pursue it,' Eleanor says. Her tone is calm, reasonable; her forearms rest on the rail, the white, aged, crepe skin eased into delicate linen folds. They look thin; food shortages remain rife. Governments hungry for war must starve their people as weapons cost more than corn.

'And if we do infiltrate? We don't even know they'll want us. We're searching for them, putting ourselves at huge risk for the idea, but the truth is, we could find them, and they could just slam the door in our faces. All this for nothing.'

'Is there a destination for this change in direction? Or are you suggesting becoming directionless?'

Prisha's square jaw tightens – she joined the Sisterhood, she told me only very recently, because her brother, Aarav, was arrested when he was only eleven. The family were hungry, so he stole a loaf of bread from the market. The patrols picked him up and he never came home. 'This is a war on children,' she told me.

I can't bear the palpable tension. What has happened to us, I want to scream. 'I have a good mark. He's worth pursuing.' I don't add that this week I saw him in the prole quarter. We walked past each other and if Smith noticed me, he didn't say. To be in the prole area shouts renegade.

'But your mark is the same man who is probably responsible for Ruby's arrest,' Cecily says. 'He's probably TP.'

I look at Cecily with new eyes. She blinks her apology

back. Pretty she might be, soft tones she might use, but it would be a fool for someone to think this attractive, gentle woman was a pushover. I shake my head a little – perhaps I'm the fool. I cannot believe she's betrayed my plan.

Leona covers her face until Eleanor touches her, to remind her.

'Sorry, I don't want to upset anyone,' Cecily says. 'But he will kill you too, Julia, and then Leona.' She places her hand on her back. 'Sorry, darling.'

Leona's eyes, like Eleanor's, track the girls below. 'So, um, if we are talking about things, this is probably the time to mention that I've had a change in work. I'm in muni-tions . . . now. I'm working with explosives.'

We are all silent, but I think this is only news to Eleanor. Below us, Sophie, a girl of eight, trips and lands on a knee and starts howling. 'Shall I go down?' Leona asks Eleanor in a clear, well-enunciated voice.

Eleanor smiles sweetly. 'Comrade Leona, so caring,' she says in a real voice, designed to be heard. 'But look, let an AS leader develop their responsibility.' She gives a graceful hand wave as an AS leader of eighteen reaches the near-hysterical child. 'You're kind to be so attentive, but remember, Big Brother gives her all she needs. We provide nothing.'

We watch the scene, listening to the jagged cries before Leona continues, 'I'm on a line, assembling bombs. Permission to take parts in increments.'

Assembling bombs. I knew it because I'd been told it, but for me to hear this from Leona requires all my strength not to speak, not to react. Leona's words are explosives themselves: could it be that the Sisterhood finally, after all these years, will access something real? Something that can have a meaningful impact on Ingsoc?

Eleanor doesn't speak immediately. She's smooth, I'll give her that. If you weren't standing next to her, you wouldn't know that Leona had just done the equivalent of exploding an A bomb in an ocean because for Eleanor, there's no ripple of reaction.

Inwardly, I brace myself for the reaction.

Grief-stricken Leona might be, but broken she clearly is not. In fact, I notice her small chin has a lift of determination I never saw before. She looks older, her own weight loss giving new definition and a maturation to her face. I realize that for the first time in such a long time – perhaps only since Eleanor assembled the Sisterhood – that I have a real glimmer of hope.

None of us speak for several minutes as we wait for Eleanor. We listen to the girls whoop and shout in the nave below.

Then she speaks: 'No target.' It is all Eleanor says in reply.

Leona's reply is quicker. 'But permission to take.'

'Not safe.'

Eleanor is correct. Leona will be watched with scrutiny.

'I know where the cameras are. I've spent years studying the blind spots. And no AI.'

No AI is allowed in the Minipax. Big Brother told us Eurasia failed to control its AI in weapon production and it cost them many, many lives. We've all been shown the footage of the blackened, blistered flesh of just-alive children near the epicentre of a nuclear blast enough times. *Life is a Blast!* is still a Sunday night favourite at the flicks. People even cheer when the mushroom cloud rises.

'No point. No target.'

'But—' I want to argue with Eleanor, but I've said too much. We *do* have a target – a Big fucking Brother target. A *bomb*? Now that feels like the kind of progress I've been looking for. If we had explosives, we could find a way of hurting Big Brother and that would be worth dying for. The Sisterhood would finally achieve something more than sewing and waiting, ad nauseum.

When you live with death, it is a grey, coarse pall that smothers. It's always omnipresent. It's rough against my eyes. It presses foully against my tongue, crowds my mouth, gags my throat. It's pervasive and never – *ever* – lets me breathe. Sometimes, sometimes, I think waiting for what feels like an inevitable death (is it? Or will I never get detected – because I'll never stop my rebellion until either I die tortured to death in Miniluv or in old age tucked into my bed?) is more torturous than death itself. In my darker moments, I almost envy the dead, envy that for them, there is nothing left to fear.

Down in the nave, my macabre thoughts are broken by another troop member, Verity (plaits, eczema, whiny). She is escalating an argument with one of our ASL leaders, the older teenagers we delegate a bit of responsibility to. Janine (unwashed hair, assertive) is giving her what for. Verity's complaining and Janine's bass retorts, echo and slap from stone to stone with rude repetition. I'd call down to support Janine, but I don't want to get caught in something; don't want to encourage the troop members to remember our presence and run up the steps to us, bringing complaints.

'I'll store,' Prisha whispers, clearly thinking of her cellar. I think of the rusting biscuit tin holding the contraceptives and wonder how safe it would be to store explosives in the damp, underground space beneath her house. All my Sisterhood are so brave.

Eleanor doesn't pause. 'No target, so no use. Too risky to take and store with no reward.'

No.

'There would be reward, a new direction for us,' asserts Prisha. 'One of direct action. Female owned. Independent. Not skulking in the shadows waiting for the Brotherhood that – let's face it – might not even exist. Or even bloody want us, if it does.'

This is a muscular change. Led by ourselves. Violent. We never swore against violence, but it wasn't in the vision; we haven't thought beyond making contact with the Brotherhood.

'Assuming she wasn't caught . . .'

Eleanor's right, it all feels dangerous. Since Ruby, we are losing our nerve. The *no* is all I can hear and then when Verity's fresh whine soars up to me, I feel, in a moment of spite, the desire to really give her something to complain about.

'Eleanor,' Cecily says, 'you built us, the Sisterhood, out of nothing. But without something real, we are nothing more than a sewing circle, full of dreams. The needles we wield are the biggest damage we will create; our threat to

Ingsoc nothing more than stuffing and velvet. All we have is a belief in change, but without change.'

If we needed a minute to digest Cecily's words, we're not given it because Eleanor's jaw tightens. 'Action follows belief.'

Prisha speaks. 'Our belief is that we will die anyway. For nothing. Eleanor, we want to die for fucking *something*.'

'Agreed, but we need to be rational.' Eleanor's voice has developed an edge.

Prisha rubs her forehead. 'Then we are at a stalemate.'

I expect Eleanor to say something soothing, something to salve the tension; instead, she says, 'Then yes we are, because I am not changing my mind.'

'Then we can't go forward,' pushes Prisha.

The air is charged. Below, the troop have stopped running and are mostly sitting on the pews. They are tired and getting bored – we have little time left. 'Eleanor, perhaps ... given the ... unusual circumstances,' I say, choosing my words as carefully as possible because this is feeling like an argument and we have *never* argued, and we can't end the meeting like this. I need the Sisterhood. Without it, I am that smashed woman on the pavement. 'We should take a vote on this.'

We have never voted before. This in itself is an act of rebellion, but I cannot let the Sisterhood die.

'If you vote for this, then you know she will . . .' Eleanor turns to Leona, her fingers spread across her mouth, but we hear her when she says: 'L, you will die. It's probably a trap.' She pauses, then: 'And what about Julia? What about her mark? Doesn't that count anymore?'

'J – we don't want you to do that,' Prisha says. 'Sorry, but I think we should vote on that, too. Your life, but every time one of us is caught and sent to Miniluv, we are all at risk.'

I glance at Eleanor. 'I vote yes to chasing the mark.'

'Yes,' says Leona.

'Yes,' says Eleanor.

Both Prisha and Cecily vote *no*, but it doesn't matter.

'No one misses Ruby more than me,' says Leona. 'I hid my job from you because of shame. But I want you to know the truth now, so I can do this for her.'

'There is no shame in your oppression, but you must know if we take it, we can't use it. We have no access to the government, so we can't use it against them.' Eleanor stops and looks at me.

She does know! She knows about me! The panic in me is wild, loose and free. I remember her pressing against my shoulder and the word *trust* being breathed against me. I can't speak.

'Vote for L taking the explosives,' Prisha murmurs finally. 'I say *yes*.'

'*Yes*,' Leona exhales before Prisha has even drawn breath again.

Cecily says *yes* before going down to the nave to resolve yet another dispute and then dear Cecily takes the steps back up again. Then I say *yes* and then it doesn't matter what Eleanor says because we can't fight for democracy and then ignore it.

We realize this perhaps at the same time, because there's an ugly pause. 'Eleanor,' Prisha says, 'your turn.'

Eleanor doesn't say anything and then I think one of us will say something intelligent and deep to encourage our leader to vote, but in the end all Leona says, in a voice storm-clouded with tears, is: *please Eleanor* and Eleanor answers her with a *no*. It's unclear if the *no* is her vote or if it's a refusal to taking part in the ballot. It's just *no*.

The air is charged and miserable, so when Cecily claps her hands and says in a real voice, a voice meant to be heard, 'Is it time for biscuits yet? Eleanor, your sugar biscuits are what *dreams* are made of,' I could kiss her with relief.

Eleanor gives a weak smile and directs us downstairs where she has made three dozen of her biscuits, a triumph given the food shortages. She doesn't have one herself. I watch her, trying to find evidence of how she feels, but she's a blank. She's not showing me she's okay – which means she isn't. I know Eleanor: she's so intuitive that she'd know I would need to know she was fine. She would find a way – a small smile, perhaps, or an offer of a biscuit.

But she doesn't. She takes the lid off the biscuit tins (just like she does for me in the cellar every month), but doesn't offer them round, instead just sits them on a pew for the gannets to flock, which they do.

It's my own knife that twists inside. I'm surprised by my anguish. I bolster myself, tell myself that no one's expendable in the fight and as the rest of us are united, it must be the right decision. But even after we've eaten the biscuits and have shepherded the children home, my words (they *were* mine) *we should take a vote* still shout on in my mind, a salvo of bullets committing an act of treachery against Eleanor's command – it's all I can hear. I see the pain on Eleanor's face – in hindsight it's all I can see – and I feel like the worst kind of defector. I feel like I killed her leadership. She was like a mother – and yet I still stabbed her in the back.

The pain and guilt remind me of what I am capable of – I am (*Mother rubbing my hands: 'You're such a cold fish, Juliet!'*) ruthless. And she was right: cold, too.

It's like I killed my father again. Now I've thought that, made that connection, now that memory is all I can hear, all I can think. Eleanor's pain, my words (*we should take a vote*), his pain, my killing an old man in bed by pressing a pillow against his face, is all very blurred in my mind. How he took something from me that wasn't his to take. How I repaid him.

How can it not all come back to me?

What kind of person (*cold fish*) am I?

Back at home, I'm glugging from the gin bottle before I've even taken off my shoes.

Julia, you seem to be thirsty. The ideal drink to quench thirst is water.

'Thank you, Big Brother,' I say, then ignore it. The stress of the Sisterhood disintegrating in front of my eyes is like death. My friends are all I have now. Are they gone?

I neck my drink. It's the proper stuff Ephrem gave me. None of that Outer Party oily gin. This stuff is like the stuff my mother used to drink with her friends. I think of them now, twittering about what they bought, who had what, where they were travelling to next. I watched them from behind the secret panel and learned.

KATHERINE BRADLEY

I drink more – much more than I planned, but I want to forget.

But the more I drink, the more I think about Ruby. The sadness is intertwined with the terror that Eleanor knows about me. If she does know about me, then I have nothing left. And with all that's been taken from me already, I won't survive their loss.

Julia, you are crying. Big Brother doesn't want you to be sad.

'I'm not sad, I'm angry!' I hear the blur in my voice, the lurch of my emotion and know I'm dangerously drunk. *Good.* I always have to hold myself so tight and I'm tired, tired, *tired* of it! I lift the bottle to my mouth: nothing comes out. I've finished the bottle. I throw it and it hits the wall, bounces off and lands on the floor. I cover my eyes like a child, thinking it will break, smash to smithereens. I even imagine pointing at it, dramatically announcing to Big Brother: 'My heart!', but it doesn't break.

Later, after I've found another bottle and had several more slugs of gin, Big Brother speaks again: *Julia, you should go to bed. Immediately.*

'Fuck you, you can't tell me what to do! Who do you think you are, my father? Let me tell you, you are not—'

Julia, I am opening the front door as we have assistance arriving.

I'm up and lurching towards the bottle. They're coming, I think. The men in uniforms. I'm going to defend myself. I grab the fallen bottle by the neck and smash it against the wall. I hit it hard, vaguely believing it couldn't be broken, but it smashes easily.

I hear the ping of the lift. They are here. But I have lost courage now and know I can't fight them.

I hear a helicopter (is that real or the one that's been haunting my dreams?), remember Ruby's legs in the scrum of the Thinkpol – how they buckled. How I didn't save her. How I didn't save Chloe.

You're not taking me too, I decide. I'm holding the broken bottle by the neck and I press it against the skin of my wrist.

Chapter 17

I am in a warm bath. I was doing fine – I was okay – and them, *bam*, I drank too much gin and fell off an emotional cliff. I didn't even see it coming. I keep myself tight and together hour after hour, day after day and year after year, but two days ago I failed. I understand why I failed. Ruby; the pressure of Smith perhaps being Thinkpol: betraying Eleanor and crucially, getting drunk and remembering things from my past . . . things that made me who I am but I'm not going to think about. I'm *not*.

I came home from St Paul's, got drunk and got frightened. I didn't mean anything by it – fuck, *yes*, I did because I know Eleanor is *right*. I wanted to be drunk so I didn't have to think about how Leona will die because they are probably going to catch her taking from the Minipax assembly line. I feel sick with the thought of the nailed eye (Ruby's?) and its trailing optic nerve and how I voted for Leona's future to be the same. I also feel fear that Eleanor is losing control of the group and I made that happen. I follow Eleanor and I should not have stepped away from that by suggesting a ballot.

Day after day, I carry with me so much pain and loss and I cope – just cope. To be permanently grieving, yet publicly fine, requires so much effort. But I can do that. Like all of us living in Oceania, living in London as Outer Party means that you live with fear all the time. Sometimes, fear becomes all you can feel, but you don't show it on your face – you don't commit facecrime. I can cope with pretending.

But I have memories – I couldn't cope with that.

I didn't really want to kill myself, I just wanted to feel something else – something overwhelming to make me forget – and physical pain let me do that.

The warm water makes me sleepy; it surrounds me like love. Keeping my hurt wrist on the side, I slide the rest of me down and shift deeper. Silken heat moves over my skin. Aside from my arm, only my knees and nose and mouth rise, an archipelago escaping the embrace.

I'm drifting again, but this time, only with sleep. It feels like it might be like last time, perhaps. Just alive, just conscious, only just above the water, and so much so, it's almost a mirror event, but tonight it's the other side. Sunlight over shadow. Life over death.

My thoughts drift back to the clinic they took me to. Someone must have called my brother because he came to visit me this morning. 'Please don't do this again,' he said and I told him I wouldn't. He must have said something to get me discharged. Really, I owe him my life. Without him, I'd be locked in some nameless place of no returns. Mental illness is thoughtcrime – it suggests the love of Big Brother is not enough. As I walked down the long corridor to the doors, clutching my things with my bandaged wrist, every step was torture. Every step, I thought I would feel the firm grasp of the hospital nurses and I would not make it to the exit.

I have always liked my feet – my mother said I had her feet and she used to like her own. It's like a connection between us. Fuck – I am thinking of my mother again. Just like crumbs into the wood, the past calls me back, back into the shadows. But I can't get lost in the past.

Perhaps I always have been. Perhaps I never left.

Do all roads lead to the same place?

I am thinking about this again when Big Brother speaks. My heart rate must be up.

Julia, my love for you is huge. As such, I require you to attend a clinic now to get your dressing changed.

Clinic.

My eyes open. 'Now?' The bath has cooled, and I am fully awake.

Yes, Julia, you need to leave now to make it on time. If your wound is not checked and cleaned, it could become infected. You need to be fit for work tomorrow.

Am I going back to the place of the locking doors, the smooth white plastic walls and the needles? Where the screaming is so frequent, no one turns their head to wonder where it comes from?

Julia, please get up.

Obediently I get up. I let the water drip off me and for a long second I stand there, too frightened to get out.

Julia, this is just a wound care clinic at your local healthhub.

It sounds caring, but it doesn't care.

Doesn't love.

'Thank you for thinking of my health, Big Brother,' I say instead and reach for a towel.

I love you, Julia.

I rub myself dry with my good hand. Dutifully I add: 'I love you too, Big Brother.'

Chapter 18

Today is the day I hunt Winston Smith. As I sit at my desk, tapping away one-handed, I'm glad I have something to do that is for the good of the Sisterhood. I need a focus, so I don't collapse again. But snaring this mark is bigger than me – I need to prove this is worth it to help restore harmony to the group. That's my role now. I want to get Smith to bring good news to Eleanor and then she will forgive me for my treachery.

Unless she does know my secrets and then nothing I do can be enough.

My arm hurts, beating a relentless tattoo of pain. I went to take some painkillers, but my bathroom cabinet is now empty of them. Suspicious but desperate, I tried to order some via Big Brother (I could go to a shop but what would be the point if I wouldn't be allowed to buy them?) but was told *Julia, these items are not currently available to you. Is there anything else you require?*

The only thing I require right now – other than some shit-good opiates – is Smith.

And today's the day I snare him.

The doubt is there that Ruby might not have even meant Smith – but somehow that has become less important. The Sisterhood's unity is everything. I take a deep breath; I will not let paranoia consume me. Reaching deep, I know I'm ready, my note's ready, and now he's on time and in place, he's ready.

I noticed him ages ago, as there are telescreens placed all around the office and corridors, but the big one that's easiest for me to see is in the corridor ahead and he passes it directly in my line of sight. He's been something of a figure of amusement to me, something to observe and mock when I'm bored. At work, I'm frequently bored. Drink at the watercooler, trip to the loo; once in there, Smith will stay there nine minutes exactly, before heading back down the corridor.

Dullard that he is, it's the same time every day. He's a train on a timetable – the eleven o'clock to Shitsville. I assume he spins the time out because he's wearied by work – I hope that's it or he's got something wrong with his digestive system. He also goes twice after lunch as well, but they're quicker visits. A straight in and out, so quick, he probably doesn't even wash his hands. Really, you're not allowed away from your desk more than twice a day for five minutes, which makes me think that he's got a medical need.

I will get up in six minutes, head to the water dispenser, take a drink from a paper cone, refill the paper thimble, drink again – because it'll buy me some flexibility – and then I'll return down the corridor. As I do so, he will be coming out of the loo and will be heading straight towards me. Our paths will cross – if I time it right – between telescreens.

I dislike the managerial responsibility I hold, but here it pays me back because it means I won't have to ask permission to leave my desk. As a section manager – pretty much as high an office as a woman can hold in the Party – there's no one near me to ask. I casually check the clock on my computer ... four minutes. The camera on my computer stares back at me, recording my every move.

Smile for the camera, dear.

Fuck you, dear.

The Fiction Department, FICDEP, has the east section of the floor, next to the greyed out, screwed shut windows. I'm in charge of the Pops for Eye-Spye and the Bangz for Party Parley, little nuggets of celeb info that are pushed via proles' smartbands, 24/7. We can push up to ten Pops per hour. It's dizzying.

Of course, that's why Ingsoc decided this as a change in methodology – the proles were becoming depressed with the constant dull drone of noise about Eurasia and Eastasia, the world territories to the East that are not under Oceania's control. Yes, 'War is Peace' as the slogan goes, but the cruelties of Eurasia make for depressing reading. Rumour has it, suicide rates rocketed. They tried lacing the mains water with antidepressant, but it didn't last. Not only was it expensive, but it interfered with the twice-yearly flush of contraceptive proles unknowingly drink with their mandatory morning glass of water.

Prole numbers must be managed.

Not many people know that – I pretend I don't.

If there's too many of them, Big Brother's projections make for anxious analysis, particularly as whatever is affecting the fertility of Party members is unknown, and why proles' fertility is undamaged is even more unclear.

To manage the mood, the Fiction department stepped up instead, and increased its output. In addition to the Eye-Spye Pops and the Party Parley Bangz, there is also the Knew-z, who produces a constant feed of My-Dog-Ate-My-Frog type stories. My role includes hooking up with Big Booqz team and then we heavily push the Pops and the Booqz to the masses.

No one actually writes them – there's no law prohibiting a person writing, but it's thoughtcrime, of course. So, Big Brother gives a loving helping hand and the Booqz content is created by algorithms; the team put in the location and genre and the prosificator pulps out some crap. I oversee it all, including spannering the nuts from the back panel and fiddling with the wires, when the prosificator breaks almost weekly.

But today I have a bigger weapon than my spanner – today I have my note.

Three minutes now until I potentially self-destruct. I hold the note dampening in my hand and push it up into my sling. Pretend to tap away with one hand. Since I hurt my wrist, it's all I can do. I've noticed they've not given me a speakwrite; I don't mind but it accentuates my paranoia: is it because Big Brother wants to punish me for hurting myself? It's almost as if I want it to notice – after all, no one I work with has questioned my injury. I'm half glad and half sad. No one cares. I'm a paradox – the women in the Sisterhood would care, but I don't want them to know. For yesterday's painting session, I told Cecily I sprained my wrist after falling drunk. I think she bought it – she knows I drink too much. Hopefully I'll be in long sleeves and no sling before our next meeting.

One minute to launch. It's hard not to go now. I feel the tension in my jaw muscles. I relax my face – nothing to see here – but my heart is whamming too fast. If I make a break too early, I will pass him too far up the corridor and the banks of cubicles might see us. I keep typing.

Thirty seconds.

I breathe, in and out, in and out.

I have my note, I have my note, I have my note.

It's time. I get up out of my seat and head towards the water dispenser.

Chapter 19

My spine feels rusty as I get up from my office chair. It doesn't want me to go. I try to walk as if I wasn't going to my certain doom, but I seem to have developed an atypical wonk to my gait as I cross the floor.

I feel that even if I wanted to turn back from this crazy mission, I couldn't. I head towards the watercooler, just as I do several times a day. This is why I settled on this as a plan – because it involves everything I do normally.

But I am free to sit back at my desk. In a world where I am not free to speak, to think, to vote, to love, to leave, to not exercise, to loll in bed, to complain, this feels overwhelming. I have this tiny choice – to continue down this long corridor to the watercooler and what that might mean, or . . . not to. I could just go and sit down.

It's a tiny choice with gigantic possibility.

I think suddenly of my father – he would be so cross. It almost makes me laugh to think just how cross he would be with me right now. I think in some ways, he would be crosser about what I'm about to do than what I did to him.

Yes, he probably would, I decide.

I'm here. With my left hand, I reach for a paper cone. Hideous things. Why are they designed to be so impractical? With my right hand, fingers fumble for the note; I panic – *it's not here! I've lost it! It's dropped out and will be found and then they will look at the surveillance footage and they will* – I feel the note. I relax. With crabby fingers, I pull it from its hiding place and slide it further into the damp flesh of my palm.

I genuinely need to have a drink – but not water or Party gin; the real stuff. The paper lip feels too big against mine. The water is too cold. I gulp it down clumsily, spilling a little from the corner of my mouth. Wiping at it, I cast about to see if my messiness or Party disloyalty is evident. I can't rush back but instead must spend nearly two minutes here. I pause, try to appear relaxed. There's a woman I recognize from the canteen (who might work in Surveillance?); she is walking down the corridor and sometimes we chat a little. *Typical.* I turn away a little and, in desperation, start to pick my nose. Who wants to talk to someone picking their nose? She'll probably consider me forever revolting and never talk to me again, but I cannot risk her throwing me off with conversation.

My timings are crucial.

I wait until she's passed by and then fold down the little plastic tap, releasing more water into the cone cup. A huge bubble of air wobbles upwards and bursts, disturbing the surface. I watch it and think: *a little thing can make a big noise*. I have to believe that.

I finish the second cup and keep my gaze on the carpet

tiles. My face feels hot. Stiff. The note presses a corner into my flesh. My palm is so sweaty, he'll not be able to read it – he'll unwrap it to find blurred ink. But I have to hold it tightly: my life is in this note.

Time's up. I am now able to throw the cone away and make my way up the corridor. I've not been looking – can't bear to, it's too much – but I have to. If my plan is going to work then I need to know exactly where—

He's here! He's here! Smith is in front of me! I have either been too long or he has been quicker than usual.

Panicked he is about to pass me, I lurch forward, aiming for a small trip, but in my alarm, achieve a mammoth fall far more spectacular than planned and instead half spill to the ground.

I hit my bad wrist against the floor. Pain is blue, bright electric fire. My eyes shut against it and then I have a fleeting glimpse of a possible future – it's weird, it's as if it's old film, running slowly and silently, playing out my fear for me to see. In it, just in this split second, I see how the pain could have made me lose my note which falls to the floor for everyone to see.

But I open my eyes and the image is gone; I can still feel the note in my hand and there is nothing on the carpet except for this drab, dull dishcloth of a middle-aged man I want to squeeze for information.

I lift my face up to his and wonder what his reaction to me will be.

My momentary feeling of fear – that I had let go of the note and it would be seen – gives way to something else.

Something unexpected.

It's jolting. Up close, the recognition is instant. Winston Smith reminds me of Arthur Ryman.

Arthur Ryman. I wish I could say that I haven't thought of him in a long time. I have a disconcerting fragment of a memory flash before me, of me crying about him over my gin bottle. I hope, hope, hope not.

'Are you all right?' Smith asks.

'I'm fine, thank you!'

'You're hurt?' he says.

'It's nothing. My arm. It'll be all right in a second.'

'You haven't broken anything?'

'No, I'm all right. It hurt for a moment, that's all.' I've not seen Smith properly close up, only from my peripheral vision – it doesn't pay to look at people directly. But I am now, and I see him differently.

I hold out my hand and he accepts the invitation. As Smith clasps my hand, his face is the image of concern, his touch surprisingly warm and sure. Standing in the corridor holding his hand for the briefest moment, I feel displaced. I'd always dismissed Smith as a shabby man, of little physical interest, but now he and I are looking at each other, I can see a vulnerability about him. He has the reddened cheeks of a gin-soaked liver, and his blondish hair has no vitality to it, more of the colour and coarse texture of building cement sand.

But his eyes, his expression, tell another story. They suggest intelligence, suffering and perhaps the soul of a poet. Just like Arthur.

I blink. His hands are on mine, and I know this is my moment. The note is now between our palms and I smooth my fingers downwards, ensuring as I release him, his fingers find the square of paper. It's a deft movement, fitting of the best thief of Cook's cakes in the entire house. 'Swift tongue, swift hand', she used to say to me through the narrow eyes of one who knows where three iced buns went but can't prove the deed.

'It's nothing. I only gave my wrist a bit of a bang. Thanks, comrade!' I say, knowing I've got to get going, despite my sudden desire to linger.

I have to go, although it hurts to rip myself away. But the note's been transferred, and it's happened, it's happened. And because my timings were wrong, it's all been done in front of a telescreen.

Now anything could take place, anything.

Anything at all.

Somehow, I get back to my desk. I drift back, the sharp pain and dull ache that exist in my wrist no longer bothering me. I'm puzzled. As I reach the suffocating mundanity of my desk, I'm surprised to learn that I'm fundamentally different to when I left it.

Winston Smith. I am a woman, tilted.

Chapter 20

Arthur Ryman was my music tutor's son. I knew him from the age of fifteen, fell in love with him when I was sixteen and by the time I was eighteen, it was over. We were destroyed at the same time and we were destroyed in the same way. He is as much the story of myself as anything else: he changed me and my family; my ideas about Ingsoc; my ideas about myself; my ideas about love. He changed everything.

Arthur made me who I am today.

He was a young man three years older than me and was given to a deep reflection and intensity I never understood. But he and I did share a commonality: our infatuation for music. When one loves music, it is more than simple adoration – it is much, much more. It is how one is put together, how one functions and when it is killed, then that person is destroyed alongside it.

I'd had a delight for music since before I could remember. I played both the clarinet and the flute well, but the piano was different: *era la mia passione*. Whereas my mother used to nag Ephrem to practise, with me she had to scold me to stop.

In term time, I was at an all-girls' school, and as such, we were a hot bed of longing, some for our teachers perhaps, and some for the fifth formers, but I was different. I only cared for music. I began to dread the long breaks from learning and my father, when he realized the impact on me, employed my school music teacher as a live-in tutor for the holidays.

My music teacher was a Mr Ryman, an older, bearded man, who was given to mumbling, sudden outbursts of throaty laughter followed by even throatier coughing, and a love of pickled onions. Despite his obvious foibles, he drew my respect as he was very possibly a music genius, not least evidenced by being a conductor in a national orchestra before public playing ceased. At my father's request, when the terms finished, he'd pack a trunk and take up residence in our country home to teach Ephrem and I. Mr Ryman, being a widower, asked to bring his son, Arthur, too, and they took up residence in a set of rooms in the north-east wing.

He taught me daily for years, sat next to me on my stool. He was kind, shared a hard round, smooth mint that he always seemed to have but wouldn't say where he got them from. He called them 'Imperial mints' after my piano, the Imperial, as we would always have them sitting at its stool. I loved them, loved letting them sit on my tongue, pearl on oyster, for as long as they would last. I should like to have had my own stash, but there was nowhere to buy sweets and I dared not ask my parents for I had started to understand – sheltered existence that was mine – to realize that such sweets were outlawed and Mr Ryman might be in some unidentifiable trouble for bringing them into my father's house.

Sweeter than the mint was the realization of how they revealed a glimpse of a naughty side to Mr Ryman. But after a year, one day, there was no mint. 'Imperial?' I asked hopefully when there was no usual offer, after doing my scales.

He pretended to pull the contents of his pockets out. 'Juliet, they are finally all gone,' he said sadly. 'All used up. One daily for both of us ... it had to happen eventually.'

'All gone?'

'I was given a rather large quantity,' he said with a tired smile and an apologetic shrug, 'from a friend. He'd had a sweet shop before—'

'A shop that sold sweets?' I said, incredulous.

'Oh yes!' His face instantly lit up – the memory clearly a bright and happy one. 'Only sweets! Jar upon jar upon jar, all lining the shelves, every colour you can imagine, dark sticky liquorice, blue space invaders, yellow sherbet—'

'A real shop that sold only sweets? How is that possible?'

'Well, when I was a boy, things were a little different. I'm an old man now, but back then, when I was young, you understand, it was before ... things changed. You'd go in and ask for a quarter of toffee crumble, or perhaps rhubarb and custard or—'

'They sold pudding, too?' It all felt very confusing and for me, the Imperial (mint and piano) was completely sidelined.

He laughed a little impishly. 'Juliet, rhubarb and custard were hard sweets. Like our Imperial mints, but bigger, pink, sweeter.' He looked upwards and sighed, but happily. 'I'm not sure they particularly tasted of either rhubarb or custard, but at the time ...' He smiled, his voice just for himself now. 'At the time, they were all a kid wanted.'

'Where did all the sweets come from?' Ideas of such excess seemed impossible.

He was still smiling into some unseen mid-distance, but when I asked him again, his spectacled eyes refocused and he answered: 'Why, someone simply made them. But we need to focus on your study. Shall we ...?'

I wasn't ready to change the subject. 'But how was that possible? That a whole shop could sell only sweets?' I couldn't imagine a world where such abundance could be real. 'And why aren't there any now?'

My questions sharpened blade against flint, and he was then sharp and alert. 'Now Big Brother gives us what we need,' he said carefully, his gaze flicking around the room. 'It is more,' he said, announcing his words for emphasis, 'than we could *ever* want. I think you should not listen to the ramblings of an old man. My memories are a palimpsest; age and time, dear, lay error over error.' He patted my hand. 'You'll understand yourself one day. My ideas are incorrect and childish. No more than a foolish relic's confusions.'

'But the Imperials? Your mints?' I was determined. 'They came from somewhere?'

'A friend. Anyway, they are gone now and like memories and ideas, sometimes that's the best way. We are better rid of frippery and foolishness. Now, Juliet, no argument, you must apply yourself to your piano. Turn to page twelve. We will attempt the arpeggio. I want to hear your progress.'

That was the end of his memories and the mints. But the idea of jar upon jar upon jar of sweets did not leave me. Mr Ryman was an utterly trustworthy man, and he awoke in me some ideas of what the past had been – and his son awoke in me ideas of what the present could be.

Arthur took on gardening jobs in the summer months under the direction of Bridges, the gardener, and in the winter months, completed odd jobs under the supervision of Jacobson, who at the time ruled the under-house with sound and fury.

Arthur and I didn't speak for the first summer and winter holidays. Despite this, I always felt acutely aware if he was ever in the vicinity. Like a torch in the dark, he drew my gaze to him and when he caught me watching, it would make him blush to his follicles.

It wasn't until I caught him playing my piano that we spoke – and then I shocked him so badly, he could have keeled over in front of me. He might have done, if my shocking him wasn't as frightening to me as it was to him. He caught me doing what I shouldn't – and I made him promise to keep my secret.

Shared secrets are the bedrock of the best love affairs, I have since found out.

What lured him in was the Bösendorfer Imperial Grand; my father loved Bach so much he indulged me with the huge grand piano, the Imperial, both rare and impossibly wonderful because of its extra keys (in beautiful black! What a masterpiece!) at the bass end of the keyboard. Because its unusual ninety-seven keys meant I could play some of his favourite Bach pieces in full – so much better than the usual eighty-eight keys. When I played, it made me feel I could change the world.

The person who advised him on his purchase was Arthur's father, so Arthur knew when he came to our house that we had the beauty. Of course, Mr Ryman saw it every day; he instructed me on it and tuned it, but Arthur hadn't seen it until that evening.

The Imperial was in the drawing room. What Arthur didn't know was that the drawing room contained a secret – a big secret that perhaps no one but my father and I knew.

The piano was well placed there, so I could entertain the endless stream of guests my father had. He had groups of men, white and middle-aged like him, visit the house weekly. Sometimes, they would stay a few days, in the many, many bedrooms we had.

When I reached fourteen, war was brewing again. There has always been a war somewhere, and the military were very active. My father was a military man, just as his father before him had been. He had a conference room that I was never allowed to go in and I never once went in there. When I was a little girl, I asked him once why all these men came to the house, and if he was in charge of them. He laughed, a huge rolling sound, and he told me, 'No, Juliet. This was my father's house and it's big enough to host an army – of course I should be the one to open my house when we need to be together. What would they think of me if I didn't?' I never went in the conference room, not because I was obedient, but because I already had a better source of information.

I didn't need to understand what was going on from my father because my unwitting mother gave me everything I needed to know. If the men arrived for dinner, they always brought their jewelled wives with them. When they did, after dinner, my mother would take the ladies to the drawing room and they would sit and talk openly. It was not the demure discussions of watercolours and sewing – oh no, they would be free with what they thought about their husbands and the war. And with regards to the war, as the wives of the most senior command in the country, there was nothing they didn't know.

In turn, that information fell to me through the special secret of the drawing room.

Our house was very old with part of the house dating back to the Reformation, and like some of the houses built at the time, it had its own priest hole. Ours was hidden in the drawing room. I was shown it by my father when I was about ten, after he'd had too much whisky. He probably didn't even remember telling me – certainly, he never checked to see that I ever used it.

But I did.

It started one day when I was fourteen, when Cook became terribly upset. Seeing her frightened, whispering to me in the pantry, begging me for her life, made me realize that the world I had been so confident in was a lie. The trust I held in the version of the world my parents told me about changed. I wanted to form my own opinion and began to use the priest hole in an attempt to detect the truth. It worked – I learnt more sitting in that small dusty place than I'd ever been taught about the world at school.

By then, the politics had heated up further, and the visits from the men became at least weekly, which then turned into huge parties where their wives would join them. The world had become a dangerous place – more bombs could be heard dropping over the cities. Adults started having all their conversations behind closed doors and, again, just as after my pony disappeared, I wanted to understand more about the world around me.

One evening, after a night of more bombing, I decided I'd listen to the evening conversation – and the routine was established. It was addictive. I would be asked to play the guests something on the piano, before they all went through for dinner. As they drank martinis, I would play them Mozart – my father loved Bach best, but also adored Debussy and Mozart (but never Beethoven, my father wouldn't hear of it). Ephrem had given up the piano by then, and my parents had given up pretending it mattered, so it fell to me to charm the guests. After they clapped, I'd say goodnight and they'd troop into dinner, so then I'd later slip back into the then empty drawing room.

Just as my father had shown me, I pressed two different bricks on the fireplace hearth at the same time, which released a small section of the oak panelling on the wall. Inside there was a lever, which when pulled, opened the panel fully. It revealed a half-height door, plenty big enough for a girl to climb through.

Inside, it smelt of ash and earth. Small stone steps led up to what could only be described as a space – where if you wanted to, an adult could draw up their legs and sleep on the floor. But it was warm as it sat in what should have been the alcove for the huge fireplace's chimney, the flue diverted somewhere up and to the left. It was also dark, but I didn't mind; I found it peaceful.

But I didn't come for peace – I came to learn.

Every weekend, I sat on the bottom step, close to the empty knot of wood which served as both eye and listening hole. I would take a snack and a cushion, sometimes a rug, and would spend the evening thoroughly entertained. The women would always drink wine and I would sit, sometimes stifling my giggles and gasps as they talked about the realities of sex and war.

After they'd gone, I'd wait until I thought my parents would be saying goodbye to their guests out on the drive, then I'd ease out of the hidey-hole and sneak up to bed in time for when my mother looked in on me, before she retired.

My life changed when I met Arthur. Without him, perhaps I would have carried on my trajectory of doing exactly what I was supposed to in life. A little naughty perhaps, a little too rebellious for my mother's tastes perhaps, but nothing that in time couldn't be undone.

But Arthur couldn't be undone.

And he never has. When he tied a ribbon around my heart, it was double-tied, treble-tied – tied for life.

The evening I spoke to him, I was bored yet again. Bored because my parents were away, bored of the estate, even lonely enough to miss an absent Ephrem, so I decided to investigate the priest hole to see if it held any other secrets I'd missed. I was poking around, desperate to discover an escape tunnel or a skeleton when I heard music playing: the

Moonlight Sonata. I froze momentarily – who dared play Father's hated composer? And on *my* piano?

Alarmed, I hurried down the steps in the dark, tripped over my feet, and half fell, half rolled through the panel, out onto the drawing-room floor.

I looked up horrified to see Arthur's fingers stilled over the keys, his eyes rounded with fear that he had been caught sitting uninvited at our very expensive piano.

And that's how we discovered each other's secret.

Piano and the priest hole pressed our lives together and, in many ways, from that moment on, we were ruined.

Chapter 21

After I give Winston the note, I sit down at my desk, but appearances must remain deceptive. To be killed for face-crime after all I have done would be laughable. So I remain Icelandic ice and fire: my face remains frozen, but inside I am volcano. I am alive with *Arthur*.

I am alive with *Winston*.

I can't do this. I can't act like I've done anything other than go to the water fountain.

My work frequently bores me, and there is nothing to distract me. The telescreen drones on with dull muzak filling the space between the update from this year's Housing Success Strategy and the hotly anticipated HSS for next year as if the world is unchanged.

But everything has changed.

I'd planned on rinsing Winston Smith for information. In Thinkpol or not? In the Brotherhood or not? Guilty or not guilty? But now I see him differently. One meeting had changed everything. It had made him more than real. I'm good at my job because I can remain focused. My focus could have stayed true with any of the scenarios I've imagined: Winston not having anything to do with the Brotherhood; Winston really being undercover Thought Police; Winston being part of the Brotherhood and either welcoming the Sisterhood or dismissing us.

But not this.

Not seeing Winston – really *seeing* him – and that reaching out and growing a neural pathway between my now and my past.

I think of my note, how it declared: '*I love you*'. It was meant to be simple – a clear expression of the forbidden. Designed to harpoon. Designed to say, I will adore you and will have sex with you and make your dreams come true, so how can you resist?

I write an e-comm that I don't even think about, my fingers achingly slow as I type one-handed. All thoughts of the speakwrite are gone; I can only think about the note and what I have done. How it feels like the words shadow some feeling from another time. Was it the past with Arthur? 'I love you. Arthur.' Or was it, I think, recalling Winston's clear concern in his eyes, the sure touch of his skin, was it some portent of the future?

No.

No, I don't love you, Winston. This is ridiculous. I'm believing my own propaganda. A sign of nothing but mental shutdown.

Now ... *urgh*. I'm losing my mind. I know it because I know the signs. Subconsciously, I reach out and touch my wrist and find my sling. The camera watches me on my computer – it knows everything, sees everything. Knows what I did – nearly did. But my thoughts are my own, I have to remember that, here at least. And maskface I can handle, too.

But after Arthur, I know what I can't handle is love.

Ombra Mai Fu. I think of Handel's aria. Winston, just as Handel wrote, you are a plain tree, there is little to admire other than your shade, but ... fuck, *what* shade.

Fuck.

What have I done?

Chapter 22

Arthur sat at the piano and I picked myself up off the floor. He didn't move to help me, so I dusted myself off and said the only thing I could think of. 'Hi. My name is Juliet.' I put my hand out to shake his and for a moment he did nothing. After a full bar's rest, he finally extended his hand.

His grip was sure – not what I expected. His skin was dry and warm and as his large hand circled mine, I wanted to keep contact. I'd never had any experience with boys, let alone held a boy's hand. When he let it go, my hand was colder for its absence.

'I'm Arthur,' he finally managed.

'I know, your father teaches me piano.'

He didn't answer but rose to go.

'Don't go! I thought . . .'

'That I shouldn't be here? I'm sorry, very sorry, miss. And embarrassed. I'll leave first thing in the morning, so you'll be saved—'

'No, please don't. I won't say anything.' I crossed the room and pressed the oak panel back into place. 'I have my own secret, as you can see.' I grinned at him. 'Arthur, that's my private little door and no one knows I use it. It's important to me that no one finds out. Might I possibly rely on the courtesy of your discretion?'

He looked surprised I'd asked. 'Of course, miss, I wouldn't say a word. It's none of my business.'

'Juliet, please.'

'Juliet then.' Each syllable was carefully spoken as if trying out a new score for the first time. I waited for him to ask about the priest hole, and if he had, for some reason (loneliness?) I might have confessed what I used it for, but he didn't, so we lapsed into silence.

I broke it first. 'The extra bass keys are quite something, aren't they? A joy that they should be black – apparently it's the only piano of its type, with black extra keys at the end. Have you heard that?' I rattled on. 'Apparently, they originally had a little cover to keep them safe.'

He didn't react to what I thought was an interesting fact and when he spoke it was as if to himself. 'I should have played Bartók while I had the chance.' He held his fingers above the keys as if he wanted to touch them again but was winning some battle of self-restraint. As someone not given to self-control, I stared at him anew, impressed and a little puzzled.

He had thick, wavy hair, just one shade on the brown side before it burnished to auburn. He had freckles, too – I alone in my family had freckles and I'd always longed for the even skin of my mother. But seeing them on him made me understand the beauty of them, even on myself. Even seated, he was tall, clearly long-bodied, and he had large hands, quite the largest I've ever noticed, and his fingers, whilst not slender, as they hovered held grace. He gazed at the keys with such a look of intense longing in his brown eyes, that suddenly, at fifteen, I had an abrupt insight: I wanted someone to look at *me* like that.

No. It was more than that: I wanted *him* to look at me like that.

For a moment, I was stilled with the magnitude of this. Then as he took a deep breath, straightening his shoulders, I realized with panic that he was about to leave. 'You could play Bartók now? I have a score somewhere for his Allegro Barbaro.'

'I . . . couldn't.'

'Because you don't want to?'

His brow deepened, making him look older than his eighteen years. 'Because I shouldn't!'

I didn't say anything. I didn't know what to do with this notion of self-constraint – particularly as it was after the horse had bolted. 'I won't tell.'

He looked at me, as if annoyed. 'I would know.'

I didn't tell him that he'd come in here uninvited, and it was a little late for illogical indignance. 'You like Beethoven?' I said instead, excited to keep this new company, particularly as it was forbidden company with high cheekbones and brooding brown eyes.

Clearly it was obvious so he didn't answer my question, but said instead, 'I was warming up. Those extra keys . . .' He stared at them, still at the piano stool. 'They're so beautiful. So enticing – I couldn't bear just to immediately . . . I've never had the opportunity to play those bass notes before. A genius to have added them.'

Again, he stumped me. I was a go-for-it-girl: act first, think later; the idea that someone should want something, but hedge around it instead of diving straight in was an anathema.

'Carpe diem,' I said, shrugging and gesturing at the piano. 'It's mine, so consider yourself free to play.'

'It's your father's.'

'It is *not*! He can barely play Three Blind Mice; he bought it for me for my birthday.'

Perhaps it was the hauteur in my voice, but my indignance meant that he was distracted for the first time from the magnificence of the piano and looked at me properly. He regarded me, not with judgement, but with an unblinking interest and then he looked back at the black, shiny grand. 'You are a very fortunate person,' he said.

I did not hear that he recognized my fortune without condemnation or awe, but rather that he regarded me as a person. I wasn't a 'person' to anyone – I was a daughter who lacked the appropriate disposition for a girl my age; a lesser thing in the shape of a sister; a pupil who needed to improve. I was so used to provoking disappointment that the idea at fifteen that I was a person, really made me *feel*.

But Arthur was already looking back at the keyboard. 'The extra bass notes,' he said in a hushed tone, 'are black. I wouldn't have thought the delineation would have been accentuated. But then . . .'

I huffed with frustration. I'd heard it before – how beautiful it was. Hadn't I said so already? I'd hope to have moved past it. Yes, it *was* beautiful with its internal cara-mel spruce, juxtaposed against the dark black shine, but I felt impatient for him to notice me. I sat next to him. 'This is a little prettier than the Allegro anyway.' I played a few opening bars of Haydn's Sonata, then when he didn't say anything, I continued. I could feel his heat next to me as we sat together on the stool. It was dizzying. To play beside him felt like taking my clothes off. My father's friends were fools, their opinions worthless, but Arthur was suddenly an audience that mattered. The music, Arthur's forbidden and unexpected presence, my parents' absence, all added to a whirl of intoxication.

Eventually, remembering to be the generous host, I paused. 'Now you can play something. If you still want to.'

Finally, Arthur turned to me. 'You are talented,' he said, and as he blinkingly, finally, really saw me, I knew I was in love.

'Thank you,' I managed, but he had turned back to the piano. His fingers had returned to the keys and he glanced at me, only to check my permission was still granted. 'Do you know this piece?' he asked, before playing, and when he finished, I admitted I didn't. I think he could have played me Moonlight again, and I wouldn't have heard it. I could only think of him.

'I thought it would be fun to use the low octave for Liszt's Ballade.' He played the low key again, seeing if I could catch the tune.

'It was thunder,' I whispered, not just talking about the rolling, vibrating bass notes. *Thunder and lightning.* To me, it was as if the air was charged with positive ions.

Sitting there, listening to Arthur play rolling thunder, I remembered my father looking at the blue-black sky when

I was a child, saying: 'There's going to be a storm, Juliet,' and then the rain crashing the biggest drops I'd ever seen to the earth almost the second he'd spoken. Then, he'd seemed so wise and strong, and watching Arthur play, I still believed that. But I could also see what he would think of Arthur sitting next to me like this, on the stool he'd bought me, at the piano he'd given me, in his house, and I knew that now I was predicting a storm.

Lesser people – or perhaps greater, depending on one's point of view – would have excused themselves from Arthur at this point and I genuinely (although sadly) believe that if I had, Arthur would've never looked my way again.

But for me, I was ready for thunder and lightning, and longed for the excitement of electricity forking my world. Arthur with his talent, his brown eyes and most importantly, his longing, was just what I was looking for.

'Come back tomorrow,' I invited him. 'You can play me a whole something – choose whatever you like. My parents don't return for ten days.'

The following day, he did return. And the next. And the next.

And just as I planned, by the time my parents returned, although he had yet to lay his fingers on me, Arthur was finally granting my desire and looking at me like I was the Imperial.

Chapter 23

The canteen stinks of the usual meat and gravy swill they serve every day. Even though it's early and more than half empty, it's still cymbal-smashingly noisy. It's like the acoustics in here have been designed to be torturous. Or maybe it just feels like it is: with my hangover and the humiliation of the removal of my stitches, any noise feels like it's feasting on flayed nerves.

It's underground; with a low ceiling and crap aircon, it always feels like breathing with one's face pressed into a stranger's armpit. There's not even a reprieve by way of a window, let alone a view.

Sometimes, all you want is to breathe freely and see a view.

Even taking the shuttle train here, the train beats trochaic against the tracks: *we're* trapped, *we're* trapped, *we're* trapped. Sometimes as it travels underneath London, the metal-on-metal screeches: trapppppeeeeeddddd!

Sometimes, I think I will die for the lack of space and freedom and green in my life; the lack of real trees (not the strangled, lifeless ones that are the only type that seem to survive in London). I think I long for home.

I want my mother.

I want her to say she is sorry, that she was wrong.

I shuffle forwards holding my tray, trying to see today's offering. There used to be heat bulbs heating the food, but one by one, they died. It doesn't matter – lukewarm shit tastes only marginally worse than hot shit.

I look into the metal containers and finally don't have to fake enthusiasm – today instead of gristle and gravy there's bean stew. I love bean stew. Bean stew hasn't been on the menu for so long, it feels like seeing an old friend.

Even better, I look up to see Issy Davy, just the sunniest person I know, and one of the few true believers that I actually like. 'Hey! Issy!' I've changed my shifts recently and I haven't seen her in ages. She smiles so easily, and it lights her face now.

After dumping her tray she winds her way through the tables towards me. 'Hey, Julia, I haven't seen you in ages. How's things going? Got anything special on for Hate Week?'

'In our ASL troop we made a huge papier-mâché of Goldstein's head two weeks ago, then found out that there's a troop of Spies creating a model of Big Brother's head, but the silly children have only made theirs two metres wide. Our Goldstein was double that, but there is no way he could be bigger than Big Brother, so one had to change. Because the little darlings couldn't be disappointed, we had to crush ours and start again.'

'Oh, how annoying! What are you going to do?'

'We've made a smaller one. We're thinking of cutting it back open so we can fill it with maggots. Then maybe it can be smashed open on the marsh and all the maggots fall out.'

'To show there's only rotten thoughts in his head! I love it – you've got to do that.'

I shrug, trying not to show I'm happy she likes the idea – it was mine. 'Feels like, now it's smaller, we've got to do something special, you know?'

'That's so cool! I love that. You should definitely do the maggots. But if you can't do that, what about filling it with sawdust? To show there's nothing in his head?'

'That's a great idea. You think people would catch the joke?'

'Sure, but who gets to smash the head open?'

'We were thinking we would just hold it up on a pole and then get a tannoy announcement to invite people to join in.'

'Oh, that's great. I'd love to do that. Who doesn't want to smash Goldstein's head in? But it could be dangerous, though – for the person holding the pole. Everyone's going to want to do that; stuff like that drives people mental. Although what an honour to be trampled to death in the name of smashing up Goldstein.'

The queue inches forward. 'An honour,' I agree and think I'll suggest that the troop gets to do it – hopefully some of the little brats will be squished by the crowds. I think of Gerta. No, Chantelle. No – *both*. Today just feels brighter and brighter.

She squeezes my elbow. 'Ministry of Plenty's done so well for us again – bean stew!' she says. Before she leaves for her desk, we agree to meet for a lecture later in the week. I need to spend more time with Issy, I decide. If I keep going as I am, all spy work and no play, I'll be dead before the year is out.

Perhaps I need a bit of balance.

Waiting for the till, I casually look around the canteen – I'm looking for Winston. Even as I do, I'm conscious this no longer feels like just work. Truth is, I'm looking forward to seeing him. Like bean stew and Issy Davy and squished Chantelle, I need the scaffolding to hold me up. I can't quite do it myself.

I've seen him a few times over the last few days, but it's not been safe enough to make the next approach. It's just been bad timing: him entering the canteen as I've been leaving, him coming in when I'm already seated with the other girls from Fiction. Yesterday was the nearest we came. He almost made it to my table but looked spooked and ended up sitting somewhere else.

I clear the till and head towards an empty table. I'm still hoping to catch Winston but even if he isn't in today, I think, putting down my food and clearing someone else's spill with a water-repelling serviette, today's going to be a good day. It's not just that I want it to be. I can feel that it will be.

Although I can't deny I'm not looking forward to seeing him, it's not the craziness it could've been. I must have been high on endorphins or something after my little drunken bathroom escapade, but now I'm back down to earth. I don't love Winston. Of course I don't love Winston! Even the memory is shaming! What a fool – he just caught me when I was down. Seeing (Ruby's?) nailed eye–

–there's something in my eye–

–What are you looking at?–

It was the cruelty of those body parts in the children's playground. The image just whirled around in my mind, the memory mixing up with fears of Arthur (*and my father, but I am not thinking about that now because today is a good day*): the disharmony within the Sisterhood, the dreaming of that helicopter every time I shut my eyes, the feeling of betraying Eleanor, and then I had too much gin.

Thirsty.

I touched my wrist. Smith doesn't even look like Arthur, I'm sure.

And then, just as I start eating, I can see Winston heading towards my table. We're about to have our second meeting. Brotherhood or Thinkpol? Help or persecutor? Not guilty or guilty?

I'm ready to find out.

(Like Arthur or not like Arthur?)

Winston Smith sits opposite me, but I don't acknowledge him. We are just two strangers sitting in a canteen eating our lunch. I eat a mouthful of beans; they mush between my molars, crushed to nothing. The telescreen is far enough away to make it possible. This is going to happen now.

He speaks. 'What time do you leave work?'

I don't look at him. 'Eighteen-thirty.'

'Where can we meet?'

Keeping my voice low, I say: 'Victory Square, near the monument.'

'It's full of telescreens.'

He's spoken too quickly, so I wait a while, just eating the

stew. 'It doesn't matter if there's a crowd,' I say finally, perhaps just as he's given up hope. Just as Eleanor taught me, I will teach Winston. Unless he knows this already and is the ultimate Thought Police spy just effortlessly hoovering up bad guys. There's no way of knowing yet.

Following my lead, he pauses to eat before asking: 'Any signal?'

'No. Don't come up to me until you see me among a lot of people. And don't look at me. Just keep somewhere near me.'

'What time?'

'Nineteen hundred hours.'

'All right.'

Our conversation is over. I finish my lunch, pick up my tray and leave without looking back.

It's about to start.

Seeing Issy, bean stew *and* an evening date with Winston Smith . . . today *is* a good day.

Chapter 24

I'm feeling good as I tramp to the market on Gresham Street. The sun is out and I sunflower towards it, feeling the heat on my face. I have to meet Winston in half an hour and I can't stop thinking about it. I'm thinking about the wrong things but ... it makes me feel better. I rub my arm without thinking; I badly need to feel just a tiny bit positive, so I'm prepared to indulge myself.

Perhaps everything will go right from now on. It feels like good luck. Winston has improved my mood. Perhaps Winston will be the connection the Sisterhood needs – perhaps all roads lead to this point and ...

I don't have to finish the thought. The feeling of hope is enough.

I realize that I'm desperate that he will be Brotherhood – more than before. Not just for my safety and the future of the group, but because then, perhaps we could be friends. I keep thinking of his poet's eyes; I shake the thought away but I don't hate myself for it. Instead I choose to let it be. Focusing on the now, I know I have to kill the next thirty minutes and make it seem natural. There are maybe two hundred people here – this market is a popular one. There are samey stalls selling samey stuff – it varies depending on what there's a glut of. Sometimes, you can't find any potatoes for months, so we eat rice, rice, rice, then it changes and then there's only potatoes piled into high, peaty pyramids, but no green veg at all. And then again no rice – once, for nearly two years. Then when the rice finally returned to the markets, everyone celebrated: 'Big Brother provides! He provides!'

I still find it bewildering that people can't judge what's in front of them – it's like the optics don't count. If it looks like a shit situation, and it feels like a shit situation, then why don't they rise up? Why are they determined to not see what's in front of them – no rice for two years?

But the confusion can't touch me today, not with the sun, not with the progress made with Winston, and thinking of him lights me from the inside, too. I'm not even going to fight it right now – I'm just going to enjoy it. After last week, I need it.

At the bread stall, my luck continues. I can see Eleanor there, her back to me, dressed in her camel, belted coat. Excellent! I can update her. I wasn't expecting to see her for two days. We're due at the same leaflet-writing evening for the Women Against Freedom. This is better because the other members of WAF are chicken-headed, obedient dullards who obsess over the Party's 'Freedom is Slavery' maxim and truly want less freedom in their already castrated lives. They debate endlessly how they can reduce it and fail to understand they can't, because they already have so little in the first place.

I will tell her about my success with Winston. I think of the right phrasing to convey the situation. Shall I say netted? Or on track? No, too explicit. Subtlety is everything. Yes, but it also needs to be more personal – we do know each other, after all. It needs to be about something we would actually bleat if we were subservient sheep – something like: *our plans for the WAF are good, Eleanor*.

I stand behind her and pretend to be interested in the grey cardboard loaves. I miss Cook's fat bloomers, sour-doughs, and honey and rye.

I pay for my cardboard loaf. Then Eleanor turns and two separate things happen in unison. The first is I realize that she's become older, so much older, and I never noticed. As the sunlight hits her, I notice her hair as if seeing her for the first time. The ASL meetings are usually under the limp light of energy-saving bulbs, but outside, the spring sunlight is vigorous, casting her hair as luminous, the thin skin of a silver birch. Whilst the colour is lovely, under the bright light, her parting yields soft, pink scalp.

As I see this, as I look at her, our eyes meet. And she looks at me blankly. The two thoughts collide. She's an old woman who doesn't know who I am. She just stares at me with the empty stare of an uninterested stranger. Doesn't she know who I am?

No, she *doesn't* know who I am! Alarm grips me. Her lovely grey eyes are voids. There's nothing in them.

Nothing.

Eleanor, always so perspicacious, is now . . . not there?

She looks at me and her gaze slides away, as if I am just another grey face in the grey crowd.

I make a mistake. 'Eleanor! It's me!' My shock makes me react. How could she not recognize me when I'm a metre in front of her? Her gaze moves back to me.

Blank face.

Blank face.

Then: *bam*! Recognition. After a brain power cut, it's like all the electrics buzz back into life. It's startling: her eyes focus, even her face moves from slackness to a tighter, more held and familiar Eleanor. 'Of course it's you, Julia,' she says smoothly. I detect a hint of annoyance at my small exclamation. 'I have been considering the text for our leaflets this week.' She touches my arm. 'They will be our best yet.' And then I'm excused, and she's gone.

I watch her disappear into the crowds milling around the market; dowdy, broken old people, too cold, too hopeless. Amongst the grey hair, the poverty of it all, I'm discomforted: it ages her. Greatly. It's as if she's gained a decade – more – before my eyes. How did Eleanor slip from steely, wise elder into generic, confused frailty without me noticing? Is this what our last meeting did to her? (*we should take a vote*) I am responsible for this? (*I know about you, Julia*) Under callous sunlight, she is reframed.

Reframed into just another old woman buying bread in the market.

My breath catches on the inhale; are we, the Sisterhood, really slipping away? The possibility feeling more like reality is a sudden, cold clasp. Never more have we needed something real, something substantial. Winston Smith, I dearly hope you are Brotherhood.

Chapter 25

My parents were taking their annual trips to the Alps; they left on Tuesday morning, early, and as soon as their car had driven through the front gates, I'd run from my bedroom, down the south wing, avoided the main stairs, feet flying up the servant staircase into the attic. The south attic corridor was dense with stifled, warm air; motes explored the beams of light that fell unchecked through curtainless windows. The servants were accommodated far away in the colder attic rooms of the east wing. Arthur and I could be as free as the motes, moving unseen.

Our liberty was strengthened because Arthur's father had also taken advantage of the holiday season and left for Kent the day before to visit his sister. Arthur had been supposed to go, and normally, he said he would have enjoyed his aunt's company, but at this point, we only wanted to be together. So, Arthur had told me that he'd planned to cry off sick. I couldn't find out if he'd managed to get out of it until my parents had left.

With held breath, I ran all the way to his room and banged on his door.

Instantly, he pulled it open. His cheeks had a candyfloss pink to them, flushed with the same delight I felt. He took me in his arms and spun me round with delight. 'We've done it!' Time alone was a treasure chest; dragon-greedy, I grabbed him to me and I swore then that nothing would ever separate me from him.

He was careful enough to post me back neatly on my feet by the door. To step into his apartment alone felt like a barrier we weren't yet ready to cross. Then I realized what I'd missed. I felt his gradual release of me and I stared smiling into his face and saw him anew – he was older, I realized. I'd seen him yesterday, seen him the day before that and before that, but today I saw him afresh. I realized that the then eighteen-year-old man-boy I had first met two years previously – moody, impatient, without social graces – had become something else. Arthur had, under my watchful gaze, grown up.

Something in me, deep in me, moved. Uncoiled and became awake. So awake, so suddenly.

What had been sweet, suddenly had an undertow of sour. But rather than spoil the sweet, it only served to subtly emphasize. To embellish.

I think I exhaled audibly.

He'd had a haircut – perhaps that'd triggered the fresh eyes that I now viewed him with. His always lovely cheekbones were now newly drawn. His jaw, sharper. But these badges of manhood, along with his height, weren't what drew me. Nor was it the intensity of his stare – Arthur was given to brooding, rolling clouds bruised with Tyrian.

It was fitting that I thought of Tyrian and Arthur. Strong, intense and royal.

It was my old history teacher, Mr Jenkins, who told me that Tyrian was the purple colour saved for royalty; it came from the glands of molluscs, harvested from their rectums. Old Jenkins told us that was symbolic of people's feelings – that no one ever loved their royalty. That the kings and queens of the world persecuted their people. Because the poor always felt their tyranny, the colour was selected from the arseholes of sea bottom feeders. A statement of their true place. It didn't matter anymore because there was no royalty left. The top feeders, he told us, were long since gone.

Sensing his discomfort, mischievously I'd put my hand up. 'Where, sir? Where have they gone?'

Jenkins had a nervous twitch and an unmistakable twang of BO. His skin had a livid quality, as if shaved with a blunt razor or an unsteady hand. Half the teaching staff drank too much. I didn't know if they were becoming more nervous or if they'd always been like that and I was only becoming more self-aware. All I knew was that school seemed to be increasingly a world of dropped answers, bad hygiene and nervous glances.

'Juliet, does it matter where they've gone?' he spluttered.

Of course it bloody did, I felt like answering. But Jenkins had an irritating habit of answering a question with a question – a classic technique of avoidance. I'd been schooled young and well.

Arthur was the antithesis of my school life. He was strong, healthy, talented, authentic and honest. His shoulders were broad, and I lifted my chin a little just to look at him. Just to be near him.

I leaned in a little. Only inches between us now.

We spent many hours kissing. This should have been familiar territory. But my breathing heaved and slowed – this felt new. His mouth parted, and he didn't close his eyes as he narrowed the gap between us.

The kiss was slow, but deep. His other hand found my back and pressed me closer. I realized our other kisses until now were childish, innocent explorations but nothing more. This was different. I could hear his breathing was different. *I need to be loved by you*, I thought.

He pulled away. 'Juliet?'

I nodded a little.

And then he kissed me so long, standing in that dusty top corridor, that I thought he'd misunderstood.

But he hadn't.

Chapter 26

'Never doubt that a small group of thoughtful,
committed citizens can change the world;
indeed, it's the only thing that ever has.'
Margaret Mead

After I had lain with Arthur, the inevitable happened. Of course, I knew something of the mechanics of life. They didn't explicitly explain at school, but if one managed to stay awake long enough during Dr Shay's lectures, the rudimentary facts were explained. What they didn't explain was that I learnt two into three results in a whole new number. A number one.

That number one was Chloe.

But I didn't know it, of course, when I held the pregnancy test I had stolen from Matron's office.

Cindy Galton had told me that Matron had pregnancy tests locked in her drawer for emergencies.

Cindy Galton was the type of girl who knew about emergencies.

And as I stood in the dorm bathroom, the light leaking weakly through the north-facing window (where if you stood on tiptoes, you could look down onto the hockey pitches), I realized that Cindy Galton wasn't the only girl now who knew about emergencies. And I realized that looking down from the bathroom window was about as close as I was going to get to playing hockey, for a long, long time.

But the funny thing was, I didn't even care.

My hand pressed against my lower belly. There was a lightness to my being. I felt reborn.

Once, when I was a child, I made a heart out of clay and carefully painted it red. I had been captivated by an empty walnut shell that Cook had given me. We had a walnut tree, of course, and it soured the ground beneath it just as my tears later would, but I didn't know that then. I collected walnuts for Cook in return for being allowed to sit next to the huge Aga and rattle on, pontificating about my life. She liked what she called wet walnuts and made many things from them – none of which I tried, for I hated the things as they furred my tongue sour. But she gave me a whole shell that was empty and I liked its wood feel, its intricate design, and fancied it something beautiful. The two pieces fitted together snugly and suggested to me a deeper idea. The tiny, painted heart was placed onto a scrap of velvet and then the top lid of the walnut pressed tight down on it.

It felt magical; that concealed heart felt like a secret withheld from the world.

I don't know what happened to it – one of the bloody maids probably swept it up just as they seemed to do with anything not nailed to the floorboards – but as I pressed my hand against my belly, it reminded me of that precious heart, locked tight in its bed of velvet so carefully arranged, and I felt – I vowed – that I would take better care of it. This was my privilege then as a daughter of the Inner Party. Confidence. I knew nothing then of society – never heard, even, of the term 'prole'. I only knew of my home and my school and the chauffeured car journeys between the two. My friends were the same and had no insight to offer me of a different reality.

I was confident, too, of the men in my life. Even though I hadn't told Arthur, I was certain of his love. And even though I hadn't told Father, I was certain of his love also.

This heart within me, later to be Chloe, would be cared for better.

I vowed it.

I fucking vowed it.

Chapter 27

Chloe was my secret for seven months.

In the end, I couldn't get out of hockey for I couldn't declare the truth. If anything, I became a better player; I felt alive with energy and power pumped through my legs, and in defence of my little heart inside, I became more fierce, more furious an opponent. I endured sickness, puking in loo breaks, vomiting once on the hockey field, claiming it was the effort, whilst Janice Withers pointed and told me I was getting too fat to play well. Perhaps it was Janice in the end who gave it away. I don't know.

I remember the sharpness in Miss Smith's vulture eye as she regarded me closely, after Janice's observation, choosing to take me herself from the hockey field to the Matron's office. But Matron's top drawer was never unlocked, because instead of a test, my mother came – we were only two days before the end of term – and took me home early. Perhaps it was nothing to do with Janice Withers; there was a lot of sickness around at the time – flu and fear and the combination made people wary. So although Arthur was stuck at school painting fences not knowing anything

(I wanted to tell him when we were alone), my trunk and me and Chloe all went back home.

But it was the end of my secret. Mother knew. I suppose I was showing by then, not much, not as much as I feared, not to the casual eye, but Mother knew me well. Mother was very gentle and told me to go to bed.

'I'm not ill,' I told her, with a touch of strong jaw and a flash of cold eye.

'I know,' she said. She turned, started to head out of the room, then stopped, paused and turned. 'I need time to think. Your father will be back from his Russian trip on Friday. I need to think what to do, before he comes back.' Her brown eyes were kind. But she pressed against them briefly, as if pained. I wondered if she was thinking of Ephrem; how much easier she must've found him than her wayward eighteen-year-old daughter.

I did stay in my room those few days. My mother and I didn't discuss it – I don't know why. Instead, she took to reading to me. I wish I could remember what it was that she read to me; I wish it was something that moved me, resonated and deepened my understanding of the world in some way, but if it did, they were lessons lost to me now. I don't remember. What I do remember is that her words washed over me; they comforted me like a warm bath. She sat at the foot of my single bed, and settled into a comfy position and read to me far beyond where others would have lost patience and quietly shut the book. Instead, her soft voice continued, even after the tea, bread and jam – or better, sometimes scones – that Cook sent up to us. She kept me company and when

Mother wasn't with me, I gazed out of my confinement, watching the sky beyond.

I didn't think of school – Arthur was still there, but would be back at Eltringham Hall soon. The last two terms of my education felt like they had already drifted away. The etiquette training and deportment classes, which had replaced history and science and maths since I was sixteen, always made me feel that I was being folded into something smaller than I was and I cared nothing for missing it.

More disturbingly, when I was younger, I was able to access the school library. There, finding a box of dusty books removed from the shelves and placed into storage and forgotten, I found all the knowledge that I knew no one was allowed to know at school. When I was younger, the librarian, soaked on gin and asleep, didn't know that I smuggled them out and then read them under the covers at night. The old, forgotten books stolen from the library taught me more about the old world than I have learnt from any other single source.

So, missing the library, with no school, I lay there in my bed and thought of Arthur. I hadn't yet been able to tell him, so Chloe was still held tight within the walnut shell and only I held her inside my fist. But it was temporary. I saw those days in my room as a pause before we would cross – all three of us together – into some point in the future where everything would be settled.

Really, that pause was only waiting for my father to return. I wasn't so naive that I thought I was in control of my life: I understood a little of the world I lived in. But, in retrospect, I was a terrible fool. Fool to lie in bed instead of fleeing barefoot from Eltringham Hall. Fool to believe that the person who would help us was my father.

I thought my father loved me enough to withstand any arctic frost, any tsunami, any drought. I thought that money and privilege insulated me against the realities that others faced. I thought being cherished meant I wouldn't be burnt.

And I knew my father was a powerful man – it seemed to me that there wasn't anything he couldn't do.

I thought if I held my breath and waited, he would return home, scold me heavily before sweeping up the untidiness of my life and leave me restored and safe.

Youth is an insulator. Lack of experience smooths and plumps. The wrinkles of later life are only the metaphorical expression of a deeper understanding – a capturing of the repeated anguish, pressed and folded into us. Each one a record of individual incidents significant enough to leave a mark.

When my father did come home, instead of helping, he gave me a terrible mark, one that folded deeply into me and made me who I am today.

I will not think of it now.

I will not.

I will not think of what he did to Chloe. To me.

I can think of his face though: the famous face, moustached, stern. When everyone sees Big Brother looking down from them from a poster, I see it differently because Big Brother's face is my father's face. When Big Brother talks to me in my flat, it is the voice of my father.

My father, George Ivor Berkshire. Commander of

Ingsoc. Dictator over Oceania and its armies. Ruler over the Inner Party. Big Brother.

Until I killed him.

My father is not Big Brother anymore. How can he be, when he is dead and Big Brother lives on? I take comfort that it can't be him who talks to me in my flat, who watches me, that it can only be his CGI shadow that remains.

I know that shadow can't be real because Big Brother never laughs. I remember my father who laughed frequently; the joy that could sparkle in that man's eyes. I remember when I used to ride around on his shoulders when I was a little girl, calling him my pony. When my mother led me blindfolded out into the paddock and pulled the scarf away, I can still remember his shining eyes as he presented me with my brand-new pony Snowball. Then later, when he kissed my hands as he revealed the Bösendorfer Imperial Grand piano wrapped in the biggest red ribbon I've even seen.

I was his favourite, but he never looked at me again after he found out I was pregnant. Instead he killed me. And that's why I killed him.

I know, because of him, I am capable of anything. When I am his blood, when I know what I've done, I know there is nothing I cannot do.

For it is an inescapable truth that even dictators have children. And it is this cold fact I struggle with at night, alone. (I don't even fear that Eleanor has guessed my bloodline – because how could she? How would she not slit my throat if she knew?) It's a terrible secret to bear alone: that Oceania's dictator had one daughter – and I can never forget it is me, Julia.

Chapter 28

Winston Smith looks up at me; he is bent low as he gathers flowers from the verge.

I shake my head – *don't say anything.* Instead, I lead him back into the woods. The smell of oxygen is powerful – I've been too long in the city and feel light-headed. He follows behind me and I'm grateful for his silence, not least because I'm in control. It feels strange to be back in my father's woods, to where Arthur and I used to meet. It's been so long since I've been here – and yet it feels like no time at all.

All my hopes have been pinned on this – Smith and my first meet away from London, away from cameras. Until now, it's just been building communication to this moment. I wasn't sure he'd make it. We arranged it when I met him during the evening earlier in the week. I thought he might change his mind and not show, or perhaps he'd get trouble from the patrols as he travelled here by train. There was every chance I'd find him here mob-handed with the Thought Police. But so far, so good. He's now dutifully following me, matching step for step along the muddy path, as if I'm leading him through a minefield rather than through a wood.

I have told him about this place – but I have not been honest with him.

We step over the fallen tree that I told him about. On the other side, I push aside a mass of rhododendrons, to reveal the place I know so well. It's a grassy knoll, a quiet, peaceful place. The leaves are thick, olive-green leather; together with coppiced trees, they provide natural screening. Even better, these woods are private – no one trespasses in them. Here, there is space for a picnic rug and little else. The memories of Arthur and I picnicking here make me weak – I had not expected to feel this *much*.

But right now, Winston, with his poet's eyes, will be more than enough to just *feel*. To just be in this moment – not in my head, its echo chamber of fear and paranoia. But just to be back amongst the leaves and the birds, the breeze and Arthur's – *Winston's* – kisses on me. To feel real.

To find the truth for Ruby; for Leona. To find the Brotherhood for Eleanor, so she can find forgiveness for me and safety for us all.

I turn to face him. In this light, he looks older than I remembered.

'Here we are. I didn't want to say anything in the lane,' I say, 'in case there's a mic hidden there. I don't suppose there is, but there could be. There's always a chance of one of those swine recognizing your voice. We're all right here.'

'We're all right here?'

Fear leaps like fleas, high, easy, blood drawn. 'Yes, look at the trees.' I pointed to the coppiced ash. 'There's nothing big enough to hide a mic in. Besides, I've been here before.'

He appears to be sweating lightly – is that a sign that he is friend or foe? He takes my hand and says, 'Would you believe that, until this moment, I didn't know what the colour of your eyes were?'

The line seems corny, and I'm a little disappointed. I'd hoped for something more poetic; I'd thought him like Arthur.

He continues, 'Now that you've seen what I'm really like, can you still bear to look at me?'

'Yes, easily.'

'I'm thirty-nine years old. I've got a wife I can't get rid of. I've got varicose veins. I've got five false teeth.'

He's still holding my hand, and is looking at me so earnestly whilst saying these dreadful things, that I struggle not to laugh. What was I thinking that he was ever like Arthur! He really shouldn't talk of collapsed veins and false teeth before we've even kissed. False teeth! 'I couldn't care less,' I say. And I don't – if he's Brotherhood, then he can have a full set of false teeth and I'll soak them for him.

If he's responsible for Ruby's death, I'll hold him down whilst Leona chokes him with them. It'd take a pair of pliers and a little time, but still.

With that thought in mind, I reach up to him and kiss him very lightly on his mouth. His lips are surprisingly pleasing: firm, but not too firm. He puts his arms around my waist and we kiss for a while. After a little encouragement, he pulls me to the ground and we lie there kissing.

'What is your name?' he finally asks.

'Julia. I know yours. It's Winston – Winston Smith.'

'How did you find that out?'

'I expect I'm better at finding things out than you are, dear. Tell me, what did you think of me before I gave you that note?'

'I hated the sight of you. I wanted to rape you and then murder you afterwards. Two weeks ago, I seriously thought of smashing your head in with a cobblestone. If you really want to know, I thought you had something to do with the Thought Police.'

For a moment, I'm stunned. ' ...rape ... murder ... smash ...' This desire to commit violence against me is unexpected. I didn't think Winston had even noticed me. I think about him lifting a cobblestone to hurt me and wonder how or why I've provoked such desire for violence in a man, who with only a few words, can then be encouraged so easily into kissing me.

Smith is not a man of substance – he's reframed instantly into something mercurial and rather unpleasant. But it does seem significant that he mentions Thinkpol so quickly. Is he Brotherhood and trying to flush out a reaction? Or is he an agent and trying to establish how loyal I am to Ingsoc?

So instead, I do just as Cook taught me: 'Juliet, when they pull your pigtails, laugh. It is less fun to hurt those who cannot be hurt.' To me, my laugh sounds maniacal, so I follow with, 'Thought Police! You didn't honestly think that?'

'Well, perhaps not exactly that. But from your general appearance – merely because you're young and fresh and healthy, you understand—'

—because I'm fresh you'd rape me?—

Perhaps he senses my ire because he's blushing and sweating now. I must not kill off this contact. Play it light, Julia. 'You thought I was a good Party member. Pure in word and deed. Banners, processions, slogans, games, community hikes and all that stuff. And you thought that if I had a quarter of a chance, I'd denounce you as a thought criminal and get you killed off?' I try to sound bouncy; I think I succeed. Now that we're here, I'm glad. Let's flush out your opinion, Winston.

'Yes, something of that kind. A great many young girls are like that, you know.'

Girls? I think of the nailed body parts and the faces of the boys in the playground that were just as eager – equally interested – in my reaction to the meaty exposure of the fresh, pearl white cartilage. *And a great many young boys 'are like that', too, Winston. Men, women, girls and boys, too.*

Instead, I say: 'It's this bloody thing that does it.' I pull at my red sash. Because I need the sugar, I root in my pocket for the chocolate I was keeping for my return journey. I snap him off a piece and pass it to him.

He opens it with a childish wonder and eats it with such a look of sublime pleasure on his face, I struggle not to giggle.

'Where did you get it?' he asks.

Oh, my dear Winston, if you knew the answer to that, your varicose veins would burst on this very spot. Instead I lie, 'Black market.' Then warming to my new persona of child/woman, I add, 'Actually, I'm that sort of girl to look at. I'm good at games. I was a troop-leader in the Spies. I do voluntary work three days a week for the Junior Anti-Sex League. Hours and hours I've spent pasting their rot over London. I always carry one end of a banner in the processions. I always look cheerful and I never shirk from anything. Always yell with the crowd, I say. It's the only way to be safe.'

What's clear is, any idea that he could be attractive to me is dead. It's hideous: the fact he wanted to rape me doesn't surprise me. Whilst rapists are executed in public, there's still rumours of rife sexual violence against women. It's whispered there are dugouts in parks, into which women can be snatched; prole areas where the CCTV is non-existent; parts of homes where the telescreens do not watch. Gossip is that rape is tolerated by Big Brother – it causes pain, and pain causes more hate.

Hearing him means I want to fold the real me into a little version of myself and tuck it away inside where he can't access me. But the good news is, I'm clear and refocused: I am only here for the reason I passed him the note.

I'm here for Ruby.

I'm glad. I might be a little screwed up, but at least now I'm back on track.

He watches me as he finishes his chocolate. 'You are very young. You are ten or fifteen years younger than I am. What could you see to attract you in a man like me?'

It's too dangerous to answer this whilst he is able to scrutinize my face so clearly. Wanting to walk side by side instead, I get up and hold out my hand. He takes it and I lead him away from the hiding place. The shrubs open out a little and we walk for a few moments before I answer.

I am prepared for this question. Any Brotherhood member would want to be careful of seeking out a new contact. My mouth is dry. As soon as I speak, if Smith is Thinkpol, I will now give him enough for me to be arrested. But I cannot do nothing. Ruby is (probably) dead; the Sisterhood is falling apart; we have no way of striking at all of Ingsoc. It is not enough to strike at one or two or three of the Inner Party. We could destroy some, but it needs to be all. Who knows that better than me? I killed Big Brother and nothing changed. Instead, he lived on as a puppet and no one noticed. No, if you don't take out root and branch, the bad will just seep over into the vacuum created and nothing will change.

Ruby must not die in vain. 'It was something in your face. I thought I'd take a chance. I'm good at spotting people who don't belong.' I'd thought about this state-ment – this idea that not belonging is the bait. I go further: 'As soon as I saw you, I knew you were against them.' The word *them* has been carefully considered – it implies a separateness different to *us*. Will he take the bait?

His hand tightens against my waist, more a flinch as if I'd hurt him, a reflex against my words, but then relaxes.

We reach the edge of the woods; here the fields are loving receivers of the sun. But I don't want to go out there – it's easier to lie in the shadows. 'Don't go out into the open. There might be someone watching. We're all right if we keep behind the boughs.'

Smith doesn't mention the 'them'. Instead, he mumbles meaninglessly about the countryside around us. I do not tell him about my father's ownership of this land.

A thought occurs: if Smith is an agent, he'll know exactly who I am. He'll know all my secrets. It throws an interesting angle onto our meeting. Am I being studied by my family?

'Look!' I whisper as a thrush lands in near proximity on a branch in front of us. It sings directly to us. Its boldness is arresting. Smith stares at the bird and it seems to me that he is holding me in its sights. His hand tightens boa-tight round my waist, cinching me in. He keeps me corseted as he stares at the bird.

For some inexplicable reason, I feel it is warning me of impending danger. This feeling – this blade edge of dread – could not be more sharply felt than if it pressed against my neck. I clutch at Winston, telling myself that it's not a raven or blackbird, it's not a symbol of doom or a harbinger of evil, but still . . . its confidence, its urgency seems too bold. I even think – for a crazy minute – that perhaps it's a synthetic, a mechanized thrush concealing a camera here to watch us. I think, yes, Smith is an agent! He's holding me here so I can be filmed! This will be shown to me as proof of my thoughtcrime, when I am chained in the bowels of Miniluv next to Ruby. Paranoia flares. I see her clearly: eye stitched shut; missing ear stitched over; mute now. I will see her again.

I'm sweating now, sick. The anxiety of this situation is killing me – it's just paranoia. Thrushes are symbols of hope. This pretty bird is just a lovely thing. Is it that I can't see even loveliness clearly now?

But the bird is so direct, it fixes me with its perfidious onyx eye and tells me: Julia, Smith is the path to your death.

Chapter 29

Standing on the edge of Damp Dip Wood, where I have just left Smith behind with nothing but directions on how to get home, I am back on my father's land. It's not lost on me that I chose to start an affair with Smith here, but it's not some petulant desire to piss off my deceased father, but rather the surety of lack of monitoring equipment here. The evils of Oceania are not applied equally.

Now Smith's gone, I'm left clearer that I can have a relationship with this man. Although he's a long way from Arthur (how did I ever confuse them?), this was never about romance. Stupid of me for being so easily tilted – *no*! I scold myself.

Not silly: just fresh trauma.

Grief for Ruby is its own entity, but it also shucked open festering wounds that have never healed. I wrap my arms around myself: too many drinks, a wallow of grief and misery, and I get silly with a knife and see disappeared lovers in dusty men. But that idea is behind me now. This is only now about pursuing truth. If Smith is Brotherhood, he won't reveal that truth quickly – a whole relationship must be allowed to build up. If he's Thinkpol – well, that may be revealed more quickly.

I leave the woods and instead of heading towards the lane, which will take me back to the train into London, I find myself dragging through hedges and fields. Beautiful in early summer, the hedges are pillowed with cow parsley; primroses stud the fringes and blushing dog rose weave, reaching for the sky. Across the south fields and then, against my better judgment, I cross through the Crow Copse, as Ephrem and I used to call it, into the lower gardens of the house. The grass is still as I remembered it, longer, coarser than the lawns partnering the house. Sometimes, we would search for frogs here. I reach the lake; old friend.

Still idyllic, moorhens dunk amongst lily pads. I almost want to skim stones again with my brother. It's a nice memory, like plunging one's hand into a pocket and finding forgotten sweets amongst wrappers and used tissues.

I walk around the edge, reaching where it meets the stream. Seeing it, a different memory surfaces.

Every summer, my brother Ephrem and I would come back from our boarding schools; it was the only time we were together. Both Ephrem and I would run feral, evading our mother's grasp, trying to thieve from Cook or avoid being roped into chores and family outings. Even our father would stop work for a few precious days and join us.

One time, Ephrem and I got hold of some bamboo canes from the huge greenhouse, pulling them free from the tomato plants. We left the plants collapsing in a sagging despair (just as my mother was left some years later after I murdered my father) and scrammed with the canes before the gardener, Bridges, caught us. Using Ephrem's knife, I sharpened both sticks into sharp points and we went hunting.

As a child, Ephrem was mean but cowardly and so had no stomach for rabbiting; instead, we stood silent and still above the stream, waiting to skewer brown trout. Ephrem never caught a thing – he dithered, liking the watch rather than the action. His fingers tightened against the wood knots (so like knuckle bones themselves), teeth gritted, eyes wild. But he never moved, never tried. He would scrutinize, pensive, poised to pounce, but could never find the kill moment.

I learnt a powerful lesson. Patience when hunting is vital – but so is the ability to strike.

Ruthless, I skewered four flapping fish that afternoon and carried them home in triumph. My mother retired Cook for the evening and the four of us fried trout in butter and wild garlic, laughing as the fat spat from the pan. Father later pulled the bones from his mouth and declared them the best thing he'd ever eaten in his entire life.

There are moments that define you; moments that push thumbprints forever into your clay. The success of hunting lay marks on my skin, but the failure did something equally defining but different to my brother. It jointed him differently. Before he had all the possibilities of youth, but after, where we jumped back from the hot fat, he alone stood close to the flames. So, I think what I gained in my father's respect, I paid for, weight for weight, in my brother's bitterness.

Thinking of him now, I think we have done well to move past what was a difficult relationship when we were younger. I finish walking round the lake, ready to face the inevitable. The house – Ephrem's house now. Still my home. It rests on a low brow, golden in the evening sunlight. The stone is warmed by the cold sun; the twenty windows stare back balefully at me. *Where have you been, Juliet?*

Really, this house has no right to challenge me. This house, my grandfather's first and then my father's. My father was not entirely truthful to his young daughter, I soon realized growing up. He was in charge, taking over from his father. It was his father's revolution and my family, the Berkshires, were the filthiest in our country's history. It gives me a connection to Ingsoc so nefarious, if it were revealed, I would be killed by my friends. No one has been born into a family as basted in blood as mine.

I look at the window that was my parents' bedroom and think of me in there, pressing the feather pillow against my father's face until he stopped breathing.

No wonder I am what I am.

Chapter 30

My feet crunch against the gravel path. If the world was different, this house should really be half mine. I think of the modern flat at Manor Towers, such a cheap offer in every sense of the word, although so much better than staying here. I stare at the house and realize that Winston screwed me and never even thought to ask where I lived. Here, I could've told him. The land on which you stand is half mine. I could've said that, could've taken him by the hand and led him to gaze upon the magnificence of my seat. *Look upon my house!* I could've cried. He wouldn't have thought it was mine. He's right, of course; my gender has harmed me many times in my life, not least when it comes to my home – I inherited nothing. Ephrem, as a male, inherited everything. Ephrem could have been my younger brother and it would've still have been his. Again I think of my flat with its snake eyes watching me, and know there is more than one way to get screwed.

It's a dangerous game, but I can't help it as usual, and walk towards the house. I wonder who amongst the old staff is still here now. Cook has died. Father could never keep his butlers, so there is not a single one that I could pick out and think of now. The maids were mice; neat movements and largely unnoticed. As I walk, the lake falls behind me and I reach the formal lawns. They stretch broad and proud; they are the last bastion between safety and the past, but still I walk on.

The early evening sun lovingly lights the stone of the house, warming it in a way I never appreciated when I was young.

This was my home from seven until eighteen. Really, I was hardly ever here from nine, as I went to school most of the year. But this was home in the holidays and in my heart. I spent long summers in the gardens and the fields beyond. The house itself was my winter playground, with its seventeen bedrooms and attics that ran further than my imagination.

I want to go home now, I realize. The longing is a sudden and real pressure in my chest; it wrenches air from me. I really, *really* want to go home.

I wish I could cross the lawns. Bridges used to roller the lawn, obsessed with its flatness. For some reason, I used to love finding lumps – worms, really, but once there was a mole outbreak – and I loved to tell the old gardener, and see the pain in his face. For some reason I no longer remember, I used to love seeing the real pain over something I used to consider trite. It occurs to me that I was not always a nice child. That it was not a kind thing to do, to wish to see an old man suffer. I stare at the sun reflected in the windows, sheets of burnished gold, lighthousing me home. I wonder why I was cold, perhaps even a little cruel. I remember I am a Berkshire. The real me is not clear to even myself, at times.

I would like to find Bridges now, and tell him, my hand gripping his, that the lawn is lovely. I wonder why I am thinking now of Bridges. I never gave him a second thought when I lived here. Really, I should want to go home and see my mother. I should long for the ghost of my father. Or even the family cat, so long gone now.

I really want to go home.

Then, I feel overwhelmingly sad: it's not home I want to go home to. I want to go back – back to when I was young and innocent still.

Before.

Before I knew about the way of the world, before I had some understanding about how society was and my place within it. I want to go back, perhaps even before Arthur. I loved Arthur and I loved what we became, what Chloe gave me in our short time together. But I can't. I am trapped here in my present and there is nothing I can do about it. It's just that the past feels so tangible, here, looking at the house. As if I could reach out and touch it. As if I could be ten and walk into the kitchen and pull up the stool and sit by the Aga, where Cook would chide me but eventually feed me something nice.

Or I could be twelve and go riding with Ephrem. I would jump Snowball better than he ever could.

Or I could be sixteen, sitting next to Arthur on the piano stool. Or eighteen, lying next to him under the spreading chestnut tree.

I'm crying now. I have tears running from my eyes. Surprised, because it has been so long since I have cried, that I touch my eyes to check if this is true.

193

It is true.

Like anything, I tell myself, looking across the lawns, there are some things in life that one doesn't get to decide, and some things that one does get to choose. Perhaps I could go home. I could walk across the lawn and walk straight in, either through the kitchen door to the right, through the boot room, or I could circle round to the front and formally ring the doorbell and ask for Mother. It has been so long since I've been here that while I do not personally know who the butler is; I would put money on that he would know who I was, without the need for me to introduce myself. But I can't see her – can't trust myself if I did.

Instead, I allow myself to absorb the beauty of the building: the huge, floor-to-ceiling windows; the sandstone terrace resting under the portico that runs the length of the building. As a kid, I played games there, dodging being caught by my parents who were worried about a ball or foot breaking the glazing. Eltringham Hall was my home; it was also my prison and my persecution.

I turn away. I will not go back and see her, I won't, I won't. My mother would love to see me, but I can't.

I steal back to the cover of the woods, a stoat slipping through the trees into the shadows. I have come here for Eleanor, for the others, and I will return for the others. We might be breaking away, sandstone under the cruel wind of time, but I will still try.

Taking the path under the trees, I start the journey back to my flat. My never-home.

Chapter 31

Have you had a good day on your day of rest?

I am prepared for this. We each have one day off in every eight, but are expected to be productive for the good of Oceania during it. 'Productive, thank you, Big Brother. I took a walk in the woods near my family home.' (Never yours – you're an algorithm.) 'And then I handed out leaflets for the ASL. Hopefully it'll yield sponsorship or new members.'

I have practised this little monologue over and over in my head. I think the microphones in this most modern of flats are designed to pick up any nuance in my voice; perhaps this flat is rigged for picking up body temperature change or it can detect my heartbeat. This is possible. The tech is available – there's no doubt only the broken finance of the country that prohibits its standardized use. But here … I've realized it's no coincidence that I'm housed here in Manor Towers.

How was your walk, Julia? Was it a long one?

'Adequate. I don't like being alone.' It's essential I emphasize this. Ownlife is slightly dangerous – a taste for solitude or any pastime that does not further the goals of Oceania. 'However, I have been wrestling with a question and have not been able to solve it. Besides, Big Brother, exercise is the route to a strong body, and a strong body leads to a healthy mind.'

Julia, the Party loves you and wants you to be healthy.

I wait for it to ask me what I am wrestling with, but it doesn't. It shuts off and the normal ranting of the telescreen increases to its standard volume. There is news of steel imports and the speaker is full of statistics that tell us how successful the Party has been in negotiating greater levels of steel; great swathes of building are predicted, furthered by greater prosperity.

I peel potatoes with a blunt peeler. I used to have a sharper one but whoever took my painkillers also removed my sharper kitchen implements. The effort of the dull blade (combined with anxiety ... will it ask about Smith? *Will* it?) means I smash my knuckle against the kitchen counter on more than one occasion. I suck at the blood, knowing it reveals my nerves. I cut the potato, white, smooth flesh, into lumps, before dropping the pieces into a saucepan of water. I watch the water heat; nothing at first, then eventually, it starts to shimmer. It agitates and then finally bubbles rise and break; I'm glad of the distraction. It is slow, but it means I can keep my back to the telescreen. In the older flats, it is the only point of surveillance, but here there is more than that.

There's one in the hall; I spotted it once when hanging my coat. It is a tiny black, shiny eye. It's the size of a rat's eye; rodent-like, it watches me in the shadows of my hall.

There's at least one in my bedroom, too. There's not meant to be – no telescreens in bedrooms. But this little camera tells me that the rules might be different in Manor Towers. It is in the top-right corner, furthest from the window and door. That one I spotted one morning last year. When I woke, the June sun had worked its way through the blinds, finding a new angle, and the timing of my waking and the angle of the sun that morning meant that I opened my eyes to see it watching me. Snake eye.

I had only just moved from slumber but as soon as I saw it – I spy – I was awake. I had to let my gaze edge away as if I'd seen nothing, though. I lay under my thin sheet and pretended I didn't know. I don't know why it was important not to know but it's just doublethink – to notice I was being watched would be admitting that it was unusual, wrong or it mattered in some way. I don't even know how I know to do this – I can't ever remember being taught this. In my dusty, draughty, high-ceilinged classrooms, I don't ever think we covered what to think or how to act. I don't ever remember it being a conversation at home either – so how is it that I know it would be dangerous to notice it then? At what point did I internalize how to exist in this society?

Rolling bubbles rip seething through the water. I've been watching the potatoes, but not noticing them; they are starting to cloud and fragment. I sieve them free, the steam billowing and celestial. It dissipates, leaving for somewhere better than the sleek confines of my flat.

The telescreen is now discussing wheat yields, a monotonous voice discussing how Big Brother has cured wheat of some plight by splicing a gene with a gene from a spider. It sounds vile but apparently will now be more resilient against frost. The voice predicts much larger yields as a result. It is dull, pompous and unrelenting. Listening to this crap would drive anyone to self-harm.

Still, I wait for my father's voice to ask for more details about what I have been doing today.

I mash a grey fat (I haven't seen butter in the markets for a long time), into the waterlogged lumps. I make a note to ask Ephrem for some real butter when I see him. He's kind; he keeps me in real coffee and chocolate. I am a mash myself – the emotion of sex again, in the same place where I used to meet Arthur. It wasn't the same thing, of course: it was angry sex, more akin to fighting – not each other, but like Winston and I were both disgusted by it all, disgusted by our situation; our sweaty, smelly selves.

I mash and think of what Winston told me. Before we parted company, he was obviously in the mood for confessions. He said, 'I don't know, I feel bad saying it now, but I saw you throw the Newspeak dictionary and all I could think about was how I wanted to tie you naked to a stake and flog you to death.' He chuckled a little to himself, before he added: 'Silly now, but I wanted to ravish you and cut your throat at the point of my—'

He looked up at me and smiled. 'It is because you're so young and beautiful. Your red sash, you see. Your commitment to chastity. It somehow made me hate you – made me want to shoot you with arrows. Can you believe it?' He chuckled again.

From love to hate in one afternoon. Smith, it's been

eventful – and now it occurs to me, perhaps too eventful. It's almost as if he's purposefully provocative. Just who is it serving?

I mash. I think of Cook, of course. So close to her again, both now in action but also reconnected after the revisit to our home. My mother was a good mother, but it was Cook I went to for warmth, food and comfort. Not that she would ever give me any hugs or any sign that she even liked me, but she would feed me and chide me and I knew she was always pleased to see me because when I turned up in the kitchen, she'd pull out the little stool from its nook and set it by the Aga. 'At least it keeps you from under my feet there,' she'd say.

I mash. I think of my father as he lay dying in his bed. How he didn't even move away as I held the pillow. Does Big Brother know that? I wonder. There were no cameras at the house (neither he nor mother would never allow it). Nor did I take the pillow away. Of course I didn't – I am my father's daughter.

Instead, I continued to hold the pillow that had choked the air from him until he was gone. His face was grey, his lips were blue and yet I did not stop because in the end, I hated him. And that is how I know it cannot be him who talks to me now, because I saw him dead.

I loved him more than anyone in the world all my life, but not at the end. After I was done, I put the pillow on the bed next to his head, and looked at his open eyes. I did not stop to close them, nor to remove the stray sole white feather that had settled against his cheek. Instead, I left the room. I wanted to say something impactful, something suitable, but in the end, it was not my statement to make, so I did not make it.

Where I stood earlier, I could see the window of his bedroom where he died, burnished in gold sunlight, and I didn't wish to change anything that happened that day. Really, I should have regrets.

But don't I? He always loved me so much. Before Chloe, he always adored me. I remember him laughing and cheering me as I jumped Snowball. 'Bravo, Juliet!' He'd clap. I loved to make my daddy proud.

The potato!

It is mush. The proteins have broken down under my vigour and it is now glue. I add liberal salt; it's a precious and rare commodity for most people, but I have ample – thank you, Ephrem. I need this nursery food to reconnect with some part of myself that I feel I am in danger of losing – and scrape it, along with my misery, into a bowl.

Now I must turn around and face the certainty of the camera again.

I sit on my sofa and spoon the gluey potato into my mouth. If I was looking for nursery food nostalgia in this mash, I have not found it. I sit on the edge of the sofa and try – and fail – not to remember the night my father died. I try – and fail – not to wait for his voice, carefully modulated through computer software, to ask me what it was that I was trying to resolve today. I am an adult but feel like a child waiting for an inevitable paternal remonstration.

Except that it's not like that at all.

I look around my modern, tastefully furnished flat – but know it is my tomb. I am in the first stage of death but it's taking a long time to die. My little going-too-far with my wrists last month and now sex with Smith is making me morose.

I give up and get ready for bed. I fall asleep almost instantly.

Chapter 32

Julia. What is it the question you've been wrestling with?

I wake. My father speaks to me. *Daddy? Are you home?*

No: wake up properly. My father never called me Julia – only Juliet. This is Big Brother. My eyes search blind in the dark. There is only the clock to show me it is the middle of the night. Somewhere, the reptile eye watches me. Shiny, black and unblinking in the dark.

He knows. They know.

What is it the question you've been wrestling with Julia? It repeats.

I work my mouth; it is stiff, my practised answers have dried my mouth. Talking to me when I am sleeping is a first. It's trying to catch me in a lie. 'Thank you for asking, Big Brother.' To give myself recall time – what was I going to say? – I lever myself onto my elbow. Recumbent feels less vulnerable than flat on my back. 'I am worried about my ability to grow the ASL. I feel we need to reach more people and leafleting feels so . . .' I hear my heart; it gives me away. 'It feels not *enough*. I am not *enough*. You give so much, and I feel like I'm failing you.'

I wait, like a good daughter anxious for paternal reassurance, but eventually, after what feels like a long time, I realize I have been dismissed and only then, lower myself back to my pillow.

I lie awake in the dark and only have my breathing to listen to. I want an answer but there isn't one. I keep my eyes open, staring at the ceiling for the longest time.

Chapter 33

When I awake in the morning, there is a single feather resting on my cheek.

Chapter 34

I have been ill for nearly a week, worried sick that the feather signifies there is now mind-reading technology. If there is – then it will be in Manor Towers. In the end, to stop myself cracking up, I've had to decide that worrying about it won't change anything I've thought in the past. It is done. I have to move forward or my mind will collapse. It is with great will that I decide all I can control is the future. I keep my focus on the Sisterhood.

Today, Leona and I have a small group of girls from the ASL troop. We are leafleting again on the importance of Goodsex, sticking our leaflets through the letterboxes of a few rows of dingy, pre-war terraces. When people see our red sashes, they tend to drop their heavy net curtains and stay back from the windows. Fine by me. We often do this once a week, but Leona and I are doing an extra drop because we want to talk to each other. She desperately wants to hear about Smith.

'I can tell you Smith is rude and yet vulnerable. He says he's never met another woman before – that could be lies, but he's certainly bad enough with women to believe it. My gut feeling is that I don't think he's either Brotherhood or Thinkpol,' I say into my thick woollen scarf. It's late May but has turned freezing again.

'He's rude to you?' She also has a thick scarf – Eleanor knitted us all one for this very purpose. With our mouths legitimately covered, it's much easier to have a proper conversation.

'Put it like this, the first time I slept with him, he confessed that when he used to see me around at work, he wanted to rape me and smash my head open. Can you believe it?'

'Julia! How incredibly vile! I'm so sorry I've asked this of you. Perhaps Ruby's contact is a different person – she would have said if he was disgusting.'

We both pause as we march up another path, post a leaflet and check on Gerta and the two other girls with us. They're behaving, making good progress up the street. They like small-minded preachy tasks like this. They try to look through the letterboxes – they dream of catching someone having sex so they can report them.

'Don't worry,' I say to her. 'He's a punk but largely harmless. I have learnt Smith is separated from his wife and he acts as if he's keen on me. Both these facts make it easier. Anyway, I've not seen anyone else who fits her description of her contact. But I was thinking that if he was TP, I don't think he'd try to repel me – he'd try to solicit harder? You follow?'

She shakes her head a little and delivers another leaflet.

Back together on the pavement, I try to explain. 'If you were TP, you wouldn't want to repel people you thought were guilty of thoughtcrime. Telling me that he wanted to slit my throat whilst raping me – I mean, who says that to a woman?'

'A wanker?'

My smile is only seen by my scarf. 'Agreed, but definitely not a sophisticated spy. Surely if he was TP, he'd want to reel me in with his charm. He'd try to make me relaxed and open up.'

Her heavy sigh is audible – she understands. 'But if he is the same guy, you'll tell me so I can kill him, right?'

'Without hesitation. We'll slit his throat and the last word he'll hear is Ruby's name.'

'I'll never be able to thank you enough – I haven't forgotten my end of the bargain. Next week, it won't be Eleanor who'll give you your injection, it'll be Prisha. She'll have something to show you. Know that it comes with my deepest thanks – thanks to *you* for all you do in Ruby's name. I honestly believe your actions have saved my life.'

The wind howls down the street, and Viola, a rather sneaky girl who simpers up to adults but pinches the younger children when she thinks we're not looking, approaches us. 'Miss, please may I have more leaflets? I've already handed mine out!' Her small mouth squeezes into her I'm-so-fucking-pleased-with-myself look, making me want to dump the whole bag of leaflets over her head. Really, I should not be in charge of these children.

I peel a thick wad of leaflets off my pile to keep her away from me and Leona remembers to call after her to praise her for her work. When she's gone, Leona sounds nervous when she speaks: 'You don't think there's any point in seeing Smith anymore, do you?'

'I'm going to stick with him for a bit, see what turns up – he could still be Brotherhood.' *But only because you want me to,* I don't add. *You and Eleanor.* 'Don't forget, we don't know this contact was the reason Ruby was arrested. He might have had nothing to do with it.'

For twenty minutes, we just deliver leaflets and interact with the girls. We show them the Anti-Sex Awareness Badge they're working towards by delivering the leaflets and will be awarded – they're excited. But not as excited as I am to see what Leona's organized with Prisha.

Then, just as we're nearly finished, Leona says to me, 'I want to say, Ruby was right about you. You're so brave – the bravest of all of us. To sleep with a man who might be TP – honestly, I'm in awe of you. Ruby always said you were ruthless. She said you were the only one in the group who'd be able to kill our enemies whilst looking them in the eye. Just you – not the others.'

She looks at me with large brown eyes heavy with gratitude and trust. It makes me feel sick – because Leona sees me more clearly than she realizes.

It reminds me of my family, about how I must be just like them: that we are seen one way but really are different. I remember my brother telling me when I was fourteen that our father had killed our grandfather. I'd been pushing him to tell what he knew about our family. It was shortly after I had found Cook in the pantry that time, and I was still puzzling as to why she'd felt compelled to beg for her life. Why was her reading from a book, and who I was, such a dangerous combination that it suddenly changed who we were to each other? I didn't ask him this – I had sworn to protect her. But about our family, Ephrem couldn't wait to tell me.

I remembered our grandfather only a little – he'd lived in our family home, Eltringham Hall, and, at that time, we lived in another property by the sea. He'd been eccentric – and a military man perpetually in uniform. I remember us both in a tank – him driving us across the south fields at the foot of the lake, me looking out of a metal tank flap at the lawns outside, telling him what to avoid and him laughing, oh, laughing so much, that the sound bashed and crashed inside what was only a riveted metal box on tracks.

This memory is real, I think. Maybe the last I have of him. It's strange, but the smell of him, cigar smoke mixed with leather and citrus aftershave, is more tangible than even his face.

He disappeared when I was about six or seven and then we moved into Eltringham Hall, my father assuming leadership over Ingsoc. I had been so shocked when Ephrem told me our father had killed his own father that I repeated it in a fit of pique to my mother, desperately wanting her to laugh and tell me that my brother was both a liar and a teaser, seeking only to wind me up.

Instead, my mother hit me, a slap hard and sharp across my left cheek. I don't know if she was more surprised than me (she was not a violent woman), her pale face only accentuating the bright, high pink of her sudden emotion in her cheeks.

At the time, I thought it was because she was angry with me. I hadn't truly believed what I'd said as I'd said it, but her reaction told me that Ephrem might often be a liar, but he wasn't this time. The bewilderment of Father killing Grandfather was delayed by the uncharacteristic reptilian hiss of Mother's *Don't you ever dare say that again! Ever! Ever! EVER!* Her venom to my young ears was as frightening as a snake attack. But as I stand here and view it from a distance, I am given a different perspective. It occurs to me that it wasn't anger that I saw in her face that day. It was something much more dangerous.

It was fear.

But not *of* me – she was afraid *for* me. Afraid of what would happen to me if my father heard me speak the truth. She was afraid of what my father was capable of.

His ruthlessness.

And it's in me, too. Ruby saw it in me, and Leona does now. The ability to be a cold-blooded killer.

I try not to let this bother me as I walk back to my never-home flat, a clutch of unposted leaflets in my hand. I think of the way Leona looked at me when she thought I was going to stop seeing Winston, and then the relief when I said I would continue. There's nothing I wouldn't do to make her feel better. I sigh. I think I might be seeing Smith for a long time yet.

Chapter 35

Prisha opens her door. She's wearing her scarf – not unusual because often the government cuts the power for the war effort and the heating turns off – but when she grips my hand and speaks, I realize it's so she can communicate clearly. 'Quick, come in – there's something wrong with Eleanor.'

'What?'

'Don't know – it's weird. Just watch for a bit.'

She yanks me into her small dark hall.

Around the table sit Leona, Cecily and Eleanor. They show me how they've carefully hemmed Eleanor's enormous *Fuck Sex* banner so two poles (borrowed broom handles) can be slid in to help hold it aloft.

I make pointless chat about Hate Week, which we spend all our year preparing for, but really, I am observing Eleanor. I'd come here, full of anticipation to see what Leona has got hold of, but now I can only think of Eleanor. Prisha's right, she seems ... different. I can't decide if it's because she's annoyed that someone else will administer my injection, but I suspect that she doesn't know – she who before knew *everything* about the Sisterhood.

Now it's gone in a different direction. It's funny – I thought if anyone got hold of the steering wheel and yanked us off in a different direction, it could only have been me. Prisha possibly. I realize now that I was quick to assume that Leona was frail and Cecily too gentle. But that's bombs for you – they blow things apart. Even assumptions, apparently.

When I came in, I asked what I should do to help. The papier-mâché head is finished.

'Would you like a job, Julia?' asks Prisha.

I tell her I would.

'Do you remember the maggot idea? That when Goldstein's head gets smashed, maggots could fall out, but we didn't have the right material? Well, Cecily's been able to get some white cotton and we thought we could start them tonight.' Prisha opens the sideboard door and takes out a small stack of folded white material. 'We couldn't get silk, of course, but we managed to get hold of old pillowcases.'

She puts them in front of me. 'They're very damaged, but careful stitching – or darning – could hide the rips. It doesn't need a perfect job because of course they're going to get ripped to shreds in the parade.'

Eleanor looks up; she's hurt, I can tell. 'I could have done that.'

Cecily sits next to her and places her hand over Eleanor's. 'Eleanor, your embroidery is the best among us. Your work on this flag is what best serves Big Brother.'

Eleanor nods, and I notice her clavicles – rising like bridges, they show how much weight she has lost. I want to seize her other hand and hold it to my chest, tight. Eleanor, Eleanor, Eleanor, she who launched us from nothing. She who built us from suds, scrubbing brushes and hope.

I pick up the pillowcases. I find white thread and decline a Victory coffee; I have no taste for it. I just had a real one at the flat; I would share but I wouldn't survive the questions of where it came from. I start to join a hole together and then I remember what I am here for. I've been so distracted by Eleanor – it feels like a broken heart.

'Julia, you might try a darning mushroom to make your sewing easier – for the holes,' Leona says.

'Oh, I've seen that,' offers Prisha. 'It's in my dresser in the hall. Help me, Julia?' And I do as I am told. If Eleanor's raised her head and is watching us, I don't want to know, don't want to, don't want to. Surely she's realized that it's that time again? Surely she realizes she's been replaced?

And if she hasn't realized, that's even worse.

I follow Prisha into the darkened hall. I can't wait to see what Leona's brought the Sisterhood.

Chapter 36

In the hallway, I let the door fall behind me, shutting off the telescreen. Then we move quickly. We pull the shelf unit out and then take the steps into the basement.

In the cellar, the familiar damp air sits heavy against the back of my throat, like a fetid cloth. But I barely notice it because all I can see is that on the shelf are the explosives. They remind me of the soft modelling clay I had as a child; there are seven clear pillowed pouches that reveal a grey substance. It invites me to squeeze it. I don't. From each pouch is a wire that connects to a central wire. I think I was expecting something smooth, cylindrical, something with fins and marked BOMB. Perhaps even bearing a skull and crossbones for good measure.

But there is no time for gazing – business first. I reach for the rusting metal biscuit tin and open it up, before drawing up the contraceptive. 'Hit the muscle like throwing a dart. Keep your wrist firm, but a little fluid. I'll show you where.'

I'm already pulling down my trousers – we have about one minute left. I pull my pants to one side and point at the

214

top outside quarter of my buttock. 'There. Now. Depress the plunger when it's in.'

If Prisha fumbles, I don't see because I'm staring at the explosive. She hits me with the needle a little too hard and then depresses the syringe too quickly. The feeling is unpleasant, but she's done it.

'She did it,' I say, pointing at the grey pillows and wire.

'She did. Enough to take out an entire ministry. Maybe more. Some new developmental explosive called TD4.' She pulls a neatly coiled wire from the top shelf. Attached to it is a crocodile clip at one end and a silver tube the size of a pencil at the other end, with the spring load at the furthest point. 'This clips into here,' she says, bringing the two together with a healthy gap between them, 'and this is the button. Simple. The wire's short though – ten metres is the limit.'

'And she was able to just take it?'

'Taken in increments. She put it together here.'

'They'll be watching her.'

Prisha's eyes drop away and she seems to refocus on the syringe in her hand. 'Probably. She doesn't care anymore, I don't think. She didn't seem to care about the risk – the only thing she cares about is finding out what happened to Ruby. Do you think you'll find out from your mark?'

'I don't know. Truth is, when I talk to him, he only seems interested in sex. He talks about the Brotherhood, but it's just a desire to join. I think if he was a Thinkpol agent, I would've been arrested by now.'

She nods. 'Good for you for trying. You're a loyal

friend.' She covers her face briefly. 'Fuck. That's a shame. I was hoping she'd get closure. This is killing her.'

I don't need to ask what's killing her – it's everything and it's killing us all.

Chapter 37

I slip the mushroom under the pillowcase and use it to darn the broken material. 'It works well,' I offer, not daring to meet Eleanor's eyes; I don't know what she's doing – I haven't dared look at her since I sat back down.

I need time to think. There's an explosive sitting in the small room dug out below. I think of it there, wondering about what will happen to it. Now we've got it, we need to move quickly because it's likely that Leona will now be being watched.

I darn away, thinking, thinking, against the backdrop of the telescreen's perpetual prattle. It pours forth information on the water shortages in Eastasia. It lists endless facts as to how the ideology of the Obliteration of the Self has caused these shortages and how the degenerate leadership failures are leading to the deaths of its citizens. It's sobering stuff. Even when a little girl is interviewed, crying for water, begging for Ingsoc to invade and save her life with water and political sustenance, I am not diverted. I am a dragon on gold: we have an explosive. The thought glows; it has its own heat, its own energy. *We. Have. A BOMB.*

I darn; I listen to children crying and I realize that I will die soon. I've known it for a while – this is not an original thought. Instead it's like a mouth ulcer and my tongue keeps returning to interrogate the necrotic idea.

Eleanor says, 'Isn't it wonderful that we don't have to worry about water? That we can turn on the tap and it comes gushing out, unlike those poor children?' She has tears in her eyes – I don't think she can take much more emotional stress. It's not just Leona who's dying from stress. We're all folding in on ourselves.

I think the waiting for arrest might be so much worse than being arrested – or perhaps that's showing my naivety.

'Can't anyone help them?' she says.

'This is what the war is for,' Prisha says firmly. 'Big Brother wants us to fight for the safety of these poor children. You must not lose hope.'

Eleanor looks confused. 'But we are not at war with Eastasia. Are we?' Oceania covers a third of the world; Eastasia and Eurasia are yet to be governed by Ingsoc.

None of us draw breath – she's not crimestopped. How deep is her confusion?

Once it would've been Eleanor who boosted us; now it is us that must boost her. Cecily laughs. 'I love your humour, Eleanor. Of course, Eurasia is our enemy, but Eastasia are simply not governed as well as Oceania. It is helpful to hold both ideas in mind when appreciating the greatness of Oceania.'

I need to find out if Prisha or Cecily have plans for the explosive – if they have a tangible target and any kind of strategy for placing it there. Eleanor was right – to have it and not use it would be too dangerous. We need to strike quickly.

Cecily must be reading my mind – I hope I have not become too easy to read – because she suddenly says, 'Isn't it wonderful to know that everyone is so united on delivering a fantastic Hate Week?'

We murmur our agreement, but really, I'm waiting to hear the point.

Prisha makes it. 'Let's meet tomorrow? Instead of supplying small hammers for people to break open Goldstein's head, I thought we could make a huge hammer – we could make it big enough to paint *Ingsoc* on the side. Wouldn't that be brilliant for showing the power of the party?'

Eleanor raises an eyebrow but says nothing.

'That's a great idea, Prisha,' says Cecily, 'but is there time?'

'We could chicken-wire the frame tomorrow. You're welcome round here. Then we could take it to the ASL for the next meeting. The girls could papier-mâché it in one evening. The following week it would be dry enough to paint. Even if it causes us great strain to make at such notice, we need to set an example to our troops: that nothing is greater than the hate we feel for Goldstein.'

Cecily takes the baton. 'The crowds would love a giant hammer. We must do it.'

Eleanor has said nothing until now but suddenly speaks. 'I can't make tomorrow. Remember I have United Against Faith on Tuesdays.'

Prisha moves quickly. 'Eleanor, I so admire you and your commitments – shame, though! But Julia, can you make it? You're great at shaping chicken wire.' Cecily and Prisha both look at me – Cecily's eyebrow raised in polite enquiry and Prisha's deep, large eyes fixed on me.

Really, I have misunderstood these women. While I've been busy with Winston, they've been busy, too. 'I can make it,' I say, enjoying the camaraderie with them.

I keep my eyes on my darning. I've darned and fixed three pillowcases before Eleanor speaks again. 'Perhaps a hammer is too heavy a metaphor – I still think a more delicate touch can be more effective.'

Her voice is clear and gentle and is a return to who she is: I tremble for it.

'Shaping a huge piece of chicken wire,' she says, continuing, 'means you risk injuring yourself. Wire cuts. I urge you to reconsider. Enjoy what we have – the Goldstein head being smashed apart is already a powerful symbol of hate.'

We all know Eleanor is really talking about the bomb. She obviously knows we've got it. I sew and wait for Prisha to reply. All this sewing will kill me. I don't even like it.

But it's Cecily who replies. 'It's got to be up to us, Eleanor. You are a true sister; your kindness is perfection. I thank you for your care from the deepest wells of my being. But ...' She sighs a little. 'I expect to get cut from the wire. We accept it. So deep is our love for the Party that we will not hesitate to use the full force of our intent against Goldstein. So you see' – her face dips back to her embroidery – 'the hammer will be made. I hope you can accept it.'

The telescreen has changed subject from water shortages to the clever planting of Big Brother resulting in unusually high yields of leeks and cabbage. It's true – I've eaten leek soup every day for two weeks. I'm sick of it.

We listen about vegetables until I can stand it no more. 'Eleanor, please.' I reach out across the table for her hand. She sees it and gives a smile like weak tea. Takes it, squeezes my fingers for the briefest of moments and then releases me. My hand is left upturned and empty, colder for having felt the warmth of her touch.

I try to make eye contact, even more desperate for reassurance, but she doesn't look at me again, even as she is packing her things. The telescreen couldn't notice any difference in how polite we are when she leaves, but it is me who realizes Eleanor leaves without looking back, letting us go.

Chapter 38

Prisha, Cecily and I meet at a hardware store. Prisha applied for chicken wire under the Hate Week munitions requests, and it was granted. She must have applied before she mentioned the hammer to us two days ago because normally munitions requests take at least a week to process – longer at the moment.

For our tokens, we're allowed two large rolls, each the size of me. Heavy and cumbersome, we take turns to carry them back to Prisha's terraced house. It's uncomfortable work: the now warmer weather sees us sweat, while the wire is annoying and the edges catch on our red sashes. But going slow gives us the perfect excuse to talk – stopping to rest means we can place our mouths against our shoulders.

'It's big – it could take out a whole ...' Prisha pauses, waits until she can say the word without being detected, 'ministry.'

Prisha pauses to take the roll from Cecily. Cecily says, 'We can't get it in. The security's too intense – we wouldn't stand a chance.'

We walk down a side street saying nothing, until we turn back onto a busy street. Cecily takes my roll; it's heavy and catches at our clothes. 'Where else is a target?' I ask.

'No target,' Cecily says.

I make a palaver of the transfer. 'It can't stay in the cellar.'

We start walking again, the mood between us silently sombre. 'Let me take your roll,' I say, reaching for Prisha's wire load. 'They must know you have it. You have to get it out.'

'They don't definitely know. Leona says she was very careful. We could go in Hate Week.'

'We would only hit civilians. We need to take out the Inner Party. Not just one either. It's all or none because otherwise we'll achieve nothing.' The roll is transferred and, frustrated by the reality that what Eleanor said about needing a target was correct, we fall silent.

Two streets later, we have sweatily swapped the rolls between us three more times, but we haven't furthered the conversation.

By the time we get back to Prisha's, I've made my mind up. We haul the wire – now so, so heavy after the carry – up the three steps to her front door. Inside, it will be too late to say as we will step back in front of the telescreen, so I say it quickly:

'I have a contact in the Inner Party. I think I could get access to either one of the ministries or some other target. I will report back.'

'Your man?'

For a moment I'm confused. I realize she means Smith.

'No,' I say before the door is open. *It's a lot more compli-cated than that*, I wish I could say, but even that would be an understatement.

Chapter 39

I am looking for my brother – there is no choice now. I have to go to the heart of Ingsoc. To the leader.

Since he rescued me from Eltringham Hall and set me up in my never-home flat, I've always seen my brother once a month. They're obligatory meetings that he insists on, cold affairs of polite society over afternoon tea, before a presentation of packages of real salt, sugar and coffee, followed by prompt dismissal. I could take the bomb to him and kill him now (myself too), but there would be no change. Big Brother would live on through the Party. Besides, I quite like Ephrem.

No, a more delicate, finessed plan is needed. This meeting will be the start of it.

I've never wanted anything from him before. The flat, my job, the rescue – I've never asked for more than a pat of butter. When we were kids I never wanted his company other than to best him – we shared a combative relationship that eased into indifference as I became a teenager. If he was provoked that I was a better hunter, rider, pianist than him, I was provoked that my ability made no difference to the outcome of my life.

I remember when I learned this. My father, Ephrem and I were in the drawing room. Father stood in front of the mantelpiece after a recital of Chopin, and since I had finished mine, Ephrem was playing at the piano. Although my brother's rendition of the Nocturne was typically thick-fingered, afterwards my father grasped his shoulder and said, 'Ephrem, my boy, you're going to inherit the world.'

'And me, Daddy? Am I going to inherit the world, too?' As his favourite, I thought he'd say yes. I certainly had the right attributes, bolder than my brother, I would take bigger risks on the jumps, was even more ruthless when I wanted something. My brother, on the other hand, was spoilt and cruel – lazy, too, if he thought my father wouldn't notice.

My father's hand stayed grasped to Ephrem's shoulder. 'No, Juliet. It is your brother who will be a leader – and that's how it should be.'

I was stunned. My father had always been my applauding audience. I was never given to singing and dancing like other little girls, but if I ever wanted him to watch me jump Snowball in the paddock or admire my archery skills, then he was generous with his praise.

'I'll be a leader, too,' I added, stupidly slow. Or stupidly tenacious.

'No, Juliet, you are made for different things. You will have a family and will raise boys – I know it will be boys you will have – and they will be generals, too.'

My brother was never an attractive child – he struggled to control his curls, and with his upturned nose and close-set eyes, he had a face easy to dislike. I called him Piggy when I really wanted to get to him. But this time, it was him who wanted to twist the skin. He smiled at me meanly, looking for a pinch. He swept his hand towards the French windows, gesturing to our country house, and towards the tennis courts, the stables and the field and said: 'This will all be mine, Juliet. You shall marry some man that Father will find for you.'

I thought he was joking. I looked at my father, waiting for a denial, a reproach to Ephrem for teasing me, *something*, but instead, my father, sensing my disbelief, simply nodded. 'It is true, Juliet. Ephrem's future is secure, but I will choose a husband for you – when the time is right – and your future will be more than secure, too. I will find you someone who is high in the new world order that has been created – a leader.'

My father's voice was kind and he meant well. I looked at his hand on Ephrem's shoulder and said nothing.

Ephrem, unable to help himself as usual, said, 'Unfortunately for you, Juliet, you're so ugly, no one will marry you.'

His stupid face grinned. So, I stepped forward and punched him square on his nose. I cracked it like a knuckle under my own. Ephrem bled all down his shirt and cried; I was roundly flogged. I think, though, my father was crosser with him than me.

Aside from understanding the inequality of my gender, I gained two further things from that evening. One, a new insult for Ephrem: 'piggy' became 'piggy *nose*', the emphasis on 'nose' reminding him I'd broken his. With it, I could turn him pink and steaming in seconds. But the real gain was understanding the benefit of my situation. Then, I was given to sunshine rather than storm clouds, so it wasn't long before I understood the advantage of being female. Less was expected of me – less to the extent that I almost didn't count. And not counting meant I could slip below the radar.

But here I am, purposefully choosing to reengage, and as I stand outside his current office base in Frugal Street, a narrow prole street, I pause before I go in. My life is about to change. I do this for you, Eleanor, I say to myself. I do this for you, Leona. For you, Cecily. For you, Prisha. But most of all, I do this for you, Ruby.

Chapter 40

This is where he is at the moment: a butcher's shop in Frugal Street, over by Lambeth Bridge. A blue sign, with the name in gold letters – 'Whymper's Meats' – above the display of slimy, sinew-coloured sausages, racks of ribs, and dark, shiny kidneys. This is a prole shop, and the meat must sit in the window because who can afford to buy it?

I first met him here last month, and again the little brass bell above the door announces my arrival; I realize I'm nervous.

Ephrem is behind the glass counter, holding a meat cleaver. He is expecting me. His crocodile smile deepens as I step inside the cool, small shop, where the iron tang of blood hangs thick. Then to emphasize the point, he brings the cleaver down on the bloody block and holds up the rabbit's head by the ears. It drips globes of crimson, the sound pattering like small rodent feet. 'Have you come for tea, Juliet?'

'It's the first Saturday of the month, Ephrem. You always expect to see me then.' The timing of two days ago and today feels too fortunate. After the explosive and now not having to wait a month to see my brother, it feels like a cheat – too easy. Like a crossword puzzle where all the words are ones you've just used.

Gloves off, he washes his hands, removes his striped apron and ridiculous straw hat, before turning the shop sign. 'I hope you like my little get-up. Come upstairs. We can talk privately there. Remind me to give you some coffee to take away – I've had a consignment and it's excellent. But now we need tea. I've got some lapsang from Eastasia. Wonderful quality. Dealing with kidneys always makes me curiously thirsty.'

I follow him up the narrow stairs, thinking of my father, wondering what he would make of his son dressed in his white coat and hat and blue striped apron. Not much, I decide.

I follow Ephrem into an office and it's a strange contrast. There's a huge desk – the mahogany one that he has his flunkies move from site to site. On it are a bank of three large screens, giving him access to too much. He ushers me impatiently into the green leather upholstered chair. I've sat in this chair many times before; like the rest of his office furniture, when he moves, he simply gets it all packed up and transported somewhere else. I once asked him why he does this and all he would say is that he easily tires of a view.

He talks to me about coffee and tea yields and then a synthetic comes in with a tray of tea. He waves it instantly away, before he fusses with a tea strainer and a little milk jug. Ephrem is tall, now in his early thirties. Gone is the piggy look I teased him about when we were young;

although not handsome, he has a strong bone structure, and his blond hair and dark eyes make for an arresting image, but he's a deeply controlling man and something about his spirit has corrupted the way he holds his face, so instead it's a hard, mean face. Perhaps it always was.

He passes me the cup and saucer. Despite knowing I prefer lapsang black, he's added milk. But I am not here to argue. I'm here to check in like the good little girl I am, and this time . . . I'm here for the Sisterhood.

'Like the tea? It's a new blend. It's grown on the slopes of Eastasia.'

The smell of real tea, compared to the blackberry leaves the Outer Party drinks, is overpowering and it tastes as good as it smells. I tell him this. Ephrem was always someone who liked praise too much.

He regards me for a second and I wonder what he sees when he looks at me. Maybe Mother. 'How is Mother?' I ask dutifully. It is more than that – I miss her terribly and wish I could forgive her so I could see her, but I don't want Ephrem to know anything about my daily pain. It's just if I don't ask, he will reprimand me for it, so ask I must.

'A little frailer, Juliet, I must confess. She's not old, is she? Only in her late fifties for goodness' sake, but she had flu last month. Do you remember? I just don't think she's got over it. She's taken to afternoon naps – something she started when she was ill, and doesn't seem to want to give up.'

I don't say anything – I can't. I think of watching her from the priest hole; seeing her laughing with her friends as they all drank Martinis and gossiped. She always looked so elegant in evening dress. Sometimes she wore long gloves – oh, how I loved them! I swore I would wear them every day when I was grown up, but now I am, I have never worn evening gloves once. I don't even own a pair. How differently my life has turned out to how I thought it would.

'Okay, you don't care about Mother, I get it, but you could at least pretend.'

'I do care, I've just got bigger things on my mind.'

Ephrem raises an eyebrow, but he doesn't ask. He'll want me to tell him, I know.

I take a deep breath and it comes out in the nervous rush I feel. 'I want my life back. I want to be Inner Party again. It's my birthright.'

I thought my brother would spit out his tea everywhere, but instead he just sips and looks at me over the top of his teacup like I'm an interesting animal.

'I want to be involved. I'm smart, hardworking – and you know, very reliable.'

'You're a girl!'

'Woman.'

Ephrem laughs. 'You are funny, Juliet.'

Eleanor's words come back to me. I take them and make them my own. 'There might be a role for me. Women have worth. We are strong.'

'Is that so?' His voice is quiet. He sips and seems to think, and then says, 'The thing is, Juliet, as sweet as your offer is, we just don't want or need you. The Inner Party is fine, and we don't use women for men's work.'

'Please – *something*. The truth is, Ephrem, this life isn't working for me. I know I did wrong—'

'Understatement. Your leader is your leader. You went against your leader and that is unforgivable. You can never come back.'

I hope this is about Chloe and not about my killing Father. He can't know. No – if he did, I would have learnt about it a long time ago. I don't let his words shake me – I knew I'd have to beg. But if I don't come back, then I'm never getting access to anywhere that the bomb can make an impact on the right people. I need full access to all of the Inner Party. 'Look, please, Ephrem. Take pity. Trust me – you know you can. You know it! Help me out.'

Ephrem turns abruptly, swivelling round on his chair. He faces the sash window that looks below onto the narrow street. He doesn't say anything for a long time – several minutes – but I know better than to break the silence. Eventually he does it for us: 'Everyone down there is so busy. I find it fascinating, that even if I stare hard at someone, they don't notice me looking down on them. They don't know they're being watched. Or maybe they don't care about being watched. Do you care, Juliet? About being watched?'

This feels like part of a test. 'I suppose I might care more if I didn't want anyone to see what I was doing.' After a pause, I add more. 'My life is dull, Ephrem. I work in a dull office, supervise annoying children in my spare time, and spend my spare time sewing or campaigning or making things that are going to be smashed up. It all feels pointless. That's why I'm here.'

'You are not here for that.'

I feel my pulse beat in my head. I'm unsure how to react so I say nothing.

'You are here because you want something. But I can't give it to you because I can't trust you.'

I knew he would say this. I control my thoughts in case their mind-reading technology has been carted in here like all the other tech and continue smoothly, 'You can trust me, I'm your sister. If you can't trust your own family – then who can you trust?'

He steeples his fingers and rests his chin thoughtfully on them. 'A ... sweet idea. But I'm not sure I can. You can understand, if I were to advance you any further in the party – if you were to be the first woman in the Inner Party – for that to happen, I'd have to trust you implicitly. I'd have to be able to trust you with my life.'

I feel sick. Ephrem is always one step ahead. Of course he is, he is the head of Ingsoc, just like my father was, just as his father was before him. There is no one more powerful than Ephrem. And like many dictators, I suppose, he is eccentric and paranoid. He won't set up office in a normal location in a ministry – he considers it too dangerous. Instead, he moves around, making people either go to Eltringham Hall like Father and Grandfather did, or visit his little 'field bases', as he likes to call him. And his paranoia is extreme – he's never going to be able to trust me ... unless I can force him to.

'I want you to be able to trust me, Ephrem. I want to come in and be loved. I miss you. I miss our time together. I know you would never want to go out riding like we used to, but I miss that in my life. Don't you?'

I've got him. His eyes – for the briefest of seconds – show a softening. He does miss it. Perhaps that's the reason he makes sure I visit once a month. I will go further – I have to. Prisha and Cecily are counting on me. 'I want you to be able to trust me. I have a secret – and I'm prepared to give it to you and you will see that I'm making myself very vulnerable by admitting it.'

Ephrem's face brightens. 'A secret, Juliet? What secret could you possibly have in your dull little life?'

I can't work out if he knows – if he's known everything all along. I look at the bank of screens and have always understood that there's a chance he knows all my secrets: the Sisterhood, Smith, the cellar. I think of the feather on my cheek and believe the truth is that Ephrem knows everything.

But if he doesn't, then I would be turning Smith in to suffer goodness knows what. That would be a cruelty of betrayal – if Smith doesn't work for Ephrem. Whilst I'm sure now Smith isn't Brotherhood, I'm not certain he's not an agent. I think probably not – but I've stayed in his orbit until I'm sure. I always felt I couldn't allow Leona to kill an innocent man, but can I allow Ephrem to? It's hard but what is clear is that I have to offer up something, otherwise I will never get closer to the Inner Party, and then we can never destroy them.

Ultimately, I must accept there can be no choice between Winston Smith and the Sisterhood.

'Ephrem, there's something I would like to confess to you. I have a secret I will give you as a sign of my desire to return to my rightful place – by your side. Your sister. Part of the family.

'As our father said, I am the daughter of the Party – I'm

the *only* daughter of the Party. Father would never have wanted me cast out – he never did it. I did it to myself, but now I want to return. I am not challenging your governance, but rather wish to support it, uphold it, strengthen it. Think about it – is there anyone you can really trust as much as me? Apart from Marguerite and Mother, who else can you truly trust?' Ephrem was paranoid even when he was young – I'm counting on that only worsening as his power has grown.

'I trust no one.'

'Marguerite, I hope. Mother, too?'

'Marguerite's not well.'

'Oh? I'm sorry to learn that.'

'Nervous exhaustion. She's been confined to room rest for many years.'

Inwardly I wince for my brother's wife. Marguerite was always a silly woman; despite being attractive, she reminded me of a sheep. She had a long face and wide-spaced eyes; even her blonde hair was curly. She irritated me, always agreeing with Ephrem, no matter what, and would just talk over the top of someone else, reiterating his views in her words. When they were courting, I was a teenager, in love with Arthur and the piano. Marguerite was older than me, had no musical ability and was a terrible snob, so I knew she'd have no time for Arthur. Then, I still believed I would find a way of marrying him. So, I dismissed her as frivolous.

She changed before her wedding though, became quieter, which my mother remarked was a sign of normal pre-wedding anxiety. She certainly seemed nervous, large eyes watching doorways as if expecting someone, always. But by then, I had stopped noticing her. I was pregnant with Chloe, although not far along, but enough that the dress fitter complained I'd put on weight when I went for the final fitting. I'd known by then and had been clever enough to make sure that whenever someone saw me, I had a biscuit or a cake in my hand.

But I didn't like to think of Marguerite under house arrest. I imagine her seeing me from one of the bronzed windows as I stood looking up at the house just weeks ago. I was trapped; I wonder if she looked down at me and saw me as free.

Ephrem rubs his thumb against his chin and narrows his eyes. 'Tell me your secret, Juliet. Then I will decide.'

So I do.

Chapter 41

When I gave birth to Chloe, it was the single most painful, confusing, exhilarating day of my life. I was eighteen and in my bedroom at Eltringham Hall. Ephrem was away then, combining a six-month tour with honeymooning with Marguerite exploring all of Oceania. Mother read his letters over breakfast, and the last one I'd heard had hinted of an earlier return; Marguerite was ill and my mother had winked over boiled eggs at my father (who himself had only just returned from a trip away, temporarily releasing me from my confinement) that they were going to be grandparents before the year was out.

So, Ephrem was to be a father. I was not so foolish as to conflate my parents' delight at Ephrem's news with my own situation. But as I put down my spoon, filled with the sudden certainty that this was my moment, within it the smooth albumen wobbled, condemnatory of what I was about to do. I asked the footman to get more toast from the kitchen.

My mother said, 'Juliet, you silly girl, there's a rack of it in front of you.'

'Please,' I pleaded again, tears so thick suddenly I could only see the suggestion of him, 'please get me fresh toast.' I can't remember his name, or even if I knew it, but I loved him then, dearly, as he left without hesitation and shut the door very gently behind him.

'No, Juliet,' my mother said in a strangled voice, now aware of what I was about to do. She had been careful – she'd told me to sit behind the table before Father came to breakfast and had brought me ill-fitting dresses. She'd known about my pregnancy since just two weeks after Ephrem's wedding; she'd collected me from school due to the whispered ideas by my hockey teacher, but I was under strict instructions not to tell my father.

But I ruined it. Because then I told my father, that what Mother had said about them becoming grand-parents was true.

The week that followed, the sun hid behind clouds.

The days that followed my telling him were marked by screaming matches – all conducted without him looking at me once. He'd demanded to know the name of the father before he smashed me twice – once on either side of my face hadn't broken my resolve, even if he had broken my cheek-bone and my heart. I'd gone from Daddy's little girl to nothing. Worse than nothing. It was him refusing to look at me that I found the most painful. But I wouldn't tell, not even when Mother said he wanted to throw me out.

If I'd told, they would've killed Arthur, I know. At first, I'd been completely naïve. I thought if I held out on that knowledge, they'd move on. When it became clear that wasn't going to happen, I simply planned on running away with Arthur and my baby at some point in a misty future.

Of course I noticed sharply that Arthur and his father hadn't returned to Eltringham Hall. I hoped then that Mr Ryman had simply been asked, like most of the servants, to stay away for a while. In some ways, it was a relief. There had been no time to tell him about my pregnancy and I'd begun to fret that if he saw me, he'd give himself away. It was easier that he was safe and unknowing somewhere else.

As the last weeks arrived and I grew like a pumpkin on a vine, my father did not have to witness it as he left again within days of my announcement and did not say goodbye. I never saw him again, until I came back and killed him.

After he left, I was moved up to the attic. There were no servants to keep me company – I was carefully deposited in a room in the eaves of the west wing, away from what remained of the staff. We kept the one butler, two maids and Cook – the least staff we'd ever had. If my mother complained, I never heard it.

I was in confinement, and I felt at the time the blunt end of shame on a daily basis and I know my mother wouldn't have wanted to add to it. The low staff numbers were to reduce the amount of staff who could tell that the commandant's daughter was giving birth without a husband by her side.

I woke early in the morning with pains low in my abdomen; dawn was streaking the sky pink – a shepherd's warning. I should have known; I should have known.

I curled round my belly and counted through the

contractions. I kept it to myself as long as I could and by the time my mother brought my breakfast tray to me, my bedsheets were already soaked in sweat and my silent cries were replaced by the lowing of the late stage of birth.

My mother stayed and helped, giving me a wooden spoon to bite down on. At the end, I was mad with pain, but I never uttered a cry – I would not give her any indication of my torment.

Eventually, Chloe slithered into the world and into my bed, but not my heart.

Because she was already there.

I had one month with her. Just four weeks. Then, my mother told me it was time to get up and get moving. 'You need fresh air.'

'I haven't got a pram or a sling.'

'I'll look after the baby. You take a break. The walk will do your muscles good.' She suggested I make it a long one – something to wake up my spine. 'Why not walk out to the folly and back?' I was no longer bruised and bleeding, and the thought of fresh air after months of confinement in my room did seem appealing.

I gave a sleeping Chloe just one last kiss before I left and set out across the lawn towards the lake and beyond.

I did enjoy the air. After nights of breastfeeding, I enjoyed the chance to have some head space. Being cooped up under the eaves with my new adult life did not suit me. I made plans, decided that I would ask for somewhere to live in London, just like Ephrem had been given. I would work when I could, perhaps do Party work whilst Chloe slept. I would use my meagre savings to live on. It was impossible to assume that I could scrape out any kind of independence – as since the revolution, women had no independent access to finance. But I would try, I would do my best. The main thing would be to give Chloe what I could. I didn't want to leave Eltringham Hall; it was my home and I wasn't so stupid to not understand that I had great privilege. But the truth of it was that I hadn't really been anywhere else. All my life I had travelled only between school and home and now I had turned nineteen, really I was expected to marry. The last of the universities were long gone, since Grandfather had banned women first, and then prole and then Party men from having a free choice of education – the numbers weren't sustainable.

Sometimes the war is from within. I'd learnt from the school library books, and a little from Mr Ryman, that the government had tried to shut down their free speech in the preceding years and there had been large, widespread protests. There was talk of banning protests, but by starving the numbers of those who could attend, they collapsed the last bastion of free thinking anyway.

Power is always fought through the balance book because economic control is the cleanest, my father said, when I asked him about it. At the time, I didn't understand, but walking towards the folly, realizing the reality of my own financial situation, I realized that I did understand it now.

I vowed to do something about it, but wasn't sure what. Considering my post-partum bleeding had only finished a few short days earlier, I found I was able to get as far as the folly. I took the stairs up to the top and looked out through the arrow slit window. In those days, the trees on Hillcrest Ridge were younger and you could see across to Eltringham Hall. I had done it – I had walked three miles. I'd been super fit before giving birth and found that I enjoyed the feeling of only me in my body.

I stared at the house. The sky had grown redder, and I realized I'd come without a coat. In the distance, the horizon was bruised with an approaching thunderhead; the cloud, immense and jutting, reminded me of the imposing force of my father, and the bruised tissue of my face after he had hit me over my breakfast.

Shutting my eyes against the memory, I felt peace from all the worry and concern now it was behind me. Chloe was here; she was well and there were no more secrets to shield. I had weathered the storm and even if the rains came whilst I was out in the forest, I had a new life perspective. For a few minutes I enjoyed the solitude of only birdsong. The walk had rubbed the tension from my muscles; tension from the months of ebbing anxiety due to the inevitability of encroaching events. Then the reality of the situation and cruel confinement. I missed Arthur, but as the dying sun pressed warmth against the thin skin of my closed eyelids, I still believed in that moment that we would be together again. We would find a way.

I don't know what it was that shifted the tone for me – one moment I was at peace listening to the birds, and the next . . . like the slow awareness of a distant hum, a feeling of discontentment eased into my being. The sun was cut off by the clouds and a new breeze licked goosebumps on my skin and the noise in my head became at once full tilt roaring. I just somehow *knew*.

And then I wasn't at peace anymore – at once I was immersed in panic. I realized what I should have known – that Chloe was back at the house, my precious girl, under my parent's watch. Fear flooded my bowel and acid my stomach. I didn't pause; instead, I turned and flew down the stairs and then ran back across the field into the woods.

Twice my feet caught on roots, and I fell – once badly, cutting my lip and banging my knee. But I didn't stop. I got up and ran and ran; my poor body had not run for months, but if it suffered, I did not notice.

Breath burned in my lungs and my arms and legs pistoned. Like a piano, the tuning pins turned within me, the strings tightening as I ran. Tightening, tightening. I covered bracken and grass and lake and gardens and with unbearable tension, I arrived back on the veranda and flung open the glass French door and I knew before I'd even hit the hall, before I'd taken the stairs and made it upstairs to my bedroom. I knew that the crib would be empty when I got there. Seeing it in my mind's eye, the gap of her greater than even her presence, meant tension pulled tighter than anyone could bear. My desperate lungs dragged in gaping breaths and I opened the door to my room.

But when I did, it was worse, much worse than I feared. For the crib wasn't empty at all.

The crib was gone.

And my strings snapped.

Chapter 42

'My baby! Where's Chloe?' I screamed out and screamed it again. I spun round the room, every moment in surreal time – slow, so slow the edges blurred, yet so fast, so fast that my breaths lasted a thousand minutes. 'Chloe! My baby!'

At first nothing and then my mother came in. Bizarrely, Cook – who'd never, in the years I'd known her, ever been upstairs – appeared fleetingly (or perhaps stood there for hours) in the doorway, looking in. My mother didn't see her because her howl echoed my own and she tried to capture me, an angry, confused octopus, in the net of her maternal authority (love? Not sure) and tried to quell my waves of tears and questions. 'Better this way, better this way,' she uselessly repeated.

I fought her, screaming, howling, emotions a mess of visceral pain and when I glanced again at the doorway, Cook wasn't there but instead a large woman, a tank, advancing towards me. I didn't have much time.

'Mother!' My exclamation was a question above the

woman strongly seizing me and puncturing my skin with something sharp.

'For the best,' my mother answered.

My grief, cellular. At once, throughout me, deep within in my marrow, my tissue, my heart; more me than I was myself only moments before. I let forth a scream of understanding that Chloe, my baby, my daughter, my true love, was lost to me forever and the stars heard my pain; they moved aside so my cries could reach out unfurling into the cosmos, expanding like dark matter into everything.

And then there was nothing.

And I was almost glad.

Chapter 43

For a long time, I stayed in bed. I don't know how long I was administered drugs. I don't know much. I lay on my side and faced the wall and tried to sleep as much as I could. I hated being awake. I was dead and wanted to be dead.

My father never visited – if he had, I would have killed him then. I would have ripped his throat out with my teeth and chewed on his flesh. He was behind it – nothing happened without his authority. My mother did visit, but I screamed at her and batted her hands away with my own. My relationship with her was never restored and I am glad, even now to this day, about this fact. They had tricked me and had done it with guile and planning. I had breastfed for only two weeks until my mother started to complain that the baby would get the wrong idea, and when I slept, she took to feeding Chloe bottles of formula. Of course, I now understood that it was either to enable the baby to be given to someone else without risk of her not taking a bottle in my absence, or because they were drugging Chloe, filling her with a slow murder, the delayed termination they had wanted. I prefer to think the former; when life is bad, I think the latter.

Sometimes I dream of my mother holding my baby, wrapped in the green and yellow patchwork blanket I sewed when I was in my confinement (I wanted my baby to see the sun and the trees in everything), telling me: *I will look after her, I promise. Go for the walk. Get the fresh air.*

I will look after her, I promise.

I stayed in my bed many months, long after they told me, then begged me to rise; long after I was near-forgotten. Perhaps Cook kept me alive with her bone broth; I don't think I chewed any food for months.

Sores opened on my bony hips, weeping yellow fluid against white sheets, solidarity with my wept tears into my pillow.

In the end, it was Ephrem who changed things. He came in one day and told me, 'Get up. I have arranged for you to have a flat in London. You will move there now and be free of your past. Pack your things and I will drive you there now.'

He left my room and for two minutes I thought about it. I knew moving away would mean leaving where Chloe had last been, but I mistakenly believed going somewhere else might mean more privacy, and I would have a chance to contact Arthur.

With regards to what I was giving up, however, I was under no illusion: I would no longer be Inner Party. Theoretically no child born into the Inner Party will automatically stay – but in practise they do. Allegedly there is an exam one has to take at sixteen, but if it happens, I've never known any of my male peers to take it. Although as a female, I could never be in government, the Inner Party would be a passport to the freedoms of life: fine wine and food, books, entertainment, no telescreen, foreign travel. Freedom of thought; freedom of being. I would be giving up a life of plenty for a life of poverty. I knew that – I did not know how bad it would be.

But even if I had known the realities of life outside the pamper of the Inner Party, I wouldn't have hesitated. I had to find Arthur, then together we would be able to find Chloe. Perhaps she was dead, perhaps she was no longer in Airstrip One, but even if this was the case, the not knowing was worse than the grief. I needed to know. I hoped for Arthur and his help. Even if we could not be a family together, just the sheer unification with him and then the consequential unification of our grief would make us a family – us two missing our third.

I got up, packed a suitcase and let my brother drive me from my prison. When Mother tried to bid me goodbye, I was rough, more unpleasant than I intended. It didn't help that my father refused even to see me. I was well and truly cast out and the pain hurt terribly. I'd planned on quiet dignity, but I became febrile and failed. I'd wanted to see Cook but she wouldn't want to see my sweaty fringe and teared eyes, and besides, after my feverish little performance on the flagstones of the hall, if I had gone to see her, my mother would have been cross with Cook for seeing me. So, I left deciding I would see Cook on my return, but I didn't, because I only returned to Eltringham Hall properly one further time in my life and when I did, Cook was dead.

Death spread wider through the house, beyond Cook, and was held in a hot breath-stained feather pillow, which, when I was finished with it, I threw into the bedroom fire and watched it burn, the cotton smouldering, releasing the feathers, the vanes blackening and curling, as the quills hissed and cursed into submission.

I was Julia then. Outer Party. I wanted nothing to do with Juliet Georgina Ida Berkshire – her pain was too overwhelming.

Chapter 44

When Ephrem saved me from my prison, he drove me to Manor Towers; he didn't offer to help me move in. Instead, he pulled up on the corner of the street, muttering something about having to get back to his wife. All I had was a single bag with clothes – I hadn't wanted to take anything else. The things I would have taken, like my books and knick-knacks, I decided I could go back for later.

Manor Towers was a modern building, still in the last stages of construction. Like a clean white tooth in a mouth of broken decay, it stood out proudly against the grey, grime-smeared squat blocks of flats it neighboured.

Bewildered, I crossed the road, lugging my bag and entering the building; scanned and admitted, I went up to my one-bed flat. Looking around, I hated the fact that there was no place for my daughter – it felt like an admission that she was never going to join me here. Of course she wasn't – she was missing, dead even, but hope like moss continued to gain a foothold in the smooth precipice of my despair.

My melancholy only grew with Arthur also missing. All

my hopes were pinned on finding him. I had never even told him I was pregnant. After being rushed back from school, at the time I was naïve and thought he would return to Eltringham Hall if only I did not admit who Chloe's father was. But of course, he never arrived. As a woman, I had no tech permissions, so wrote to Arthur, and then when I didn't hear back, Mr Ryman. I had no reason to think they were not at the school, but when I received the first of many letters returned to me, with 'not known at this address', all hope was finally lost to me.

Chapter 45

The crowds gather, impatient for Hate Week because the bombs are falling again. It's not lost on us that the enemy attacks intensify as Hate Week approaches.

Eleanor has just witnessed an attack on the way to meet us; she is covered in grey dust and attracts attention, because we've all heard the bombs landing and the telescreens show the attacks. We tell those looking: 'This comrade has just witnessed a bomb blast! Down with Eurasia!'

'Down with Eurasia!' they reply, patting her as they pass. We are a nation only united when Hating.

Cecily holds Eleanor and they stand by the Thames in an embrace. Their shoulders shake, and we group around them like herd animals. We know what this means for Cecily, too – her entire family were bombed when she was sixteen. At that time, a neighbour saw the shell in the ruins and started screaming that she had seen them on the Minipax line she worked on: 'These are *our* weapons!'

Apart from Ruby, Cecily says that was the only time she saw someone arrested in daylight.

The neighbour, three months later – with a scar on her head and two stone lighter – knocked on every door on the street and Cecily, who by then had been taken in by a near neighbour, said she repeated the same lines over and over again. 'I have been mentally unfit. Disregard anything I have previously said. Big Brother brings strength and love.' If someone asked her a question, she would only repeat her lines back to them. Cecily says that even as she endured the indescribable grief of losing her family, it still disturbed her seeing the transformation of the neighbour who had been a family friend for years – and the dead-eyed gaunt ghost she had become. 'When I tried to take her hand, she pulled away but I'd seen already: they'd taken her fingernails.'

Eleanor finally lifts her head and Prisha feeds her water. Cecily has found a handkerchief and uses the water to wipe the dust from Eleanor's face with such careful dabs, I can see what an amazing mother Cecily would be.

'I had just walked by a waste ground,' said Eleanor. 'Kids were playing there. Boys of about ten or twelve, all kicking a football about. One of them kicked it too far and it went over the fencing, over the road and into my path. I threw it back and when it went back over the fence, they cheered me. I think I must have gone a little up the road when the bomb fell. It was a huge noise – *huge*. I hit the pavement, just as the ground shook. I landed on here—' She gingerly gestures to her jaw. Her ear is bleeding and the side of her face is badly swollen.

None of us suggest hospital – no one goes in out of choice.

'I got up from the pavement, and I couldn't see at first. There was dust in my eyes.'

'There still is, I think. Here, let me ...' Cecily tries to clean her eyes again.

'The fence was blackened, raw twisted metal ... flattened. I got closer and could see a huge, jagged hole where there had been none. Clouds of ash just fogging everything.' Her voice is leaden, almost robotic. 'I couldn't think – if you'd asked me my name, I don't think I would know how to answer. Then I saw a kid, and he was just standing there, bloodied, arm missing and he was staring at me. His arm missing from the shoulder, just a neat nothing.'

She blinks, her eyes rounded shock, and I can see that really she's still there. Leona grips her hand and Prisha feeds her more water. 'The dust dissipated a little by then – it's windy, isn't it? The alarms were going, too, and I think there were more people coming out of the houses, but all I could see were the bodies of the scattered children, all knocked down like skittle pins. I counted them. Twelve of them. All dead. No adults; this was where the kids played on the Hinckley Road. One had a jaw missing; another had his bowel hanging out. I wanted to save them, but there was only the boy and I couldn't see him then – he'd gone. It was a terrible, terrible sight – I shall never forget it. Never.' Eleanor makes a keening sound and more people notice her again. 'I want to know what happened to the boy.'

Her hair is still thick with dust, and I remember I have a comb. She lets me comb her hair. I do a bit, but I'm awkward and I'm grateful when Cecily gives me a gentle smile and takes the comb from me and does a proper job.

'And then there were people, and I don't remember how I got here. I just knew we were meeting and I remember thinking that I had to tell you so . . . and I didn't know what else to do so now I'm here.'

We are all changed by the recent rocket attacks. The news last week was full of an attack on a crowded theatre; it had been bombed and buried over two hundred people under its collapsed brick walls. The beams pinned others who were trapped, and the cameras showed them being burnt as the fire reached them. An outcry of Hate towards Eurasia surged and the funerals were screened for all to see.

The hate is rising; it's a tangible rotten smell that permeates everything, almost every conversation. Huge posters of Eurasian soldiers are pinned all over London, showing their cruelty. The posters are attacked: ripped down, graffitied with racist language, or wiped in dog poo. People take a delight in it – it's as if it becomes a competition as to who can be the most vile. The timing is clearly too perfect – yet no one questions it. Perhaps no one wants to question it. Perhaps the unification is just too intoxicating to Hate together. I'd put it to Winston that I thought the government were dropping the bombs as a way of keeping people frightened. I was surprised he'd not considered the idea himself – I'd thought that many people would have assumed it, but he had never contemplated it.

I cover her hand with my own; it's cold and her skin feels feathery, delicate bones underneath. 'Eleanor, I think you should go home. We can take you.'

Cecily nods. 'I'll take you.' She looks at me. 'You and Prisha can stay here.' I understand the point.

'I'll help you,' Leona says.

Prisha and I watch the three of them walk away, Eleanor well supported between Cecily and Leona. We start walking; like driftwood, we follow the river. We are careful how we talk now. 'Your connection to the Inner Party. Any good?'

'Solid. Will yield after a task I've got to complete.'

'Yield what?'

'Full access to full target.'

We fall silent as we consider what that means. She doesn't ask me how I've arranged this, and I'm glad. Better that there are no lies between us. I think she also knows how this will end for me now. Perhaps it is simple: there is a bomb and only I can carry it to the Inner Party. Perhaps I will be able to escape. Perhaps. But without Arthur and Chloe . . . perhaps I can simply only leave things better for whoever comes after me.

I think of the boy who left his house to play football – then all his friends killed, his arm gone. He didn't want to be bombed either. Perhaps in war, the only privilege is that for some, there is sometimes choice. At least I have that – he had none.

'And your Brotherhood contact – is he?'

'No. It was a mistake. He is nothing.'

'Will you tell Leona?'

I shake my head a little. 'I have to stay with him, till the end.' I owe Smith that. I owe it to myself, too – I need to know how this ends for him because of what I've done.

For a few minutes, Prisha doesn't ask anything, although she has opportunity. Then: 'C wanted me to talk with you.

J – I'm ... we ...' She smiles at me, just briefly. When she speaks though, it's to the river. 'We're worried about you.'

'I'm worried about all of us,' I quip.

She doesn't say anything for several minutes, and then she says, 'We cheered ourselves up the other day. We realized we needed a dream to shoot for. We decided that when this is over, Cecily and I want to open a school. She said her aunt lives in a beautiful rural village by the sea. There's this big manor house that's sat empty since the rebellion. We thought we could do it up, take in kids that need help. We could offer them an education and fresh air and nature.' She smiles, a little abashed. 'I might even dig out a pond; I always wanted a little bit of water to keep ducks. Have you ever had a duck egg?'

'I don't think I have.'

'Jules, they're amazing. Maybe you'll come and visit. Perhaps Eleanor will live with us, and she'll bake for the children.'

We walk in the sunshine. The pavement is grey, the water is grey, the faces of those around us are grey, but we enjoy the sunshine and the thought of duck eggs and schools for orphans. 'What would you do, Julia, when this is all over? Perhaps you would choose to live with us?'

I hear the 'would' – not 'will'. This is a hypothetical question for me – she knows it, too. Prisha is a smart woman – savvy, analytical. She knows if I'm buried so deep that I have Inner Party connections and a bomb, then I'm not going to be feeding ducks by their lake. I feel a surge of emotion for what I want – but will never have. On a whim, I tell her about Chloe and about Arthur. I do this without mentioning much about my family, and if she is shocked, she doesn't say.

When we finish our walk, we stop and look at each other, properly. We can't say much but she does briefly risk taking my hand for a gentle squeeze. 'I'm sorry for your loss,' she says, in a voice that shows she is.

On the way back to my never-home flat, I wonder if she just means about my little family that nearly was, or what I still have yet to lose and most certainly will.

Both, perhaps.

Chapter 46

'Juliet,' says my father's voice, waking me.

'Yes, Daddy?' I answer, opening my eyes into the night. I'm confused and blinking – I was just with my father. But no – a dream of a memory from long ago . . . a memory of golden, glassy-sided fish. Leopard-pocked flesh browning in the pan. Brown butter rolling chestnut-coloured bubbles.

'Juliet.'

Did he say Juliet, not Julia? Daddy? But another blink and reality breathes heavy.

–it's not him–

After reality hits, fear dumps cold. For a small fraction of time during the transition of reality and then fear, I realize something I knew but did not know: I miss him. Seeing him in my dreams and now hearing him . . . A long time ago, I decided not to miss him because of what he did to me and what I did to him in return, but the feeling of missing him is real.

Reality wakens, crystal salt ground in meaty wounds. 'Big Brother . . .' My throat is dry.

'Julia.'

The feeling I am in trouble is cold. The image of a delicate, slender, steel instrument drilling into an unanaesthetized skull wakes me fully. What is corporeal becomes clear. 'Thank you for waking me. Perhaps I have been asleep too long.' I know this isn't true because no light leaks from the edges of the blind. It is an indeterminable time of the night – but it is night.

'Julia, I am by your side whether you are awake or asleep.'

Twice now, waking me in my sleep. This is new. Why? I listen to my breathing, it's becoming faster. Could fear make me unconscious in my own bed? I'm waiting. Although it doesn't answer straightaway, it will. As I wait, the space, the darkness, seems to gather mass; it presses on my face, my neck, my chest. It's hard to move, harder to inhale. It feels like pushing against a murderous pressure.

'Our great leader has a question for you.'

I try to think only of Winston as I have already given him up – I *must* think of nothing else. I must protect myself from thought surveillance and when I am tired – and I'm so very, very tired – it would be easier to slip up. 'What is the question?'

'Our great leader asks ... are you still prepared to go fishing for him?'

For a moment, I think I'm having a seizure. I'm having an electric shock. My muscles become rigid. My hands flatten, then claw, knuckles locking, then flatten again. My spine feels like cold metal. Urine releases and is warm underneath me. Sweat breaks and is cold on my skin.

I can't order my thoughts.

It's true, it's true! This is proof. It can now read my thoughts. Or my dreams. Or both.

No. We did discuss fishing between us when I agreed to the task – but I don't know. I don't know. I pray for certainty.

When I speak, my voice is dust. 'Yes.' I want to say more, but all I can do is repeat the single word again. 'Yes.'

Yes, I will go fishing.

When in my life am I not hunting for something?

Chloe, I miss you the most.

Chapter 47

Two months after Ephrem drove me from my parents' home to my new flat in Manor Towers with a heart full of hope and a desire for action, I was left with none of that; instead, just those few weeks left me an empty husk. I knew I wouldn't hear from Arthur again. After writing to him and receiving 'not known at this address', I hadn't given up. I'd even gone up to my old school on a pretext of looking for a lost trunk. In the entrance hall there were several dark wood boards with gold lettering – each year's head girl, each year's sporting heroes and house champions, and there was also one with the staff names on. As soon as I stood in the stone-flagged entrance hall, I saw that the head of music's name was now Dr Lessing. Mr Ryman was gone.

If Mr Ryman was gone, Arthur would be gone, too – but I still caught another music teacher in her room, a colleague of some years of Mr Ryman's, a small, rather silly young woman who played the oboe beautifully, but was completely unable to cope with rambunctious students. But if she ever knew it was me who had locked her in her storeroom, she didn't seem to remember and greeted me like an old friend. I had to tolerate talking with her for half an hour – or rather, her talking at me as she listed a seemingly unfettered catalogue of whines and woes about her pupils – before I managed to manoeuvre my purpose, my question into the conversation.

'Mr Ryman's gone now, I see,' I said.

Miss Viele's forehead, which had been mountain-and-valleyed with her frustrations, instantly smoothed to blank.

'Arthur, his son, went with him, I suppose?' I pursued.

'I don't know who you mean,' she said evenly.

'You know, Mr—' I halted, suddenly aware of the precipitous change in our conversation. Mr Ryman and Arthur weren't just gone, they were abolished; they were now unpersons. Every record of their name, every photo, every proof of their birth, education, employment, would've been expertly expunged. They joined the long list of the never-here. To even acknowledge they had ever existed was dangerous. I found new respect for Miss Viele, who continued to gaze at me as if nothing verboten had occurred.

The silence between us was as painful as nails screeching down a blackboard.

'Miss Viele, forgive me . . . I, I don't know what I'm talking about – I realize I've completely confused two places of my childhood. Please, tell me your plans, would you, for the summer concert this year?'

If I detected a sheen on her top lip, I was probably correct, because she launched into detailed and hurriedly spoken plans for the school production. It was dangerous for me to enquire about Mr Ryman – but just as dangerous for her to be asked.

I left quickly with a promise to return in the summer to see the school's orchestra, a promise I knew I would never keep. Instead, with a decaying heart, I decided to head straight for my father. If Arthur Ryman had been abolished, then there was every chance my father knew that Arthur was Chloe's father. And if that was known, there was every possibility that Chloe was a never-known, too. And if there was one person I could discuss that with without fear of the firing squad, it was my father, head of Ingsoc.

Our great leader.

Within the hour, I was on the train from school to the nearest station and power-walked the four miles to the house. I did not want my parents to know my intentions lest they block my arrival, and sped along the country lane as if my sheer presence would trigger alarms and sirens. My arms were the soldiers' arms I'd seen practising the grand march for my grandfather's birthday along The Mall. Like them, I imagined having military precision, but anger probably over-stoked my engines, and if I'd encountered anyone on the journey, then I probably looked more like the reality of what I was: a woman about to commit murder.

My father had taken my baby (my mother clearly countenanced it, but like all Ingsoc women, she was very much the subservient wife), and now had killed my lovely piano teacher and the love of my life. With Arthur gone, there was no one left to help me find out if Chloe was alive or dead. My dreams of a family were over – and I was going to make my father pay.

When I was small, I didn't realize the impact he had, as we watched from the balcony of the enormous palace: the rolling tanks and the swathes of soldiers marching, first for my grandfather and then, after he disappeared, marching for Big Brother, who to me was my father. They were the same face and no one could explain to me how they were different.

When I was thirteen, a new teacher joined my school and as I played hockey, I could see the man and my PE teacher conferring on the side of the pitch and the PE teacher indicated me when they thought I wasn't looking. I was, although pretending not to, because by then I had started to become aware that the teaching staff treated me differently to my peers. It was a delicate difference, but if any of my peers noticed it also, they never mentioned it to me, and I was not able to define exactly what the difference was. It was certainly not favouritism, nor dislike by any stretch – it was more a very subtle swerve away from me. As if I had what us children called 'cooties' or 'fleas', the childish game of believing that if one got too close to another person with lice, for instance, one could catch the undesirable.

That moment when awareness became understanding was when I saw the new teacher indicate with an indiscreet finger and then I could see him say – not hear because I was too far away and the shout and hollers of my fellow hockey players would have made it too impossible – *is that her?* And then my PE teacher nodded and looked away, as if my even catching them speaking about me might in some way endanger them with a contagion.

Only Mr Ryman treated me as if he liked me, when he started coming to the house and engaging with me in his warm, affable way, delicious with his air of shambles and confusion. I'd always loved the piano, had been told I was gifted many times, but because he talked to me like I was just anyone, I tried all the harder for him.

I loved him for it, and now he was gone because of me.

Dead? I did not know. Gone was worse. I didn't know what gone meant then. Although I had left school and home and had the promise of a job, I knew nothing really of the realities of the world.

But as terrible as losing the kind, decent Mr Ryman was, to lose my Arthur was worse. The rawness of Chloe being taken had not ebbed even a molecule in the last month. I cried for hours every day, struggled to eat, didn't want to get out of bed. Big Brother talked to me constantly and it tortured me to hear my father and know he was watching me, after what he'd done to me by taking my daughter; still surveying me even though I was no longer in his house.

I tried to kill myself twice. Once with painkillers but then I was no longer trusted with them and instead they were dispensed two at a time by the synthetic who prowled the corridors of Manor Towers. Secondly with the kitchen knife, then they were all abruptly removed by the synthetic, too, and I was left with spoons. One evening I was close to figuring out how I could kill myself with a spoon when I suddenly realized it wasn't going to help Chloe or Arthur. What I needed was to do something to make the rest of my life purposeful – make it useful to ensure that the world did not carry on being where women had no choice over whether they got to keep their children or not. It had occurred to me that I was not the first. I was determined that I had to try to be the last.

I thought of faceless, nameless women who might in the future suffer the same fate as me and felt my need to change our world for them; this bolstered me, gave me a wider sense of sisterhood. I felt a belonging, almost a shared consciousness: a sistren networked like a map of stars that spread wider than me alone.

Outer Party families were actively discouraged – propaganda promoted the utebubbles despite their failure; and for those who did have children, their offspring were not encouraged to look upon their parents with any love. It made me angry that it was different for the Inner Party where children were cosseted and nurtured and loved, with male children expecting to inherit the world. But not for women. Not for me. Not for my daughter.

And there was one man whose fault it was – and I was going to make him pay.

I marched down the country lane, with the mind I was going to get there and he would be in his office at the back of the house and I would grab a knife without even saying hello to Cook (because she'd know just by looking at me that I was in what she called 'a cream puff' and would talk me down) and then I would find him and change this world to be a better place.

In my mind's eye, the vision of the confrontation was so clear that when I arrived at the house and saw my brother's car on the driveway, I was crushed. The vision of me versus my father was so vivid, there was no space for this unexpected reality. My brother being here would change everything. As I stared at the huge chauffeur-driven thing, just like my father had, with its blacked-out windows, I paused. I did not want to see my domineering brother or his shallow, vain wife, Marguerite, who cared only for ribbons and rubies.

But after a minute, I decided that I wouldn't let it have any impact on my plans. My father had taken both my child and the love of my life, and he would pay. I was dead anyway, I decided. In front of the heavy front door, I nearly rang the bell; I had never stood at the door of my home like a visitor, and I was in such a rage that I would not start now, so I opened the door.

Chapter 48

I stepped into the hall of my true home; the hall was large, with its huge oak staircase stretching up into a triple height space. Although there was a large fireplace, the room was always cool as it was always unlit, the front too full of stone and lack of light to heat, with any warmth dragged up by the high ceiling at the back. But despite its lack of natural warmth, complete with the heads of hunted animals hung high above the cold fireplace, it never felt intimidating or cold to me – it always felt like home.

With Ephrem, I had skidded in games on the stone flags; we'd played hide and seek around the staid furniture and trailed teasing wool in front of the endless cats we had across the room.

But standing on its threshold now, I saw it for what it was. I had only stood there seconds, when my mother walked down the staircase, hands wringing, and when she saw me, paused briefly before she said, 'Juliet, about time. Where have you been? Your father has not got long,' and then she reversed her journey and headed back up the stairs and off in the direction of the west wing, leaving me agape like a beached carp.

What did she mean? Was she expecting me? And what did she mean that my father did not have long? But the deepest interrogative and the one that pushed me onwards, was why did she look so utterly, utterly *frightened*?

I followed in the direction she'd headed, towards where her and my father's bedroom suite was. I didn't see anyone on the journey – not my brother, not Marguerite, not a servant; it was as if the place had turned into a ghost house. With a feeling of foreboding, I made my way through empty corridor after empty corridor. As I neared my father's bedroom, I heard my mother talking to a servant. She was giving orders for my father's things to be packed – he was going away.

'What's going on?'

'Your father is very ill – not that we ever heard from you to show you care – and a helicopter is coming any minute to take him to hospital. Dr Sanders is taking him to a special institute in the mountains to recover. He's going to be gone some time, perhaps many months.'

'Recover?'

'Pneumonia, Juliet. It came on overnight. One day, he was super fit, and then in hours, he got sick with a terrible virus. Do you remember last year, when he stayed out on manoeuvres overnight and got all chesty? I reminded Dr Sanders about that – I don't think he was listening to me, had his own ideas, no doubt – but he's been weaker chested since then. It's me that listens to him breathing at night, and I'm convinced I can detect this slight rattle that was never there last year. I told him to do steam inhalations and he just wouldn't and now it just won't shift . . .'

My mother finally ran out of air and looked around as if she had put something down and forgotten where she put it. I hated seeing her like that – she looked as if she herself had aged and it was like that image was a portent of a near future where she was much frailer, much older. It only made me hate my father more to see her lost because of him.

She flung her hands up and exclaimed over some crucial thing that she had failed to organize for my father's imminent departure and left for his downstairs office in a flap, walking as fast as her dignity would allow.

I stepped into the small hallway of my parents' suite. From this room there were two doors – one entered onto my parents' large bedroom that overlooked the front of the house, which in turn, led onto a large bathroom. Also off the central bedroom were two further doors, one for my mother's dressing room and the other, accessed both through the bathroom and the small hallway, was my father's private study and from that, an anteroom made up with a single bed. My father used this room to sleep in when my mother was already asleep and he didn't want to wake her. I had stepped into it expecting to find it empty, but Ephrem was in there, sitting on the winged armchair.

'Juliet, good to see you. Are you all right?'

'Not really. Mother acts like . . .' I realized I didn't want to discuss it with Ephrem. 'Father must be sick for you to be here during the day.'

Ephrem looked back at his laptop. 'Well, that's ironic coming from you who never sees him.'

He had a point. 'No Marguerite?'

'Goodness no.' He sounded like I'd offered him an enema. 'Come through and see him.' He stood, moving towards the door. 'Of course, after what he did to you, I'm amazed to see you here at all.' He turned back before grabbing the door handle as if to offer an afterthought. 'You being here – after the way he treated you and the baby – says jolly good things about you, poeface,' he said, using a nickname I had forgotten even existed.

I had seen Ephrem since he'd driven me to the flat in Manor Towers – regularly, in fact. Our relationship had changed since I had moved to London; he met with me every month without fail and gave me all the money I needed and real food packages, which made me feel looked after and connected to the family. But we never talked about what happened. Now we were both back home, our father ill, it felt right to reach out to him. 'I never thanked you properly for rescuing me. Driving me to London and getting me somewhere to live. You pay for it, I know. Thank you. And I'm sorry. I was a mess.'

He touched my cheek briefly. 'I felt for you. For the record, I want you to know that I tried desperately to talk him out of it. To kil—' He halted abruptly and flashed me a wide-eyed look of horror. 'To *take* – to take, I meant – a little girl from her mother is vile.'

For a long second, we just looked at each other. His hand stayed on the door handle. 'I better . . . go, poeface.'

'What were you going to say? What do you mean?'

'Nothing. Huge apols, sis – it just came out all wrong. I'm tired and sour for you – sorry. It was horrible to see, but totally much, much worse for you. Forget my crassness, please.'

He turned quickly and exited the room into our parents' bedroom.

I stood, unable to go forward; I felt bile rise, burning my throat, the back of my tongue. Light leaked through damask drapes, reminding me that outside this room, outside of how I felt, there was a whole other life. But none of it seemed reachable, tangible even. All I could consider was that I always hoped that Chloe had just been ... moved ... somewhere, perhaps to one of the reclamation centres for homeless children, but the stumble of Ephrem's words told me what I had feared: there was no reclamation centre for my daughter.

Chloe was dead.

Murdered.

By her own grandfather. But should I be surprised? After all, this man had killed his own father to take power. He killed him and then we moved into his house, this house. What kind of callousness does that take?

Just as my brother's had done, my hand clasped the cold, bronze handle and I followed Ephrem into my father's room. The room was hot; the huge fire had been stacked high with logs and the flames blazed big enough to roast a hog. Ephrem stood by his bed, smoothing Father's many covers, the whispering sound as the creases were chased away joining the noise of the popping of the apple logs and Father's rasping breaths.

Ephrem did not look at me as I came in and I did not look at him. I felt detached, robotic, no longer alive. I wanted to ask him questions, but I was afraid. As if joining me in my struggle to stay alive, my father's breathing rattled; it was as if I could hear the cilia working against the tide of filth; phlegm drowning them like pollution on a seaweed bed.

My father's head was back against a ridiculous stack of pillows, his mouth hanging open. He looked terrible, dark shadows under puffy eyes, contrasting with new hollows under his cheeks. His moustache – always so bold and strong – now seemed to overpower him. Before, I would have been shocked, but now I felt nothing for him. He was a rock, a stone, a toad, a lump of nothing in my life.

Outside I could hear the throb of a helicopter – it sounded different, discordant. As the sound ebbed closer, I wondered if I was drowning. I dragged air into my lungs and realized I hadn't breathed for a long time. The breath left me in a rush and as it did, I saw two small dark shapes pass the gap in the curtains. There were two helicopters and by the sound change, they were landing on the front lawn. The noise was huge and vast and since nothing could be thought of or said with it going on, I took it, and hid under it, pulling the distraction over my head like a child. For one moment, I shut my eyes and did nothing but think about the whooping sounds of chopper blades and the whine as they started to slow.

'One copter for me, one for Father,' Ephrem said, surprising me. Even though he was in front of me, he'd ceased to be noticed by me.

He addressed Father: 'I'm sorry I can't come with you to

the institute. I'll visit at the weekend.' Ephrem was saying something to him, adjusting the stacked pillows that held him almost to a sitting position, supporting him as he removed one from behind him and cradled his head to help him down to a lower position. As my father slumped back, he said in a voice gentler than I had ever heard my brother use: 'That's better, Father.'

He turned to me then and said, 'I'll leave him with you. See him out the door, will you? For both of us?'

He pressed the pillow he was still holding onto me. 'The men from the institute will be here soon.'

I held it and met his gaze. 'What did they do to her?'

He looked down, sorrow deep in his face. He shook his head a little and my father behind him rattled his breathing as if to urge his son to say nothing.

'Ephrem – please. If you know.' I was crying then, complete heaving sobs as if to keep step with my father's laboured breathing. 'She's my daughter.'

'For the best, he thought. You have to forgive him for that. He said . . .' His voice hitched, and he looked up again and met my eye. 'He said it was like Lulu's pups.'

A decade earlier, my father drowned half of the litter of our Labrador's pups in the river; Ephrem and I had screamed and screamed to find the litter by the Aga, which depleted from eight to four overnight. My father had been furious and threatened to hit us both with his boot – 'see the wood for the trees,' he kept saying, but it took Cook and Mother to explain what he meant, that Lulu didn't have enough milk for eight, so he was trying to save some rather than none.

I could hear the sounds of men shouting over the

lowering hum of the helicopters and then they fell to nothing. The blades, too, fell silent as Ephrem and I stared at each other, only the pillow between us.

My fingers closed over the silk pillowcase, digging into the smooth feather-filled shape. My brother had the decency to close the door carefully behind him. The latch clicked smoothly into the reception of the lock, and then I heard the quiet sounds of shoe leather on wool runner, just briefly before silence.

Stillness seized the room; motes tumbled in and out of the light shard that fell between the heavy, mostly drawn curtains. Watching them reminded me of being with Arthur in the attic; then I only saw the freedom of the dust motes' dance, not the prison in which they moved – that when they fell into shadow, they became blanked from existence. So easy, this movement of light to dark, life to death.

Too easy.

Holding the pillow gripped tight in my hands, I turned to face the man who had killed my daughter.

Rebirth. Is this what this moment offers me?

It occurs to me, that in this too-hot bedroom of my father's, this feather-filled pillow I hold could be how I wrest my life from a place of pain and powerlessness to something . . . *else*. Something better. A new start.

Eyes shut, he lies prone, a sick, ageing man on his bed. My grip tightens against the softness; I am actually considering this. I see it in my mind's eye – placing it across his face. Holding it down as he struggles. I imagine different versions: where he goes gently; where he fights and wins;

where someone (Mother?) walks in and finds me engaged in an undisputable sin.

A log in the hearth pops like a child's cork gun and I'm startled from my reverie.

In this damask-draped room, apart from the gap in the curtains, the fire is the only light. Now sound is smothered, the quiet only broken by the sounds of his breathing, my heartbeat, the faint tick of his mantel clock, the sounds of licking flames on logs – but together the room hushes, waiting to see what I will do. I'm waiting to see what I'll do.

I feel dangerous.

Even in the gloom, his bedroom is familiar to me – too familiar my mother would say if she knew. But she doesn't know. Just as it used to be, it's now just me and him. I am not just here now – this room, his suite, is a palimpsest of memories, each laid over each other, different images, different emotions, different times. They are all within me.

The clock ticks on.

I have not got long – they are coming. I did not come here to do this, I feel like telling him, but despite my pro-testations, I have not put down the pillow.

In the gloom I study my father's face: jowls hang, his charcoal and ash-coloured hair swept back from his forehead, smoothed out of place perhaps, by my mother's anxious hand. She could come back – or the men – and find me here. I need to decide now, while I still have time. Is my rage enough?

Ceaseless, cold and candid – my rage *is* enough. I move the pillow closer to his face. Part of me watches with horror, challenging me: you won't really do this, will you?

Yes, I tell myself. I will. Because I want the chance to start again, to become someone else. I want rebirth.

I will become Julia.

The flames whipped in my peripheral vision, and I tightened my hold.

My father slept on, his lidded eyes not sealing tight his eyeballs, showing me a white crescent of unseeing eye. His breathing rattled on, cilia waving in filth.

And I placed it over his face and pressed it there and I did not stop even when I should have.

And it was easier than it should have been, because I could see Chloe's blue eyes looking at me with a trust that wasn't deserved, and the sharp regrets of my failure as a mother made it so much easier to fail also as a daughter.

Chapter 49

The sound of the washerwoman's singing wakes me, reminding me I am in bed, in the room above Mr Charrington's shop. I keep my eyes shut in case Smith is awake. I've been avoiding him, but ran out of excuses and loyalty to Leona brought me back.

Smith let this room from Mr Charrington for the sole purpose of our affair, but sometimes I think it's just so he can spend more time with the old man. Charrington's his hero and sells Smith relics from the past. Of course, together they're both committing thoughtcrime to think about the past, but their discussions charge Smith with thoughts of rebellion. When I realized the extent of their relationship, I felt huge relief that I've never shared any truths with Smith. If I had, I have no doubt they would all be unburdened onto Charrington, and I have never even met him.

Charrington isn't to be trusted – most proles wouldn't want to talk to a Party man like Smith, even an Outer Party man. Most proles wouldn't dare let a room with no tele-screen in a prole area to a Party man either. And surely *no* prole would choose to commit thoughtcrime with a Party man? What could be a more certain way to ensure arrest? It doesn't make sense, but when I asked Winston about this, pressing the point to an argument, he won't have a word said against the old man. 'We have a special relationship,' is all he would say. 'Perhaps you're jealous that he and I were friends before we even met.'

I want to sleep, but it's hot, too hot, and the noise of the washerwoman singing is plaguing me. I wish I could ask Mr Charrington to have a word with his neighbour, but I can't. Even if I wanted to meet him, he's suspiciously never around when I am. If this room wasn't real and above a real shop, I would doubt he was even a real person.

'He's not in the Brotherhood, is he?' I'd asked earlier, suddenly in fear I've led Ephrem to the Brotherhood.

'Sadly, no. I asked him – told him I would join.'

'You didn't!'

'Well, the discussions we've had – trust me, that little admission is nothing to what we talk about.'

Now, I feel the mattress move as Winston shifts his body; the old springs gratingly complain as he presses himself closer. His breath is hot against my ear. 'Julia, I have some exciting news.'

I am tired of Smith. Perhaps I'll need to disappoint Leona after all. My eyelids stay down like the doors on a nuclear bunker. I'm out; no one is home.

'Julia—'

Go away.

He shakes my shoulder.

'Yes, my love?' I keep my voice purposefully sleepy.

'Do you know O'Brien?'

I make a noncommittal noise and the bunker doors stay tight.

'Wake up, won't you? I think I've found the Brotherhood!'

'O'Brien?' I concede one eyelid. 'That Inner Party swine? I doubt it.'

Winston's propped on one arm looking at me with a fierce intensity. 'He's reached out to me.'

'O'Brien?' Giving up, I raise myself on my elbows. 'He's a troll. He's a proper, proper swine. Stay away, Winston.' O'Brien is the contact I thought Smith already knew – I saw their shared look at the Two Minute Hate all those months ago. But if Smith wasn't Ruby's contact (and I'm completely sure he wasn't), then I was wrong about Smith's involvement with O'Brien. I feel a little sick.

'O'Brien's reached out to me,' Winston repeats, fireworks in his eyes.

'How exactly?'

'He sought me out to talk about words and has ...' He pauses, taking a moment as if in anticipation of some expected applause, then says, ' ...now invited me to his home. He has offered me a copy of the latest edition of the Newspeak Dictionary. But I think it's a pretext – I think he wants to talk to me in private.'

Now I'm awake. I feel the lurching, stomach-dropping sensation as the adrenaline fires my blood. This is it. To buy myself a little thinking time, I adjust, pulling myself up against the bolster, my face turned away. I'm afraid if he sees my horror, he'll guess what I've done. The deal I made. *I'm sorry, Winston.* This is the landing of the fish, I know it.

When I don't say anything, he adds, 'He wants to talk to me privately!'

I'm sorry, Winston.

'You don't have much to say,' he says a little huffily, clearly annoyed that I'm not instantly enthralled with his perceived win. 'I thought this is what we both wanted.'

I shut my eyes again to give me more time to think. I tell him I'm tired. I stretch and yawn to buy me extra time. I'm sick, so sick. I wasn't ready for this – I did not think Ephrem would strike so quickly.

'Darling, just get him to bring you the dictionary at work. Much easier.' I snuggle into his chest so he can't see my traitor lies.

'Don't you understand!' Winston explodes. 'Of course, he *could* give me the dictionary, but he said he wouldn't remember to bring it into work. But that must be an *excuse.* How would a man of his standing not be able to remember to bring in a simple book if he felt that's what he wanted to do? It's just a ruse.'

'A ruse to get you to go to his flat?'

'Exactly!' he says, mood easing like a passing summer squall. 'A ruse,' he repeats and rubs my back, brightening. Sometimes I think that Winston thinks I'm stupid – more stupid than the image I've cultivated. It's an interesting choice, I think, to assume dullness. My father always said it is the fool who assumes he has found a fool.

'And when you get inside O'Brien's home? What will you do then?'

Now it's Winston's turn to be unsure. He furrows his brow. 'Well ... I suppose at some point, if we are to find the Brotherhood, that's going to involve more risk – but I can see your point.' He sits with his back to the mahogany headboard and breathes deeply. 'I think,' he says grandly, 'we will have to disclose – if he doesn't first – our feelings about everything. Our desire to rebel. We've always said that it is a matter of time until we get found out and face the shooting squad ... so ... perhaps now the time has come.' He sighs, falls silent for a few seconds before visibly brightening again. He beams. 'Can you believe, he *actually* read one of *my* articles?'

'Articles?'

'Honestly, Julia, I think sometimes you don't listen to a word I say. Yes, my articles! He saw the Newspeak article I had in *The Times* the other day. He thought it was scholarly! Me! He actually used that word.' He sinks back against the headboard and repeats it with an extended sigh: '*Scholarly*. Julia, I was thunderstruck. I could only mutter I was an amateur and really just take a regular interest in the language, but still ... he had noticed me!'

'Amazing, darling. What happened then?'

'Then – and I only realized the significance of this afterwards; really O'Brien is such a smart man – he said that I write elegantly. That was enough to make me blush. Of course, I hope that I write, that is to say, I attempt to write as elegantly as possible, but the fact he said it stirred my thoughts sufficiently for me not to understand the significance of what he was saying. He said – are you listening to this, Julia? It's important.'

'I'm listening, of course, my darling, I'm listening.'

'This only really occurred to me *after* our conversation. He said that he wasn't the only person to notice that I write elegantly. He said that he had been talking to someone else about my abilities, but could not remember who that person was! Do you see?'

I do not want to burst Winston's bubble of triumph, but I do not see and tell him so.

He pushes his lips together, a hard ruled line of agitation before continuing: 'He was talking about Syme! Syme from work. Syme knew us both but is now an unperson. No one can talk about Syme since he was abolished. To even hint at him is such a huge, incredible risk for O'Brien to make, it can only be a signal – a code to me that he is on the outside, thinking about an unperson, committing thoughtcrime. He wants me to join him. And I want us to join him.'

I ignore Winston's inclusive pronoun and instead ask, 'What did he say, though, about you going to his home? Not what you think he meant, what did he actually say?'

'I thought I'd explained. But to be more precise, he said in my article I had used two words that were no longer in existence in the new updated Newspeak dictionary. Then he asked me if I had the latest edition. I said no, then he said he did at home and invited me round to his to collect it. He gave me his address on a slip of paper.'

'Do you have that with you now?'

'I've got it at my flat. It felt too risky to carry around.'

Despite the fact I had already done the damage, I couldn't help but want to save Winston. 'Darling, it's exciting but I don't think it's enough for you to risk everything.

You know how the Inner Party are about dead words. Perhaps he just wanted to make sure you didn't use them again. As you say, you do write elegantly. I will look up your article and I'm sure it's beautiful. I expect he just wanted to tell you and lend you the dictionary. Perhaps you simply managed to inspire the swine!'

'No, it's more than that. It's the fact he sought me out at work. He actually followed me down the corridor and then gave a little cough, wanting me to turn. When I did, he actually – this is O'Brien, remember – laid his hand on my arm! Can you believe it? Then he started walking with me; it was as if we were equals. Him! Inner Party and me! It was quite, *quite* clear he was singling me out at that precise moment. He said he wanted to speak with me – but it's more than that. This is key: he passed me the note directly in front of the telescreen. Can't you see, Julia, what that says?'

'The note with his address?'

'Yes, yes. The fact he's invited me round there ... would he do that if it was *just* to give me a copy of a new dictionary?'

'Yes! Can't you see, Winston? It's all risk based on your hopes. That's not enough for you to chance your life. Can't you see, darling, it could be a trap? He promises nothing – a book. Now you're filling everything in around it. You must be careful.'

'Darling, I haven't told you the most significant thing for me. O'Brien pulled me over almost exactly in the same place I met you – a note just in front of the telescreen, too. In the very same corridor. Two notes – both leading to great things! You have to understand the significance.' He pulled me back, kissed my neck, working his way down to my spine. He lifted his head. 'Julia, it's the only sign I need – he contacted me in the same way you did. Before you, I was pathetic. I had nothing, no real way to rebel. I only had Mr Charrington's things . . . his words. Now that seems so petty, so puerile, such a pointless rebellion against the Party. Then there was you – in front of that telescreen passing me a note in exactly the way you did, in exactly the same place. It's like a signal.'

Of course. *Of course.*

It *is* a signal.

I should have seen.

Bile rises and I feel dizzy with the certainty. When I gave Winston up, I was not telling Ephrem anything they did not already know – I had hoped I was, but he knew about me and Winston from the start. He *always* knew about Winston. They must have seen me pass the note and O'Brien simply mimicked me so that I would understand.

My secret affair was never secret.

Winston's words – *he was singling me out at that precise moment* – reverberated like thunder.

I needed Winston to stop talking. The washerwoman started up with her song again and the room felt like a hundred degrees. Like a lobster seeing the darkening as the lid closes the pot, I knew my time was close. Lying on my back, I stared at the water-stained ceiling. If they knew about Winston, they were watching him and if they knew about me passing Winston the note, what else did they know about? Nothing? Perhaps they were just watching me? Everything? Some variance in between?

A sicking thought: if Smith wasn't connected to Ruby, but was already being watched, by reaching out to him, did I inadvertently just lead them to me?

It's a tangle in my mind. But whatever the truth, the Sisterhood is not safe. And perhaps none of our secrets are – including the bomb.

Chapter 50

Winston has made a grave error. I know it because we are outside O'Brien's mansion block and Winston doesn't seem to understand he has walked into the stinking centre of the rat's nest. How or why he would think that the Brotherhood would exist here, in the Inner Party region of town, I cannot imagine, but it tells me what I already know: Winston is a romantic. And like all romantics, he only sees what he wants to believe, instead of what's in front of him. And he has terrible taste in company – me, Charrington and now O'Brien. It's as if he wants to be arrested.

I can – if I angle my head – see Manor Towers from where we stand, but here, the surrounding area reeks of high living, expensive tastes and inherited privilege. Power prevails and like a catty schoolgirls' clique, is impossible for outsiders to penetrate.

Winston doesn't know the Inner Party like I do – to live it is to know it. But the knowledge only brings sadness; it takes a special kind of person to know that others are suffocated of the basic needs of life, whilst one sits round a table, calling out for another whisky in a raised crystal glass overflowing with want.

But now I am here between two stone pillars, on this doorstep covered in a checkerboard of black and white tiles, I know that there is no going back. Why am I here? If Winston came alone, he could simply change his mind at the last minute and just ask for the dictionary and leave. He knows this but I think he must have insisted that I come so that he can't change his mind, can't release himself from the self-dare at the last moment.

I now look at his lightly lined face, this dusty man who I have known as a person separate from the machine. This dry man who had been hiding away so much hurt has come alive in confidence, daring and ambition in the time I have known him. *They are coming for you!* I want to tell him. I nearly did as well but he was so happy, so glowing with the possibilities of O'Brien seeking him out that I knew he wouldn't listen.

They want to wrinkle out not just Winston's deeds but his thoughts, too. And that makes perfect sense because they want everything. They want the full crime. They want the dissected biology specimen, intricately cut open and pinned so that every component of wrongdoing can be mathematically examined. That's what they want – it's not to give a bullet in the head. It's the control of wanting to carefully eviscerate; they want to establish the focus, the lens, before they either refocus or cut one into neat meaty bits to lay in a buffet of public dissection in a children's playground.

They want it all.

I glance at the camera in the top-right corner of the over-hang, but in an effort to escape it, I drop my face and let my hair fall across my face a little and hiss, 'Why would a Party man align with the Brotherhood? Think, Winston – it doesn't make sense.'

And I turn my head to see, fixed up under the portico beams, yet another black, shiny lens of yet another camera and know even here – *especially* here – my brother has followed me.

Chapter 51

When I was eighteen, Ephrem had his own substantial house given to him by my father, so when my parents were away, he had little reason to visit Eltringham Hall.

With only servants then to keep watch, it was easy to – and I did – become sloppy about Arthur. My parents frequently went away at the weekends, and I loved it when Arthur and I could be alone. Mr Ryman was also no keeper of us: he had a spinster sister who lived forty miles away, which was perfect because it was close enough for him to feel obligated to visit often and far enough away for him to want to make these visits overnighters. I remember then being confused that Mr Ryman could have such a relationship with a sister that he would choose to leave his very comfortable flat and undertake a difficult journey (we were so remote at Eltringham Hall that if you didn't have a car, you were dependant on public transport which was unreliable at the best of times) to stay with her.

Inevitably, my deep, deep obsession for Arthur made me sloppy. Oh, how I could only think of him! My brain ached with the constant obsessive thoughts of him – if I wasn't with him, and I took every opportunity to be with him, then I dreamed of him. I woke to my first thought being of him and hated myself that there was no other space in my mind except him. It was as if I had been drained like a waterskin and filled only with him. There was no me left. He was an obsession to me, and I was helplessly drawn to him, captivated by his pull. I don't think I could've fought the urge to be in his orbit if I tried.

But I didn't want to try.

Our infatuation was both mutual and decadent. We wanted nothing more than being together – preferably with our clothes off, but we luxuriated even in the mundane together. We could muck out the horses together and be in a state of deep, deep contentment.

Over the summer holidays we had plenty of opportunities for everything we longed for and ran laughing, dodging from the servants. It was easy – the servants had their jobs and were uninterested in me; the house was huge with acres of attics and the grounds stretched for miles. At the sight of a servant, to suddenly duck behind a bush or round the corner of a corridor, holding each other tightly, hands gripped over each other's mouths to hide the escaping laughter, was an indescribable joy.

As Arthur and I fell so deeply in love, the real world retreated, becoming blurred, and the only thing we could see clearly was each other. And when we lost focus on everything else, we made a mistake. Ephrem could have caught us in many compromising situations. but in the end, he caught us at the piano.

We were playing at the Bösendorfer Imperial, me on the

right and Arthur on the left, as was our custom. As a break from playing Bartok's Piano Sonata, which was Arthur's latest obsession (he adored any piece that had been specifically composed for the Imperial. 'She cries for it: these beautiful pieces are her birthright. It's our job to deliver'), we'd been working on a transcript of Tchaikovsky's Romeo and Juliet overture. Arthur had taken the orchestral piece and transposed it for the piano as a gift for me. We were reading Romeo and Juliet at school and I was entranced by it. It felt as if it spoke to me directly. I was Juliet Capulet, torturously in love with someone my parents would never approve of, daring to love, daring to challenge our fate.

Our hands drifted over the keys as we played a favourite refrain, with my hand and his hand acting as a single pianist.

'I love you, Arthur.'

'And yet I love you more, Juliet.' He kissed my cheek as he played. 'O, I am Fortune's fool!'

I paused and ruined the playing. 'You've learnt a line!'

'I can't have you thinking I'm a philistine.'

'It's not your fault, I told you.' Shame at the memory of a previous discussion burned my cheeks. 'I just didn't know that what I learnt at school wasn't the same as what you learnt at school. I didn't know I was receiving a different education to other people.'

I missed a note and he corrected with me. 'It's not your fault, either. You've been tucked up in a feather nest. It's because of who you are.'

'Who I am? What do you mean?'

'Sssh, Juliet, my darling.' He picks up my wrist and

kisses the inside where the skin was thin and blood pulsed close to his lips. I wanted to know what he meant but when I went to ask, he kissed my wrist again, and then again further up. He looked at me as he pushed my sleeve out of the way and I watched him kiss me again, this time in the dip of my inner elbow, then I didn't think about what he meant anymore.

After a while we broke away and continued to play. As much as we had passion for each other, I accepted that Arthur burned to sit at the Imperial. When my parents and his father were at the house, he couldn't get within three hundred metres of it, so as long as he loved to play with me, I still knew better than to try to compete.

We played a little more of Arthur's arrangement but perhaps neither of us were thinking about the music too much more. 'Did you enjoy your school?' I asked, curious. I was due to return soon as the holidays were in their closing days and I felt the dragging weight of knowing how much I would yearn for Arthur. At least I could see him sometimes, glimpsing him from a distance at the school. But a glimpse is all it would be. There, we would not take risks: his father's employment rested on Arthur's own professional conduct and I knew that his concern for his father scaffolded almost his every thought, aside from me.

'It was okay. Different to yours. I went home every day; we never had any music and' – he laughed; I loved his laugh, it was baritone and freer than he somehow ever was – 'and we definitely did *not* learn Shakespeare. The food was the same, though. Spuds and gravy nearly every day.' We played on and I thought the subject was left behind then he added: 'Although at my primary school, we still sang hymns. The teachers locked the door and we had to promise not to tell anyone. Of course we loved that! I like hymns.'

He shut his eyes and had such a look of peace and contentment that I wasn't part of, I felt a dagger's twist of envy. I wanted to know everything that Arthur liked. 'Hymns? What are they?'

He played on even though my hands had fallen to my lap. 'Arthur?'

'You're Inner Party. It's not for you. It's not for us either – it's gone now for everyone. They probably shot the teachers.'

'What do you mean?'

'Hymns are songs sent to God. You're Inner Party so . . .' He looked at me with a full stop held in the stillness of his face. 'Come on, finish the piece. And then we can go and find something else to do.' He winked, but I was not to be put off.

'Who is God?'

Arthur blew through his lips, an extended sigh. 'My father has told me not to get into stuff like this with you.'

'Why not?'

'I can't, Juliet.'

'Why not, Arthur?'

'Because my father asked me not to. He feels it's dangerous and I love my father so . . . so please don't ask me.' He looked at me a little sadly and then I wanted to know what it was that made him feel sad. Was it his father? Was it me asking? Or was it something else I didn't understand?

'I don't like not knowing. That doesn't feel fair.'

He looked a little amused now, warmth back in his burnished conker eyes. 'And fair is what bothers you so much?'

His amusement did not settle me – the opposite. 'Actually, Arthur Ryman, I happen to think that fairness is a very important thing. Not to be trifled with. *Actually.*'

Perhaps I was worried he would do what all the men in my family usually did, but he didn't do anything like pat my head or send me to my room, or the equivalent that he might have done.

Instead, he took my hand and spoke to me levelly. 'We cannot talk of these things, not because I don't want to treat you fairly, but because—' He extended the word as if searching for the answer. 'Because you are Inner Party. And because we're not supposed to talk about these things. I'm very serious about you, Juliet. If I could have married you by now, I would. But do I ever think I will be allowed? My father is a teacher – I'm likely to be recategorized as a prole when he retires as I don't have an Outer Party profession.' He gave a little smile. 'What I do know is that breaking the rules is not going to win me your father's favour. And your father – just like Lord Capulet – does care what you do very much.'

I was flummoxed. Embarrassed. I had never had any friends outside of school and Arthur was the first person I had known who was not Inner Party. His father had been the first person who'd hinted at mysteries not known. But Mr Ryman's musings were always things from the past, hard white sweets and shops that were long gone. And now his son was doing the same – extending my knowledge outside of the careful construct of my childhood – but it felt different. Arthur knew stuff about now. And sweets, well, that was small enough to put in your pocket, but who received songs sung to them? And Arthur knew his music and for him to look like that, they must be special songs in some way.

I did not want to embarrass myself in front of Arthur, but I did not know what a prole was, or hymns or God. The books from the school library had not covered such things. I knew I had huge gaps in my knowledge. I remembered Cook crying in the pantry, her fear, and felt that this was in some way connected to that. Perhaps there's a point in everyone's maturation when they are introduced to unexplored territories and feel shamed by the lack of knowledge, but I was not used to being the one who did not know. In our relationship, aside from music, it was me who gave the gift of knowledge. It was me, enthused by *Romeo and Juliet* at school, who came home and read it to Arthur and inspired him. We'd worked out some time ago that my schooling told me things that were kept from Arthur: Greek classics, French and German language, Latin. All these things that were taught at my exclusive girls' school, as if someone had decided that this was what the daughters of the Inner Party should know.

Now I was eighteen, school had become duller with subjects like French cooking, deportment and etiquette becoming foregrounded. We were destined one day to be Inner Party wives and would need to sit and converse with others and clearly should not appear unknowing.

Resentment bubbled because although Ephrem had long

left school (he was now employed in some official capacity, which meant he wore a uniform and joined Father and his comrades for their long, secret meetings), I know when he had been my age, his secondary education had been centred on philosophy, politics and economics. 'You can't run this country unless you've done your PPE,' he said.

'Father didn't do it.'

Ephrem sniggered. 'Politics was different then. Before.'

I didn't know what he meant about what had been *different* and when exactly was *then* and *before*. I could ask, but if Ephrem thought I wanted to know, he wouldn't tell me. I'd either have to beg for the information or bluff him. I wasn't the type to beg.

'Things aren't so different,' I said with narrowed eyes like there was really meaning behind my ambiguity. 'Things just look different.'

He made an amused *hmmm*. 'Maybe you're right, little sis. Maybe the steel grip is now just hidden in a velvet glove.' He looked at me as if waiting for me to say something else, but I had nothing more to say. 'Anyway,' he added, unable to resist a retort, 'as a leader now, one needs a certain education to know how to hide steel in velvet. You, on the other hand, just need velvet on your dress so you look pretty enough to attract a decent husband.'

When Arthur later told me of his education, how he'd been taught none of the things I learnt, I also found out it was different to my brother's. Arthur's school days consisted of rudimentary mathematics and carpentry and crop rotation, rather than Ephrem's PPE. But it seemed that Arthur still had the advantage over me. Now it was

Arthur hinting at things I did not know. I did not know about God and hymns and proles any more than I knew what economics actually was, and it seemed to me that someone had decided my life based on my gender. It infuriated me, not least because, although I never managed it in my own family, in front of Arthur, I was used to being the sophisticate and I liked it. I was so keen to impress Arthur, to appear worldly and clever. But now I was the one who did not know, and again felt just like the silly girl the world was determined I stay, and it stung because I liked Arthur too much to want to appear silly.

We played on and my thoughts drifted to our most regular of conversations. 'I still want to run away,' I told him, hearing the resolute stubbornness in my own voice.

'And I still don't,' he said lightly. We only made it a few more bars before he sighed and left the keyboard and took my hands. 'Juliet, if we run, they will find us. You don't know the world at all outside this house and your school, so I want you to take me at my word. I promise you they will find us. And when they find us . . . then . . .' He looked down briefly as if he didn't want me to see what he was thinking. But then he looked up, calm and resolute, and said, 'Then I would not be able to offer any reassurances of decency. Your father would be quite right to have me' – he paused again, his mouth working a little as if searching for the right word – 'banished.'

'Just like Romeo.'

He sighed as if he was disappointed in my answer, when I thought I was being clever by observing the textual alliance to our life.

'It's serious,' is what he said.

'Yes, but—'

'There is no but. They will catch us.'

'So, you want to tell my father.'

He let my hands go and turned back to the Imperial. He played a few bars on his own before stopping again. 'At least it's honest. Foolish, but honest. Sometimes, all that's left is what's right.'

I didn't understand then. In truth, I loved the romantic notion of running away, of finding our own little bolthole, a little room somewhere. Practicalities like money, and work and staying unfound didn't really figure in any material way. I pushed him again to follow my dream.

'But we won't survive. It would be glorious and then it would be over. We would be arrested some sunny afternoon and then ... I don't even want to think about what would happen then. Juliet, we have a choice. We either put this behind us and forget it happened before we get caught or we try to turn it into something real. If it's going to be real, it must have your father's agreement. I don't think I could ever regret trying to turn it into something real.'

'I think he will kill you.'

He pressed his forehead briefly against mine. 'I don't think I could ever regret,' he repeated, 'trying to turn it into something real.'

For a moment, there was silence.

The impossibility of our situation was the wall we kept slamming against and it was becoming increasingly painful. Every time we discussed it, it only reinforced how we were trapped. The good sense would've been to end it, but that was the only option neither of us could bear. The pressures were increasing, too – I would leave school this year and my father was likely to end Mr Ryman's tutorship of me. Mr Ryman himself was always rubbing his back and complaining that it was time he retired. With Mr Ryman retired and me no longer in school, Arthur and I would have no opportunity to see each other. I saw a future where I would be strong-armed into a dead marriage and the thought made me feel like putting a plastic bag over my head and screaming into it until it all went away.

Eventually, to make myself feel a little better, I told him that the school was due to put on a production of *Romeo and Juliet*, and I was to try for a part. 'Obviously, we all want to be Juliet,' I burbled, 'but will you come and watch me anyway? You'll be back at school in September.' I stated the fact as if to ward off the nebulous nature of our future. But the subject only reminded me of the impossibility of our situation; the suicide of the star-crossed lovers seemed to foreshadow some awful event in our future, although since we had no priest to help us, simply running still seemed to me the most plausible and positive option.

'My father,' said Arthur, 'says that they are taking me back for this academic year, but this time I'll be on the grounds maintenance team. I think I will like it better being outside, but I don't know if they let grounds main-tenance staff come and watch the plays.'

'All the staff watch, so you will get a ticket even if it's for the ghastly practice where we all fluff our lines and sweat our pancake make-up off under the spotlights. But I don't think I'll be your lovely Juliet – I bet I'll end up as Tybalt because Miss Jenkins doesn't like me.'

'Miss Jenkins does like you, I'm sure, she's just scared of you.'

I stopped playing abruptly. 'No, she's not.'

He looked amused, but not unkind. 'Juliet, they are all scared of you. Don't you know that?'

I did, but chose not to think about it. Although I had noticed, I had no need to think about it – life rolled on with the surety of tanks and my reality was consistent. But now, to hear someone speak of it, felt frightening – no one else had spoken of it before. If my friends had ever perceived some nuance in the way the teachers interacted with me, they never commented. To hear it spoken aloud, as if it were an undeniable truth, felt disturbing. It now felt real – a noticeable reality.

Perhaps he realized he had frightened me with his veracity, because he lifted his hands away from the keyboards again and put his palms against my cheeks. 'You are the loveliest Juliet in the world, and you do not need to get the role because, Juliet, to me you are already the sun.'

And he kissed me then.

I didn't yet know I was pregnant, but when I look back on this memory, I think about the three of us, together, next to our other love, the Imperial. It was, aside from holding Chloe for the first time, the sweetest moment in my life.

When we finally broke apart, we looked up to see Ephrem standing in the doorway.

I don't know how long Ephrem had been standing there,

and I can only assume that Arthur didn't know either, but I never found out because after the longest of pauses, where the sounds of a plane droned overhead and then somewhere, deep in the house, a door banged, Arthur simply put the lid down on the Imperial, so carefully, as if gently laying down a baby for the first time in a crib, and then got up and quietly left the room. He shut the door behind him.

I never saw him again.

Chapter 52

A replicant admits Smith and I into the mansion flat entrance hall; like all replicants, his manner is smooth, unruffled. We're expected. I imagine O'Brien watching the CCTV only moments ago, before giving the command to let us in.

Now we're waiting, as he has disappeared through a door.

I glance at Winston. He looks excited, eyes shining and chest puffed out like a dodo bird. This is his bad idea.

The black and white tiles are echoed inside, this time in marble. A huge chandelier hangs; a painting of my father – no, of Big Brother – rests in a gilt frame. O'Brien lives in a mansion block only for the wealthy. It's clear that us being here isn't right – so although my guilt pervades, I tell myself with a plier grip that Winston needs to own the responsibility of his own decision. Why can't he read the signs that this is dangerous?

How can sitting here in such luxury not twitch and pulse his nerves?

Everything here to me, screams: *get the fuck out*.

I promised myself that I would accept that he's created

his own flightpath, but I lose my grip and murmur through dead lips, 'Winston, stop. This isn't right.' Cupping my mouth with my hands, I add, 'I could leave now. You could just get the book and leave.'

I tried, I tell myself, I tried.

I think of the Sisterhood, the secrets I keep for them. Perhaps Ephrem knew about Smith, perhaps this is only a trap laid for me. Perhaps I gave up Smith and he never knew about him, but I can't regret telling him about Smith. If I didn't give one of them up, then I could never gain Ephrem's trust.

And I need that trust – *we* need that trust or the explosive has no home to go to. It will instead sit and gently decay next to the biscuit tin on a shelf in a forgotten cellar and will ultimately yield only a promise of something. I remind myself that in war, there are difficult decisions to make. I remind myself that no one has forced anyone to do anything that they do not want to do. Winston is here because he wants to be.

'This is *it* – I can feel it.'

Winston reaches out and briefly squeezes my hand. He smiles gently at me, and I see the excitement in his eyes still, but also some new nuance I have missed before. And I understand something that I have missed: he is not unknowing.

I study the bridge of his nose, the redness of his cheeks and realize I haven't really noticed the man for a little while. But seeing him sit here, taking a risk on everything in his life because he's driven by the compulsion to do the right thing, I realize again what I had forgotten: Winston is a comrade in arms. If he's naive, I can see now it's driven by bravery. He's pursued risks, broken rules, dared to be. He's a man driven by dangerous desires and has been committing small acts of defiance before we ever spoke to each other. His desperation has driven him to this point. Perhaps – if he is real and not some trap laid for me – he is no different to the Sisterhood.

We are the same.

Forgive me, Winston, forgive me.

The replicant is back. 'Please follow me. Mr O'Brien will see you now.'

We stand and follow the replicant further down the hall to the first door on the right.

'Please,' he tells us, opening the door for us. 'Do step inside.'

Chapter 53

Inside O'Brien's flat, I feel strangely at home – his furnishings remind me of my father's study. The wallpaper is a rich forest green, and the dark wood panelling is very similar to my father's tastes. There's a large mahogany desk and on it is a large sand timer, also very similar.

Smith looks a little lost, but O'Brien walks to the telescreen and flicks a switch.

'You can turn it off!' he said.

Poor Smith – there's so much he doesn't know.

O'Brien stands waiting; he's tall and a little heavier than I remember. He doesn't comment on my being here – I imagine I'm expected and Ephrem has told him everything. It even smells of Ephrem – the type of cigars which I only associate with him. Madness lurches – perhaps he was just here! Perhaps he's just left!

I can't speak – I'm so sickened by it all, it seems I only have the power to watch and wait. When the pause extends, I realize that O'Brien is waiting for Smith to incriminate himself. I came for the dictionary, I want him to exclaim! I don't know who this woman is – she followed me in!

O'Brien gives Smith a broad grin and then with his thick middle finger, pushes his glasses further back on his nose. He's sweating slightly, I notice. It's warm in here, too warm, but I wonder now if perhaps it was true, and it was Ephrem's cigar I smelt. That he left just as we arrived for our appointment.

I remember how Ephrem used to like to spy on people. Perhaps I was no different, with my priest hole, but I would argue I was. I would spy to learn things – things that as a girl I knew even then that I will never be party to. Ephrem would spy just to know things. He was once beaten because he fitted a camera in the kitchen. Why he wanted to spy on Cook, I would never know, but the camera was found up in the corner, hidden on a shelf above the Aga, and somehow my father knew it was him. Something I learned after, suggested that Ephrem had done something similar before with Bridges. In punishment, he was given a sound beating – enough for me to even feel sorry for him. My father could be a cold disciplinarian and he hated cameras. I shiver, despite the warmth of the room.

'Shall I say it, or will you?' O'Brien says.

'I will say it,' says Winston. 'That thing is really turned off?'

'Yes, everything is turned off. We are alone.'

'We have come here because—' He pauses.

For the dictionary! The dictionary! It is not too late, my mind cries, although of course, it is the evening of our lives already. Winston knows this – he sees the dusk drawing in and I think again that perhaps we are alike. That we simply cannot bear letting the night fall on us without trying something, doing something, even if it is impossibly futile.

'We believe,' Winston continues, 'that there is some kind of conspiracy, some kind of secret organization working against the Party, and that you are involved in it. We want to join you and work for it. We are enemies of the Party. We disbelieve in the principles of Ingsoc. We are thought-criminals. We are also adulterers. I tell you this because we want to put ourselves at your mercy. If you want us to incriminate ourselves in any other way, we are ready.'

He's said it, I think dully, and behind me is the soft sound of the door carefully being opened. It's the replicant and when I see it, I'm pleased. I realize I thought it was my brother.

The replicant is carrying a decanter and glasses, and he brings it into the room.

'Martin is one of us,' said O'Brien impassively. 'Bring the drinks over here, Martin. Put them on the round table. Have we enough chairs? Then we may as well sit down and talk in comfort. Bring a chair for yourself, Martin. This is business. You can stop being a servant for the next ten minutes.'

The replicant sits down, seemingly slipping his servant role as easily as a man removes his coat. Tellingly, it is O'Brien who fills the glasses with wine, and I understand something – this is not any replicant. I don't understand it yet, but as I watch O'Brien serve Martin, I understand that the hierarchy is off. Winston doesn't notice and it occurs to me that O'Brien doesn't even notice his little slip-up either.

Thinking of his mistake, I realize that I've made

my own. From old habits, I've swirled the glass and smelled the wine.

O'Brien looks amused – he knows I've given myself away. 'It is called wine,' he says drily. 'You will have read about it in books, no doubt. Not much of it gets to the Outer Party, I am afraid.'

I loathe this man. I loathe that he caught me in an unconsidered habit; I loathe that he has patronized me in a room where I have no power – and loved the opportunity despite knowing that if I was a man I would be his better – and I loathe that I have to let him. I feel an urge to break him like I could break the glass in my hand. I imagine it briefly, vividly. The image is bloody, messy, visceral.

I am my father's daughter.

He raises his glass in a toast. 'I think it is fitting that we should begin by drinking to his health. To our leader: To Emmanuel Goldstein.'

Wordlessly, we take a sip. Then I watch Winston gulp his wine in one, like a child with fresh milk. 'Then there is such a person as Goldstein?' he asks eagerly.

'Yes, there is such a person, and he is alive. Where, I do not know.'

'And the conspiracy, the organization? It is real? It is not simply an invention of the Thought Police?'

'No, it is real. The Brotherhood, we call it. You will never learn much more about the Brotherhood than that it exists and that you belong to it. I will come back to that presently.'

He looked at his wristwatch. 'It is unwise even for members of the Inner Party to turn off the telescreen for more than half an hour. You ought not to have come here together, and you will have to leave separately. You, comrade' – he nods at me – 'will leave first. We have about twenty minutes at our disposal. You will understand that I must start by asking you certain questions. In general terms, what are you prepared to do?'

'Anything that we are capable of,' said Winston.

As Winston speaks, I feel a punch of irritation. Of course I should leave first, just so Winston is vulnerable and exposed. But if I thought I was only to be excluded from this conversation later, I realize I am wrong because O'Brien actually angles his body away from me and towards Winston. He only looks at Winston, only speaks to Winston. 'You are prepared to give your lives?'

'Yes.'

I expected O'Brien – still – to turn to me to ask me, too. To give my life? But he continues, only asking Winston for both of us.

'You are prepared to commit murder?'

'Yes.'

I cannot believe the way Winston answers without pause.

'To commit acts of sabotage which may cause the death of hundreds of innocent people?'

'Yes.'

No! I feel like shouting. No! We will not let innocent people die. There is no need. That is not the way. I think of Eleanor, her determination not to do anything to hurt even one person. That is the way of the Sisterhood – not a single innocent person should perish. All life is valuable – and none more so than those outside of the Inner Party.

'To betray your country to foreign powers?'

'Yes.'

'You are prepared to cheat, to forge, to blackmail, to corrupt the minds of children, to distribute habit-forming drugs, to encourage prostitution, to disseminate venereal diseases – to do anything which is likely to cause demoralization and weaken the power of the Party?'

'Yes.'

No, no, no, Winston!

'If, for example, it would somehow serve our interests to throw sulphuric acid in a child's face – are you prepared to do that?'

'Yes.'

No! They don't even notice my distress.

'You are prepared to lose your identity and live out the rest of your life as a waiter or a dockworker?'

Obviously if he is prepared to throw acid in a child's face then being a *waiter* is *acceptable*. How can one follow the other? If you are prepared to leave a small person screaming in pain as their face opens raw in fire and burned tissue and sinew, then being a dockworker under a fake name is obviously and clearly effing fine. My bile rises and burns brightly.

How can they even have this conversation? I wish Winston shouted *no* – actions such as hurting children are much worse than the Party's obsession with thought. Everything in this world is hopelessly back to front. O'Brien's odious positioning just jabs my revulsion deeper.

I hate them *both*. They are both disgusting. But I'm

meant to feel this. This is designed to debase him, make me realize what a fool I've been to associate with Smith.

'You are prepared to commit suicide, if and when we order you to do so?'

'Yes.'

Behind Winston and O'Brien, I see a sudden movement. The telescreen, a huge shiny panel, suddenly silently turns on, changing from black to colour. But it isn't showing the usual running news and proclamations – instead, it is showing silent footage of me.

Me.

Me in my father's bedroom. Me holding the pillow over his face. Me killing the great Father of Ingsoc.

O'Brien and Winston continue with their ridiculous question and answer session, oblivious, their backs to the noiseless screen. Only Martin looks at me, his expression placid. Dangerous. He's probably recording my reaction and uploading it to the Party as we speak.

As my world disintegrates, O'Brien keeps his monotonous – almost torturous – investigation going: 'You are prepared, the two of you, to separate and never see one another again?'

Winston starts to move – perhaps he has noticed movement on the telescreen from his oblique position to it, or perhaps the question has merely made him uncomfortable.

'No!' I cry out, desperate to stop him from seeing me so clearly killing my father. It works, as now he looks at me.

At my cry, the telescreen winks shut, returning to a black obelisk, sleeping – not off at all. O'Brien lies.

Winston, oblivious, looks back at O'Brien. He wants

to speak, tries to speak, but struggles, silently. I realize he wants to give me up, wants to be the good child. Wants to say, *yes, I can give up Julia*. But because I've shouted out, he thinks I've asked him not to.

'No,' he says finally.

Don't worry, Smith – they'll just get you to agree to that another time. Poor, sweet fool.

'You did well to tell me,' O'Brien says. 'It is necessary for us to know everything.' He turns himself towards me and adds in a voice with somewhat more expression in it, 'Do you understand that even if he survives, it may be as a different person? We may be obliged to give him a new identity. His face, his movements, the shape of his hands, the colour of his hair – even his voice would be different. And you yourself might have become a different person. Our surgeons can alter people beyond recognition. Sometimes it is necessary. Sometimes we even amputate a limb.'

In other words, pass off someone who isn't Winston, as Winston. They totally misunderstand how I feel about him. If I wasn't so angry I could laugh. He's so inconsequential that as I turn to face O'Brien, my rage coursing, thoughts of Winston fall away and I can only think of what's really important to me. Hiding my face from Winston, I mouth: *I want to see my brother.*

His fleshy face nods. 'Good. Then that is settled.'

From a box on the mahogany table, O'Brien offers me and Winston a cigarette. I take one only because O'Brien would expect a woman to decline. When the box moves to him, Winston's hand pounces – I expect he was a greedy child. He accepts the light and puffs his chest, dodo bird again, inhaling with an audible satisfaction.

'You had better go back to your pantry, Martin.' O'Brien sits. 'I shall switch on in a quarter of an hour. Take a good look at these comrades' faces before you go. You will be seeing them again. I may not.'

Martin pauses briefly, scanning our faces; a replicant scanning information and using it to complete some file somewhere.

O'Brien continues to pace, smoking his cigarette to a fiery point. 'You understand,' he says, 'that you will be fighting in the dark. You will always be in the dark. You will receive orders and you will obey them, without knowing why. Later I shall send you a book from which you will learn the true nature of the society we live in, and the strategy by which we shall destroy it. When you have read the book, you will be full members of the Brotherhood. But between the general aims that we are fighting for and the immediate tasks of the moment, you will never know anything. I tell you that the Brotherhood exists, but I cannot tell you whether it numbers a hundred members, or ten million. From your personal knowledge you will never be able to say that it numbers even as many as a dozen. You will have three or four contacts, who will be renewed from time to time as they disappear. As this was your first contact, it will be preserved. When you receive orders, they will come from me. If we find it necessary to communicate with you, it will be through Martin. When you are finally caught, you will confess. That is unavoidable. But you will have very little to confess, other than your own actions. You will not be able to betray more than a handful of unimportant people. Probably you will not even betray me. By that time, I may be dead, or I shall have become a different person, with a different face.'

Before he even finishes his cigarette, he is reaching for the silver box again. He almost lights one from the other, but my narrow-eyed stare catches him in the coarse act and instead, he grinds out the first in a green onyx ashtray, before lighting the next, afresh.

He continues his diatribe talking about death and disease as if these are friends of his. He paces to and fro over the carpet, his heavy feet softened by wool. With his smoking hand, he pontificates with authority, punching at the air on occasion as if to underline the authenticity of his beliefs. If I didn't know O'Brien, if I didn't know of my brother's involvement, I realize I could have believed it.

But I grind out my cigarette and know that I don't.

Winston looks at O'Brien with eyes shining with deep love. He has waited years for this.

O'Brien continues, 'You will have heard rumours of the existence of the Brotherhood. No doubt you have formed your own picture of it. You have imagined, probably, a huge underworld of conspirators, meeting secretly in cellars, scribbling messages on walls, recognizing one another by codewords or by special movements of the hand. Nothing of the kind exists. The members of the Brotherhood have no way of recognizing one another, and it is impossible for any one member to be aware of the identity of more than a few others. Goldstein himself, if he fell into the hands of the Thought Police, could not give them a complete list of members, or any information that would lead them to a complete list. No such list exists. The Brotherhood cannot be wiped out because it is not an organization in the ordinary sense. Nothing holds it together except an idea which is indestructible. You will never have anything to sustain you, except the idea. You will get no comradeship and no encouragement. When finally you are caught, you will get no help. We never help our members. At most, when it is absolutely necessary that someone should be silenced, we are occasionally able to smuggle a razor blade into a prisoner's cell. You will have to get used to living without results and without hope. You will work for a while, you will be caught, you will confess, and then you will die. Those are the only results that you will ever see. There is no possibility that any perceptible change will happen within our own lifetime. We are the dead.'

What he means is: *You, Winston Smith, are the dead.*

He continues rattling out diatribe before he mercifully checks his watch. 'It is almost time for you to leave, comrade,' he says to me.

I don't say anything, but I do think that Winston should ask then, what is the point of the organization? What is it that they hope to meaningly achieve? It's a typical Party idea – all thinking and knowledge with no action. But it shows the lie – no such organization would exist since the sheer inactivity would mean the risk wasn't worth the outcome.

It makes me think of the Sisterhood and our desires for action, even at the expense of the group. I can't think of them, fearful of thought-reading technology, but I do realize that we are full of heart and hope. I lift my chin against this fear-peddling fakery.

'Wait. The decanter is still half full.' He fills the glasses and raises his own glass by the stem. 'What shall it be this time?' he says, still with the same faint suggestion of irony. 'To the confusion of the Thought Police? To the death of Big Brother? To humanity? To the future?'

'To the past,' Winston says.

'The past is more important,' agrees O'Brien gravely.

You are wrong. You both are. I think of my baby's eyes and know that the future is the most important thing. That is what the Sisterhood fights for.

Drinks finished, I know I am now free to go.

O'Brien takes a small box from the top of a cabinet and hands me a mint, telling me that I shouldn't go out smelling of wine and cigarettes. I don't tell him that any decent member of the Brotherhood wouldn't risk their meeting with wine and cigarettes, but I don't.

I'm just glad to leave and when I do, I don't look back to say goodbye to Winston. And if he notices (' ...*to throw sulphuric acid in a child's face – are you prepared to do that?' 'Yes.'*), I don't care.

Outside in the hall, a side door opens and Martin reappears. I'd expected no one or if someone, Ephrem. But Martin is carrying something and for one terrible, terrible moment, I think it is Chloe's body. Both his arms are stretched out and what looks like her baby body is laid between them, wrapped in the green and yellow patchwork quilt I stitched by hand. I would know it anywhere. I reach for the wall, overcome.

'Julia,' he says smoothly, 'I have been asked to give you this.'

It is Chloe's baby blanket, and as I take it, I see it is bundled around her toy rabbit – the one that was mine and I gave to her to keep her company in her crib.

I take them, press them against my face. For a moment I can only breathe in her scent; the remains somehow, amazingly, still clinging to her things. For a few seconds I can go back, and it seems real. It feels amazing, the closest I have been to my daughter in so, so long. I just want the moment to last, but eventually I cannot sustain the illusion and I am back, standing on the marbled floor, looking at a replicant.

'I have,' says Martin, 'been asked to tell you this.' There is a click to signify the start of a voice memo. 'Juliet,' says my brother's voice from Martin's mouth, 'I rescued these from Father. I know you are worried about what you did to him, but I thought you deserved these so you should know you were justified. Please take them with my love.'

With his love! Oh, the hypocrisy of the Party! As O'Brien breathes hate, his own boss sends me messages of love! I don't care about the games they play, all I care about is that I have Chloe's things.

I turn and almost run from the rat's nest lest they take back what is now most dear to me.

Chapter 54

Later, after I have smoothed and sung and cried and touched and examined every inch of Chloe's blanket and her bunny has been kissed and squeezed and sobbed over and rocked, I am content to let them rest across my face as I lie in bed.

I am star-shaped. Now, this moment, is the closest I've felt to contentment in so long – perhaps since Chloe was killed. I suppose to an outsider they might think that the retrieval of her things would just open the meaty grief wound, but it's not like that. It was never shut. It's always been in me, festering, fussing, never resting. Now, to have her things is a little salve. Sometimes, it was as if I imagined Arthur and Chloe as the gap in years widened between us, as the gap in who I was then and who I am now widened, too. Those days at home in Eltringham Hall, blurred by the soft focus of time.

But now her bunny is back with me, Chloe is back in clear focus.

I stretch my star pose wider, enjoying the stretch through my fingers and shoulders. Now I feel good about giving up Winston – he's clearly not the man I thought he was. Hearing him confirm he's happy to harm children turned off any loyalty I may have had to him. He's yet another man looking to get what he wants from me. Well, this time, it worked both ways. I decide I will stay close to Winston until I am given the signal – they have brought me in just as I asked to be. There will be a further test, I suspect, but I will be ready for it. It occurs to me that for the first time I am a double agent – with Winston as the collateral damage.

Chapter 55

It's finally Hate Week. I'm standing with Cecily in the crowds. Since getting Chloe's things back and clarity on Smith, I feel more in control than I have in a long time. Our lives feature constant risk, but the atmosphere today is contagious. This has been a long time in the planning, and we intend to enjoy it. London's main parade strip is packed tight with people. The mood is charged with expectation: the highlight of the calendar, the only time of celebration, is finally here.

The Sisterhood's excitement is not the same as others, however. It's not the sights of Hate Week we want; instead we're looking forward to planning together. We still have no plan for the bomb, but here we can continue to move our ideas forward. *Always forward in safety.* The masses means that we have reasons to be together and the saturation of people means that we will be able to have full conversations. Thought Police will be everywhere, but the chances of them hearing anything are close to zero because the crowds are chanting. The crowd's chants catch and grow and then ebb until something else replaces them. At the moment, it's: '*We are Strong!*' Over and over again, everyone with a tight fist raised high. We punch on every word. Children on shoulders nearly topple with the vigour of effort, their jeopardy barely noticed because of the united and all-consuming love for the Party.

The CCTV is sophisticated enough to zoom close onto our mouths, and additional drocams fly over us, but compared to normal life, this feels safe.

Most people in the crowd get a good view of the road. We're about five metres in from the front of the crowds on Pall Mall but we'll see the tanks. My favourite is the marching soldiers, but first it'll be the fighter jets.

'When's it starting?' I ask. I have to speak directly into her ear otherwise she won't stand a chance of hearing me. My lips graze the shell of her ear. When we talk privately, we'll start moving through the crowds.

As if in answer, there's a roar and overhead there's a diamond nine of grey fighter jets. They're loud and fast and exhilarating to watch as they fly in formation over us. The crowds go wild. Flags are waved, whipping the air into figures of eight – one so frantically, there's a clunk of pole to scalp, but even when blood beads, it goes untouched as the victim's fingers reach like all the others to the sky.

When the jets' exhaust trails turn crimson, the patterns the jets fly create the illusion that they are slicing into the sky, cutting their own injury. The display goes on for long minutes. Our screams and yells are vivid passion. *We are strong*, we all cry. We can win this war. Just as the jets leave, we are treated to their sonic booms. It sounds like mortar bombs exploding and around me, hysteria breaks out as one woman faints, folding slowly as the pressing hordes buffer her fall. Others are left crying and laughing at the same time.

The skies, now empty, bring a brief lull filled with the crowd's buzz of excitement. We know from the leaflets handed to us that the army parades are next. There's the sound of a thousand feet against tarmac. It's faint but growing stronger. Every head cranes to see and with the visibility less now that the entertainment isn't above us, the jostling turns rough between two men. One punches the other and for a moment I think there's going to be a full-blown fight. Fights are commonplace in Hate Week; everyone loves a bit of personal violence. A fist in the kidneys is the party bag everyone expects to take home. This fight doesn't progress, however; the one who's been hit backs off, his head shaking, mouthing inaudible complaints.

The military march moves into view. The soldiers goose-step with flexed, bulging military muscle and it's beautiful. My mother told me their march step – the *stechschritt* – is ancient and originates from Prussia.

I want to get closer, and pull Cecily with me. I get an elbow to the ribs and someone else stamps on my foot, but we gain another metre. It's an impressive sight: the soldiers dressed in dark green uniforms create an X with their scissored legs and the angle of their rifles. Row after row after row after row march past. *We are strong!* We start up again; it feels exhilarating.

It lasts for seemingly forever – it's unbelievable how many soldiers there are. It's a mass of coordinated control. It's chilling; it's impressive.

Then, when it feels like it can't be topped, a huge flatbed truck rolls past with a vast rocket strapped to its back. It's black and the size of a bus – longer perhaps, sleeker of course, and the sight of the nuclear warhead pitches the crowd into a fresh frenzy. Another three roll by and for a crazy minute, I really, really love Big Brother. The feeling is bright, fireworks in my heart. I can understand how easy it is to fall.

There's a lot more soldiers and the atmosphere is celebratory. And why not – life is dull and grey and hard. But today the sky is blue and after exhausting, endless weeks of preparing, everyone now has the week off. Tomorrow, the Sisterhood is involved in a parade, where we'll march with our banners, our Goldstein head and the big hammer, but today is just a free day. With the march finished, Cecily and I decide to find the others and get food. Most of the time, the nation is balanced on the cusp of starvation; it's not uncommon to see skeletal bodies exposed in summer. But in Hate Week, we are catapulted from famine into feast, and it is only a fool who would not take part.

Chapter 56

*'The best protection any woman can have
is courage.'*
Elizabeth Cady Stanton

Eleanor is back in charge, and it feels good. Not in charge of the Sisterhood, but as she orders children around as the leader of the ASL, it feels good to hear her voice ring out in command. I'd expected her broken after the bombing she witnessed, but it proved to do the opposite. She simply turned up at the next meeting looking more focused. 'I'm back,' she said simply. 'I had a chance to think about the hammer on Goldstein idea, and now I can see how it's the only way. Sometimes one has to get tough.' We know that she is really talking about the bomb. Somehow, even though the hammer is just a chicken wire shape, it's become our code word for the explosive still in Prisha's cellar.

I can't remember being more pleased about anything. Our hands found each other's and we squeezed them tight, smiling so hard, our eyes smiled, too. In the end, I think it was the bombed boy with the dismembered arm who perhaps finally moved her away from the academic's theoretical fight against bad government to the more personal one that I experience because of Chloe. Which is just as Prisha sees it because of her brother, Aarav. It *is* a war on children – every single one, including, perhaps *especially*, those who are indoctrinated in hate.

The girls are standing in uniform listening earnestly to her as she outlines the plan. They infuriate me, but they are simply products of this society. I watch Prisha: she is keeping them in line and the sun catches the dark of her hair so that it shines in the light; we are all shining in the light.

It's sunny again today – endless blue skies – and I'm glad.

We are gathered within sight of Victory Mansions. The parade will move up Pall Mall and culminate in Victory Square. We will parade our giant Goldstein head – which looks in the light absolutely fantastic – and at the Square, we will smash it open. The pillowcase maggots will be released, and the girls are invited to throw the maggots into the crowds. One girl, Jill, is only seven and has just found out that she will not get to keep a maggot. I don't know where she got the idea from – I find the things they get in their heads baffling. No, she is told, they are to be thrown. They are maggots. No one should want a maggot. Jill starts crying, noisy howls of disappointment, and it doesn't stop until Gerta, the jug-eared twelve-year-old, smacks her across the face.

Nobody admonishes her – it's Hate Week. Violence is rife and it's permitted. If someone challenged Gerta, even we would probably receive a kick in the shins. Everyone runs on a little too much rich fuel – there's too much meanness in the mix. It's okay as long as it's aimed at Goldstein, but invariably, there's a couple of murders and many, many fights in Hate Week. All are blamed on the Brotherhood's corruption.

I don't think of the Brotherhood today. I don't think of O'Brien or my brother or our explosive. I need a break from the stewing pain of my life. I'm taking a holiday. I lift my face to the sun and realize this might be the last time I am happy; the end is near, the tangles in my life becoming so deep and tight in their knots, I know they will never be undone. But right now, my face is warm and I don't feel the shadows.

I can tell that Prisha wants to talk to me about business, but I'm not playing ball – I just want to sit on this kerbside and watch everyone else do their thing whilst I feel the peace of the moment. Chloe's things have wrought a change in me; it's as if my grief is bookends – the taking of her was the start of my burning, churning anger, and the restoration of her belongings, the end. I am left with something else, but what that something else is, I'm not sure – I don't yet understand the shape of it. It feels like acceptance. It's been ten years – perhaps this is what happens after a decade. Perhaps not, perhaps it's only respite from my pain, but whatever it is, I need it.

Later, the world will explode; later I will need this moment to return to.

Jill has stopped crying and the girls are now in lines. I'm walking at the back, Cecily on one flank of the troop, Leona on the other, with Eleanor at the front accompanied by the girls chosen to carry our flag. It's black with a scarlet red band to symbolize our red sashes. Two girls have been given drums and they will walk behind the flag bearers. Prisha and Chantelle and Jade will be in the middle and will start with the hammer; if it gets too heavy, it will be traded amongst us. Chantelle and Jade are such toads, they would rather be squashed than give up a symbol of destruction.

Other troops are joining now. This parade is the Virtues. All groups that oppress love and promote Big Brother are gathering in groups. Behind us will march the MCCs, Men Committed to Celibacy, a dull collection of men who dress with brown vests over their boiler suits and pretend to themselves their celibacy is self-elected. They've brought banners, but compared to us, with our giant hammer ready to smash Goldstein, and our endless flags and banners including the FUCKSEX on broomsticks, they are shown to be the dullards they are.

In front of us, we will be following the Starves. Their flags depict a crossed-out gin bottle, and they're avowed not to eat or drink anything that tastes nice. They are the most limp, joyless group of men and women I've ever had the misfortune to meet.

Prisha, and now Cecily, keep trying to catch my eye, but I manage to look anywhere but them. I'm happy. I want to stay in the moment for just a little bit longer.

A representative from the Ministry of Truth comes over

and saves me from any danger of conversation. Using his megaphone, he starts to organize us. We are finally ready to meet the cheers and the boos of the crowds that have formed down Pall Mall and round Victory Square.

A whistle blows and we're off. The crowd is noisy and we all enjoy the march. It takes an hour and it's hard work. The hammer does prove heavy, but we all pitch in to help carry it above our heads. We think we look great in our uniforms, with our whistles, drumming, the flags and banners, and of course, the Goldstein head on a pole. People in the crowd clap and cheer us. We hear shouts of 'fuck sex!' and hisses and boos at our Goldstein as he passes. A man, drunk, rushes at us at some point, trying to take the hammer from us, but the girls are magnificent and kick and punch at him. The two drummers use their drumsticks to beat him. Viola, our sneaky pincher, finished him off by twisting his ear right round and he howls and gives up. Afterwards she pulled her I'm-so-fucking-pleased-with-myself look, and I even managed to tell her well done.

At the end, we gather around a new monument erected of Big Brother sitting on a throne, and in front of it, the girls are finally allowed to group around the hammer and crack it against Goldstein's head.

It doesn't break, so Prisha, Janine and Gerta help rip it apart. The maggots are chucked everywhere and the crowd go wild trying to catch them. Even Jill is happy as she gets a maggot and rips it to pieces with a hearty 'I hate Goldstein!' I finally make eye contact with the rest of the Sisterhood. We grin at each other, happy. It's a great moment – everything has worked out better than we imagined. The Anti Sex League are a hit and I dare to wonder if this might foreshadow that our future plans, laid side-by-side with the parade plans, might be equally successful.

Chapter 57

By the end of Hate Week, our mood has dipped. Ingsoc has announced – by making it seem as if it had always been the case and therefore no change, even though it's a huge change in reality – that Oceania is at war with Eastasia. Not Eurasia, but Eastasia.

Now Eurasia is Oceania's ally, and the perpetual war has moved to us against Eastasia. We are all expected to believe that we have never been at war with Eurasia. Now it's presented that we've always been at war with Eastasia, when only last week, Eastasia were our allies. Badly governing of their own people, yes, poor providers of water and food, yes, but our allies against Eurasia.

We can only speculate as to why they would make such a fundamental change and pass it off as if there has been no change, but it feels as if it's to fuck us up into thoughtcrime. Big Brother just want to confuse everyone. Confusion is a means of control. Lack of certainty causes people to withdraw.

We are no different. Disorientated, Eleanor witnessed the announcement during a Hate Week speech. But she said it wasn't announced, but 'just simply mentioned as if it had always been that Oceania was at war with Eastasia. Everyone just took down their banners. Banners that proclaimed hate for Eurasia. Nothing was said. Can you believe that? The people in the crowds just looked confused for a moment but then just carried on screaming their hate. They didn't seem to care.'

We whisper our discussion now as we head towards the final Hate Week event. Even that fills us with trepidation because it was initially billed as a mass execution of two thousand Eurasian soldiers, followed by a firework display. But if Eurasian soldiers are comrades in arms with Oceania, who will they hang instead?

We journey to Victory Square through the back streets, presumably safer for our conversations. We are supposed to be together – we've signed up for tickets and are now on our way to see the hangings. It's the biggest event, bringing a close to Hate Week. Allegedly so many tickets have been issued, it's expected that the crowds will spill out from Victory Square in all directions. You can apply for front row seats if you've taken part in the Virtues, Military Might or any other of the Ingsoc-approved Hate Week activities. Leona dutifully filled our applications in for us; if you don't apply, one risks Thinkpol kicking in the door. How can you not salivate at the victory of the Party over its enemies?

The unknown looms ahead as we troop there together: Prisha, Leona and me, with Cecily walking behind talking with Eleanor. None of us are in a good mood – we fear what Big Brother has in store for the masses.

'We haven't seen you since the march,' Prisha says to me. 'We thought you were trying to avoid a proper conversation.'

'I've just been busy. I was called back into work because of the war change. All Minitrue workers had to go in. My team had to go through every novel produced that mentions the war with Eurasia and replace it with Eastasia. Allegedly,' I say, my voice thick with hushed sarcasm, 'some bug in the system caused it. I was only excused today because the Junior Anti-Sex Leagues were in the Virtues parade.'

Leona grips my elbow, revealing herself too much. 'We're worried about what you'll do with the bomb. We don't want you to get hurt,' says Leona, sounding upset. 'I've been wanting to get more detonating wire but there hasn't been any to take.'

I grab her hand briefly and let her go. We must continue to take all precautions. But she's fragile today. She hasn't said, but I think she's worried that she'll witness Ruby being executed.

Prisha places a calming hand on Leona. 'Julia will have a plan.' She turned to me with big eyes and mouth unguarded. 'You do, don't you, Julia?'

She looks at me for the longest moment. Her large brown eyes are earnest and full of desperation.

'I have a plan,' I confirm, sounding more confident than I feel.

'Where you won't get hurt?' asks Leona.

'I have an Inner Party contact – a good one. I admit I haven't been given the opportunity yet, but it's a … close contact, so I'm hopeful.'

'Is it that man?' asks Prisha.

'No. In fact, I had to give him up.'

Leona is quick and nervous. 'You don't see him now?' she says, not understanding what I meant. I don't want to tell her the truth.

'Yes, well, no. He wasn't anything to do with Ruby – I'm sure of that.' They are all looking at me and I can't possibly unpick this for them.

'But we were so sure he fitted her description,' she says, clearly devastated.

'Well, if he is guilty of betraying Ruby, he's dealt with – that I can promise.'

Cecily and Eleanor join us. 'He's gone?' asks Cecily.

'Not yet. Nearly, I think.' The waiting is painful, but I feel I owe it to Smith to see it through. Besides, it's like wanting to watch the needle when receiving an injection – if the pain is coming I like to know exactly when.

They are looking at me, wanting more information so I'm forced to add what I didn't want to: 'I had to give him up to my Inner Party contact.' As soon as I say it, I regret it. When they fall silent, I realize I want to offer them something else: 'It was him or the Sisterhood. It was a bargain of trust. I chose to protect the Sisterhood.'

We walk in silence for a while, and I wonder if I'm the only one trying to think of something to say. Eleanor gets there first. 'Incredible, isn't it, the change of enemy,' she says, returning to our earlier conversation. I'm not sure if it's because her memory is poor and she's forgotten we've discussed this, or because she wants to help me by moving the conversation away from my treatment of Smith.

'I was at a night rally when it happened,' Eleanor continued, repeating her point from earlier. 'The crowds were on the verge of savagery – really, the screaming, salivating for violence was really quite disgusting – but then the speaker, you know, that disgusting Party man, Wilfred Nardis—'

'The one who looks like an angry troll?' None of us want to tell her that she has already told us this story. Eleanor's memory is just one more thing to worry about.

'The same, well, he obviously got the message somehow – I don't know, I was near the back and really there must have been three, maybe four, thousand people there – and suddenly someone came on stage, passed him a note and Nardis changed tack mid-speech and said that we were at war with Eastasia. Not Eurasia anymore. All suddenly changed.'

'What was the public reaction?' I ask. Although she has told us, I'm keen to keep the conversation away from the bomb, my plan and my betrayal of Smith.

Eleanor laughs a little; a dry laugh that reminds me of the crackling of crisp leaves. 'The funny thing is that no one questioned it. They just dutifully stamped and ripped the banners that derided Eurasia and carried on. It's almost like they just want war – the enemy doesn't matter.'

We are nearing Victory Square; the closer we get, the more crowds increase in density, iron filings pulled towards the magnet. 'It's unifying,' I said eventually. 'We're all fighting the same thing – except it's nothing.' Even Smith hadn't considered the possibility that the bombs dropped periodically were released by the government as a way of convincing the masses that we were at war. And if he, who hated the government, couldn't see through the Party propaganda, then what hope did the faithful have?

'I wonder what they'll do about the hangings – the Eurasians are no longer war criminals. If they hang them, they'll be hanging allies now,' Cecily says, patiently making the point we have already discussed.

'I thought the same,' Eleanor adds and smiles at me, a glorious, beautiful smile. And I smile back.

I love these women.

Chapter 58

We take our places, just to the right of the stage, third row from the front. The platform has been created specifically for Hate Week, covered in scarlet material with a microphone placed in the centre. To the far side, a noisy brass band plays some overbright pageantry that jangles my nerves. The eighth and last day of Hate Week had been billed as a mass hanging of Eurasian war criminals. But now there is no such thing as a Eurasian war criminal – because now the war is with Eastasia – something had to change. Although we were no longer expecting rows and rows of gallows this morning, we suspected there would be some substitute savagery instead. Something to show the might and menace of Big Brother. The edging unease of anticipation has been sickening, so to see just five shooting posts jutting up like rude fingers from the stage is – almost – a relief.

Not everyone feels the same. As we, the sisters, entered the square, around us we could hear conversations of disappointment that the gallows are missing. After the days of military might – parades, stamping, shouting, burning of effigies, smashing of Goldstein's image, the rallies and speeches, the thunderous flypasts – the masses wanted the catharsis of a tight grip round two thousand throats. This is war and they want to win.

Adding to the gathering swarms are an endless stretch of troop upon troop of Spies. There are possibly a thousand, more even, bussed in for the week, from around the country. They have the centre section stretching all the way back through Victory Square and perhaps beyond. It's then I notice that their flags are flying, not just in the crowd but the Spies' uniform colours are the stage backdrop – blue, grey and red. My unease deepens.

The huge screen at the back of the stage flashes into life. There is a picture of four smiling Spies, two boys and two girls aged between about seven through to twelve, and the words *Our Future!* blazes beneath them. Is this an event for them? This event is to drain the abscess; the people have been building towards this for so long. It wouldn't be safe for the government to gather so many here and build so much venom with no place to vent. But to place children at the heart of Hate Week?

Another image is shown – it's a near aerial shot showing the upturned faces of the more Junior Spies; underneath the caption is: *Their Safety in Your Hands!*

This event *will* be about the Spies. I try not to but exchange a glance with Cecily next to me. How I wish I could reach for her hand.

At the change in image, the Junior Spies, in the midsection directly in front of the stage, create a huge wave of stamping of feet and the hubbub of noise rises higher. They clap along with the drummers in the band. It's a carnival atmosphere. I am in the company of the mad.

Tension is creasing knife points into my shoulders, but my maskface hides the truth.

Over the next half-hour, there are more images of Spies and a montage of videos from troop leaders discussing their work; parents and teachers extolling the benefits of belonging, as well as Spies telling anecdotes of their ways of serving Big Brother. All designed to make them seem cute, vulnerable and perfect. A final picture flashes up of a troop of Spies with the message: *Welcome to the Child Hero Celebration Event today!*

Just as the crowd becomes restless, a short, thin man, with a huge, near-balding skull, with strands that flap when he shouts, takes centre stage. The crowd goes wild, and Eleanor stands and cheers. 'This is Wilfred Nardis – the amazing speaker I told you about. He's amazing, you're going to love him!' she shouts, enthusiastically clapping as he accepts the applause open-handed. We understand her message: this was the man who announced the change of enemy from Eurasia to Eastasia. We follow suit and I punch the air and scream, 'Come on!' I've always been good at being the loudest cheerer.

'Ladies, gentlemen and the dear Spies,' he begins and then launches into a vile spew of Hate. He lists the murders our country has seen in the last twelve months, blaming all on Goldstein. As Nardis speaks, Goldstein's face is projected onto a screen behind, and the crowd screams their Hate. 'Death to Goldstein!' we chant, our bile rolling to a boil in Nardis' every pause, which only lessens to a simmer when he speaks. He starts spouting new dispiriting statistics of crime and subsequent suffering, puncturing each one with a question. 'Is that the land we want to live in?'

Everyone jeers in response.

'These murderers, these stinking, shrivelling rebels who plot against the state – against the happiness of you and I – should we *allow* them to continue without challenge?'

'No!' we all cheer in response. Leona has both fists raised, and she's beating the air as if it's a door that refuses to open. '*No!*'

'Look upon these children in front of you! These beautiful, strong young people whose dedication puts us all to shame!' Nardis extends an arm that seems too long for his body; a hand also out of proportion sweeps gesturing to the children. 'Should Goldstein's whores hurt their delicate futures?'

The Spies go wild. A sea of grey shirts and red neckerchiefs almost blur at the recognition. The brass band starts up again in a celebratory ta-daaa! But it is drowned by the joy of the children as the rest of us howl for their protection.

'Their future is being persecuted by those who want to bring down the being that they adore! Do you know those whores are amongst you now? *This very minute?*'

It's us; it's us. As the crowd howls in horror, I feel with a sudden drilling certainty that we've been tricked. *This* is why we are near the front. Within a second, I imagine us being electro-prodded out of the crowd and tied to the post. We have been tricked. For a fleeting moment, I even wonder if it was Smith who gave me up. But no. It is *I* who am the traitor.

'Traitors of these children; traitors of the state! Who are they *amongst us?*'

The burst of adrenaline, as Nardis echoes my thought, weakens my legs and my bladder simultaneously.

'Is it fair that these children – *good* children, *loyal* children, decent, *law-abiding* children – have to suffer in silence overseen *in their own homes* by traitors of the state?'

It's not us. The relief that it's not me is followed by shame at myself and disgust at what is now suggested to come, all hitting at the same time.

'Can we allow this . . .' Nardis is forced to pause because the roaring of the crowd is so loud, he can't be heard over the amplifiers. But the little troll is not concerned; instead, he smiles, a grimace of twisted hate, and raises both his hands above him in a gesture of encouragement.

He is the mockery of a priest intoning a pseudo service. But of course, there is nothing good in this state-sanctioned religion – the only religion not banned is the worship of Big Brother. Of course, they have to outlaw any faith, any worship of God, anything that detracts from the love they want people to feel for the state would only weaken them. For control, they need control of everything. Only they must be followed. Narcissistic governments are greedy. To achieve loyalty, they must lie and cast fear in equal measures. Around me, the crowd accepts the offering, hands reaching for what is given.

Nardis is patient and finally the crowd dims a little, hungry to hear more. 'Can we allow for Goldstein scum to corrupt innocence in the very homes where children should be nurtured to love Big Brother?'

The crowd roar *nooooo* in answer, but I wonder if they even understand the question.

'Quite right, quite right,' he says and asks the crowd for calm. 'I have a little surprise for you all, you see. There was going to be yet another huge execution of war criminals – did you hear the rumours?'

The crowd start stamping their feet. After a few seconds, there is a rhythm found by matching the drum beat of the band, and it sounds like an army stamping its way over the back of their enemy.

'Well, that was true! We were going to have two thousand Eastasian prisoners – two thousand, can you believe? Ready to be hanged, but you know who got to them, don't you?'

GOLDSTEIN! the crowds roar back.

I want to scream back, *you lie! They were Eurasian prisoners, don't you remember? Can't you remember the facts?* The fury within me is huge enough to almost trick me that I would be heard.

'It's true! He sent in his own traitors, and they set them free! In the night, they broke in, destroyed the cells the prisoners were held in, killed the guards and *desecrated their bodies!*' This last phrase brings Leona to a scream. 'Do you know where those war-prisoner-scum are now? Those vile criminals safely rounded up by us to keep you all safe? Goldstein has freed them, but where – you must ask! – are those rapists, and murderers, and torturers and children-stealers now?'

The crowd wants to know, it yells back, a homogenous force captivated by its captain.

'Well, those murdering scum are amongst you!' Nardis' bony finger jabs the crowd. 'They are standing next to *you* in the crowd right now! Blame Goldstein. They will be hiding under your beds, ready to rape your wives as soon as you are sleeping. Blame Goldstein. They are burgling your house as you stand here, right now! Because someone, someone we know all too well, set them free! We *must* blame Goldstein!'

Around me I see a man punch his neighbour. Another to my left pushes a woman and then is set upon by two other women. The hysteria that the enemy is amongst them riles the crowd more than it can bear. Goldstein's name is strangled on everyone's lips.

'The escaped war criminals do not want you to punish the guilty! They do not want you to see justice! They do not want the law of the land to be served!' Nardis' voice rings out, strangulated to a squeal by his vehemence and the struggling sound system. He punched his hand against his palm. 'Well, I say *enough*! Enough! Do you say *enough*? Do *you*?'

ENOUGH! returns the crowd. The fever is boiling now, and we are ready. I dread what is next.

Bizarrely, a man in a boiler suit carries out a mannequin. Perhaps it is left over from the mannequin raffle, when each lucky winner of a called raffle could axe apart their own wax mannequin wearing a Goldstein mask. This one is wearing the blue overalls of the Party. After the assistant leaves the stage, Nardis addresses the crowds again. 'This is an example of one of Goldstein's whores – they hide in plain sight. They hide amongst us wearing the unform of the Party. Who would ever guess?'

The crowd roars its disapproval.

'But we have a weapon amongst us people! We have Spies! Those who are courageous enough to call out traitors even when they find them within their own home! Amongst their own parents!' The crowds cheer, but Nardis quietens them as he produces a piece of paper. 'On my list I have the best amongst us – the very best! First up is Johnson Jones. Johnson, are you here?'

'Me, Me!' A little boy amongst the crowds waves his arms.

'Come on up, Johnson – you are a lucky boy because you have been picked!'

Johnson is thrust through the crowds to the front and then he climbs up onto the stage. Nardis grins and bends down, pushing the microphone under Johnson's mouth. Johnson is a little blond boy of about seven. 'Tell us, Johnson, what did you report to your troop leader?'

'That my parents are traitors of the state,' says Johnson calmly into the microphone.

'Do you think that you would like them to be destroyed?'

'Yeth.'

'And when would you like to do that?'

'Now?' he asks, looking up with questions in his eyes at Nardis.

Nardis pats him on the head. 'Comrades, this boy is already committed to the principles of Ingsoc and hunting down all thought criminals! Want to practise' – Nardis gestures off stage and a different assistant brings Nardis a machine gun – 'with this?'

The boy yelps his joy and the crowd cheers. After a brief pause where the assistant helps position the gun over Johnson and shows him how to point and shoot, Nardis then directs him towards the wax mannequin. 'If this was one of your traitor parents, what should you do?'

We can't hear Johnson's reply because Nardis has kept the microphone. Nardis turns to the crowd and holds out the microphone to us instead and yells, 'Tell him, folks, what should Johnson do to his traitor parents?'

'Shoot them!' everyone shouts. I can't bear to, even if it means arrest.

Nardis and the assistant stand between the front of the stage and Johnson opens fire. There's a loud *chugger-chugger* of the machine gun and, if the boy wasn't supported by the assistant he would've gone flying back. The wax figure is cut in half and the crowd goes wild. Nardis bends down and says something in the boy's ear and then in answer, Johnson bows and the crowd cheers louder.

'Now,' says Nardis, gesturing for calm, 'I think what this audience really wants to see, Johnson, is you do the same to your thought criminals. Is that what you want to see?' he says, turning back to us. The masses predictably start chanting *yes, yes, yes*.

'And do you, Johnson, want to rid yourself of your so-called parents who as you rightly – courageously – denounced as traitors?'

'Yeth!' shouts the boy with outstretched arms. The

crowd roars its approval. Immediately, two hooded people are walked out onto the stage. Their hands are cuffed behind their back and because of the hoods, they could be anyone, but I fear not. I want them to shout something, a warning to their son, but under the hoods, I expect they are gagged. Perhaps drugged. I want to hold Eleanor's hand as Nardis and the assistant stand behind the boy. Nardis screams: 'Now show your allegiance to Big Brother!' In reply, the boy opens fire.

They react differently from the wax figure, which stayed rigid even when the bullets sliced through its torso. Here, the blood gathers and their legs give way beneath them. They've been tethered to the poles and their bodies slump forward, their heads rolling almost comically, one to the right and the other forward. It's impossible, because of the baggy clothes and hoods, to tell which is which, but it doesn't matter now because it's ended the same for them.

From my angle, I can see that young Johnson is confused – this is not what he expected. His little mouth is an 'O' and he blinks. But he's not allowed to pause – the band starts up and Nardis turns the boy around as the assistants remove the gun from his hands. Nardis holds up one hand in the air as behind them, a team of assistants come and cut free the bodies and, feet first, drag them from the stage.

Johnson doesn't see this and for a moment he doesn't realize because the crowd and band are celebrating him. Eventually, Nardis shows that he is to return to the audience and then, only then, Johnson turns back to check on his parents. I'm close enough to see doubt in his face; his parents are now gone. Was it real? But he hasn't time to question it because his mouth has been plugged with a lollypop, and the stretching hands of the masses reach up for him and gobble him up.

Nardis is reading more names out and this time five children come from different parts of the audience. More assistants arrive with more guns, and it's repeated, this time with ten parents, all hooded, two to a pole.

The bloodshed goes on and on and on. The swing between cruelty and joy sickens me. When one girl bursts into tears at what she's done and is collected by the assistants instead of returned to the crowds, I've never been gladder there's a bomb in my friend's cellar. And I'm the one who's going to use it – and when I do, I vow I'm going to do it for little Johnson Jones and his friends, who shortly will start to comprehend the reality of what they've done.

Chapter 59

Winston is sitting in bed, his back up against the head-board, reading his new obsession. Open in his lap is his copy of the secret book he believes has been written by Goldstein. He was given it, via a bag swap, during a rally at Hate Week. I wasn't going to come because I couldn't bear to see O'Brien continue to paw Winston before the inevitable happens. Cruel enough for me to give him up – crueller perhaps for me to turn my back on him before his destruction.

So I'm here, pretending to sleep next to Smith in the bed in Charrington's room. I'm broken after the horrors of last week. Work has been my entire life as the Minitrue employees tackle extended hours – some even sleeping in the office – to clear up the information. Any record of the war with Eurasia or the alliance with Eastasia, had to be expunged. The work was made harder because no one could even discuss it.

Everyone is flat after Hate Week is over; they don't real-ize they've been tainted by it, that we are all darker into the shadows for what we've seen and done.

Winston continues to read; I keep my eyes shut. Now he feels he's in the Brotherhood, now he has Goldstein's book, he has what he wants. Winston is driven by curiosity – he now needs something new.

I don't want to be here, but I'm injured after yesterday and couldn't face making the decision not to come. It felt easier to turn up as expected. I haven't got the mental space to work out how to do Smith and me differently. Besides, there's value in being in a space with no telescreen.

The downside is that I have to listen to Smith read this book aloud. I think O'Brien probably wrote this book. I hear Winston read: 'At the apex of the pyramid comes Big Brother. Big Brother is infallible and all-powerful. Every success, every achievement, every victory, every scientific discovery, all knowledge, all wisdom, all happiness, all virtue, are held to issue directly from his leadership and inspiration. Nobody has ever seen Big Brother. He is a face on the hoardings, a voice on the telescreen. We may be reasonably sure that he will never die, and there is already considerable uncertainty as to when he was born. Big Brother is the guise in which the Party chooses to exhibit itself to the world. His function is to act as a focusing point for love, fear and reverence, emotions which are more easily felt towards an individual than towards an . . .'

I stop listening. It's not true. Big Brother was just my father. How quickly people forget. People would've known, because he stood on the balcony at Oceania Palace during the processions, waving to the crowds. But this is a managed mass consciousness, supported as Ingsoc are so sharp at managing their records. If someone wanted to check if there was any war with Eurasia, there is no reference of it anywhere.

I drift but keep coming back to Johnson, remembering his glee shifting to confusion every time I shut my eyes. There's no rest for me.

Smith reads: 'Between the two branches of the Party there is a certain amount of interchange, but only so much as will ensure that weaklings are excluded from the Inner Party.' Ephrem loved to call me a 'weakling'; thinking of the boy he was, again I struggle with the contrast of the man he must have become. I think he has added that as childish dig.

Smith continues reading and then I get what seems to be another message:

'A Party member lives from birth to death under the eye of the Thought Police,' says Winston. 'Even when he is alone, he can never be sure that he is alone. Wherever he may be, asleep or awake, working or resting, in his bath or in bed, he can be inspected without warning and without knowing that he is being inspected.'

I'm looking at you, he's telling me.

Always the sneaky spy. How alike we are.

I awake to the sound of the washerwoman singing outside, surprised I've slept. After the horrors of the parent massacres, I hadn't been able to sleep. I was exhausted, but wake now feeling like I've slept for a year, instead of the couple of hours the clock says have passed. I'm starving and leap up offering coffee to Winston, who's also been asleep.

The little camping stove has gone out and is cold to

touch. It's surprising – normally it lasts longer. I give it a shake. 'There's no oil in it.'

'We can get some from Old Charrington,' says Winston.

I resist the urge to make a familiar barb about how he must be scared of women as he avoids me, and instead tell him that it's colder and I'm going to get dressed. I feel uneasy. Something's not right but I can't put my finger on it; being naked and nervous is not a good combination.

Winston has put on his overalls and goes to the window; I join him and lean in against him. The sky is empty and leaves me, for some reason, feeling hopeless. I don't want to feel like this, but standing here, looking at the blank sky and listening to the washerwoman's repetitive singing, jangles my nerves. Winston obviously doesn't feel the same. He says the woman is beautiful and I make a quip to disagree. I don't want to be told there is hope and beauty when I can still see the bullets blossom scarlet against the blue overalls, and Chloe's blanket is cold and desolate like the sky.

He refuses to dim his joy, caused by his acquisition of the book, and continues, 'Do you remember the thrush that sang to us, that first day, at the edge of the wood?'

'He wasn't singing to us,' I reply, hearing my own grump. 'He was singing to please himself. Not even that. He was just singing.' I don't even feel mean, just cross that Smith has allowed himself to be tricked by me. It's my fault but then I remember Ephrem's voice through the pages, telling me that we were always watched. He always knew about us. I never gave Smith up because they already probably knew.

The sky remains bleached fresh and vacant and wrong-looking for a reason I don't understand; I also don't feel better for the realization about my betrayal of Smith.

'We are the dead,' Smith says with amusement.

Hearing him repeat O'Brien's words with amusement disappoints me. Smith now thinks he's in the Brotherhood and one of them. His elation will be short-lived. But the disappointment is for me, too – I came to Smith looking for the Brotherhood and all I have found is empty words, empty of hope. An empty man who would hurt a child with acid if he was told to. It all feels hopeless. I wonder when it will end. I find myself repeating it, feeling instead that it is true. 'We are the dead,' I agree.

'You are the dead,' says a steel voice from behind us.

And I know it is finally over and my first feeling is one of relief. The waiting for this inevitable moment has been endlessly eroding. Painful. I've stayed with Smith much longer than I would have chosen – not least because if I caused his demise, I had to be brave enough to see his end. I owed it. It has dragged, but it's over now.

And that is why I am glad.

Chapter 60

'You are the dead,' repeats the metallic voice.

I don't turn around. I don't want to see but I am gifted with sudden clarity and understanding where the voice is coming from – I know what I missed and what I so nearly saw. 'It's behind the picture,' I whisper to Smith. It seems obvious now – that there has been a telescreen or mic there all along.

It hears me because it repeats my words, confirming the reality. 'It was behind the picture,' it says. 'Remain exactly where you are. Make no movement until you are ordered.'

Smith stares at me with something close to excitement, commingled with fear. Anticipation bristles and fizzes. His whole life he has been asleep. I realize he is now awake. He realizes it, too.

Behind us there is a crash, but we don't turn around even then. We will wait until we are told to. I think the picture has fallen to the floor, but I don't know; it doesn't even matter. I just stare back at Smith, wishing I had a fraction of his excitement. It's because he doesn't know, but for me there is no mystery. There is nothing I don't know – I even knew this on some level. I lied to myself because I needed to, but it's over. This is Ephrem. Of course, he would get to me here. How like him to press his eye to the keyhole.

'Now they can see us,' I say, because I owe it to Smith to hold his metaphorical hand as much as I can.

'Now we can see you,' it says. 'Stand out in the middle of the room. Stand back to back. Clasp your hands behind your heads. Do not touch one another.'

We do that and I realize I'm so cold. We overslept, I see that now. The cold stove, the wrong light to the sky, it's all so obvious. Smith judders behind me and I don't know why he's shaking. I wonder if it's the cold or the fear or the excitement – probably all of it. There was no Brotherhood – there was only this.

I think then that when I blow them up, perhaps it won't be Johnson's confusion I picture – perhaps instead it will be the joy on Winston's face as he cradles the book on his knees.

Oddly I notice the washerwoman's singing – how can she sing when our lives are ending? Then – as if in answer – she stops. There are voices and then a crash and I hear a small cry, perhaps from her.

It's then that I hear the approach of a dozen tramping boots – across the yard bricks, up the stairs and then they're here. The Thinkpol have come for me, just as I always knew that one day, they would.

Chapter 61

'The house is surrounded,' Smith says.

'The house is surrounded,' the voice confirms.

We perhaps have only seconds together before we will be parted. With Smith standing behind me, I wonder if I'll ever see his face again. I don't think so.

I feel my heart bruise. It will not be broken by the loss of Smith – not even near – but I am very sad. I think of what this man means to me – so many things over the course of the last few months. First, he was an opportunity to avenge Ruby or to find a connection to the Brotherhood; then perhaps it seemed almost-love when he reminded me so much of Arthur; next revulsion at his sometimes-callous behaviour – but also lover, confidant, friend, as we drank coffee together next to our little stove. Really, we were partners united by a desire for both real human connection and a desire to leave the truth of our lives. Escapees, together.

Together, we created this little home away from our not-real homes. We created this throwback to the past when two people could come together and just be free of surveillance (so we thought) and the constant telescreen reminder of our lives. Winston, older than me, impulsive, spoilt, curious, brave, rebellious, is gone from me now. We have had our time, for what it was worth. 'I suppose we may as well say goodbye,' I say.

'You may as well say goodbye,' says the voice.

And then I know he is here, because he finally speaks. 'And by the way, while we are on the subject, Here comes a candle to light you to bed, here comes a chopper to chop off your head!'

My grandfather taught us the rhyme, but Ephrem turned it into a prank against me. When we were kids, that was the point that Ephrem would karate-chop me on my neck. I remember my mother catching him doing it and it was the only time I really remember her losing her temper with him. She saw him and slapped him, telling him it was dangerous to hurt anyone's neck (something very much out of character, my mother usually the placid personification of calm), and Ephrem, twelve, cried from shock, until my mother told him to blow his nose lest my father catch him snivelling. Many times after that, he chopped my neck, as if to prove he didn't care what our mother said.

Now Ephrem is here, he could give me away. I desperately don't want Smith to know or misunderstand my betrayal. I have not done it out of any sisterly loyalty to Ephrem – the opposite, I have done it to preserve the Sisterhood and to get closer to the Party so I can find a source for our explosive. But how could I ever tell Smith the truth?

There's a scraping sound and then the top of a ladder smashes in through the window. A man appears at the top rung, and using a baton, he smashes out the rest. As if in answer, there's the sound of boots thumping on the narrow stairs and bursting into the room are more black-uniformed Thought Police, with electrobatons in their hands.

We are surrounded.

One of the men picks up Smith's glass paperweight he bought from Mr Charrington – something he's always loved – and throws it to the ground where it smashes.

I can't see his face as he is back-to-back with me, but the meanness of the action galvanizes me out of good behaviour. Meeting the man's eye directly, I mouth: *bastard*.

In response, with his electrobaton, the man smashes me in my solar plexus. He discharges electricity and this combined with the force means a fire roars through my torso, breath chased instantly from my lungs. Trying not to vomit, I hit the floor and fold around my white-blue pain. Around me, I can see the black boots of the men; no one helps me. Winston does not help me. He does not even look at me.

I remember our conversation, when he said that once they get hold of us, there will be 'nothing' that either of us can do for each other. I tried to convince him that they can't get in our heads if we choose for them not to control us. Our feelings, I told him, can remain if we choose it. He agreed that was possible, but now as I look up at him, his face deadpan, eyes focused dead ahead, skin sallow and lifeless, and I'm desperate for something, not even heroics or pointless bravery, but just some flicker of life to show he cares. But there's nothing. I realize that perhaps he didn't really believe it, but instead agreed with me to please me. He does not even look at me when the men pick me up by my knees and shoulders, and like a corpse, I'm carried from the room.

As I'm carried away, I twist my neck to see his face one last time – but Winston is still turned away from me, already obedient, already compliant.

And I know that we have already been severed.

Chapter 62

The men carry me down the stairs – I don't fight them. I'm dazed from the pain of the electrobaton and disappointment in Winston.

At the bottom of the stairs they put me down in the small shop of curios. I want to lean against a glass case, backed in black velvet with shelves filled with stuff my mother would have liked, but I know that I won't be allowed and neither do I want to show the weakness. Sitting in an old-fashioned buttoned wing chair is my brother, wearing, a little bizarrely, a velvet jacket. In his hand, his fingertips agitate an old-fashioned cane topped with a brass round.

'Hello, Juliet,' he says and gives a curt nod to the uniformed Thought Police, who then leave.

'It's Julia now' – I narrow my eyes – 'and your men electrocuted me.'

'I don't employ them for their sweetness. Besides, you needed to get roughed up a bit. Can't risk Comrade Smith up there,' he says, raising his eyes upward, 'guessing you ratted him out, can we? He'd love to know how easily you gave him up, wouldn't he?'

'What's going to happen to him?'

He got up, and sighs as he smiles. 'Winston and I are old friends.' He runs his fingers through his dark hair. 'Although he might not recognize me.'

The pain has made me dull, and I realize my mistake. '*You* are Mr Charrington.'

He smiles a smile that means nothing.

'You wore a disguise.'

'I did. Do you like my jacket, Juliet? It's a rather dapper look, isn't it? I cultivated it for the part of Charrington and I must confess, I shall be rather sorry to give it up.'

'Were you not being a butcher?'

'Butcher, baker, candlestick maker?' He laughs, always too easily amused by childish rhymes. 'Yes, I still am – but the butcher is not for your benefit; it's for someone else I'm monitoring. But no matter, she is not part of your story. Perhaps Winston will meet her in due course. You know I enjoy creating my little vignettes – it's so diverting and so much more humorous than spreadsheets and strategic plans.'

'You're nuts.'

The smile again – colder, even, this time. 'Not at all. Father spent too much time behind a desk. He lost touch with what his own soldiers thought; what the proles thought. All that standing and waving – he was just making himself a target. Grandfather's error was even worse – he didn't spend enough time with Father, and lost sight of what his own child was thinking. Look where that got him? Believe me, staying in touch not only makes my day a little more interesting, but the people I talk to are honest with me. Understand the people and you understand what controls them.'

He stands up. He looks at me for a long time. Then when I think the moment is going to last forever, I see a flash of the old Ephrem, the angry, petulant boy who just hated losing to me, and suddenly he strikes me hard on my temple with his bronze-tipped cane. '*That*,' he says in a cold, quiet voice, 'was for being my sister and yet still being a disgusting slut. You're an embarrassment.'

The pain is bright and hot. The force knocks my forehead against the glass cabinet and I fall to the floor. My hand flies up and I press it against the bleeding. Instantly, my palm is slicked with blood. Reeling, I turn to the cabinet. The force of my head hitting the glass has cracked it. There's enough of a reflection that I can see a long cut from my temple up to my forehead where he smashed the cane against me. I can feel the blood run down my cheek. I feel sick and dazed and the pain is very, very bad. I re-press my hand against my head hoping to staunch the flow but the blood is now running down my wrist.

I hear him tell his soldiers who stand guard outside the room: 'She's yours now. You know what to do.'

Then as I hear his feet on the stairs going up towards Smith, as the world greys against the edges, my last thought is that, for Smith's sake, I wish my brother wasn't walking away from me.

PART THREE

'I am not free while any woman is unfree, even when her shackles are very different from my own.'
Audre Lorde

Chapter 63

Beeping.

Pine. Not the pine smell of the trees though – more like . . . mouthwash. Floor cleaner.

Beeping. I listen to the rhythmic electronic sound – it's soothing . . . until it's annoying. Very annoying now. Have I left the fridge door open?

I awake into a dream. The room is smooth white and there is shining metal and strong light. Although I am lying down, I realize my back hurts a lot. Then *alarm*! My thighs are in stirrups and separated and I can't move my legs and I'm pulling on them but they are stuck and now I realize my wrists are pinned down either side of my head – just as a new-born sleeps.

Chloe.

I struggle, *help me, help me!* Panic flares. Terror, terror! I want to shout. I try. But something – a mask? – is placed over my mouth and, and, and—

Chapter 64

I'm back lying on my attic room bed, looking at the same wall I have stared at before. This isn't my childhood bedroom – that is downstairs. This room, up in the eaves, is the room I was taken to when I was expecting Chloe. It's under the same roof, but now it's not my father's but my brother's. I'm listless, back-achy from lack of movement (is it? Is *that* the reason?), feeling like I've not done something I should have, feeling like I've not attended a meeting or not kept a promise ... or *something*. A loose thread I've not followed. Really, I don't know why I feel like this – there's nothing to do, nothing to forget.

In fourteen days (the lines on the wall keep tally of my imprisonment), I've done nothing but lie here during the day, then dress each evening to play at my Imperial piano. I come down, am introduced to the drawing room full of blank-faced men in dinner jackets who already know exactly who I am and then play what music has been left out for me. It comes back to me, these pieces, washes over me, takes me back. I thought – swore even – that I would never play it after Arthur left that day, carefully shutting the door behind him, but now I have no choice. I don't speak to anyone; I finish, I stand, they applaud, I leave.

I think they're drugging me. I like to think that playing the Imperial for Ephrem's Inner Party guests might provoke more of a reaction in me than sluggish agreement. I feel I don't even care. I just don't anymore.

It's a relief.

It's restful here, amongst the ghosts; together we drift. I call this drifting twilight – it can last a long time. When I drift, they're so close, I feel my eyelids press and yet still caress them with invisible lips, invisible fingertips. We lie in silence here, together. It's not just the empty air that gives rest – their silence holds no blame. Arthur lies in front of me, our child between us. With my eyes shut, we can be together.

Sometimes, I'm more awake. Then, Arthur is less clear. Hidden behind sea fog, ebbing away; I stretch for the outgoing tide. His words seem just memory and each time I reach him, I can only see a lesser version of what was there before. Like a poor copy of a previous poor copy, he retreats further from my grasp. I can spend hours staring and thinking and staring and thinking, longing for the better being of our twilight.

When I'm more awake, I make the effort to turn from the wall, to stare at the space where her crib lay, and my hand outreaches, fingers unfurling like questions into the empty air.

Sometimes, I think of Smith and wonder if he is alive; he looked for adventure and found it. I feel sorry we couldn't find the Brotherhood; I should have loved to have done that together. Winston, I hope you are safe. I suspect you are not. I'm sorry.

I think of the Sisterhood, how they must worry and fret about my absence. The lines on my wall tell me that I have missed two meetings – or is it three? – and my absent chair at Prisha's grandmother's walnut table will terrify them.

There's a knock at the door and it opens.

I can't see who it is because I'm looking at the place where the crib was and I don't care enough to drag my eyes up, even when they start to speak.

'Comrade Supreme Commander Berkshire has asked you to visit him in his office now.'

They come in then and someone pulls me out of my bed; they make me stand.

Pull yourself together, Juliet! says my mother, or perhaps it's Eleanor or perhaps it's Cook. Whoever's voice it is, it's steel. And I stand straighter for them, stand tall, because they can see me and some part of me knows I need to do better.

'So! Juliet – can we dispense with the Julia nonsense now? – here we are again, after all these years, back in the house together.' Ephrem is sitting in Father's chair, behind Father's desk, with the same steepled fingers Father favoured. He looks like Father now, I realize, almost as if he has metamorphosed into him without me noticing. I swear, now Ephrem is older, moustached and a little heavier, I could look from him to Father and then back again, and almost not be able to tell which is which. Perhaps it makes no difference.

'How have you enjoyed your rest?'

I don't say anything.

'You've been doing a wonderful job of entertaining some very important men. Having you play has really enlivened our evening meetings. I've been very pleased at their comments – Juliet, I'm talking to you.'

I drag my gaze away from the space above his left shoulder.

'I want to thank you for your beautiful recitals. I want you to keep going. Since Grandfather's time, fewer and fewer people are playing instruments – and because of Father's insistence that you keep up your lessons, you now have something very rare.'

My focus is wide, fuzzy and unspecific. His words compete with a distant humming.

He snorts, irritated, picks up a pen, writes something on something and then picks up an old-fashioned desk phone and a man comes in and takes away the note Ephrem passes to him.

'I've just made a request to adjust your medication. Perhaps we've been ... too focused on your compliance over the last few months.' He pauses. 'You're not even listening to me, are you? Juliet?'

Months? It's been fourteen days. Have I been confused? I feel confused. Heavy, foggy. I want to go back to bed. I want to find the space where my twilight world is. Chloe and—

There's a sudden pain in my arm. My head, heavy on the spine, lifts and slides round as if on ball bearings; I blink to focus on my brother who stands with a fountain pen in front of me. He has just stabbed me with it.

I look at the blue ink puncture wound as it allows a scarlet drop to ease into existence. 'That hurt.'

'Good.' He repeats it again to himself as he sits down. 'You've had a procedure, and for a moment then, I thought that the ... Forget that. I need you for more than piano playing, Juliet.' He takes my silence as my invitation. 'I need to plan my succession. We Berkshires have had a proud lineage and ...'

Ephrem's voice has been a telescreen churning words out in the background, but perhaps whatever they've given me is starting to fade, or perhaps his words are different, or perhaps because Mother? Eleanor? Cook? is standing in the corner looking cross with me (not really! I'm losing my mind!). *You need to focus, Juliet*, she tells me sharply. It works. Like a slap in the face from my mother or my head dunked in a bucket of water, like Cook did once when I was hysterical about something and she really wanted to sober me before my mother found out, my mind is focused.

It occurs that perhaps my numbed mind is self-elected – but why would I do that? This feels like a loose thread on a jumper I should follow but I can't see where it goes and Ephrem is talking again and so I make an effort to meet his gaze.

I cannot. It's easier to drop my stare to his desk. On it is a curious thing – some sort of calendar. It has two glass domes set onto a wooden base. One date is today – one is set in the future.

Ephrem sees me looking at it. 'This was Grandfather's and then it passed to Father. And like everything that was theirs, now it is mine.'

I blink, staring at it. 'I've never seen it before.' I'm tired and I want to go back to my room, but Ephrem obviously wants to talk to me, and I struggle to think of what to talk about other than the calendar. 'Why does it have two dates?'

'To show the truth and the truthlie.'

My eyelids are heavy. I shift myself in the chair in an effort to stay awake and then I see Ephrem staring at me, like one does when one discovers unexpected mould. I've forgotten what we are talking about . . . then I notice the calendar again. 'What will happen on that date in the future?'

'Juliet?'

'What's the significance of the date in the future?'

He points to it. It says 4 February 2084. 'That's now. Today.'

I blink, so very confused about everything. *How long have I been here?* is my first thought, then I realize that's ridiculous. 'I'm . . .'

'Confused? You've spent too long with the plebs and proles. You knew the truth once, I think.'

I blink, my eyelids wanting to drop again. I want to sleep but I also want to understand. 'You've changed the date.' I point at 4 February 1985. 'That's not now. But people think it is. Why lie?'

'Because confused people are easier to manipulate. The bombs didn't even start dropping until 2032. Then there was the Darkness that followed. When old systems tried to re-establish, Grandfather started the revolution. Poor Juliet, I suppose he didn't even bother telling a girl about that?'

I shook my head, wordless.

'Strange, you and I – we live in different worlds. So close and yet so distant in our knowledge.' Ephrem looks pleased. 'Grandfather reset time.'

Grandfather reset time. Even that statement makes me want to sleep for a hundred years. 'How did he do that?' My words are a blur and I'm surprised they're mine.

'He told me it was easy once they had control of the information systems. It's just a mop-up job afterwards. Deleting records, replacing them. Hacking broadcasters; hijacking key IT channels; book burning; controlling phone providers; taking charge of the media, the influences, shutting down social channels that wouldn't comply. Once they seized the water systems and the Big Pharma, it was easy to control the populace.

'Really, Juliet, the people wanted to be controlled. After the wars, the chem weapons, the viruses, the economic collapse, the people were conflict-dozed and battle-weary. There was space for a new world order. When wars leave people fatigued, hungry, homeless, frightened, they'll accept any real sign of leadership. And don't be mistaken: the tougher, the uglier, the dirtier the leader, is just what they want – because it gives them hope that that person will have the iron fist needed to drive them forward. When people have suffered and suffered and suffered, they're less fussy about the things they should be fussy about.'

Ephrem's words roll round my skull like spiked metal balls. It hurts – I want him to stop.

'After Grandfather had taken control, the first thing he did was kill his enemies. He slaughtered them all and then slaughtered everyone they were associated with. He slaughtered their wives, their children, their comrades, even the people who cleaned their houses and their children's schoolteachers. Then he called on others to come forward and they did, and he purged them, too. After it was over, he replaced every truth with a truthlie. They were terrified and accepted everything he told them. The changed time; the war—'

'The war is a lie?'

Ephrem laughs, his teeth yellow. 'Sister, no more. You've either been listening or you haven't.'

'What about Big Brother? Why that?'

'That came later. Grandfather put the infrastructure in and then Father's paranoia to keep control saw the advances in CCTV, digital tagging and monitoring, finessed by the telescreens. Once the monitoring was in place, total control was achieved. No one goes anywhere without us knowing. When Winston Smith went prancing off to the woods, we tracked him. I knew where he was going – after you'd given him that note, of course I knew. Then I sent in my little friend and you smiled right into the camera towards me.'

A better Juliet than me would say something clever or witty, but I am no longer that woman. I'm not Julia either. I'm whatever came after that. 'What do you mean?' is the extent of what I manage.

'You and Smith admired the latest in animatronics. The thrush you stood and watched. Oh, how easy it was to capture your attention! It sung to you and you both smiled into the camera. It was too perfect. I'm amazed you didn't understand it was singing for you just so I could capture your moment. Appalling naivety.'

I remember the bird's black onyx eye and remember my suspicions – perhaps Smith had them, too. I think I even remember thinking that Ephrem had known about Smith before I betrayed him, but perhaps not. It doesn't matter, it was too late. They already knew, just like we thought they did. At least it means I didn't give him up. I didn't give up Smith because *they already knew*.

I shut my eyes against the noise of knowledge. I do not want to know anything else. This is all too much. Mother?Eleanor?Cook says: *Juliet, wake up!*

I am being yanked up out of the chair. Ephrem is still seated and next to me are two uniformed soldiers. A man I've seen before is drawing up something in a syringe and Ephrem is yelling at him: 'This is your doing. Of course nothing is going to work when she is such a mess!' He tells them to sort me out and then there's another jab in my arm and I'm settled back into place. I blink, the men are gone and I draw air into my lungs like there's no end to it. I'm awake.

'Better?'

'Yes,' I say, and I realize I am.

'Shall I go on?'

'Yes,' I say because that's what I'm meant to say.

Ephrem looks at me as if he wants me to beg him to continue. In a way I do. I will never learn the truth about Oceania if I don't hear it from him. I don't have the appalling naivety that he accuses me of to think that he only tells me the truth, but he got me out of my twilight to come here and sit in this chair and listen to him – and I must try.

He's been talking about something, and I pick up midway through: ' …We have given the people something better – something to hate. Hate is so much more unifying than love. With Goldstein, we have created a common enemy—'

'Goldstein isn't real?'

'Maybe he was once,' Ephrem equivocates. 'Then Hate Week was introduced and the telescreens were rolled out. Hate has unified the people better than love ever could.'

'No. I don't believe it. Love brings people together.'

'Rolling around on some dirty bed with some dirty man? What do you know about love?' Opprobrium tightens his face with disgust.

Every syllable is an acid-dipped arrow. *My cheeks will not burn my cheeks will not burn my cheeks* – Ephrem saw the whole thing. Dark images now flash in my head – things he had seen that I wouldn't want anyone to see. Private things. Shame will not violate me, though. No, it will not – not this man. He will not cow me after what he has done. 'You watch everything all the time – you were always the same, spying on even those in this house. I expect you've rigged up this house now like Father would never allow.'

Ephrem shakes his head. 'Wrong. I wouldn't trust it not to be hacked. I have one trusted, latest tech drocam and it is all that I need.'

I change the subject. 'How is Marguerite?'

Ephrem wrinkles his nose in a sniffy, irritated expression. 'My wife is defective. This is what I've been trying to explain to you.'

I am surprised – I didn't know we had been discussing this at all. Although the injection has woken me up, my mind is still in a fog. I sit straighter, breathe deeply and give myself a little pinch on the arm. The last thing I need is Ephrem deciding that it is me who is mentally defective and carting me off in the back of a van to a corrective hospital. Possibly, I must be careful how I establish how long I've been here – perhaps a direct question would give me away. 'I'm sorry to hear that.' I steel myself for the lie. 'I always enjoyed Marguerite's company.'

'Her company is just fine, but that's not the issue – the issue is, she's like so many women in the Inner Party. It turns out that you're a rare jewel, sister.'

'At trout fishing,' I say, for reasons I don't understand.

Ephrem hits the desk, his fist slamming, and he swears at me. I don't want to be strapped to a trolley (again? Has this happened?) and I'm not so foggy that I don't realize that I'm in real danger of that. He's talking again. I don't know what he's talking about, but the fog continues to clear and I'm trying hard to understand. He's looking at me as if expecting me to speak. I must try to seem sensible. 'What is it that's defective – if you don't mind the polite family enquiry?'

'Shall we start again?' He doesn't wait for me to comment but talks with the slow emphasis of one who speaks to a stupid child. 'Marguerite is sterile. I'm sterile. Many Party people are. You are not. I have one child but I want more. Grandfather, who started the revolution, Father, and now myself, must be followed. I want several boys because if others perceive a lack of strong succession, they will try to seize power. Someone always seeks to fill a vacuum. You are helping me with my succession plans. Are you following me?'

I had not forgotten Marguerite was pregnant at the same time as me but they did not live at Eltringham Hall then, and within months I was expelled to Manor Towers, ensconced in my job at the Ministry of Truth and I never saw my family again. My grief for my own lost child meant I never thought of my brother's family – I could only think of my own lost one. 'I follow you.'

'Chloe is now ten. Would you like to see her on the screen?'

Chapter 65

'Chloe?' I manage, my face on fire – all of me suddenly engulfed, consumed in raging, hungry fire. I'm awake – finally, I'm awake.

My brother opens a desk drawer and brings out a model of bluebottle fly. He places it on the desk. 'This is the only camera I need in this house.' He places his fingertip against the back of it and says: 'Activate.' It flicks into life and starts crawling around on the desk. The action also turns on what looks like a telescreen, but isn't, because it's been a silent ebony obelisk this entire time. Now the screen shows this office from the point of view of the fly.

'FlyCam seek Chloe,' he says to the fly before he gets up to open the window. 'This is the only downside. My scientists are developing a version that can collapse and crawl through tiny gaps, but we're not there yet.' The fly takes off; the screen is a blur of action until it shows a ten-year-old girl, dark, swinging, shiny hair cut to the shoulder, with the most beautiful brown conker eyes I haven't seen since I looked into Arthur's. But this girl can't be mine – my daughter had blue eyes. I must have said this aloud because

Ephrem laughs. 'You really don't know anything, do you, sis? Babies' eyes sometimes change colour from blue after they're born.'

'Is Chloe—?' ... *my Chloe?* I haven't the courage to finish the question. I can think the words, but can't say them. But now it's not from fog – it's from fear. Fear from the answer.

Ephrem's eyes narrow to piggy disdain. 'You're really not listening to me *still*. I'm sterile, Juliet. Marguerite is sterile. Most non-proles are. Our top scientists labour day and night to find out why infertility is exponentially increasing. Currently sixty-eight per cent of the Party population is infertile. Furthermore, we can't yet create a productive, reliable utebubble. Frustratingly, proles seem largely unaffected, so we live in this curious dichotomy of giving them contraceptives to control their numbers whilst Party members' ability to procreate deteriorates.' His fingers drummed the mahogany desk briefly. 'It's a battle between controlling who falls in love, and yet making sure the right people have children. IVF is highly successful without the mental contamination that sexual desire seems to provoke. So, it's not a national disaster yet – but for me, right now, it is. What's worse is, I can't let my generals know the situation, or else they'll move against me.'

Chloe. I feel everything, the press of the chair against my back, my bottom, my legs. My feet in their socks. My palms resting against the smooth wood of my chair's armrest. I breathe, inhale – exhale. I can live but I cannot comment, cannot move, cannot speak. *Chloe.* I watch the screen and at Ephrem's command, the camera zooms out to reveal she is in the garden on a rug. She is just metres from me. I know our garden – she is just outside the drawing room. I was in there last night and she is metres from where I was. So close to me now. She is *alive*.

I want to get up and run to her, but I will be stopped before I can reach her. Then I will be thwarted. But to not try to run to her means I have to struggle against my every sinew, every tissue, every muscle. I have never been more awake and focused.

Chloe. She is reading; I can see enough from the cover that it's not some Minitrue ephemeral crap, but instead that it's a real book. I wish I could see which one it is, I would dearly like to know what she is reading. I'm reminded of how differently the Inner Party live to the rest of Airstrip One. The privileges they have of access to banned material. I look at my daughter and am glad she is alive, am glad that she has access to the same books that I had. How fortunate I was and never appreciated it.

I did try to tell you, MotherEleanorCook says from her corner, but my eyes do not move away from the screen.

My eyes are hungry. They are ravenous, starving, insatiable.

Later I will rage, later I will scream and cry, later I will kill Ephrem for what he has done to me, to her, but at this moment I just want to sit in this seat and look at my daughter on the lawn, reading in the sun and download every millisecond of that into my mind.

We will never be together, I know that. There are mountains and seas between us, and although I will fight and explode everything to be with her, I know I will not succeed. This is not a world of happy-ever-after. This is a world of lies, hate and tears.

But these are concerns for the future. Right now, I have this moment where I can drink in the vision of watching my beautiful, beautiful daughter read a book and this will nourish me later; it will sustain me in the fight and through what must come afterwards.

The camera widens its focus and now I can see Marguerite sitting on the terrace. Time has been harsh. Her red hair is now completely white and she is thin. She is not reading, she is not watching Chloe, she just focuses into the middle distance. Her whole demeanour is one I recognize from my bathroom mirror – she has been drugged. I am certain of this; clarity is now mine. My adrenaline, and whatever I was last shot with, has cleaned out any sedative in my own blood. I have never been more sober now than I am in this moment.

'*You* took her from me.' I did not know I was going to speak until I did. '*Not* Father.'

'It was not Father,' agrees Ephrem. He gives a voice command, and the black, shiny obelisk is returned.

I want to beg him to return it to Chloe – but I don't want to beg for anything from this man. This puppeteer of my suffering – so much suffering to lose my child, to believe she was dead and now to see her, mothered by another woman I never even liked, whilst I was left without, never knowing. I have never felt such suffering as I do in this moment. Joy, too – that she is alive and well. Joy that she is growing up in the same home in which I grew up, reading perhaps the same books that I did, perhaps even attending the same school I attended, but this joy is really on pause.

'And Mother, too?'

'Her idea, actually. Marguerite had been pregnant many times and each time it ended in early miscarriage. Tests revealed she wouldn't take a child to full-term. Then you get pregnant by the piano teacher's son and ha! It seemed so fortuitous! Mother was right – Chloe was the child we should have. You couldn't have her, and it was better that she was kept in the family.'

'Better for Mother.'

'Much better for her; much better for me.'

'And Father . . .?'

'Father didn't even know. He was away on operations for most of your pregnancy – probably on purpose because he was so disgusted with you. When he came back, Mother told him you'd miscarried at eight months and she'd sent you away to recuperate. Do you remember Mother moving your bedroom to the attic? That was when Father was due back. He was in the house and you were ensconced in the eaves, up out of the way. Then you attacked Mother, and although Father knew nothing of the details, he was back by then and that was why you had to go to Manor Towers – to save you all from each other.'

'And Mother now?'

'Mother is dead. She died last year, Juliet. Pneumonia. She was a fine mother, wife and sister of the Party. You would have enjoyed her funeral. She requested Beethoven's Moonlight Sonata. A curious choice, don't you think, given how Father felt about Beethoven?'

I concentrated on my breathing and know that although I have to take this news in now, I must deal with it after. I am now only focused on the truth of Chloe. Mother can wait. *I can wait*, MotherEleanorCook reassures me. 'So when I killed Father ... I didn't have to. He had not taken my daughter.'

Ephrem laughs. 'No, he did not take your daughter. I set you up, Juliet.'

I feel sick. So sick. I remember the pillow in my hand – the pillow he passed me – how I held it over Father's face. I was so angry and now ... and now I understand that Ephrem created my anger and then weaponized it. He suggested Father had killed Chloe – how cleverly he laid the trap. Vomit rises but I swallow it down. I will not let him see what he has done to me. I envy Smith suddenly. He's probably locked in the Ministry of Love, probably beaten and tortured. I envy him the simplicity of damaged tissue and fried nerves. Simple pain. Simple fear.

Not the loss of a mother.

Not this: to find out my own brother stole my child; that my mother helped him; that she is dead and that my daughter is only metres from me, and I can't reach her ... I would gladly take the beatings rather than endure *this*.

And that's not all, MotherEleanorCook whispers. I ignore them – if there is something else, it can't be worse than what I've already endured.

'The camera recording you showed at O'Brien's ...?' I can hear my revulsion, mixed with the burning of bile and cannot manage a full sentence.

'I wanted a fall guy if someone accused me of killing

Father. I recorded you doing it; you were my potential fall guy. No one did, and of course many years have now passed, but at the time, I wanted the reassurance of having someone else to blame if it came to it. It's a precarious time, when power is transferred from one commander to another, and Father had many loyal comrades. All went within the first weeks, of course.' He smiles a snake's grin.

'You killed Father, somehow . . .? You made me feel like I did, but it was you?'

Ephrem laughs again. I see the spoilt selfish boy he always was. Sitting here, in my father's study, always so keen to tell me how clever he was, to show off any accomplishment he made. He was always in competition with me and I understand that hasn't changed. He always wanted what I had and, it seems, he has never stopped wanting everything from everyone.

'Father was already dead when you came to the house – well, his heart was beating but it was the end. I had given him a new radioactive substance we'd developed – Lorothanium – and it shut his system down within hours. No one could have saved him. He was cooking from radiation when you saw him.'

'Did Mother . . .?' The fire in my brain stops me from finishing my own sentence.

'Of course not. She believed he had pneumonia, and after you left, she thought that was what killed him. If the doctors had any doubts, they did not express them. Luckily for them.

'I took charge within minutes and that is how it is

today. Father remains the face of Big Brother and I remain the reality.'

I can only be silent because I am unable to articulate the emotions I feel. I think of Mother dead, and don't believe that she died from pneumonia – too convenient. *You're right, Juliet, but you're still not paying attention. You think you are, but you are not,* MotherEleanorCook warns me.

I think of her idea of giving my daughter to her son and how that readjusted my paradigm on my family life growing up and what happened after. There is already some relief that I did not kill Father, that he was doomed already. Perhaps all I did was save him from a more painful death.

I know Ephrem requires me to say something, but I need to process this. Clearly, this will take time and at the moment all I can think of is that my daughter is alive and so close. Ephrem will grow tired of me if this conversation dries up, but I have nothing. Then I seize upon something. 'Winston? What happened to him?'

'We were always on to him.'

He doesn't want me to have any ownership in giving him up – as if I would want it. 'Is he alive? Is he in the Ministry of Love?'

'He has been there. He is no longer there.' He pauses briefly, but then adds, 'SysCam, show Comrade Winston Smith 574933.' The screen turns on and after a brief message – *searching system* – the screen switches to a room with many tables. A café.

At first, I think the system has made a mistake. There's a woman wearing a pinny serving, but only one customer, an old man who sits alone in a corner. The camera zooms in and the haggard face dips towards an empty glass. I can't stop my gasp.

Ephrem looks amused. 'Surprised to see your old *friend*?'

I ignore the intentional goad of his emphasis, and instead study Winston's face. He's cut off briefly because the woman serves him a gin. The camera pans out further and I can see trees through the window. I know this café – it sits on the periphery of the park. When the woman moves, the dusty lines on his face are not clear but his demeanour is still that of a man much, much older than he is. He blinks and looks up and appears to listen – perhaps to the telescreen. He nods to himself, as if agreeing with someone. Winston. Whatever they did, they truly got you.

'What did you do to him?'

'Less than you did to your own father.'

Ephrem watches me watching Winston, but eventually turns it off. He picks up his fountain pen and I watch him unscrew the lid and think: he's going to stab me again. It occurs to me that our family is very fucked up – but perhaps that's the reality for dictators. 'Did Father really kill Grandfather?' Suddenly I want to know and there's no one else who can tell me. My life is closing down, I still feel it, and I think I should like to know before I die.

Ephrem looks uninterested. 'I think he did. You must have been eight when he disappeared – I was nearly thirteen. I remember there being a brief fuss about it and Mother crying. Then we moved here and it stopped being talked about.' He gives that snake grin again. 'I probably shouldn't want a boy, should I? All this patricide running in our family.'

Don't worry, Ephrem, it'll be me that kills you. 'You said you were sterile.'

He huffs. 'I'm going to have to repeat myself. Promise you're more focused?' He checks his watch. 'Because I've got a thing in five minutes.'

I tell him I'm fine and to repeat himself.

He checks his watch again. 'I'll be brief. I need a male successor. There's been rumblings amongst my generals that I don't have a successor. A girl is obviously not enough. But any juice in the tank is now gone and I'm completely sterile. Marguerite's defective. I need DNA and a womb. You are the nearest to my DNA and you have a womb. You are going to have my baby – a boy – and then, next year, you've got to have another boy.'

All at once, I remember the white and metal room and the feeling of being suffocated. *I told you there was something worse,* MotherEleanorCook says, but I struggle to hear her sympathy over my screaming.

Chapter 66

Ephrem has slapped me hard across one cheek and now slaps me again.

I think you should stop screaming, MotherEleanorCook advises. *It might not be as bad as you think*. She pauses, her mouth in a tight line. *But it might be worse*.

But I do stop screaming. This woman's advice (or these *women* plural? I am losing my grip on reality ... or the drugs are very effective) has always been helpful when taken.

Ephrem sits back down at my silence. There must be guards outside the room, but I'm chilled that they know not to rush in. I think of Marguerite's blank face and want to rescue her.

'I actually thought you'd be pleased to give Chloe a sibling. Think of the fun we had as kids – that could be hers, too.'

I laugh at our different perspectives and then stop abruptly at Ephrem's irritated sigh.

'I need you, Juliet, to do your bit. It's not working as

instantly as I planned. You've had two rounds of treatment and you're not pregnant.'

The remains of the contraceptive injection, I think. It will be diluting each month – perhaps next month it'll stop its protection.

Ephrem gets up out of his chair and takes his military hat from the coat rack. He puts it on, looks in an oak-framed mirror – the same one that my father used for the same purpose and talks to me from its reflection, just as my father did. 'You must have another treatment. I want that son. In the meantime, you will make yourself useful by playing for my guests.'

'Who, what . . . you said you are sterile.'

Don't ask, don't ask, pleads MotherEleanorCook in the corner. They wring their hands and startlingly – because I've never seen them (when they were real people, indi-viduals as they should be) – they have tears in their eyes. *Don't ask.*

I watch them as I ask anyway – their fear has lit some-thing catastrophic in me. The missile has left my mouth now: 'Whose child will it be if not yours?'

MotherEleanorCook is now crying loudly purposefully, I think, trying to distract me from his answer. I nearly tell them to shut up (something I have never told any of them, but this isn't really them, I understand, and I don't want to speak lest I speak over him and miss his answer).

'I am pleased with Chloe. It's as if she is only pure Berkshire – so her sibling will also be from the same reces-sive genes, allowing ours to take control.'

Please! MotherEleanorCook's crying has become a

tortured fox screaming. The noise is unbearable, and I say something trying to get a fix on what Ephrem is saying.

Perhaps I asked something crucial, because he answers what I already, somehow, understood: 'Yes, the piano teacher's son. He is more useful now than he was as the school grounds man.'

'What happened to Arthur?'

Ephrem laughs. 'Is that his name?'

'You know that. You know that! *What happened to him*?'

'Don't worry about it, Juliet.'

I want to lose it, want to fall apart, but this is the focal point of my whole journey: *this*. I have to know *this*. Even the Sisterhood is secondary to me knowing *this*. 'If you don't tell me, you'll get nothing from me. What happened to Arthur?'

Ephrem laughs again. 'I promise you, regardless of your petty threats, I'll get exactly what I need, when I need.'

Everything in my life is just too much. I put my wrist against my teeth. 'Tell me or I'll bite my own veins out. You'll get nothing. I'll bleed out and you'll get *nothing*.'

His eyes narrow, but he doesn't take long to process the idea. 'He's mostly dead, Juliet. Trust me, there's nothing left of him to care about your heroics.'

The world greys but I breathe deeply. I have to know. 'What do you mean "*mostly*"?'

'Oh, relax. The brain checked out a long time ago. We just kept certain' – he smiles a little coyly – 'little bits of him going. Amazing tech. Can we move on now?' He checks his watch. 'I'm a busy man.'

'When did he die?'

Ephrem sighs.

'If you are not specific, you will get nothing from me.'

'Oh, for goodness' sake! He's been in Miniluv since before Chloe was born. I found you snogging and I had enough seniority, even then, to have him put away. To be honest, I'd forgotten about him, then recently, you approached me at the same time the generals were getting disloyal and I thought: I know, I'll make use of the piano teacher's son and Juliet. But I had to kill him because if I was going to have more children from him, he felt like a loose end I didn't want. So he's dead but I have his nuts in a very high-tech jar. I have boy sperm galore and you just need some boy receptive ova and hey-ho. I have a boy – or two? I was rather hoping for twins? If only so you can . . . be released . . . back to your life.'

In my mind, I know I won't survive this knowledge. But I will handle that later. I need to also know about Ruby – I might not get another chance and I need to know just in case I can ever get word to Leona. 'Are there Thinkpol agents in Minitrue?'

He pulls a face so surprised, it's almost comical. 'Now, I did not expect you to say that. I thought you'd start howling about the piano teacher's son.'

'Tell me.'

He gives a shrug like it doesn't matter and types into his computer. 'Tons of them.'

'Why?'

'To spy, to ensnare. There's one has been parked in front of you, babysitting you for years, by the way. Grahame Luck.'

Dreadful Grahame. An agent. If I wasn't so miserable, I could laugh.

If there are so many, I can never know. I can't tie this thread off neatly because I can't risk alerting him to anyone in the Sisterhood.

Now I can howl about the piano teacher's son. Oh, Arthur. I cannot bear it. Then he leaves me to the atavistic screaming and screaming and screaming from MotherEleanorCook; their noise is terrific and overwhelming but when I ask them to stop, I realize that they have left me too, deserted me in this moment of anagnorisis and with that knowledge also comes the understanding that the dreadful noise is coming from me.

PART FOUR

'And the girl with dark hair, the girl from the Fiction Department – she would never be vaporized either.'
George Orwell, *Nineteen Eighty-Four*

Chapter 67

I am in my room singing. It's a song Cook used to sing in her rounded vowels and it makes me sound happy. In a room with a thousand mics, it's important I sound cheerful.

Instead, I promise myself that at some unspecified point in the future (when it's all over?) I can end everything. Until then, there is maskface and singing. It has to be that way. I can neither see my own daughter who is so close or weep for her father because after I started screaming in Father's office, the doctor (Egris, I have since found out; he is both my shadow and my nemesis) stuck me with another needle. The drift from reality was a long, low tide and it took a long time for the sea to turn and reach the shore again.

But that is behind me. Now, I cheek my tablets and am careful to lose my laced hot milk down the kitchen scullery sink. The notches on the wall are gone, and on my bed-side table are flowers I picked from the woods. And I sing, mostly ''Tis for Thee', certainly not from super state pride, but because we always sung it as a Sisterhood. I miss them incredibly. It makes me feel united with them.

But I remember not to sing too much.

After I refused to eat, Ephrem relented and let me out of my room during the day if I agreed to stick to the servants' areas and the servant stairs so that Marguerite and Chloe don't see me. I move like a ghost around this house, sometimes catching Chloe's laughter – never Marguerite's – at wonderful moments. I have seen them a few times from the window, looking down on them on the lawn. They are often static, Marguerite gazing into nothing and Chloe usually reading, but she sometimes mills dreamily around the garden, poking at things with a stick or picking flowers. She will be eleven soon and I expect Ephrem intends on bearing her off to boarding school. I wonder what he has planned for Marguerite then. Pneumonia, I suppose.

The kitchen is a good place to hang out because the staff all talk to me – they either feel sorry for me or they're too scared not to. When I don't do anything to alarm Ephrem, I push again, clear-headed and careful. 'Look, it's not good for me physically to be cooped up inside all day. You should let me walk round the garden – with a guard if you need, I don't care. I get no natural vitamin D and perhaps my muscles will atrophy.' He said he'd think about it, but what he probably did was talk to Egris.

Egris is desperate; Ephrem who usually talks very quietly has taken to screaming invective at him every time it's clear I'm not pregnant. The doctor probably fears the rope drop if it doesn't happen soon. Ephrem later told me that not only should I go for a walk round the garden, but I could take daily long walks into the woods if I wanted. It had to be a specified route and time so not to bump into Chloe and Marguerite, but I gladly agreed.

If he was setting me up for a test, he failed. Every day, I set off for long walks and expect to be followed by a black onyx-eyed thrush. I always return because, after all, I have a better plan than simply to take off, panting and fearful into the countryside or to stand on the back lawn and yell to a girl that I'm her mother.

Since Ephrem realizes I can go out all day and still return, I walk daily; I smile more and during the endless evening piano recitals, I've taken to embellishing my performance with little introductions about the pieces I play for the uncultured, and I wear make-up (especially over the long scar that now graces my temple to the forehead, thanks to Ephrem's cane) and wear my dresses a little lower. Ephrem seems pleased with me and he claps me with increasing vigour.

I'm singing and sewing. 'Let me do something useful, Ephrem,' I mewed, so now he allows me to sew blankets for soldiers in the war that isn't real. But Ephrem thinks that I've accepted my life and I smile more – but not too much.

What he doesn't know (perhaps, perhaps – I watch carefully for the bluebottle) is today I managed to get the fourth waitress uniform I need for my plan. It's taken weeks. I stay close to the laundry and I'm careful. I secreted it under my jumper and walked it to the priest hole and left it in there. Later on, I heard yelling in the kitchen and the housekeeper was tearing into someone; perhaps it was about the uniform. But I should be above suspicion – why would Commander Berkshire's sister take a waitress uniform?

I feel like singing *I know something you don't know.* Ephrem hated that when I was a child. But I do know something he doesn't know. Something very, very important.

It came to me one morning – flicked the switch within me. It was a very simple thought, but clear. A lighthouse beam falling like a path over dark waters. If Ephrem is spending all this energy trying to get Egris to get me pregnant, then he doesn't know it's unlikely – which means he doesn't know about the contraceptive tin rusting gently in Prisha's cellar.

And if he doesn't know about that, then there's a good, good chance he doesn't know about our bomb.

Bang.

Chapter 68

I'm finally out.

Ephrem took some persuading, but when I told him I'd take a soldier escort into London, he relaxed. 'I want to clear out my old life,' I told him. 'You know I enjoy being back in our home, my real home, and truth be told, I'd love to be pregnant again. But there's still a few bits and pieces I want from my old life. I might have a girl next and if you want a line of male heirs, then you want at least one more child after this one.' I touched my stomach as if my mere hope would bring it forward. 'Then I'm here to stay for at least a couple of years. Maybe more. So let me get my things. If I really wanted to go anywhere, I would have tried to escape a long time ago.'

These days, I have learnt not to bully Ephrem until I get my way. I say my piece and then I let him mull it over or talk to whoever he talks to.

He went away two days later, on a trip with his most senior staff. It seemed rather hurried, but as he left he told me I could return to the Minitrue office and empty my drawers, and also return to my flat to get my things.

'I also want to say goodbye to the children I've worked with for years.'

'Fine, fine,' he told me, his mind already on something else. 'But you take a guard.'

But as I change out of my real clothes back into the Outer Party Overalls I will be expected to be seen in, I know I'll go alone. Half of Eltringham Hall's staff are sick – a vomiting and diarrhoea bug.

I grab my coat, keen to get going. I try not to smile as I think of the faeces I edged from under my thumbnail into the beef stew pot last night.

Sorry, guys – easier if I travel light.

Chapter 69

When I arrived at the reception of the Ministry of Truth, my pass no longer worked; the receptionist was coolly pleasant and passed my desk contents over to me in a box. The message was clear: my brother had called ahead, and I wasn't welcome to go up to my floor and say goodbye to my comrades.

I pulled a sad face knowing a million cameras were scrutinizing my expression. I sometimes saw the bluebottle at Eltringham Hall, but here, the CCTV system was extensive anyway. I knew Ephrem would be checking me from his trip. I wasn't strictly doing anything we didn't agree and Ephrem wanted to trust me. My carefully planted idea that I could be productive – but not too reliable – meant that he would have to watch me for years. Ephrem liked to watch me, I knew, but being a jailer took time and energy that he couldn't always afford. He knew if he was going to get what he wanted from me, then I needed to be fit and healthy and being coshed under heavy drugs did not result in a productive baby-making machine.

The March weather makes for a miserable walk from

the ministry to my old flat. Glad of the warmth as I step into the marble-floored lobby of Manor Towers, I step into the lift unchallenged. The smoothness of the lift and its scent (wood, polish, cigar smoke) feels both familiar and from another lifetime; I float up to the top floor. The penthouse. I was always taken care of, but as Cook was fond of saying, a silk shroud is still a shroud. As I let myself into the flat, my father's synthetic voice welcomes me. *Welcome back, Juliet. Can I help you with any aspect of your packing? Is there anything specific you would like me to relocate?* Juliet, not Julia. It knows I'm going. Of course, my previous life is over.

I want to ignore it but maskface must continue. Ephrem must think I'm happy (but not too happy). It's programmed to detect any ripples. 'I'm fine, thank you, Big Brother. I would like to thank you, though, for all your help over the years.'

That's been my pleasure. I will miss you, Juliet. You are going back off grid, so I won't see how you get on. Maybe you might let me know in the future?

'Yes, I will. I promise.' *Don't you worry, I will definitely send a clear mess—* I cut the thought.

Just in case.

I grab a few favoured clothes, and Chloe's things because Ephrem expects it, but I don't really want or need anything because they're just things and you can't take them with you. I inhale deeply; events have moved me on so far, I would not have believed it possible.

Before I leave, I glance round the place I have lived for ten years. It might look pretty with its smoked glass and cool chrome but it's a place of cruelty. Here, I've been a trapped rat in an observation box tortured in a thousand ways.

I let the door bang behind me and carry two bags into a lift. I came with one black cloth shopper, and I'm leaving with one more. Everything I'm taking from the flat fits in a single bag. I'm glad to be gone from Manor Towers.

I have two last stops to make. I check my watch. My planning means I am right on time.

Chapter 70

Sometimes things work against you and sometimes they work for you. I think this as I ring Prisha's doorbell. I picked this day because it's a Sisterhood meeting – or at least officially, it's the steering group of the Junior Anti-Sex League. I don't know if it's worked out for me until Prisha opens the door and blinks at me. She hasn't seen me for months but she's so together, she merely says, 'Come in, Julia.'

It's painful to hide the joy we feel to see each other, but maskface is everything today. The Sisterhood have become so professional – I'm so proud of us.

After stepping into her dark hall, I purposefully drop the black cloth bag in the shadows without breaking my pace. Then I go through to the small dining room and take the empty chair that I've dreamt of. I ease myself into it and try not to look at anyone. Prisha sits down and picks up her sewing.

I select some material set out in the centre of the table, then reach for a cotton spool and a needle from the mountain of choice. I gather myself and decide to pointlessly tack

406

a hem. 'I can't stay long,' I say, finally meeting their eyes. I look at Prisha first: steady, bold and receptive.

Then Leona. Like her name, delicate, but her face is more healthily padded (so difficult to tell in this light); I won't be crass to say time is a healer. My mother used to say it, but it's not true. I look at Eleanor on my right.

Eleanor gives me a brisk nod that feels like a salute. She seems relaxed, welcoming. Sharp, even – I see nothing of the earlier confusion. Perhaps today is a good day or perhaps they've been united in my absence to their betterment. I'm glad. They've had no way to use the explosive so perhaps that calmed the fire.

Cecily's expression is careful. She's suffered with worry for me, I can tell, but she still smiles at me. It's fractured, cautious even, but there's only genuine emotion in it. It's easy for me to return it. Leona blinks, keen to cover her feelings.

'I've been away because I've been honoured. I'm in service to the Inner Party. I can't say too much, but you might imagine I feel incredibly proud to promote the values of Ingsoc in any way I can. Big Brother has been good to me.'

I asked my brother recently why he perpetuates the Big Brother construct when he could so easily take centre stage himself. He looked amused at the question as if no one else had ever asked it – perhaps because the answer was so clearly evident, there was no need for it. 'Real people are liable to make mistakes. Real people are clumsy, messy even – and most certainly open to criticism. If people are in love with nothing then there's nothing to disappoint.'

After my father's face leaves the screen, bland, tinny music plays instead. We sew in quiet conversation, sometimes stopping to listen to the updates on the telescreen when they punctuate the noise, sometimes the Sisters breaking the silence to share anecdotes of the children in the ASL. It's relaxed and comfortable to be back together and it leaves me feeling both disorientated and nostalgic.

I have been through so much since I was last here. I couldn't articulate the horror if I wanted to. How could I even start if the telescreen was turned off? What could I say about my growing up at Eltringham Hall and my recent return? How could I tell them about what I did to my father and who he is in their lives? I couldn't begin to encapsulate Arthur and Chloe and my realization that my daughter is being raised as my niece and that Arthur . . . I just couldn't. I couldn't even find the words to express how much I have missed them. So, it's easier not to try; it's easier to sit and sew and just be.

I think sometimes, one doesn't have to explain everything anyway. My being here, perhaps they know intrinsically my sudden unexplained appearance is, in fact, a goodbye visit without me saying – we want to enjoy this last time together without it feeling like the last time. This is just any other time – just the same.

When I have enjoyed their company a little too long, I stand up. 'Prisha, I think I've left something in your dresser in the hall. I don't expect to be back for a while – it's my favourite crimping scissors – do you mind awfully if you could help me find them?'

Prisha is fast and we are in the dark of the hall, careful

to let the door fall just enough shut that it doesn't look purposeful but provides the necessary cover. Together, we remove the drawers and the unit, and I grab the black cloth bag I dropped in the shadows and with it in hand, I follow Prisha down the steps.

I take the rusty tin lid and take out the contraceptive and draw it up.

'You need this still?' Prisha's forehead deepens to something near horror.

'Never more than now. Do you think it lasts long in my system – more than a few months?'

'How long have you been on it?'

'Years.'

She shrugs. 'Eleanor's the scientist, but I think she told me if you've been on it a long time, it can take a while for fertility levels to recover.'

This is what I thought I remembered her saying, too. Perhaps I'm infertile now, or perhaps it's just knocked my system out. Either way, I'm pleased to have another dose. 'That's good. Really good. Listen, I have some things to tell you, but no real time to explain. I need you to listen. On a particular date, I need you all to come to a specific place and wear what's in this bag. All the information is in the bag – instructions, date, time, everything.' I pull down my trousers and indicate she is to jab my buttock, before taking the needle back and putting it back in the tin. Really, it's a wonder I've never caught anything from it.

I pass her the cloth bag. I outline my plans and add, 'Leona can come to the house, meet with me, but she will need to go somewhere else after. There is a map in here and instructions of what she must bring.' I thrust the bag at her. 'We've been too long already.'

I take the explosive out of the tin, and using a bandage I stole from the kitchen first aid, I wrap it round my waist. 'Here, help me.' Prisha does and then I add the coiled, too short detonation cord. I tell her the rest of my plan in seconds and I'm glad I picked her because she doesn't ask any questions, and she does not beg me to discontinue. I've told her everything and she's repeated the salient points back to show she understands and now I should go, but the impulse jolts like electricity and in desperation, I grab her shoulder. 'Please. I have to say it again – promise me, *promise*, you'll make Cecily swear to do it. *Just. As. I've. Said.*'

'I promise. Julia, I will help her – we all will.'

'Thank you.' I grip her shoulder. 'Please don't back down – don't let any of them back down. There is no other way – this is what I want.' I think of Winston and think of the last words (O'Brien's words) he ever said to me before we were arrested. He did not really mean them, but I rephrase them to Prisha now and I do mean it. 'Tell her I'm dead.'

Prisha – who is iron, stone, rock – has tears in her eyes and takes my hands in both of hers. They are warm and wrap mine with the nurture of a baby blanket. 'I swear it, Julia.'

'You say it, too. Tell me so I know you believe it: tell me I'm dead. So you don't try to stop me. To show me you accept I'm gone.'

Prisha, who knows how short the detonator lead is and

the implications of that, doesn't hesitate: 'You're dead.' Her tears are diamonds.

'Don't cry. I have a debt to pay.' To my father for my murderous actions; to Winston, for giving him up; to my mother for not saving her from Ephrem. 'And tell Eleanor – she can trust me. She always could.'

Hands bound in love, eyes united in respect, our word is our bond. We are the Sisterhood.

We are strong.

Chapter 71

But after we move quickly back up into the hall, the dresser unit back in place, scissors in hand, I don't retake my seat at the table. I might be strong, but I am also weak.

I grab my remaining bag with Chloe's things in it and don't look at them as I tell them I am leaving. I want to say something appropriate, something momentous to reflect the depth of my emotion. I have worked with these women for years on little things and big things: soothing crying children; gluing velvet letters; perfecting plans to quell governments; parading; spying; sewing; plotting; whispering; scrubbing.

I have much to say to acknowledge our work, our sistren. The words I want to say pile up, stones into a drystack wall that now sits as a barrier between us.

It is the cruellest of goodbyes when it's public but one's feelings are private. The silent tumult. The pain of the unsaid.

Clutching a pair of scissors I don't need, I turn away to save me making eye contact. I am a coward. Hating myself, I open the front door and slip out into the chastising cold, pulling the door shut behind me with unnecessary care, as if to leave it ajar might allow their confusion – or worse, themselves – to trail after me.

Taking the step down to the street, I think of them at the table, sewing in silence. What they must want to say, want to do, and yet must not.

It's hard to go, but I know that sometimes it's harder to stay.

Turning my coat collar up against the wind, I turn my mind to the last exigent visit I must make. With the explosives strapped round my waist, I am a human bomb.

I turn towards the park.

There is no reason why I should see Winston, but I just know that I will. It is why I am here in the park: I have come to find him. The savage wind howls between the trees and lampposts, and despite my thick hat and gloves, it bites at my ears and my fingers, too. I've got two pairs of socks on and my winter shoes but as I clump round the park, my toes are still cold. It matters not to me, though – it's not the sadness of saying goodbye to the Sisters that I feel, but the forming fire of my next steps.

This keeps me warm as I look around for Winston. He loves the park and the Chestnut Tree Café was where Ephrem's camera found him. It was always a place of fascination to him – the people who went there on the edge of society. From what Ephrem showed me, he'll fit right in.

It feels important to see him. Our relationship has been complicated. I needed him to help me find the truth of Ruby's arrest. Although he wasn't who I was seeking, he started a journey to something bigger. Briefly, for a fleeting moment, I thought I could love him, but Smith could never be a man I fell in love with. At the end, I stayed with him out of guilt. I sold him and felt obliged to see how he paid for my entry into Ephrem's trust. I'm glad I know, he was moribund anyway, having started that journey towards his arrest before I even met him.

I never loved him – sometimes I didn't even like him, and I often hated him, but he has mattered. More than that, I feel I owe him this: a confession and a goodbye.

Really, I could miss him by minutes; he might not even come here anymore, he may have new routines, but I just feel it in my marrow that I'm going to see him. It's just a certainty that cannot be explained but fits with the finality of my day. Everything has been straightforward and smooth, and I pray that it continues.

I have given an hour to this; I walk around knowing that I will be watched by a hundred electronic lenses unblinkingly conveying images back to scrutinizing human eyes, but my behaviour will not cause concern. I spend each and every day walking for hours; it's my job now to be as fit and healthy as possible under Dr Egris' supervision. I adjust my bag over my shoulder – now only one bag – and dig deep into my pockets. The wind strafes my exposed skin, but after months of being imprisoned indoors, I welcome its insolence.

Then I see him on the path in front of me – I don't realize it's him immediately. Not dressed for the weather in only thin overalls, he moves slowly on the path with the air of the ancient elder looking for a lost thought somehow dropped on the path in front of him. He's thickened in stature, but he moves with a caution, as if he's worried he might break. He hasn't aged ten years in almost a year, he's aged twenty. More.

What did they do to you, dear?

He's coming towards me, but he hasn't seen me yet; his eyes are screwed up against the wind like a hairless mole, staring at the ground in front of him.

He's changed. *So* changed.

I can't help it – I can't look at him. I can't bear it for him. The ruination of him. His whole body has revolted against him, and he's not recognized me, perhaps because of my hat and now we've passed each other.

I just couldn't bring myself to speak because I'm afraid. He is so different, so, so different and it's my fault.

Not your fault. The Thought Police had identified him, O'Brien had identified him and Ephrem / Charrington had snared Winston *before* you met him. You simply sensed in him what they did – his rebellion. Winston's hamartia was his inability to hide his true self.

Lost in my usual internal conflict, I'm suddenly aware that he's behind me. He must have realized it was me and turned and caught me up.

I turn off the path and hope he follows me onto the grass. I know there's a space behind a clump of shrubs that's a bit more private. I know there's no escaping the cameras, but habit and instinct drives me to seek out the shadows. He follows me.

I stop and turn and try to smile. I expected Winston to smile or say something, but he surprises me by reaching out and putting his arm around my waist. I did not expect this.

It feels wrong – assumptive and inappropriate. We haven't even spoken yet – not even a word of greeting. I remind myself that I came to see him; this is the right thing to do. I'm here because I owe him this.

His face is so different it feels as if I'm with a man I don't know. His nose, mouth, everything seems thickened; his lips are now purple-tinged, his nose and cheeks liver-coloured. His hair is gone, and his scalp looks scalded from the cold. I want to pull away not least because his fingertips are pressing against where the explosives are bandaged tight. He might notice but that's not it: I don't want to be held by him anymore. He feels and looks so different it's as if I have no connection to this man. O'Brien was right – people can be changed so they become unrecognizable. I remember rejecting freshly washed clothes as a child because the housekeeper had ordered the wrong washing soap and the different smell made me feel like they weren't mine anymore. This is how he feels to me now – not mine.

And I am not his. After weeks of lying in the twilight world with Arthur and Chloe, I couldn't feel like anyone else's but theirs, ever again. That strange time restored me emotionally to my family and I never want to leave them in any sense, again.

But he's still holding me and staring at me and the words I want to come, can't. Not here. I make a break, hope he doesn't pick up on my annoyance with him for his grabby hands, and leave the shrubby area. I've misjudged this. He follows me – still silently. Winston always loved to talk. It can't be just his physical body that's changed. Has he had a lobotomy? This is a man more broken than his wearied wrinkles suggest. He is silent and strange, and I need to be somewhere that other people can see me – just in case. I lead him to a park bench instead. It's more in the open.

We sit next to each other on metal park chairs; the cold iron presses through my overalls to the backs of my legs. Better than a bench though – I'm glad for the enforced gap two chairs provides. He stares at my feet, and his silence and the intensity of his stare make me nervy. I realize it is me that must speak first: 'I betrayed you.' This is what I came for: to confess this. I cannot tell him the truth – who I am, my family, the Sisterhood and why they had to be protected above him. I cannot beg for his sanction of my choices which old Winston (there is two – the one before and this one, I understand this) would approve. But I can tell him it was me that betrayed him and I can tell him a version of the story that he believes and understands.

'I betrayed you,' he says. He sounds like he doesn't care, and it irks me – this new Winston acts like a synthetic.

'Sometimes, they threaten you with something – something you can't stand up to, can't even think about. And then you say, "Don't do it to me, do it to somebody else, do it to so-and-so." And perhaps you might pretend, afterwards, that it was only a trick and that you just said it to make them stop and didn't really mean it. But that isn't true. At the time when it happens you do mean it. You think there's no other way of saving yourself, and you're quite ready to save yourself that way. You *want* it to happen to the other person. You don't give a damn what they suffer. All you care about is yourself.'

'All you care about is yourself,' he replies.

He's said nothing that isn't just repeating what I've said. Winston has gone. They killed him and left these remains behind. The remains are to shame him. This drooling, shuffling chimera of past and present.

'And after that, you don't feel the same towards the other person any longer.' This is what I came here for. I didn't want him to always hanker after me, to want us to be together again. I want him to know that for me it is over.

'No,' he said, 'you don't feel the same.' His voice is dull – but there is truth in it. This new version of this man has let me go, too, and I'm glad. I like Winston enough to not want to hurt him more than they have already hurt him – if these remains can be hurt. This man in front of me is more interested in my nervous feet than me.

Perhaps Winston wants to sit here longer or perhaps not – it's hard to tell. I'm not sure this leftover man wants anything. He makes no further effort at conversation, and instead we sit, cold in our thin overalls and him with no coat. I stay for a while, expecting him to add something – wanting him to have the chance. It's like being gentle to a child or someone hurt – I want to be kind. This man gave his life for trying to break a corrupt government. His heart is still beating, but he's gone. Winston Smith died for the cause. He is a brave man and I wish I could kiss his cheek in memorial for what he did, for what we once were, but this man is not the same person and I cannot be sure. Instead, I vow I will not forget him at the crucial moment. I think this as we just sit together in silence until eventually I tell him I have a train to catch.

'We must meet again,' he says, so much like a synthetic,

I wonder briefly if they killed the old Winston and replaced him with this mockery.

'Yes,' I agree, not meaning it any more than he does, 'we must meet again.'

When I leave, I hear his footsteps behind me on the path for a while, as if he's so dull-brained he follows me from lack of knowing what else to do. As he follows me out of the park onto the street, I try to shake him off with my pace but he stays creepily just one pace behind. A small group of people gives me the opportunity to weave through and he's less successful and is slowed. I can see his reflection in the shopfront windows and for a moment he tries to make gains to catch up but when I next check, he's not there and that Winston (or what's left of him) has finally given up.

Relief is tinged with pity. Poor Winston – I feel saddened for this broken man who wanted the same as me. He was brave to take them on. Judging by the state of him, he was strong, too, held himself with integrity.

I promise him: Winston, it wasn't for nothing. You led me home, made me realize that the end should really be where it started. I shall bear your name at the end.

Chapter 72

It's been two months since I've seen the Sisterhood. I look out onto the rear of Eltringham Hall's grounds and know that today they will come for me here. As we planned.

I have yearned for their company; their friendship is not in doubt, but it's the presence of realness, of being known and understood that I miss. It feels like a hundred years have gone since I sat sewing at Prisha's. It's not – but the time feels immaterial today; now it's just the past. Everything is the past now, I think, as I move through my father's suite.

Being in his bedroom makes me feel both connected to him and melancholy. I haven't wanted to come back here, didn't feel able to, but now I feel differently. It should be safe – no one comes here and if there are cameras, what does it matter now?

It's not Ephrem's bedroom – his is at the end of the west wing. He probably doesn't sleep in here in case my father's ghost torments him. Coward, I think, and smile.

Piggy Nose.

Huge, mullioned windows overlook the lawn. This suite holds many rooms, many memories. I sit on the window seat my father let me lie on to read my books – when the sun hit that spot, I was as content as any cat stretched out in the sun. I glance in his small ante bedroom. He used it on the occasions he arrived home after midnight. It's empty now. Instead, I go to his personal study. He loved working up here, he said, preferred it to his office on the ground floor, because here, no one could bug him. I glowed when he told me, felt so special because I alone was allowed to sit in here whilst he worked.

Standing here now, I look out at the beautiful views over the land and can understand why Father would choose this space. From here, I can see most of Eltringham Hall's land. In the distance is Grandfather's folly, a place where I'd met Winston. It was there, looking back at the house, I realized Chloe was in danger. It was a building Grandfather had designed to look like a bombed, broken-down church. My father told me that his father had spread a rumour that a nuclear bomb had been dropped in its vicinity – it worked well at keeping people away.

From the window, I can see the lake and the woods, the field where I jumped Snowball, the lower lawns where Grandfather had ridden his tank, me on his lap. It is all here – all of my past.

I'd had such a blissful childhood – I had been so adored. Until Arthur.

I sat on the battered Chesterfield, surprised it was still here. 'Hello, old friend,' I said, giving it a pat. This would be where Sulky the cat would hide, or I would pretend to nap, but really would just watch my father. How I loved him.

I remember so many memories: me watching his back as he sat at the desk under the window; me sorting through his coin collection, interrupting his work as I pestered him for information on each one. Afternoon tea being served up here, whilst Mother and Ephrem socialized. Me breathless, in riding breeches, asking for feedback on jumps I'd hoped he'd seen from the window. It's always been so difficult to reconcile the adoring father he was, to the monster he has been to the people. I'm not sure I'll ever be able to.

I wish I could sit here forever. Now I'm free from the anger of what I thought my father had done with my daughter, I can see our relationship for what it was.

I'm glad I hadn't killed him; for that, I am grateful. But Ephrem started something when he passed me that pillow and slipped from the room, leaving poisonous lies in my ear. He started something and now I had to finish it.

I turn the door handle carefully, quietly. I step one foot into the corridor when I realize I have not been careful enough.

She stands to the side. Waiting.

I am in trouble.

Chapter 73

'Don't go! I've been waiting ages and ages and *ages* to see you.'

A girl of ten stands in the corridor. She has Arthur's brown eyes and my freckles, his oval face, my dark hair. She is lovely. She is lovely!

I think I am going to cry.

'Don't cry!' she says, apparently reading my mind. 'I promise not to hurt you.'

I am unable to speak or move. I don't know what to say. I have stepped from ghosts of the past to everything I ever, ever wanted in my present. The shock is indescribable. To see Chloe up close, right in front of me, is beyond what I ever thought possible. I want to touch her, inhale her. My eyes are starving – I never want to move my gaze from her. I want to tell her the same – *I have been waiting ages and ages and ages to see you, too.*

I blink; I breathe.

Chloe smiles – a bright, sudden smile that neither Arthur nor I can lay claim to. Excitedly, she's moving from Mary-Janed foot to Mary-Janed foot. She is holding a pad and a pen and claps them together. 'I knew you were real! Everyone said that you weren't, that I must have imagined seeing you, but I knew I didn't imagine you!'

'You've seen me?' I am still holding the door handle – I'm not sure how to react. This moment is both pure joy and pure terror. Looking at her earnest face, the fine arch of her eyebrows, the sweetness of her mouth, there is nowhere I would rather be than looking at my daughter. But I am not prepared for this – it is both too much and not enough.

'Yes, in the window. I've seen you many times.'

I am taken aback. How was this possible? 'How . . .'

Then she pulls her brow deeper in an expression of frustration that makes her look older than her years and is pure Arthur. 'Because when I read on the lawn, you stand in the window and watch me. And I pretend not to notice you, in case Mummy gets upset again. Obviously.'

Mummy.

I want to ask why 'Mummy' gets upset, but of course, there really is no need.

'I'm surprised you saw me. I thought I had been careful.' But not always. Sometimes the drugs Ephrem had been giving me made me sloppy; sometimes I leaned my forehead against the glass and cried, thinking the distance was enough.

'I've seen you a zillion times! See? I've written them in my book.' She looks in her notebook. 'I've been hunting for you for ages. This house is too big. It's taken a hundred years. I've been to this bit loads and loads but you've never been here, but today I thought I'd try again

424

and here you are! Can I ask you some questions please? I have an interview for you because I am an investigator, you see.'

I glance up the corridor, nervous of the spying bluebottle. I can hear it usually, or it gives itself away with its restless crawling. But if it is here, I decide, what matter? He has taken her – he will not take this moment too. So I stand in the doorway of a forgotten corridor and tell her, yes, I will answer her questions.

'Right, first one. What is your name?'

'Juliet.'

She writes it down. 'Full name please.'

I cannot tell her I'm a Berkshire too. It'll create too many questions, so I'm stuck, pinioned between a truth and a lie. 'Do I get to pass on any questions?'

'No?' she tries, unsure.

'Juliet Julia, then. That is my name.'

Her eyes narrow with scrutiny. 'That's not a real name – it's just the same name but different.' She bites the end of her pen. 'I won't tell anyone, you know. I'd get into hideous trouble if they knew I'd spoken to you.'

'Why?'

'Well, like I said, they all told me that you didn't exist. Said you must be a ghost.'

'You don't think I am a ghost, though?'

She wrinkles her nose with amusement. 'You're not dead yet!'

Yet.

'What if you don't write the answers down? Could that be all right?' I suggest.

She looks doubtful. 'I'm an investigator. This is my investigator's book.'

'An investigator has to have an excellent memory. If someone found it, they'd see all the answers and then—'

'Hmm, yes, I see. Okay, I won't write anything down.'

'Next question then.'

'Why do you live in this house?'

'I used to live in this house when I was your age and then I came back.'

'You used to live here when you were a child as well? How extraordinary!'

I nod and hold onto the door handle. I no longer feel like I am going to faint, but I need the support still.

'Do you like living here?' she asks.

'When I was your age, I liked it very much. Do you?'

'Yes, it's lovely. I think I should ask the questions though.'

But I have to know you are happy.

She studies her book, sighs, then closes it. 'All my questions are wrong now. I didn't think you used to live here – I thought you were going to say you snuck in and that was what my interview was about.'

'Why did you think that?'

'Well, it would explain why no one knew you were here.' Her eyes narrow again. 'Does Daddy know you are here?'

'Why don't you tell me your favourite book?' I have to change the subject, but I also want to know because when I think of her, I want to remember her reading something and know what it was.

'That's easy. I love *The Lion, The Witch and The Wardrobe*, by C. S. Lewis. It's brilliant. Have you read it?'

'Yes, I love it, too. But you won't be allowed to read that at school, surely? It's a banned book.'

'What's school?'

'Where you go to learn.'

'Oh, I don't need to go somewhere like that. I have a governess who teaches me here. What's a banned book?'

'Books that you're not allowed to read.'

'Daddy says I can read anything I like – he says Berkshires are different to most people. He says we need to be smart.'

Of course, the elite must have full access to knowledge. Their greed is everyone else's famine. I recall the Ingsoc slogan: *Ignorance is Strength*. My father always said the maxim was true – but was not the full line. He said that the full unshared line is: *Ignorance of the Masses is the Strength of the Party*. It made him laugh – he said that was the irony, that the people were ignorant about ignorance. He said that's how you controlled others: by blinding them about what it was they didn't even know in the first place. He once told me he banned books because they contained ideas and education. When education was a weapon, he said, why give the enemy ideas and weapons?

'And does your governess teach you the piano?'

'That thing in the drawing room? No, Daddy says he'll thrash me if I touch it. He says it rots the mind. Anyway, he's getting rid of it very soon. He says its usefulness is coming to an end and then he's going to junk it. He even said that when he does, he might have a party – apparently, he hates it and cannot *wait* for it to be gone.'

She lifts her head, hearing something. 'That's my

governess now. I said I was looking for spiders – will I see you again? I haven't asked you half as much as I wanted to, and I have so many questions.'

–He's getting rid of it very soon. He says its usefulness is coming to an end–

I'm glad she doesn't wait for an answer because now I can hear a woman's voice too, calling for Chloe, and with that, she turns and runs up the corridor, and I shrink back into the shadows.

A ghost of yet to come.

Chapter 74

'I'm going to make myself a jam sandwich,' I tell Mrs Macdonald and the fifteen-odd people who are bustling around the kitchen – none of them respond. I nearly announce that I'm going to burn the kitchen down, to see if I can raise an eyebrow or a smile – but there's no point. I've heard what they call me.

Mrs Macdonald doesn't even glance my way; the pressure's on and she doesn't handle pressure well. She's the cook, but I can't give this thin, rather nasal woman the title of Cook. Not in my beloved Cook's kitchen as well. I think of Cook now. She wouldn't have any extra staff helping – she loved big dos, and prided herself on her and her team managing alone.

But they are now all gone; no one remains.

Now, as I watch the chopping, frying, blending, whisking, I know that most of them are new hired hands, just for tonight's long-planned event. The house is teeming with strangers, all in uniform. Upstairs, there's a fleet of cleaners, polishing everything in sight. Architraves, skirtings, picture and dado rails, panelling, staircase – no surface goes untouched. The air is thickened not just with lavender beeswax but with lilies; the florist van is parked outside and they are setting up magnificent displays in the hall, drawing and dining room. I know a team of waiting staff are turning up in an hour to assist the regular house staff. They'll all be tipped off about me when they turn up: 'She's the Master's sister – stay right away, I reckon. Kind of him to take her in, but' – I can even imagine them touching their temples – 'not right in the head, if you know what I mean.'

Perhaps they'll even tell them about my latest incident. I expect most of the regular staff heard the screaming match two days ago when the housekeeper, Mrs Franfield, approached me as I sat in rehearsal at the Imperial. She said she'd organized a piano tuner to come in. Ephrem found me strangling her against the mantelpiece, wild with fury. 'No one goes near the Imperial! *Ever*! She's mine! My daddy gave her to me and if you or any of your minions touch it, I will personally bite off every fucking finger that trespasses on what is *mine*!'

Ephrem himself had had to peel me off her. 'My sister is overwrought. This piano has a . . . personal resonance for her. She's also very able at tuning it herself. Best to cancel whoever you organized with our apologies.'

'Tell her no one goes near it!'

Ephrem leaned away from my scream. His voice, though, was warm and calm. 'I think we all know that, don't we, Mrs Franfield?'

Mrs Franfield gave two, quick, small nods of compliance.

'Good, good, you see, Juliet? All is fine.'

Mrs Franfield placed her hand against her chest, inhaling like she hadn't breathed for an age. Her neck was reddened and for a moment she couldn't speak. Finally, blinking, she managed a, 'Very good, sir, I shall do as you say,' before she fled from the room.

Ephrem and I were left looking at each other. Perhaps I still looked ready to attack, because he placed a hand on my shoulder. 'Don't worry, sister, no one is going to take your beloved piano from you – but a word of advice if I may?' In my silence he continued: 'The party slogan is correct: he who controls the past, controls the future. You must not allow the past to control you – or it will determine your future. Set him free from your thoughts.' Bizarrely, he cupped his hands. 'Like a bird you have trapped . . . just release him.' He parted his hands, 'Set him free.'

He means Arthur, I thought, my breathing choking on close tears.

I'm better, calmer – even with the housekeeper. When I passed Mrs Franfield in the dining room yesterday as she stood on a chair to help the maid with the curtain cleaning, she shrank back. They all know I am perfectly capable of biting bones. I baited her (naughty of me) by even saying 'crunch' as I passed – the maid helping her with the curtains actually whimpered as I said it.

Mrs Macdonald wouldn't whimper for anyone, I think, as I watch her struggling under the burden of the heavy pan. She'd have heard though – I screamed at Franfield loud enough to take the roof off the building – but if she didn't hear that, the gossip mill would've done the rest.

She curses as a young man nearly barges her as she

431

balances the pan on the rim of the huge sink. Steam billows around her and I watch her for a moment – she's been a fixture in my life for the last few months. I've made a point of hanging around the kitchen too much – I want to be seen as a mundane feature. Of course, they all think I'm mad, even before my performance with Franfield – pale as a ghost, I've heard them say (and what's that scar on the side of her head?), hanging out in the kitchen like a skivvy with nowhere to be. I take up space – can't and wouldn't help them with anything. I just pick through the cupboards and get under their feet, stop their gossip about life upstairs.

They might think I'm lonely, purposeless and drifting, but they are wrong. It's all been for one thing. Every single visit to the kitchen; every single sandwich I've made; cup of tea taken at the kitchen table; every time I've sat on the worktop trying to engage someone in conversation and the hours spent gazing out of the kitchen window with a glass of milk in my hand – it's all built up purposefully to this one moment.

This moment here. Now.

To be able to hang around the kitchen, like it is completely normal.

I feel the wham-wham of my heart. My mouth has gone dry. This is so important.

Mrs Macdonald caustically calls to Dolly to help her, and her assistant drops her paring knife and goes to assist. Dolly knows not to help Mrs Macdonald unless explicitly commanded.

With them distracted, I slip into the old pantry.

I shut the door carefully behind me and just lean back against it, taking a breath.

This was always a special place for me. When I was younger, Cook used to send me in here to reach up to retrieve items from the numerous shelves. The shelves are empty now. This room has become redundant. No one comes in here since the room next to the kitchen was modernized. Now it's empty and dusty and forgotten – and that includes the tradesman's door on the far side. It's unlocked because I've tested it – the key was never moved from when Cook kept it on the door frame.

I open it now.

Outside, the air is sweet. It's late morning; I can hear the songbirds in the trees. I pause, indulging myself in brief seconds to enjoy the solitude of the garden. This is to the left of the house and many shrubs and small trees have grown up in this corner, shielding it from the lawns and terraces to the right. Only round this corner is the front of the house and the drive – in Cook's day, the delivery drivers used to park up just round the corner, and there was a path where they walked in the deliveries of food and coal for the Aga, to the back of the kitchen. But Ephrem had everything changed and a different, new entrance has left this one forgotten, the path grown over.

I had not forgotten though.

I step through bushes and trees and go round the back of the garages and think I'll have to wait – I'm a few minutes early.

But they are here. I see them.

My Sisterhood.

Chapter 75

The back of the garage is red brick – old, built a long time ago. It's ugly and the gardener has made a show of disguising it by growing pretty rowan, hawthorn and bay trees. The Sisterhood stand together under these trees, in the shadows. They wear both expressions of uncertainty and the uniforms I left for them in the basement. They have never been to Eltringham Hall; all they know is the instructions I left with Prisha – when to arrive and what time.

A crow takes off abruptly as I arrive; it beats its wings and caws its threats and we startle – not just at the rush of feathers, but because it feels like years since we've seen each other. It's only been weeks, but for me at least, it's been an age.

I smile at them – not the warm greeting that I thought I would give, but instead a weak affair, nervous and fragile.

Cecily, Prisha, Eleanor and Leona instead crowd round me and wrap their arms and love around me. Once, I wished for the Brotherhood – I wished for a network greater than our own. As I feel my friends' embrace, I know now that there is no network greater than our own.

We are all we need. We had it all along.

Greeting over, I lead them through the door into the old pantry. We can hear the noise of the kitchen on the other side. Eleanor locks the back door and Prisha and I carry a storage chest and quietly stow it behind the door. No one ever comes in here, but if they did, it might give the women a few moments head start.

Together we sit on the floor. 'Thank you for coming,' I whisper after I have checked the room carefully for the spy fly.

'I have told them everything I know,' Prisha whispers back.

'Thank you.' I reach out and place my hand against her face. I have so much love for her – for each one of them.

They have never let me down and now they are here. We have argued, nearly pulled ourselves apart, but we have united, here, now. I look from face to face: Eleanor's blue, clear eyes steady on mine – she is a spear that today will find its mark; Prisha leaning into my palm, her eyes briefly closing as she places her hand over mine; Leona reaches for my free hand, her grip, like the questions in her eyes, are patient tenacity; and Cecily, only she has tears in her own. I don't know if she is crying for the past or what is yet to come; perhaps like me, she cries for both.

'Julia,' says Eleanor. 'I want to tell you something.' There's something in her voice – a gravitas – that makes me remember her gripping me and saying: *Trust, Julia. Don't let me down.*

I'm going to hear it now.

'Julia, I always knew who you were. I knew you were Juliet Berkshire and I understood what that meant. I want you to know, so that you know just how much I trusted you for being you. That I believed in you. That you weren't some kind of hunter of rebels, but a true friend.'

I gasp. 'How did you know? You couldn't have, surely?'

'I saw your photo. My parents were pretty old by the time they had me. They were practised at hiding things they considered precious – historical archives that they didn't want looted when it became thoughtcrime for individuals to have their own photos. They didn't want to surrender them. Unlike everyone else, whose digital photos were simply deleted, my father had his own dark room and photography was his hobby. When they died, I had access to my parents' card photos. They had one of you when you were a baby being held by your father – on the Oceania Palace balcony. My mother had written your names on the back.'

'Then why don't more people know about Juliet?' asks Leona.

'People aren't allowed to remember, are they? Great effort goes into making sure records are changed, images created, others destroyed. Not everyone had elderly parents with a passion for academia and record-keeping. Besides, you were just a baby before you were hidden from public view. But it was your name, you see. Because then I also had a photo of you, Julia – Juliet Berkshire – captain of your hockey team. It was printed in a brochure for parents of your girls' school. How my parents got it, I don't know.'

'Brochure? Of a school?' asks Cecily, incredulous.

'Life is different for the Inner Party,' Eleanor says unnecessarily. She turns back to me. 'So you see, I was able to link you with your father. I didn't understand why you were living in London. But I saw a sadness in you. I thought someone with your background might make for an . . . interesting ally.'

'That was a risk!' Prisha says.

'Yes, of course, but the Sisterhood was about risk. My mother used to say, you couldn't make an omelette—'

'Without breaking a few eggs.' I smile. 'Cook used to say that, too. That reminds me – I wanted you to take this.' I get up, move a set of shelves, reach round in the dim light for the right brick. I find it and pull it out. Then the one above. This is a house full of secrets. Inside, I pull out a parcel wrapped in bubble wrap plastic, before restoring the shelves and placing the package on the floor between us. 'This has been here for about forever – but I don't want it to stay here. I want you to take it with you – for Chloe.'

I unwrap the plastic and then the velvet material inside. 'It's a Bible. Do you know what that is?'

'I do,' says Eleanor. 'My mother remembered all the religions – and them being banned. Then unbanned but never given back. She said that Ingsoc wanted to unify belief. If people followed different things, then they were harder to control. If they love someone more than their leader, then the leader cannot always be followed.'

'I first knew of this when I was fourteen. I came in looking for stashed cakes and discovered Cook reading it. She was, at once, very, very frightened that I had found her. Terrified. It was the only time I saw her scared. It was seeing her fear – this big strong woman who everyone was nervous of – cry in front of me, begging me not to tell my family; begging for her life she said, that I think, made me who I am, in many ways. It was certainly what made me rebel – this realization that my world was not some happy, harmonious place full of roast dinners, hockey games and ponies. That someone like Cook, who I thought my family adored, could do something that would make her afraid for her life because of them. Who were my family, really, to make her feel like that? And what was it about the book that would anger my family so? It showed me that there were things about this world that I did not understand. It was because of that, that single incident, that meant I started spying on my parents from the priest's hole.

'You see then, in a way, it started a stone that began rolling and ends here tonight.

'And this. Please give Chloe this also.' It is an old paper photograph. It is of a march with people holding rainbow flags. On the back are the words: Mum and Layla. Me aged two months. It was my beloved Cook with her mums.'

'In the days before.'

I nod. 'Cook was very dear to me – like a mother. I'd like Chloe to have it, so she knows that things can be different from how they are now. That people are different and need to be, to survive.' We fall silent for a moment; Cecily is wrapping Cook's things up. I think she might be crying. After our moment, I whisper: 'Stay here until I cause a commotion in the kitchen. You'll hear me shout – I'll cause a fight with someone and make sure it's big enough and dramatic enough to involve everyone. You'll only have a few seconds to exit. Just step out of here and look like you know where you are going.' I smile. 'Don't worry, I know how to cause a scene. And once you're out of here, you'll be safe – most of the staff here don't know each other, they've been pulled in for today's event. You look like maids, so you will have run of the house.' I tell them where the servant stairs are, and direct them to what they need to do, both before and after. They have many practical questions and I take the time to answer them clearly and completely. It's essential they are confident in what they are doing if we are going to succeed.

When they are confident, only a few minutes have passed. I give them what I have brought in here. It is a notebook. Winston gave me the idea – he had a notebook that he loved to write down his thoughts in. At the time I scoffed at it, but here, stuck up in the eaves, I found I had much to say.

I realize that the cameras would have caught every word I wrote, but Ephrem probably had plans to intercept it at some point and burn it – now he cannot.

I open the front page and read it to them: 'For Chloe. This is the truth – with all my love forever, your mother.'

Then, the addendum I added just after seeing her:

The answers to your questions.

They read it in the gloom.

'She will know you,' Cecily says and reaches for me, folding me into a hug.

Then I stand and hug and kiss each one. Each one says the same to me: 'She will know you,' and their promise is our goodbye.

Then, there are no more words; there is no more time. It is time to go.

Chapter 76

*'By propagating women's nature as non-violent
they are discouraging women from becoming
fighters in the struggle for their own liberation
and that of society.'*
Anuradha Ghandy

I have never felt so grown up as I do in this moment. The
Sisterhood are in place and all I have had to do is dress for
this evening's party. I dress carefully in the dress laid out
for me, a simple black silk gown with long sleeves. In the
long mirror I stand and realize I look like I've dressed for
my own funeral. I fasten my mother's black pearls around
my neck. She will be with me tonight. Ephrem gave them
to me, saying, 'Tonight is the most important night in the
Inner Party's calendar – and this year we have much to
celebrate. Be your very best.'

Tonight is special – for the first time, Ephrem has invited me to take the grand central staircase to the ground floor. He doesn't want me using the servants' staircase. It's been a long time – years – since I walked down here. The day I left after killing Father, I think. Yes, I decide, my hand trailing against the rail, the last time I killed someone.

The light of the open drawing room doors spills onto the hall floor – a warm welcome. I am nearly there.

Ephrem wants me in position in the drawing room as guests arrive. It's a strictly no wives event tonight. There are a hundred men attending. The full government: Ingsoc in its entirety. The Inner Party. The dining hall can only seat forty at a push; Mother always used to complain with that number it was like eating at a trough. As such, it's canapes tonight and I have strict instructions to look like I'm circulating without actually speaking to anyone. I have to be 'there without actually being there'. Ephrem has had a new picture painted of Grandfather, Father and him gathered together in front of Eltringham Hall. It's fictional because in the painting, Ephrem is the age he is now, but he wants to unveil it tonight to make a point that the Berkshires are the lineage to run the Party. If I'm there, he thinks it adds to the pretence, as long as I don't 'say anything, to anyone, at any time.'

So I do what he asks. With everyone else, I clap when the huge painting is unveiled and raise my glass in a toast to my brother's future, and then circulate around the room, dodging reaching hands and bald innuendo, never giving more than a polite smile. I linger by the long curtains that cover the windows that look over the gardens and adjust them to my liking. No one sees me do it and no one shuts them again.

I did as he asked and now I sit behind my piano, the Bösendorfer Imperial Grand. I press my hand against the black gloss top and thank it for its presence in my life. It has been a constant friend. I vowed to never use it again after Arthur disappeared, but playing it again has been a comfort to me. It unites me, past and present.

Now, in front of me sit the sixty men (*I see you, O'Brien*) and my brother. King Pig. I don't say anything, but I am permitted to nod at the staff when I am ready, and then they take their cue to retire from the room and shut the doors behind them quietly.

I wish I could feel Arthur next to me, his hand on the small of my back. I wish Cook was in the kitchen downstairs, grumbling about a sauce's consistency. I wish Mother was in the audience squeezing her hands together as she did every time I gave a recital. But they are all gone now.

I always enjoy the moment's silence as the audience waits with expectation. To start with the rustling as they have a last-minute fiddle with something and settle into their seats. I know from experience that if you wait too long to start, then the lull picks back up into murmurous, ill-concealed irritation. But that's not tonight. They settle and I take a deep breath and give a check around the room. I'm ready. Holding my fingers over the keys, I take a deep breath and then begin what actually is the end.

Chapter 77

*'A defiant deed has greater value than
innumerable thousands of words.'*
Emmeline Pankhurst

My brother probably realizes something is wrong when I
don't play Bach as agreed. Instead, I start by playing the
piano transcription to Handel's Largo from Serse, *Ombra
Mai Fu*. For Arthur. Then I see the torchlight through
the gap in the curtains and it's perfect timing. Three long
flashes follow one short. They did good.

Knowing that both Chloe and Marguerite are safe
in the woods with the Sisterhood, I start playing
Beethoven's Moonlight Sonata. I don't look at Ephrem,
who I suspect will be pink-faced and straining into his
evening tie collar.

I play on and wonder how they got Marguerite and

Chloe out from their bedrooms. Marguerite might have been easy to move if she was dosed like I was. Chloe perhaps would have been tricker. But there was nothing in the way of any disturbance all night and my Sisters are wise and capable and had time to plan their approach. For the signal to be given, I know they are all together.

I have only minutes left. There's no escaping it, but I feel calm.

In the end I have had no choice about the outcome for me, just as it always felt would be the way. But when I brought the explosives into the house, the house where my daughter slept, there was only one place where they would be safe: the priest hole.

But I knew I wouldn't be able to detonate it from there. Not just because the detonator lead Leona supplied was too short to reach, not just because the trailing wire would be seen even if I wasn't seen rigging it, but also because the stone walls around the priest hole are so thick, it would muffle the blast and make it too ineffective.

I take a deep breath knowing I'm getting to the end of the piece. Explosives have to be close to the target. When it's detonated, it needs to be as close to these men as possible in order for it to wipe out Ingsoc. I'm hoping when they're gone, there will be a quick assembly of a new order. Perhaps Eleanor's cloud has passed, perhaps it will be Prisha. I hope they will be quick to provide leadership. I warned them that there will always be a psychopath who will seize power in a vacuum, just as my own grandfather did. But perhaps not. Perhaps it can be them.

I'm at the end now. I'm ready.

I finish the piece and stand. I meet my brother's eye. He looks at me like he has never hated me more. He now realizes that these last few months where I have been the good girl are a lie. To see me play unagreed music and then stand as if to address the room is such an outrageous straying from his wishes, that it is enough for him to know. His hand is inside his jacket. I'm no fool. It gives me some satisfaction to know I was always the better shot.

I think of Winston Smith because I vowed I would. I think of Arthur. I think of Chloe, who I am glad will stay with the mother she knows. I'm sure Marguerite will be just fine when she's away from Ephrem. If she's not, Cecily is going to be close by. I know Prisha will make Cecily keep to my request of stepping into the role of Chloe's mother if need be – she promised me. They will all be a wonderful support for my wonderful girl.

'This is for the Sisterhood.' And then, thinking of Winston and in case there is a Brotherhood somewhere, engaged in the struggle just as Winston hoped, I add: 'And for the Brotherhood.'

As I say these words, I watch my brother draw his pistol from his jacket.

I think of the Hate Week's boy's face, young Johnson, and his round mouth of surprise when he realized he'd shot his parents. I think of Ruby who never came home, and the ear and eye nailed to the post in the children's playground. Of Prisha's Aarav; of the rocket-bombed child and his dead, skittled friends; their broken lives and with it, Eleanor's spirit.

Ephrem stands up to take the shot.

445

I think of my father dying in bed, poisoned by his son, and my mother, who probably met a similar fate. I think of Mr Ryman. I think of them all. But mostly I think of Arthur.

I feel the bullet punch me in the shoulder.

But it doesn't stop me from pressing the black, beautiful, bass notes of the Bösendorfer.

Chapter 78

I am dying. But as I look at the bomb's aftermath, I realize that despite destroying myself, it's all right. There was no other way. No one was ever allowed near the piano and no one alive now knows their way through the insides of that piano like I do. Whether I liked it or not, putting the explosive in the Bösendorfer Imperial was the only way.

Forgive me, Mr Ryman. Forgive me, Arthur. Forgive me Imperial.

Despite the tortured metal, littered masonry and cold flames, everything is all right now: the struggle is finished. From where I lie, I can see the stars. The roof above this room has gone, the walls where the windows were, are gone. There is a fire to the left of me.

I lie for a while or maybe no time. I hear someone call my name and I look up to see Eleanor bent over me.

Her hand is gripping mine. Love *does* exist. The house groans and there is a shudder before the sound of falling masonry; this building is collapsing around me and yet this brilliant woman has come back for me.

'Eleanor,' I try to say. She touches my shoulder, and I can see her hand is covered in blood. My blood.

I hear sounds – the sounds of people in pain, dying. 'Are they all . . .?'

'Yes, Julia, they are – or nearly are.' She glances at the roof. 'Not long now.'

'For me, too.'

She smiles a little. 'You're not on your own.'

The remains of the huge roof over the collapsing house groan again.

'You need to—'

'I'm not going anywhere. I'm staying with you.' She squeezes my hand again.

I want to speak but I can only shake my head a little, mouth *no*.

'Yes. Julia. I'm an old lady. I never had a daughter, but if I could ask for one, then I would ask for one just like you.'

She smiles her lovely smile again, the smile that reaches her eyes. It's rare – and so rewarding. I understand, I think. I wouldn't leave my daughter either. Not again. Not if I knew she was in danger.

I strain to find my last voice. 'Chloe?' I manage.

'Safe. Cecily, Prisha and Leona are with her and Marguerite. I came from them, so I can promise you *they are safe*.'

Relief.

There's a bang – a much smaller one, but it releases a lot of smoke. I realize I could, but now can't, hear the moaning of others. They've gone now.

I'm glad Eleanor's here. I lean back and realize that the

huge bulk of the Imperial – or what's left of it – pins what's left of me. But it doesn't matter: we have won victory over Big Brother, I want to tell her, but there is no need to say that either. I think it for us instead: *Always forward.*

Eleanor's coughing, struggling to breathe. There's another explosion nearby; perhaps the fire has hunted the Hall's gas supply. She strokes my forehead, an action that shows she understands that there is no point trying to get me out of this place.

I smile up at her. Eleanor bends her body around me. Winston was wrong. He thought it was better to be understood than to be loved. No. It is better to be loved.

'It's midnight – twelve o'clock,' Eleanor whispers, looking at her grandmother's watch. The Inner Party is finished. Ingsoc is gone and so time is restored. We watch the sweeping hand together, wishing for the drama of just twelve chimes to mark the moment – not thirteen. She grips my hand and I think of Arthur.

I shut my eyes; I am tired, so tired, and no longer able to watch the flames light the concern in Eleanor's face.

It's enough to hold her hand as life ebbs away and I thank God for the love I've had in my life. In just seconds my thoughts will turn to Him, but in my final moments I remember my mother, my father, Cook, Leona, Ruby, Prisha, and Eleanor with me now. Arthur, Winston, Cecily, Chloe. And I think it again . . .

I am loved.

I did this for them.

This is a love story. This is a love story.

Notes on writing

Writers are sometimes asked where they get their ideas from. Because I borrowed George Orwell's world, I thought I owed a note to say something about why I did and what my intentions were.

In March 2020, the Covid misery started. It spread across the world, creating devastation. As a teacher, I'm able to comment that it hit schools like a head-on juggernaut. Students were sent home overnight – confusion and fear were rife. Then, while most remained at home, schools returned in a haze of uncertainty, before being sent home again for another lockdown. The world was in fear freefall, with rights and certainties suspended. New laws restricted our freedoms. Taped-over children's park play equipment screamed a new societal solitude. Books in supermarkets – not considered essential – were plastic-sheeted to prevent buying. We can all remember not being able to see loved ones over Christmas in 2020.

So in early 2021, between lockdowns, when reading George Orwell's *Nineteen Eighty-Four* to Year 9 as part of a dystopia unit, Orwell's warning rang louder than ever before. Dystopia discomforts, never more so than when the world has developed parallels. In tandem, this time I read it, I noticed something I'd never noticed before. Reading the character of Julia, I became acutely aware that Julia is – in many ways – a silent character. She has no full name. Her motivations aren't explored – why reach out to Winston Smith when Winston seems so unappealing (to be fair, Winston also wonders)? At the time I was contracted to write a psychological thriller. I'd started, but set it aside, restless to examine the possibilities of Julia through a female gaze. In late summer 2021, Katherine Armstrong and S&S agreed – I could write *The Sisterhood*. Fortunate for me as I couldn't help myself – I was already 30,000 words in.

Winston told Julia that she was only a 'rebel from the waist down'. Winston was often wrong. In this story, my post-Covid misery has fired Julia's agency – and Julia has become a rebel from the waist up.

Acknowledgments

I'd like to start by thanking my good friend and editor Katherine Armstrong. I've previously credited her with being my fairy godmother – this still stands. This book was my third wish. Thank you, Katherine, for still waving the wand. I'd also like to thank the rest of the fabulous team at S&S for their support; specifically, but not exclusively: Louise Davies; Jessica Barratt and Judith Long. Thank you all for taking a draft and making it so much better.

I'd also very much like to thank my agents – Jane Gregory and Stephanie Glencross at David Higham Associates. Jane, after an illustrious career, retires this year from being one of the most successful literary agents in the country. She was always my dream agent and I remain forever indebted to her for her unfaltering loyalty and wisdom. Thank you, Jane. Stephanie, thank you for your advice, and continuing editorial insights – I'm so pleased that we are going to continue to work together. My thanks is also extended to Camille Burns and all at DHA.

Thanks to my sister, Juliet Hunter, who always reads the first draft of all my books and tells me just enough to make improvements without discouraging me. Thank you also to Dorrie Dowling who, like Juliet, is a fantastic champion of me. Thanks also to Simon Dowling for his feedback, who read an early draft and did not laugh. Thanks to Harry Scantlebury and Charlotte Sale for putting the spark into dry wood. I am incredibly fortunate to be supported by a wonderful mother, Jenny, and fantastic friends and colleagues. Thanks particularly to: Hannah B, Kate, Sara, Emma, Michelle, Hannah, Claire, Sanna, Mara. Lucky me – this is not the full list. Thank you all. Thanks to my dear, dear dad, John. Gone but never forgotten.

The nearly last word must go to my husband Brad, who has always been incredibly supportive. I'm frequently somewhere else even when I'm in the room. It can't be much fun being married to a writer – or maybe it's perfect because he gets to choose most of what to watch on TV. Thank you, Brad, for being the best man I know. Thanks also to my sons Cooper and Casper for patience and support.

Finally, my final note must be for George Orwell. He died in 1950 so was not able to give his consent for me to write directly about his created world – he might not approve. I have to accept this, but hope it is not true. I did do my best. So it is an unqualified thank you for Mr Blair. For helping us see.